Elusive Hope

ESCAPE TO PARADISE
BOOK 2

MARYLU TYNDALL

ESCAPE TO PARADISE BOOK 1
FORSAKEN DREAMS

Print ISBN 978-1-61626-597-7

eBook Editions:
Adobe Digital Edition (.epub) 978-1-62836-265-7
Kindle and MobiPocket Edition (.prc) 978-1-62836-266-4

Cover design: Faceout Studio, www.faceoutstudio.com

Published by Barbour Publishing, Inc., P.O. Box 719, Uhrichsville, Ohio 44683, www.barbourbooks.com

Our mission is to publish and distribute inspirational products offering exceptional value and biblical encouragement to the masses.

Printed in the United States of America.

"For man looks at the outward appearance,
but the LORD looks at the heart."
1 SAMUEL 16:7 NKJV

Dedicated to all those who feel they never measure up.

Acknowledgments

First and foremost, I thank God for giving me the opportunity and ideas to continue writing novels for Him. I am nothing without Him. He is the Father I never had, a more loving father than I could have ever hoped for. I also owe my deepest thanks to everyone at Barbour Publishing for believing in me and continuing to publish my books! For all the extra effort every one of you puts into each novel, I thank you from the bottom of my heart!

I could not write without the support and love of my dear author friends: Laurie Alice Eakes, Louise M. Gouge, Debbie Lynne Costello, Ramona Cecil, Patty Hall, Julie Lessman, Laura Frantz, Ronie Kendig, Dineen Miller, Camy Tang, and Rita Gerlach. There are so many more I don't have room to list here, but thank you all so much for your encouragement, prayers, and love!

Special thanks to Michelle Griep, who read this manuscript when it was raw and unpolished and loved it anyway!

And to my Motley Crew, the best crew who ever sailed the high seas! Your Captain loves you!

Last but not least, thank you, Traci DePree, for your continued expert editing and for making this book shine in places I didn't know it could.

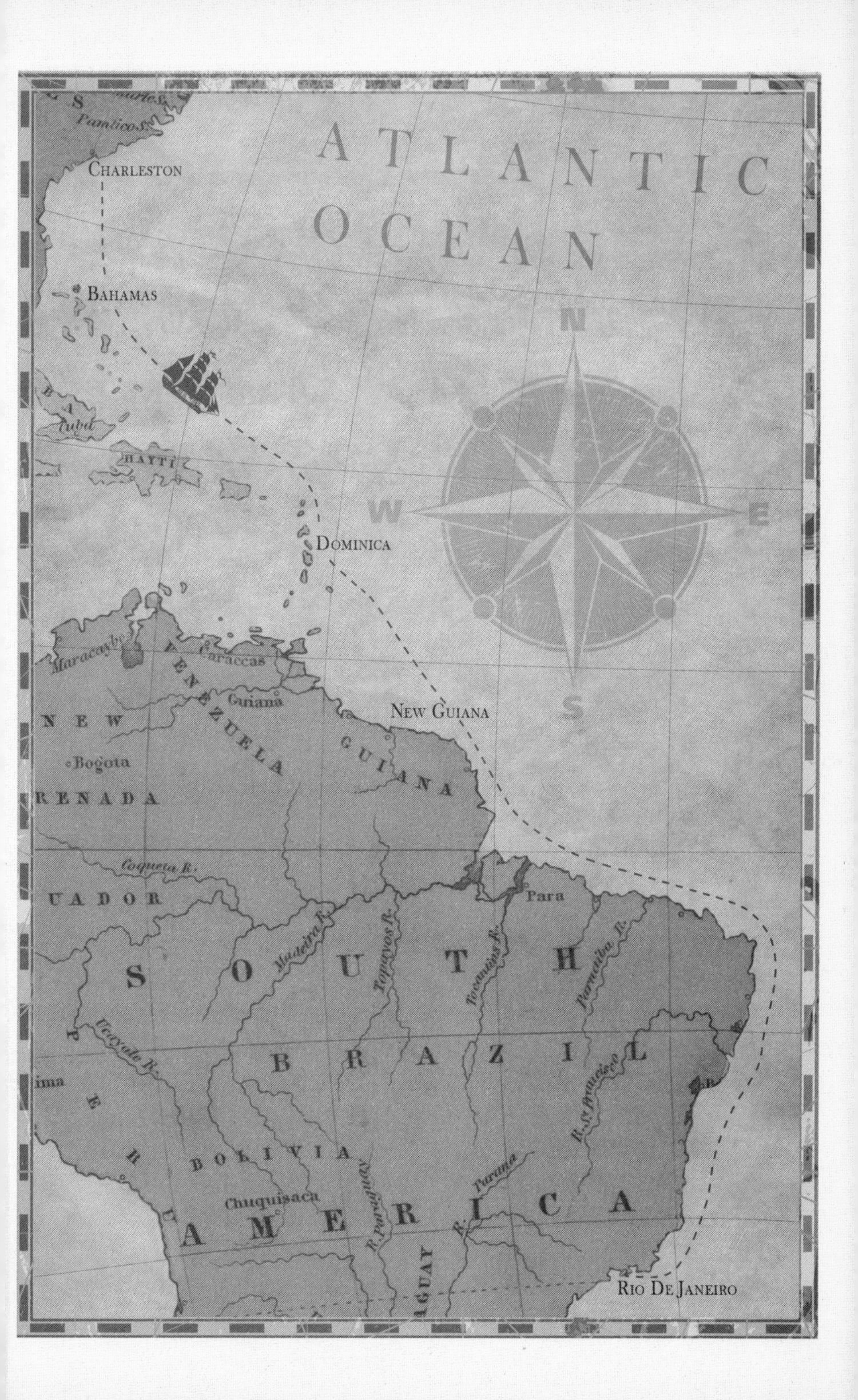
ATLANTIC
OCEAN
Charleston
Bahamas
Dominica
New Guiana
Rio De Janeiro
N
W
E
S
Cuba
HAYTI
Maracaybo
Caraccas
VENEZUELA
GUIANA
Bogota
Coqueta R.
Para
SOUTH
BRAZIL
AMERICA
Madeira R.
Tocantins R.
BOLIVIA
Chuquisaca
Parana

Cast of Characters

Magnolia Scott—Spoiled plantation owner's daughter who hates her new life in Brazil and longs to return to Georgia to marry her fiancé. Constantly belittled by an unloving, domineering father, she believes her only value is in her appearance.

Hayden Gale—Con man who is searching for his father whom he believes is responsible for the death of his mother. Bent on revenge, he'll do anything to punish the man who ruined his life, even becoming as much of a liar and cheat as his father was himself.

Colonel Blake Wallace—leader and organizer of the expedition to Brazil. A decorated war hero, Blake suffers from an old wound that causes him to limp. Blake is serious, commanding, and disciplined and feels the weight of responsibility for the colony's success. He recently married Eliza Crawford.

Eliza Crawford Wallace—Blake's wife and Confederate Army nurse who runs the colony's clinic. Once married to a Yankee general, she was disowned by her Southern family. Eliza is impulsive, stubborn, courageous, and kind.

James Callaway—Confederate Army surgeon turned Baptist preacher who signed on as the Colony's only doctor, but who suffers from a fear of blood. Feeling as much a failure at preaching as he does at doctoring, James nevertheless still pursues a higher purpose for the colony.

Angeline Moore—signed on as the colony's seamstress, Angeline is a broken woman with a sordid past that she prefers to remain hidden. Unfortunately there are a few colonists who seem to recognize her from her prior life.

Mr. and Mrs. Scott—once wealthy plantation owners who claim to have lost everything in the war, they hope to regain their position and wealth in Brazil by marrying off their comely daughter to a Brazilian with money and title.

Wiley Dodd—ex-lawmen from Richmond who is fond of the ladies and in possession of a treasure map that points to Brazil as the location of a vast amount of gold.

Harmen Graves—Senator's son and ex-politician from Maryland whose hopes to someday run for President were crushed when the South seceded from the Union. Hungry to rule over others, Graves slowly goes mad when he encounters a supernatural entity beneath an ancient temple that promises him riches and power.

Sarah Jordan—war widow who gave birth to her daughter Lydia on the ship that took them to Brazil, and who signed on to teach the colony's children.

Thiago—personal interpreter and Brazilian liaison assigned to New Hope to assist the colonists settle in their new land.

Moses and Delia—a freed slave and his sister, along with her two children, who want to start over in a new land away from the memory of slavery.

Mable—slave to the Scotts.

Chapter 1

September 20, 1866
Colony of New Hope, the jungles of Brazil

Magnolia tumbled backward and fell, bottom first, into a mud puddle. Uttering an unladylike curse, she scowled at the black sludge splattered over her skirts. Footsteps pounded. Boots appeared in her vision. She knew whom they belonged to before she looked up. "Now, look what you've done!" Warm moisture soaked into her petticoats and undergarments. Chuckling sounded in the distance. A blistered, scraped hand extended toward her. "I've come to rescue you, fair maiden." The voice strained to withhold laughter.

She glared up at the buffoon, Hayden Gale, a stowaway on their ship to this desolate place. Her gaze took in the sweat shining on his brow, the mischief twinkling in his green eyes, the dark stubble on his chin, then lowered to his bare chest visible through his open shirt—which was what had gotten her into trouble in the first place. His lips quirked into a grin.

"I believe you've assisted me quite enough." Sinking her hands into the puddle, she struggled to rise, but her ridiculous crinoline prevented her from doing so in a ladylike fashion. She would have to accept his help. But that didn't mean she couldn't have a little fun in the process. Gathering a handful of the black ooze Brazil was so famous for, she reached up and gripped his hand, smashing the mud against his palm until it trickled out between their fingers. Not a flinch, not a tick, altered his grin. Not a flicker of surprise or anger crossed his eyes.

Only a single eyebrow arched toward the sky. He pulled her to her feet then released her hand and shook off the offending slime. "I fail to see how your clumsiness is my fault."

Plucking a handkerchief from her sleeve, Magnolia wiped the muck from her hands and arms as best as she could. In all her twenty-three years, she'd never been as dirty as she had been the past three months in Brazil. No matter how often she washed, there was always a smudge here, a stain there, a bit of perspiration where it ought not to appear on a lady. And forget trying to maintain a decent coiffeur. Lifting her chin, she started walking down the path. "You called my name, distracted me. And I tripped over a root."

"You were staring at me for so long, I thought you might be in some sort of trouble." He slid beside her, his knee-high boots sloshing in the mud.

"Staring at you? I was doing no such thing." Magnolia halted, met his gaze, but then thought better of it, and instead scanned the large field where Hayden had been only moments before. Men picked and dug and hoed the earth in preparation for planting coffee and sugar. To the left of the field stood the thatched huts that formed the city of New Hope, their new colony in Brazil.

Hayden raked a hand through his dark brown hair, slicking it back. "I'm not blind, Princess. You were staring at me for several minutes. More like ogling, if you ask me. See something you like?" He grinned.

"Ogling! I was not—" Magnolia bit down her fury before she gave the insolent plebeian more reason to taunt her. "You, sir, are a cad. And my name is not Princess." Uncomfortable at his closeness, she took a step back and nearly fell again. He reached for her, but she jerked to the side, trying with all her strength not to stare at his brick-firm chest peeking at her from within his shirt. A shirt he must have hastily donned when he'd seen her topple into the puddle.

It was that brick-firm chest, billowing with corded muscle and gleaming in the sun, that had stopped her in her tracks on her way back to camp. She'd become further mesmerized by his rounded biceps and the way his dark hair hung around his face while he dug furrows in the field. Mercy me, what was wrong with her? She'd never stared so boldly at a man before. Not even at Samuel, her fiancé. Yet, she'd never seen him with his shirt off. Yes, that must have been it. Surely that was it.

Hayden leaned toward her again and sniffed.

Magnolia flinched. "Whatever are you doing?"

"Just investigating the cause of your sudden clumsiness."

Heat raged through her veins. He referred to her occasional need for spirits, of course. She glanced around to make sure no one was within earshot. "How dare you mention that in public. Besides, it's not yet noon."

"Ah." His tone was sarcastic. "Then I shall be on the lookout after dinner in case you topple to the ground again."

"I don't drink every day, you fool. Oh, never mind. Why am I talking to you?"

"I don't know. Why are you?" He cocked his head and studied her. He smelled of sweat and man.

"Because you will not leave." Her gaze lowered to his lips and the remembrance of the kiss they'd shared on the ship that brought them to Brazil sent her belly spinning. Why couldn't she forget about the silly incident? It had been nothing, really. Surely a rake like Hayden hadn't given it a second thought.

"If you'll excuse, me, sir. I must get back to camp." She skirted around him, but he fell in beside her. "I'll escort you."

"No need. I'm in no danger." *Except from you, perhaps.*

"I beg to differ, Princess. You never know when a root might leap out and trip you again."

"Very amusing," she hissed. Choosing to ignore Hayden, but very aware of his presence beside her, Magnolia forged ahead, batting aside insects as she went. There certainly hadn't been so many carnivorous, flying pests in Georgia, had there? *Georgia.* The name of her homeland soothed her nerves like honeyed tea. They'd told her Brazil was a paradise, a Garden of Eden, but instead she found it to be a seething maze of vermin-infested vines compared to Georgia's gentle rolling hills and sweet honeysuckle trees.

Why, oh why, had her parents forced her from their plantation in

Roswell, Georgia, from her servants and slaves and balls and gowns and friends and—well, if she were honest, they really had lost most of those things in the war. But regardless, why had they forced her from all she knew and dragged her into the jungles of Brazil?

And then there was the heat. Not just any heat, but a heat that was visible in spirals of steam rising from the greenery around them. She dabbed the perspiration on her neck and face and drew in a breath of humid air that weighed down her lungs, making them as heavy as her heart. She must return home. She could not spend the rest of her life in this primordial wasteland, slaving and sweating and working like a commoner. Wasting her beauty on men who were far beneath her.

Like the man beside her. A working man, a stowaway on their ship. Why, he hadn't even planned on joining the colony. And though he'd stayed and helped them clear the fields and set up camp, she sensed a restlessness in him. As if he were waiting for something, looking for something—which would explain his many long absences from the colony. No, Hayden was not the type of man to plant roots in a shoddy outpost. She sensed a kindred spirit in him—a need for wealth and success—which was why she tolerated his presence. When he found what he was looking for here in Brazil, perhaps she could convince him to take her back home.

She batted aside a tangled mass of lichen hanging from one of the trees as the sound of rushing water met her ears. The mighty river beside their new colony had lulled her to sleep many a night when her tears would not cease. It had been her only comfort as her parents snored on the other side of their hut, oblivious to her agony.

Always oblivious to her agony. Or perhaps they believed she deserved it. For the things she'd done.

"You should not venture so far away from camp," Hayden offered as he plodded along beside her. "Thiago tells me there are wolves and jaguars in these jungles."

"I was seeking fruit for our noon meal."

"And yet you return empty-handed." He smiled.

Magnolia huffed. "I couldn't find any." None she could reach, anyway. Besides, she was unaccustomed to work. Her family once owned the largest cotton plantation in Roswell. Her father even owned part of the famous Roswell Manufacturing Company—until the Yankees burned it to the ground. And he was also a member of the city council. She'd grown up with a bevy of slaves caring for her every whim. What did she know of menial work? She stared at the scrapes and mud marring what once had been white, silky skin on her hands and arms.

Hayden swept aside an oversized fern and gestured for her to proceed into the camp as if he were escorting her to a ball. Tightening her lips, she grabbed her skirts and brushed past him into the town of New Hope. Well, it wasn't really a town. Not yet. It was just two rows of thatched huts of various sizes lining a wide sandy path. Nine buildings on the left, nine on the right, and three on the end that served as the clinic, town hall, and meeting shelter, complete with tables, chairs, and a large brick oven and fireplace. Not exactly the Southern utopia they'd hoped to build, but it was better than sleeping on the ground in a tent as they'd done when they'd first arrived on the shores of Brazil. In fact, they'd found these huts already built and filled with crude furniture—or rather, Hayden had found them—just a week after they entered the jungle, apparently abandoned by whoever had made them. James, their doctor turned preacher, had declared it a gift from God.

Magnolia was not so sure.

To the south of town, the river bubbled and gurgled as it made the two-mile journey down to the sea. Eventually, it would be their easiest means to transport their crops to the ocean where ships would then take them to market. That was, if they ever managed to work the tender soil and keep the encroaching jungle at bay long enough to bring the coffee and sugar to harvest. *And* if they built the cane press and mill they needed to process those crops with only twenty-eight men to do the work. Some of whom were unaccustomed to getting their hands dirty at all. They could have purchased slaves in Rio de Janeiro if Parson Bailey hadn't absconded with all their money. Magnolia sighed, thinking of all the hardships they'd endured on the trip here and how many more were still to come.

If they didn't make a success of the colony, they'd have to return home to the devastation of the war-torn South. Fine by her since she had a fiancé waiting for her, but most of the people had nothing to return to. Even worse, they faced persecution by the North.

As she headed down the path, women skittered about carrying pails of water and baskets of fruit. Sarah Jordan, the town's teacher, lifted her gaze from where she knelt working in her vegetable garden and waved at Magnolia. The sound of hammers peppered the air as men reinforced the huts with cut branches and palm slats. Only temporary shelters, their leader Colonel Blake had said, until they could build proper homes. A luxury for which Magnolia's father was not willing to wait.

"A Scott has never lived in a hut and never will live in a hut," he had proclaimed with his usual aplomb.

Shielding her eyes, she peered into the distance beyond the town where Moses's bronze back shimmered in the sun as he erected the frame of a large house. Her father had hired the ex-slave to build them a home "away from the riffraff of town." How he intended to pay the man, Magnolia had no idea, since they hadn't much money left to their name. But she had a feeling Moses was more than happy to do the work if it placed him closer to Mable, Magnolia's personal slave. She had not missed the coy glances drifting between the two. Most unusual, for Magnolia had not assumed Negros capable of deep, abiding relationships.

But at least someone was enjoying their stay in this godforsaken place.

The home, however, was a sign her parents intended to stay. She never truly believed they would subject themselves to live like savages, but poverty did strange things to people. Poverty. She refused to accept that brand in life. If only she could return to Atlanta and marry Samuel, she'd never have to worry about money again.

Or bugs, or heat—her stomach growled—or hunger.

"You may go back to the fields now, Hayden." She dismissed him with a wave, knowing full well both her tone and gesture would annoy him to distraction.

His subsequent groan—akin to an angry bear's—brought a satisfied smirk to her lips.

"I'm not one of your slaves, Princess," he said with more frustration than anger. "We are all equal here. There are no bluebloods who plant their soft bottoms in plush carriages and spew mud on all those they pass."

Magnolia was about to kick some of that mud on his trousers when her mother's shrill voice stiffened her.

"What in heaven's name! Miss Magnolia Scott. You are covered in dirt."

"I am?" Magnolia gazed at her gown in mock horror. "Oh, mercy me, however did that happen?" She smiled at Hayden, who winked at her before he excused himself and walked away.

Her father, following close on her mother's heels, scrunched up his nose, scanned her from head to toe, and shook his head. "I realize we live in the jungle but that doesn't mean we are to behave like wild beasts."

Magnolia sighed. She started to tell him what happened—wanted to tell him that it didn't matter what she looked like here in the middle of the jungle—but decided it was no use.

"Go wash that mud off and put on something presentable!"

"Yes, Papa," Magnolia said numbly as she made her way down the street with one overpowering thought in mind. The sooner she left Brazil, the better.

Chapter 2

Magnolia poured fresh water into the basin, set the bucket down, and pressed a hand on her aching back. She couldn't even carry water from the river without causing herself pain. She was completely useless. Back home on the plantation, she'd kept busy with her cotillions and soirees and calling on her friends for tea, keeping up with the latest gossip, and playing the coquette with the town's eligible bachelors. But here in the Brazilian jungle, life was hard. Even though the sun was just peering over the horizon, most of the men had been up for an hour tilling the fields, chopping wood, and building a barn. The women were up as well, preparing breakfast, hauling water, and gathering fruit. No one was idle. Well, except Magnolia's parents, who spent most of their day complaining of the heat and overseeing Moses as he built their new house. Magnolia so wanted to help the colony. She truly did. But she didn't know how.

So, she came to the one place where she felt of any use at all. The clinic. Even the smells permeating the tiny hut—a mixture of pungent herbs and lye and beeswax—brought her a smidgeon of comfort.

"Good morning." Eliza's cheerful voice preceded the lady into the hut. "You're up early, Magnolia." The ex-war nurse and wife of the leader of the colony, Colonel Blake, never failed to have a positive outlook on life.

"I couldn't sleep. My father snores."

Eliza gave her a knowing glance. "Ah, yes, my husband made quite a racket last night as well." Magnolia grinned. Pink blossomed on Eliza's cheeks as she set down a bundle of clean cloths. "But, honestly, I couldn't care if he sang Dixie all night at the top of his lungs, as long as he's by my side."

Now it was Magnolia's turn to blush. Yet her heart grew heavy at the same time. Would anyone ever love her like that? Had Samuel, her fiancé? Obviously not or he would have sought her out after the war—would have come to Brazil looking for her by now, begging her to return. "Marriage becomes you, Eliza. You are fortunate to have such a wonderful man love you so much."

"God has been good to me." Eliza began folding the cloths, but her beaming smile began to fade. "My first marriage was different. Stanton was a beast. Cruel and heartless. And selfish." She shot a somber glance at Magnolia. "It's so important, Magnolia, whom you choose to marry. And sometimes, it's the least likely person you would ever consider."

Magnolia knew she spoke about the troubles that had almost kept Eliza and the colonel apart. In fact, it was a miracle they'd been able to overcome the obstacles and marry at all. Moving toward the cupboard, Magnolia grabbed a damp cloth to wipe down the examining table in preparation for their first patient. Had Samuel been the least likely person for Magnolia to marry? No, he had been the most likely. Young, handsome, wealthy, from a prominent family, educated, and on the path to success, who else would be more suited to become her husband? He was the perfect choice.

"You should never choose a husband based on a list of requirements," Eliza continued as if she read Magnolia's mind. "Only God knows the man for you."

A breeze blew in and rustled the loose strands of Eliza's brown hair. The woman never seemed able to keep her coiffure pinned up properly. Magnolia patted her own bun and dangling curls, ensuring all was in place as she pondered the woman's words. Samuel would make a great husband. She would never have to worry about money again, and if his political aspirations succeeded, he would usher her upward through society's ranks. Of course she loved him. Who wouldn't love a man like that?

By the time their first patient arrived, a myriad of birds, kissed awake by the sun's ascent, began their orchestra outside the tiny hut, adding a cheerful tone to the morning. Sarah, a war widow and the colony's teacher, entered the hut, greeted them both, and laid her baby, Lydia, nearly four months old now, on the examining table. Magnolia kept the child busy by making funny faces while Eliza examined her, pressing her abdomen, looking in her mouth, nose, and ears, listening to her heart and lungs with the stethoscope and asking Sarah dozens of questions.

"You're good with children, Magnolia," Sarah said after the examination was complete. "You should help me out in the school."

"Oh no, I couldn't possibly." Magnolia shook her head. "Truly, I don't care for children at all." She leaned over and blubbered her lips at Lydia, making the baby giggle. "But I make an exception for your sweet girl."

Eliza washed her hands. "Do you never wish to have children of your own, Magnolia?"

Magnolia ran a hand over her tiny waist that had been the envy of all of Roswell, maybe even all of Georgia. "And ruin this figure?" She laughed.

"There are some things more important than a good figure." Sarah's smile softened the censure in her blue eyes. Magnolia bit down her retort. Though a lovely lady and pleasant in all respects, Sarah was no raving beauty. How could she possibly understand losing the only thing that made Magnolia stand above the other ladies in her class?

"Is that why you still wear your crinoline? And all those petticoats?" Eliza asked while Sarah dressed little Lydia. "Most of the women have given up on such cumbersome underthings in this insipid heat."

"My father forbids it. It isn't proper. A lady should dress like a lady wherever she is."

Sarah hoisted Lydia in her arms. "I believe we should always be modest and look our best, but I also believe in comfort. Most of the women in Rio de Janeiro didn't wear these contraptions."

Most of the *commoners*, she meant. But Magnolia wouldn't say such a thing. She also wouldn't tell them that just because they were in a savage country that didn't mean they had to dress like savages. Mercy me, that thought sounded so much like her father, it caused her stomach to sour.

Several more patients came in with minor complaints: a cut, a sore back, indigestion, and a rash. Magnolia did her best to assist Eliza while trying to learn as much as she could about tending the sick and wounded. She would never tell her father, but she found the profession fascinating and enjoyed the rewards of healing those in need.

"You make an excellent nurse, Magnolia," Eliza said after the last patient left.

"I do?" Magnolia bent over to pick up the bandage scraps. The statement both shocked and sent a spiral of elation through her. She'd never been good at anything. Except—according to her father—being beautiful.

"Of course. You aren't squeamish. You are efficient, professional, and kind."

Magnolia almost dropped the bowl of bloody water she held. She stared at Eliza as the woman dried her hands on a towel, waiting for her to chuckle or offer a playful grin.

But it never came.

At least not before Mr. Dodd wandered into the clinic, gripping his injured hand. With a wild mop of blond hair, side burns that crawled down to his chin, a sculpted nose, and sharp blue eyes, the ex-lawman from Virginia was not entirely unappealing. Unless you were a woman and he happened to be in a gawking mood.

"What a busy morning," Eliza exclaimed, ushering him to the examining table. "How did this happen?"

"Digging. Ran into a sharp root."

"For gold?" Magnolia's mocking tone drew his gaze—a gaze that absorbed her like a sponge. The man fancied himself not only a Don Juan, but a fortune hunter as well. He'd been searching for treasure ever since they hit the Brazilian shore—*pirate treasure*, he said. And he had a map to prove it. Foolish quest if you asked her.

"And I'll find it one day too," he said. "You'll see."

Eliza handed a basin of fresh water to Magnolia. "Hold your hand over this, Mr. Dodd."

He did so, and Magnolia focused on the twig embedded in his bloody flesh rather than face the lecherous look in his eyes. "Will you share your gold, Mr. Dodd, with those who have fed and housed you during your search?"

He chuckled and reached his other hand up to scratch his blond whiskers. "I like a woman with pluck, Miss Magnolia. I do." The sharp tang of blood rose to join his smell of dirt and sweat. "But I do my fair share. I look for gold on my own time."

Magnolia wasn't sure about that and, from Eliza's grunt, neither was she.

"Now, this will hurt a bit." Eliza yanked the twig from Mr. Dodd's hand and immediately pressed a cloth on top.

To his credit, the man uttered no cry.

He *did* utter a moan of delight, however, when Angeline entered the clinic. The town's seamstress, and one of the few single ladies in the colony, froze at the sight of him. Unease. No, more like fear skittered across her striking violet eyes. Shifting her gaze away, she hastened to put a cluster of thick, fleshy leaves down on the sideboard. "Some aloe for you, Eliza." Her voice broke, and Magnolia's sympathies rose for the woman who always seemed eager to leave Mr. Dodd's presence.

"Thank you, Angeline," Eliza said.

"Good morning to you, Miss Angeline." Dodd's sultry tone stiffened her spine. "When I'm done here, I'll gladly walk you back to your hut."

Frowning, Eliza grabbed a bottle of alcohol and poured it on his wound.

"Ouch!" He leapt off the examining table. "What'ya do that for?"

Magnolia and Eliza shared a smile, but Angeline had already dashed out the door.

Raising his machete, Hayden slashed through a thick copse and shoved the branches aside, the first time he'd used the blade today. "The jungle isn't as dense as I thought it would be this far inland."

He could hear the rustle of Thiago's sandals stomping through the dried leaves that covered the forest floor. The Brazilian guide, assigned to their colony by the emperor to help acclimate them to the country, had been an invaluable aid to Hayden as he searched for his father. "No, *senhor*, much of the jungle inland has no *arbusto*. . .brush."

"Just tall, thin trees." Hayden glanced up at the trunks thrusting into the sky some sixty to a hundred feet above them. Birds, plumed in colors that would shame a rainbow, flitted from branch to branch, warbling their happy tunes. "And these." He grabbed a vine of vegetable cordage suspended from a branch, then gestured to the dozens of others hanging all around them and running along the leaf-strewn ground before climbing up the trees again. "What are these again?"

"*Sijpos,*" Thiago said as he stopped beside him. "We use them to tie wood together for buildings and fences and many other things. Some call them nails of Brazil."

"Indeed." Hayden tugged on it. "As thick and strong as ship cordage. Amazing. We should use these in the construction of New Hope."

"A good idea."

Hayden dabbed the sweat on his brow, noting the Brazilian never seemed to perspire or even breathe hard. In fact, he quite resembled a Spanish conquistador of old with his olive complexion, black hair, and strong noble features.

"What are we looking for again, senhor?" The man's dark eyes sparked in playfulness.

"A camp. Or any sign of colonists like us." Hayden uncorked his canteen and took a long draught.

Thiago nodded.

When the heat had become too oppressive to work in the fields, Hayden had grabbed the Brazilian guide and stole away for a few hours of exploring. As he'd been doing since they'd arrived at the abandoned settlement over two months ago. Trouble was, he wasn't finding anything—not a footprint, not a scrap of clothing, not a discarded bowl or pot. Nothing that would indicate humans had inhabited these forests for years. So, where could his father have gone?

The immigration officer in Rio had given Hayden the exact location of the clearing and huts that now made up their colony of New Hope. Though the colonists had been overjoyed to find fields already cleared for planting and shelters already erected, Hayden's disappointment couldn't have been more devastating. He'd come so close to ending his fifteen-year hunt for the man who had ruined his life—to finally receive the satisfaction of watching his father pay for what he'd done—that to have missed him by only a month gnawed away at Hayden's soul. A soul that seemed to grow more empty with each passing day.

He started forward again, asking Thiago about the many plants and trees that surrounded them. So far they'd seen tree ferns, bamboos, lofty palms, acacia, cassia, mango trees, and breadfruit and lemon trees. A green lizard scrambled over Hayden's boot. A thick black spider skittered up a tree trunk, while monkeys howled in the distance. The smell of sweet blossoms and rich earth wafted beneath his nose. A paradise teeming with life.

Yet, paradise or not, if Hayden didn't find any sign of a settlement in his next two trips, his best bet would be to go to Rio and ask the immigration agent if he'd heard from Hayden's father. Perhaps the man had returned to the city for supplies or to change his colony's location. Or, even worse, to book passage on a ship back home.

Perhaps Hayden could take Thiago along to Rio. Especially since Hayden wasn't altogether sure how to find the city over land. And the guide had been more than willing to accompany him on most of his treks into the jungle. In fact, Hayden had enjoyed his companionship.

"Thiago, how is it you know English so well?"

"My father is an American dentist." He chuckled.

"A dentist?"

"Yes. Much needed in Brazil. We have few dentists." He tapped Hayden on the shoulder and spread his mouth wide, proudly displaying rows of strong, glistening teeth.

Hayden grinned and stomped onward, scanning the ground for any sign of human footprints. "I see the advantage in having a dentist for a father."

"Yes, senhor. Not the least is I learn English. Though we not speak it much at home. Father want to only speak Portuguese."

"And your mother?"

"A native of Brazil. From long line of Portuguese royalty. I have royal blood in my veins. But it is nothing here. The emperor rules all."

A band of monkeys swung through the vines overhead, some stopping to chastise the humans below, no doubt for some jungle infraction, before they scampered off to join their friends. Hayden wondered about the emperor. He had seemed a nice enough fellow, but just how much freedom would they have if their new colony became a successful, burgeoning town?

"Instead of becoming dentist like my father," Thiago continued, "or working at a trade, I become interpreter for English-speaking immigrants. It is good job. I meet many interesting people."

Hayden chuckled to himself. More like the easiest vocation in the world. Thiago got free food and lodging just for talking with people and making sure they weren't stealing the emperor's lands. Hayden should have thought of that years ago. It would have settled on his conscience better than swindling people out of their money.

"Like Mrs. Sarah," Thiago added.

Good thing the man talked for a living. He was certainly good at it. "What of her?" Hayden nudged aside a thicket of vines then ran a hand over the sweat lining the back of his neck.

"She very pretty. And nice. Is she not?"

"I suppose." Hayden hadn't really noticed. The teacher was far too prudish for his tastes. Besides, she just had a baby, and he had no interest in being a father. He would probably end up being just as bad a one as his own had been.

"What happened to her husband?"

"He died in the war." Hayden slapped a mosquito on his arm and turned to study Thiago. "You have an interest in her." It wasn't a question. More an observation. And one that was confirmed by the way the man squirmed and dug his hands into his pockets.

"She nice to me."

Hayden swung around. "She is nice to everyone." Still, he smiled.

Perhaps the poor widow would find love after all.

As he passed a large tree, Hayden eyed a beetle the size of his palm clinging to its trunk. Butterflies and other more annoying pests buzzed around his ears and face. A shriek sounded in the distance. A monkey? A bird? Hard to tell above the cacophony of croaks, buzzes, and squawks surrounding him. The living jungle swayed like gentle waves at sea, and Hayden sensed a thousand eyes on him.

Then the crackling began. Barely audible at first, but heightening with each step he took. He glanced around, saw nothing, and continued. Still the sound increased like the spit and crack of a large fire. Raising his machete, Hayden scanned the foliage. "Do you hear that?"

"Yes, senhor, but I do not know what it is." Thiago's dark brows collided as he froze and stared into the jungle.

A shadow—no, more like a dark cloud—sped through a cluster of trees to their right.

Hayden pivoted in that direction. Thiago pulled a pistol from his belt and cocked it. The sound echoed in the moist air. The crackling halted.

The dark shadow sped to their left.

Hayden's chest tightened. "Who's there?" he shouted.

The leaves rustled. A large fern parted. Hayden raised his blade.

Chapter 3

Clutching her skirts, Angeline darted from the clinic, eyes on the ground, trying to get as far away as she could from Mr. Wiley Dodd. All the while, chastising herself for not staying in Rio de Janeiro when she had the chance. But how could she have made a living? She didn't speak the language. Or have any skills. Except one. And that particular one she refused to use ever again. Which brought her back to Mr. Wiley Dodd. Wiley. The perfect name for the man, for he was as wily as a fox. Surely he recognized her. He had to. Then why hadn't he told anyone else? Did he intend to blackmail her? If so, she wished he'd get on with it.

To make matters worse, he'd been a lawman back in the States! From Norfolk of all places. Sweet saints, if he were to connect her to the woman the Norfolk police had been looking for, it would all be over. Her new beginning. Her second chance here in Brazil.

Her life.

Hugging herself, she hurried down the main street, forcing tears from her eyes, and barreled into a chest as firm and wide as a tree trunk. She brought her gaze up to see a thin cotton shirt plastered against muscles bulging from exertion. Oddly, the sight brought her no alarm. Just the opposite, in fact. She gasped and took a step back, raising her gaze at least a foot to the sprinkling of dark stubble on a rounded chin, the slant of steady lips, and finally to the bronze eyes of the doctor turned preacher. "Pardon me, James. I didn't see you."

The corners of those bronze eyes now crinkled in concern. "Are you all right, Miss Angeline?" He cocked his head and touched her arm. "You've been crying."

"It's nothing."

"Something wrong at the clinic?"

"No. nothing like that." She slipped from his touch. Not because it bothered her. But because it didn't. In fact, she rather liked it. She dropped her gaze to see mud sprinkled over his Jefferson boots and splattered on his brown trousers held up by a thick belt into which a pistol was stuffed. So odd for a preacher, but then again the jungle wasn't exactly Jackson Avenue in Knoxville, Tennessee, where the man had grown up. And where she'd met him that dark, bleak night over a year ago. He'd claimed to be a preacher then as well, though he'd behaved like nothing of the sort. Thankfully, he didn't seem to recognize her from their brief encounter. She refused to ponder the odds of having met, prior to their journey to Brazil, two of the twenty-eight men in a colony of strangers. If there was a God, He was definitely not on her side.

Yet, now, standing so close to James and seeing the way he glanced around ensuring no one was bothering her, all thoughts of that conundrum, along with fears of Wiley Dodd, fled like bats in the sun. And she felt safe. As she always did in the doctor's presence.

As she had that night on the ship when he'd risked his life to pull her from the sea. The night she'd tried to end her misery once and for all. Despite her agony, despite her wish to die, she'd felt safe in his arms as he carried her, dripping wet, across the deck. He'd been bare-chested then. Why was she, now, having so much trouble keeping her eyes off him with his shirt on? *Sweet saints, Angeline. He's a man of God!*

As if possessing an uncanny ability to read her thoughts, his face reddened and he shifted his stance. A breeze tossed the tips of wheat-colored hair across his collar. "I was coming to get some water for the men working the field." He glanced toward the open stretch of land beyond the town. "Forgive me for my slovenly attire, Miss Angeline."

His sudden nervousness brought a smile to her lips. "No need to apologize, Doctor. None of us can keep up appearances like we used to."

The blacksmith's wife passed them with a nod, a basket of oranges in hand.

James swept his gaze back to Angeline and smiled. His expression grew sober. "If there is something or *someone* bothering you, I hope you know you can come to me."

"I do." But she wouldn't. How could someone like her ever think to approach a preacher with her problems?

"Well, then, I must get back. Good-day to you, Miss Angeline." He had the most genuine sounding voice she'd ever heard. As if he meant every word he said. She nodded as he skirted around her on his way to the river. And she felt the loss of him immediately.

"I expect to see you at Sunday Services," he called over his shoulder.

Sunday services. So far she'd been able to avoid them with one excuse or another. Not that she didn't believe in God. But simply because she was sure He no longer believed in her.

"I almost killed you, Graves!" Hayden lowered his machete while Thiago uncocked his pistol and stuffed it back into his belt. "What in the Sam Hill are you doing out here, anyway?"

"Just exploring like you." Graves gave a sly grin that angled one half of his black mustache down to his chin. "Difference is"—he glanced at the web of greenery above them and sighed—"I found something for my trouble."

Hayden raised his brows, his interest piqued, along with his annoyance. The mysterious Mr. Graves had kept his distance from the others throughout the entire sea voyage and now in their new town as well. He hailed himself as a politician who once ran for the senate until the war killed his plans, along with his family. And just like a politician, he refused to do any real work, preferring instead to wander the jungles in search of food and supplies. Or so he claimed. Hayden had yet to see him return with anything of value.

"Do tell, Graves, what did you find?" Hayden plucked a cloth from his pocket and wiped the sweat from his head and neck, trying to mask his irritation.

"Come and see." Without waiting for a reply, Graves swerved about and disappeared into the shrubbery. Hayden should have ignored the cantankerous man. He should have continued with his own search, but his curiosity got the better of him and he started after him, Thiago in his wake.

Graves was easy to track. Dressed in his usual black trousers, black shirt, and waistcoat, he reminded Hayden of the dark shadow he'd just seen flitting through the greenery. Or had he seen anything at all? He thought to ask Thiago about the odd mist, but didn't want to sound foolish. Probably just an illusion brought on by the heat and humidity, which seemed to rise with each step he took. He longed to take off his boots, but he'd seen too many snakes and insects to risk tromping around barefooted. Sweat slid down his back and covered his neck. Slicing a piece of twine from a nearby plant, he tied his hair behind him. What a sight he must be. He certainly looked nothing like the gallant gentleman he presented himself as whenever he'd been working a scam. His thoughts drifted to Mrs. Henley, the charming, beautiful Katherine Henley. How her face would light up when Hayden sauntered into a room wearing his silk-lined suit of black broadcloth and stylish top hat. He knew the first time he'd met her at the horse races in Louisville that he would soon have her swooning at his feet, willing to do anything he asked. He grinned. He'd made at least two thousand dollars off her. Not bad for only a few week's work. But, of course, the lady's husband was none too pleased when he discovered she'd purchased an empty, useless cave instead of a silver mine. Hayden hoped the man hadn't been too hard on her. He shrugged off a twinge of guilt before halting and glancing up at the canopy.

Thiago bumped into him from behind. "What is it, senhor?"

"Do you hear that?"

"No."

"Exactly. The birds have stopped chirping. And where is the incessant drone of insects?"

Thiago ran a hand through his dark hair and looked around. "You are right. They are gone."

"Over here!" Graves's shout lured Hayden onward, the crunch of leaves beneath their feet the only sound filtering through the trees. Despite the heat, a chill slithered down his back. He hoped he wasn't walking into a trap. The thought caused a curse to emerge from his lips as he plunged through one final thicket and nearly bounced off a massive stone wall that was at least ten feet high.

"Holy Mary, mother of God." Thiago crossed himself.

"What is this place?" Hayden shifted his shoulders beneath a palpable heaviness in the air.

"This way." Graves gestured. Hayden had never seen the man so exuberant. Which made him feel even more uneasy. They followed the wall as it curved around the clearing, no doubt enclosing something within. A fort, perhaps? But out in the middle of the jungle?

"I do not like this." Thiago moaned from behind as they came to an opening that must have been the entrance but was now merely a rotted wooden gate strangled by green vines.

"Isn't it incredible?" Graves slapped the stones with his hand. "Looks to be quite old. Perhaps built by natives."

Incredible? A different word came to Hayden's mind—*disturbing*. Though covered with moss and vines, the stone structure stood as a firm reminder that whoever built it had been trying to keep something out. "If natives erected this, it makes one wonder what they were afraid of." Hayden shifted his stance and glanced from Graves to Thiago. Didn't they feel the heaviness in the air?

"Perhaps, they feared *Lobisón*," Thiago said as he gazed up at the wall's height and then peered around the corners of the broken gate to examine the thickness of the wood. "Or something far worse."

Hayden wondered what could be worse than a man that turned into a wolf but thought it wise not to ask. He already had the urge to turn and run and never come back, to trust his instincts—the ones he'd honed living on the streets. They had saved his life more than once and now they were telling him to scurry out of there as fast as he could.

Yet, what if his father had come this way, stayed here, left a clue?

Without a word, Graves slid through the opening and disappeared within.

Hayden started after him when Thiago clutched his arm. Wide

eyes met his. "I do not think we should go in, senhor."

"Stay here if you wish, but I must see what's inside." Turning, Hayden entered and halted beside Graves. Across a courtyard infested with weeds and vines and broken pottery, at least twenty stone obelisks rose from the ground like mummies from a mass grave. Hayden made his way to the closest one and brushed aside the vines to find an engraved collage of gnarled faces in various postures of agony. His stomach clenched. He backed away, shifting his gaze to two rectangular slabs of stone, lying prostrate upon blocks of granite. A massive fire pit rose from the center of the clearing. Scattered around it lay broken wooden idols and stained blades whose handles had long since rotted off. Beyond the clearing, a crumbling building rose from the greenery like a monster from a swamp. Columns that reminded Hayden of a plantation house held up a flat roof and formed an open air portico that faded into darkness.

"Looks to be a temple of some sort." Graves remarked as he tromped across the courtyard, his tone one of enthusiasm.

Shaking his head, Hayden slowly moved toward one of the tables. In between the moss and vines, dark stains peered up at him from the light stone. His stomach convulsed. "If this is a temple, I don't think it's a Christian one."

"No." Thiago's tremulous voice came from just inside the gate where he stood frozen. "These are ruins of Tupi. They were cannibals."

Hayden's glance returned to the fire pit, shifted to the ancient blades, then moved to the stains on the table. Bile rose in his throat. Gagging, he bent over, praying he wouldn't vomit and embarrass himself in front of these men.

"Cannibals?" Graves's dark eyes flashed.

Hayden took a deep breath and rose to his full height.

Pulling an amulet from his pocket, Thiago crossed himself again. "I wait outside."

Hayden longed to go with him, but he couldn't seem to move. Instead he stared at the ghastly scene, imagining what horrors must have occurred within its walls.

A *caw caw* drew his gaze upward to a black bird with the wingspan as wide as a man was tall. The odd sight kept Hayden riveted as the beastly bird crossed the clearing and disappeared. Something about the bird, its size, the loneliness in its cry, caused air to seize in his lungs.

Graves headed toward the temple where he plucked a torch from a holder on the wall, struck a match, and lit it. "I'm going in to explore. Join me?"

"I'll wait here," Hayden said. If his father had come this way, Hayden should find some evidence in the courtyard. There was no reason to subject himself to further horrors.

Graves gave him a taunting snort before he mounted the steps and entered the building with the exuberance of a child at Christmas.

As disturbing as his presence was, Graves's absence left Hayden alone with the dark foreboding he'd felt upon entering this fiendish site. He ran his sleeve over the sweat on his brow and started his search of the area, careful not to touch anything. He'd grown so accustomed to hearing the chatter of the jungle that the absence of it spiked his nerves. Perhaps that was the reason for his discomfort. He prayed that was the *only* reason.

He circled one of the obelisks, cringing at the tormented faces carved into the stone and wondered if these were the faces of those who'd been killed by the Tupi. His chest tightened. He backed away. The crackling returned. Soft like the sound of waves, yet harsh as if a thousand fires were lit all around him. Hayden drew his machete and swerved around. No one was there.

Then she appeared. Materialized out of the torrid air like a mirage in the desert. Yet unlike a mirage, she stood before him as real and vibrant as he remembered her. Mrs. Katherine Henley, hair cascading around her head in a bouquet of golden curls. Striking emerald eyes, now swimming in tears.

Hayden rubbed his own eyes, hoping to sweep away the vision, but still she remained. He reached for her. She retreated.

"Why?" she asked. "Why did you do it?"

Hayden swallowed. *This can't be happening.* It's the heat. His thirst, this evil place playing tricks on his mind.

"I thought you loved me. You told me you loved me." Tears

streamed down her cheeks, glistening in the bright sun.

"You're not here. You're not real." Hayden clenched his jaw.

"Is that what you think? That I don't feel the pain you caused me?" Her sorrowful expression turned as hard as the stone obelisk they stood beside. Rosy lips drew into a cracked gray line. Her eyes turned to slate. "You think you can't hurt people simply because, to you, they aren't real. I know who you are, Hayden Gale. I know who you are!"

Hayden's heart thundered in his chest. He was going to be sick. Tearing away from her, he ran up the stairs of the temple and plunged into the darkness after Graves. Thoughts dashed in his mind, racing past impossibility. Someone had to be playing a trick on him. But nobody knew about Katherine. Nobody but him.

Darkness enveloped him and with it came another kind of heaviness. It pressed on his shoulders as if the air weighed more inside the building than without. A light fluttered from a dark corner.

"Ah, you've gained your courage, I see." Graves's voice echoed over the stone walls. "Come here. I've found something quite interesting."

Hayden squinted as his eyes grew accustomed to the gloom. The room extended so far back he couldn't see the end. Rotting chairs, tables, and bowls littered the cold, stone floor, along with dirt and dried weeds. A collection of handmade axes and swords hung on one wall. Hayden glanced over his shoulder and scanned the courtyard but Katherine was gone. Just an illusion. Of course. Hadn't he just been thinking of her? No doubt his guilt had gotten the better of him. He drew a deep breath of dank air that smelled of mold and agony.

The flicker of Graves's torch drew Hayden's gaze, and he headed toward him with one thought in mind—to drag the madman out of here and leave this place posthaste. A rancid smell much like rotten fruit assailed him as he passed a large pond circled in stone. Steam spiraled off the dark water like misty fingers rising from the grave. Apprehension twisted his gut and he hurried along, his gaze drawn to metallic engravings that decorated the entire back wall. Torch light glinted off a golden crescent moon surrounded by stars that hung above what appeared to be a stone altar. Thinking this must be what drew Graves's attention, Hayden faced him, intending to make a joke that they shouldn't tell Dodd about the temple or he'd strip the place of all its gold. But Graves wasn't looking at the golden moon. He was staring at words etched into the stone above an opening to the side of the altar.

"Do you know what this says, my friend?" Graves held the torch up to the lintel.

Hayden glanced at the words. Latin? How had Latin words come to be written in the middle of a Brazilian jungle? "No."

"It says 'Beware, the Catacomb of the Four.'"

Chapter 4

Back in New Hope, Hayden slid his knife across the bark and watched the mahogany curl beneath his blade. One of the many wonderful things this jungle possessed was a variety of rare, exotic wood. His good friend, a furniture maker from Savannah, would be happier than a beaver in a woodshed with such abundance. Smiling at the thought, Hayden carved another slice, carefully shaping the wood like a potter molding clay. The smell of roasted fish and fried bananas stirred his stomach to life, and he looked up to see several of the farmer's wives hovering about the massive brick fire pit at the edge of the meeting shelter. At least that was what the colonists were calling the large pavilion left by the previous settlers. Based on the table and several chairs scattered beneath the palm-frond roof, Hayden assumed the area must have been used for meetings, for sharing meals, and perhaps even for the occasional party. But why had his father's colony left after working so hard to erect the huts and build all the furniture? Not to mention felling trees and clearing away part of the jungle for planting crops?

Something had driven them away. Something frightening.

His thoughts scattered to the eerie temple Graves had found earlier: the stark silence surrounding the area, the heaviness in the air, the odd Latin phrase about catacombs. Could something from that unholy place have caused the last colonists to leave? But no. From the looks of it, no one had set foot there in years.

The setting sun speared golden rays through the web of green, casting a bluish hue over the jungle, before sinking beneath the tree tops. And just as quickly, the warble of birds transformed into the buzz of crickets and croak of frogs. Though Hayden ought to have been accustomed to it by now, the sudden onset of night took him by surprise. Rising, he struck a match and lit one of the many lanterns hanging on posts throughout the camp while other men did the same. The golden cones lit the street at intervals and made the camp look almost civilized. Almost. Settling on a bench beneath one of the lights, Hayden resumed his whittling as James Callaway, the doctor-preacher approached and eased beside him.

"What are you making?"

Hayden studied the long piece of wood he'd formed into what could pass for a table or chair leg. "Not quite sure."

"You've got talent, Hayden. We could use some decent furniture around here." James shifted on the bench, causing it to wobble. "Whoever made these didn't know what he was doing."

Hayden nodded his agreement. The ramshackle furniture had been shabbily assembled and would no doubt fall apart within a year. And though Hayden would love to put his skills to use, he had no plans to remain with the colony. He had to leave, find his father, and make him pay. But he couldn't tell James that.

"Where did you learn woodworking?" James asked.

"I spent a summer working in my friend's furniture shop in Savannah."

"It shows." Groaning, James stretched his back and gazed over the darkness that now inhabited the field they'd been plowing all day. "I tell you, I've never worked as hard as I have these past two months." He chuckled.

Hayden had no doubt James was unaccustomed to hard work, except, perhaps, for his years as a battlefield doctor. Before the war, the man had been a preacher. And a hypocrite. But then no one knew about that except Hayden from the one time he'd seen him in Tennessee back in '60. Regardless, the doctor's family came from big money. Not like Hayden's. No, Hayden had been forced to scrape and beg just for scraps to eat. Until he figured out how easy it was to swindle the rich.

Too easy, as it turned out.

Angeline's sweet laughter drew both men's gazes to the comely russet-haired seamstress carrying a platter of food to the table in the meeting house. She not only drew their gazes, but those of several of the other single men, including Mr. Dodd, who took a seat on a stump across from Hayden. Hayden hated the way the man ogled her, and he wasn't altogether pleased at James's interest in her either. Yet, what did it matter? Hayden wasn't staying long. But if he was. . .well, the woman intrigued him. He was sure he'd seen her face on a wanted poster in the Norfolk, Virginia, jail. He never forgot a face, especially a beautiful one like hers. And now that he'd discovered she had a sweet disposition and a kind heart, the dichotomy of her brush with the law fascinated him all the more.

Setting the platter on the table, she returned to the fire and began stirring a kettle. Though she claimed her family were wealthy shipwrights, she did not shy away from hard work.

So unlike Magnolia. Who now entered the clearing, flanked by her pretentious parents and followed by their slave, Mable. Wearing a lilac taffeta gown and with her flaxen hair pinned up in a waterfall of curls about her neck, the spoiled plantation owner's daughter presented a rather alluring picture.

As long as she kept her mouth shut.

Her gaze brushed over him with a dismissal that pricked his ire. He shrugged it off. He'd been engaged in verbal battle with the shrew ever since he'd wandered into her cabin on board the *New Hope* with a bullet in his side. Since then, the only time she'd been quiet was when he'd kissed her on board the ship. But oh, what a kiss! He reacted even now at the remembrance, and his knife slipped over the wood, slicing his finger. A thin line of blood rose from his skin.

"Let me see that." As if the war nurse could smell blood on the wind, Eliza appeared out of nowhere.

The doctor, sitting beside Hayden, had the same ability but the opposite reaction. Coughing, he turned his face away, and Hayden had the sudden urge to shove his bloody hand into the man's vision just to see him squirm. But that wouldn't be nice. And Hayden *did* like the doc, even if he was a bit preachy.

"It's nothing," Hayden said.

Eliza knelt to examine his hand. Reaching into a pouch clipped to her belt, she opened a jar and spread salve over Hayden's wound as a night breeze swirled around them, cooling the perspiration on his neck.

"Ouch." Pain brought his gaze down to Eliza pressing against his cut. "It felt better before you touched it."

"Don't be such a baby, Hayden," she chided him. "You don't want it getting infected, do you?"

The spicy scent of the food drew more people from their huts in anticipation of supper. The blacksmith and his wife, the baker, the cooper, several farmers, another plantation owner, and several ex-soldiers, forty-two in all. Most of whom got along just fine.

Eliza wrapped a bandage around his finger. "I believe you'll live."

Hayden grinned as she rose and looped her arm through her husband's, who had just joined them. For all his sternness, the colonel, and leader of their ragtag southern outpost, melted like wax whenever he looked at his wife. Ever since their wedding on the beach the day after the ship set them ashore, the two hadn't kept their eyes—or their hands—off each other.

Hayden averted his gaze from the look that now passed between them. A private look of promised love and intimacy.

Sarah, the teacher, announced dinner and the group moved to sit in the meeting shelter, the women at the table and the men scattered about on chairs and stools. After James said a prayer of thanks to bless the food, Thiago educated them on their Brazilian fare for the night.

"Rice, beans, *carne seca* or dried beef, boiled cabbage with garlic, fried bananas, roasted *bacalhau* or cod, and mandioca cakes." The guide smiled broadly. "Mandioca is a root that grows here in Brazil," he continued in his Portuguese accent. "It is poisonous if you eat it raw but once cooked it is safe. Known as the bread of Brazil. Very good." He rubbed his tummy and smiled, eliciting a few chuckles from the colonists. "Eat and enjoy!"

Hayden gathered a plateful, anxious to appease his hunger after a long day's work. The food tasted as good as it smelled, and he couldn't shovel it into his mouth fast enough to satisfy his aching belly. While they ate, James and Blake discussed what else needed to be done before they planted the fields, as well as the best way to organize the men and gather materials to build a sugar press, mill, and barn. With each spark of enthusiasm in their voices and each glimpse of excitement on their expressions, Hayden's heart sank. He couldn't join them. No matter how much he longed to be a part of recreating a Southern utopia in this strange new land, he couldn't stay. He'd come for a different reason, and he must keep his focus.

His gaze landed on Magnolia, who seemed as miserable as he was. Scowling, she picked at the food Mable had brought her as if it were poison. Her father leaned toward her and said something that further deepened her frown and sent her dashing down the main street in a riot of taffeta and lace. Her abrupt and over-dramatized departure, however, did nothing to dampen the jovial mood of the colonists, who continued to converse and laugh while the children giggled and played in the center of the square. Hayden shook his head at her childish behavior even as pity stung him for the way her father treated her. As no father should treat a daughter.

The soothing rush of the river harmonized with the buzz of nighttime insects to create a pleasant tune that, combined with the scent of orange blossoms in the gentle breeze, settled an unusual peace over Hayden. Despite the hard work involved in tilling the farmland and building the colony, Brazil was indeed a paradise: green and lush and teeming with life, and with more wild fruit and fresh water than a person could want. What Hayden wouldn't have given to have spent his childhood here instead of begging and stealing on the streets of Charleston. At least he would have had plenty of food and not been surrounded by hooligans and drunks intent on taking advantage of a young, innocent boy.

As if reading his thoughts, a predatory growl echoed through the trees, causing the hairs on his arm to stand at attention. Silence descended on the camp as all eyes shifted toward the dark jungle surrounding them. They'd heard beastly howls before but this one seemed closer, more intent. Thiago hopped up from his seat beside Sarah, yanked four polished stones from his pocket and headed toward Blake.

"Colonel, put these rocks at four corners of camp, they will keep out the *Lobisón*." Fear sparked in his dark eyes as he cast a wary glance over the jungle. "The man-wolf. That is his call."

"Man-wolf?" Blake stood. "What nonsense is this?"

"No nonsense, Colonel. He is part man, part wolf. Legend says if he attacks you and you live, you become Lobisón too."

James closed the man's hand over the charms as if the sight of them repulsed him. "We have no need of these, Thiago. God is far more powerful than any wolf. He will protect us."

Thiago narrowed his eyes. "You do not know what Lobisón can do, Mr. James. These rocks are part of the *Penha*, a mountain rock consecrated to Virgin, our Lady of the Rock. Very powerful against evil."

Hayden was about to remark on the foolishness of such a notion when a woman's scream split the night.

Chapter 5

Magnolia batted tears from her face and stormed toward the edge of camp. Could her father not cease his harsh censure of her for one meal? Just one meal when she wasn't castigated for her appearance or the improper way she was eating her food? She could almost understand, almost, if they were seated at an elegant linen-clad table, dining with British royalty or even with the upper-crust of Georgia—rich, eligible men of substance and power—but they were sitting on stumps in the middle of a primordial jungle eating with commoners! She was tired of being told what to wear and how to fix her hair and how to sit and walk and speak. And behave. It wasn't like she had to impress anyone except snails and toads and oh—something cracked beneath her shoe. She froze, cringed, and slowly lifted her foot, not daring to glance down. A squishy sound met her ears, sending the few bites of supper she'd consumed into her throat.

"Oh. . . I hate this place!" she squealed and glanced back at the glow of the campfire flickering between leaves. She'd been so distraught, she'd passed her parent's hut and plunged into the jungle unaware. Buzzing and chirping and croaking surrounded her like a living, breathing entity—a dark, breathing entity made up of quivering shadows and pulsating greenery. She grabbed her skirts, intending to head back to camp when the soothing sound of water beckoned her onward. Perhaps she could wash her face and have a moment's peace before she faced the colonists, who were no doubt entertaining themselves this very moment with gossip about her sudden departure.

Glancing around at the dark foliage, she took a tentative step toward the bubbling sound. Truth be told, she seemed to provide the citizens of New Hope with much entertainment of late. Just because she was different: educated, more attentive to her appearance, genteel, and refined while most of them were nothing but farmers, soldiers, and tradesmen. Why, oh why, had her father subjected her and her mother to such plebian rabble! She swept aside a branch and moved forward.

Something buzzed by her ear. "Oh, shoo!" She batted it away, hoping the insect wouldn't get caught in her hair. The hair Mable had spent nearly an hour curling and pinning before supper. Just to please Magnolia's father.

Moonlight penetrated the canopy in a clearing up ahead and sparkled over a rippling creek. The scene appeared so serene, it was hard to believe there were dangers in the jungle like the jaguars and wolves Hayden had told her about. Over her shoulder, she could still see the lights of New Hope through the foliage. Perhaps it would be safe enough to sit for a while and clear her thoughts.

Gathering her skirts and adjusting her crinoline, she lowered onto a flat boulder, allowing her billowing gown to settle around her. Moonlight transformed the tiny creek into silvery braids that rose in a mist of fairy dust across the clearing. The beautiful sight did much to calm her spirits. But she had something else that would help even more. After one last glance at the camp, she withdrew a flask from the secret pocket she'd sewn in her petticoat, uncorked it, and took a long draught of the port she'd stolen from her father. The smooth, tawny liquid eased down her throat, unwinding her tight nerves with each warm embrace. She drew in a deep breath of the moist jungle air, fragrant with passion flowers, and tried to forget her father's reprimand for the slouching manner in which she sat. "So unlike a lady," he had said.

Another sip of port and the disappointment blaring in his tone began to fade. Her shoulders lowered, and the rod that held up her spine melted. Leaning over, she untied her ankle boots and kicked them off, not caring if her stockings became soiled. Hiking up her skirts, she wiggled her toes, took another sip, and giggled as she dipped them, stockings and all, in the cool water. If her father could see her now.

A crackling sound joined the nightly hum of the jungle. Low at first, gentle like the hiss of a dying fire. But then it grew in intensity and sharpness. Magnolia sat up and scanned the foliage but the oscillating shadows of dark and gray revealed nothing. No fire. No torch. "Hello?" The crackling stopped.

Shaking her head, she took another sip. It was almost gone. And the way her father kept track of his precious liquor, she doubted she'd be able to steal more any time soon. At least not enough to benumb her mind and heart against her horrid circumstances. Not enough to make it bearable to rise each morning and face the heat and insects and back-breaking labor. Or at least her attempt at labor. No, she would have to find another source of liquor. Mr. Lewis, the old carpenter, seemed to have an unending supply. Perhaps she could cajole him into sharing.

The crackling began again. Or was it simply the wind quivering the leaves? But, there *was* no wind. At least not enough to cool her skin. Perspiration moistened her forehead and neck, and she leaned toward the creek to splash water on her face when she caught her reflection.

Moonlight silhouetted curls the color of the morning sun that fell from her chignon about her shoulders. Only one errant strand was out of place in an otherwise perfect coiffeur. Oval eyes that were almost catlike in shape reflected blue from the silvery water. High cheekbones, a refined chin, a small perfectly shaped nose, and rosy lips completed the visage that had brought so many gentlemen to their knees. One of whom had destroyed her family. And another whose suit she would have accepted—whose family and reputation could have restored her own family's name—if only her parents had not dragged her off to Brazil.

If her father hadn't been so proud and stubborn and allowed them to wed before the war, they'd all be sitting in a comfortable parlor in Atlanta sipping tea from china cups instead of drinking river water from pewter mugs.

As if reading her thoughts, the crackling turned to laughter, soft, malicious laughter. Magnolia corked her flask and put it away. No more port for now. She was starting to hear things. A shadow slithered through the greenery. And apparently see things, as well. "Hello?"

A growl rumbled through the trees. Close, but yet, not close. Magnolia froze. Her heart thundered in her chest. Her fingers grew numb. She scanned the forest, afraid to move. Something flickered in the water. Leaning over, she gazed at her reflection again.

Her beautiful golden hair began to shrivel. Like old twine left too long in the sun, it shrank and grew brittle until, strand by strand, it slid off her head, landed on the water, and floated away. Leaving her bald. Completely bald!

Flinging her hands to her head, she did the only thing she could think to do. She screamed at the top of her lungs.

Hayden was the first one to burst into the clearing, James and Colonel Blake on his heels. What he expected to see—what his worst fears imagined—was Magnolia being mauled by some wild animal. What he saw instead was the lady gripping her head and screaming, "My hair! My hair!" After scanning the clearing for a wolf, he dashed toward her, forced her hands to her sides, and led her into the moonlight to see if she'd been bitten or injured. But aside from her hair being hopelessly torn from its pins, she seemed unscathed.

Yet her eyes told a different story. They were wide and etched with fear. No, not fear—absolute, excruciating horror. They searched his as if looking for an answer. "My hair," she sobbed.

"Your hair? What about it?" Hayden wondered if she'd either gone mad or—he dipped his nose toward her mouth—had too much to drink. Obviously the latter due to the pungent scent of alcohol hovering around her. Angry, he released her.

"What happened? Are you all right?" James approached and drew her into an embrace. She fell against him and started to cry. Of course she did. Hayden couldn't believe he'd been so gullible. That was exactly what she wanted—attention.

And everyone fell for it. Blake, pistol in hand, surveyed the edge of the clearing, while Eliza rushed to Magnolia and took James's place by her side.

"My hair," Magnolia whined.

"What about your hair, dearest?" Eliza brushed a lock from Magnolia's face.

"Don't coddle her. Nothing happened." Hayden huffed as James circled the camp, examining bushes and sweeping aside leaves.

"It was gone. All gone." Magnolia's gaze shot to the small creek. "When I looked at my reflection"—she drew in a shredded breath—"my hair fell out. I was bald!" she whimpered, tears spilling from her eyes. "I was completely bald."

"Well, you aren't bald now." Eliza held one of Magnolia's long strands in front of her. After touching it, Magnolia released a shuddering sigh.

"Nothing here." Blake joined them.

"No animal tracks at all," James added.

"But the crackling." Magnolia stared into the jungle, wiping her face. "The voices. Did you hear them?"

Blake's gaze snapped to Magnolia.

"No. We didn't hear anything," Elisa said.

Hayden rubbed his eyes, angry that this woman's insecurity and propensity to drink caused so much unnecessary trouble. Yet hadn't he heard crackling at the temple right before Katherine Henley appeared? How strange that Magnolia heard the same sound before seeing something that wasn't there. But no, it was only Hayden's guilt and Magnolia's insecurity that caused these illusions. Nothing more. Then why did Blake continue to stare at Magnolia as if her ramblings made sense?

"Let's get back to camp, shall we?" he finally said.

Hayden agreed. He'd left a half-eaten supper he intended to finish. They all started back when Magnolia halted, tugged from Eliza's grip, and darted back toward the creek mumbling something about shoes.

"I'll watch over her," Hayden offered. No sense in the foolish girl keeping them all from their food. With a nod, Eliza looped her arm through her husband's as they joined James on his way back to camp.

"Where are my shoes?" Magnolia pointed toward the sand. "They were right there."

"Drop the charade, Princess. Everyone is gone, and I'm not buying it."

"Not buying wha—" She spun to face him with what looked like real tears in her eyes. Hayden grinned. Ah, yes. She was good. He'd give her that. But she had no idea who she was dealing with.

Those eyes turned to glaciers as she planted hands on her hips. "You think I'm lying? You think I made up the crackling sound and the baldness. Why would I do that?"

He crossed his arms over his chest. "For attention. Or because you've had too much to drink."

"I'm not drunk." She stomped her foot. "I know what I saw." She gazed down at the mud dripping from the hem of her gown and groaned. "And I don't care what you think. Where are my parents? Didn't they hear me scream?" Her gaze darted toward the camp.

So that was it. She'd staged this to test her parents' love for her. But Hayden knew they weren't coming. Her father had risen from his seat, seen Hayden and the others speeding by, and then sat back down to finish his meal. Did he not care for his daughter at all or was he so accustomed to allowing others to do his work, that he left the safety of his own family in their hands?

Poor girl. A wave of sympathy flooded him as a breeze swept the ivory tips of her loose hair across her waist. Standing there—silent—a look of innocence and desperation on her face, she looked like a sad forest sprite, all glitter and beauty. And something within Hayden stirred.

She swung her gaze to his and huffed, breaking the spell. "Stop looking at me like that."

"Like what?"

"Like you want to kiss me again."

"Again?" he toyed with her.

Her lips drew tight. "I know you remember." He caught a glimpse of her glassy eyes in the moonlight before she turned and began stomping back to camp, mumbling, "Incorrigible man."

But she was right about one thing.

He did want to kiss her.

Chapter 6

"Leave?" Blake looked up from his desk in the large hut that served as New Hope's town hall, looking more like the army colonel he used to be, rather than the leader of a meager colony in Brazil. A stack of papers, a gold pocket watch, a set of quill pens and ink, a tilting pile of books, and a telescope from the ship spread across the top in a haphazard manner that was at odds with the colonel's regimented style. Setting down his pen, Blake sighed as he eyed the ledger he'd been writing in then leaned back in his chair.

Hayden didn't envy the task of keeping accounts for the colony. Though he'd always been good at making money, he'd never been good at managing it properly. Or holding on to it.

Shifting his boots over the tamped dirt floor, he drew a deep breath of sweat, coffee, and gunpowder. He knew this wasn't going to be easy. So instead of facing Blake, he glanced over the shelves housing their dwindling supplies: sacks of rice, beans, flour, coffee, and dried beef. Extra shovels, picks, axes, and rakes were propped against the wall, ready to be moved to the barn when it was built. Lanterns and candles lined shelves behind Hayden, along with whale oil, extra canvas, and tar. Finally, he faced forward and glanced at James, who sat on a chair beside Blake's desk. Rays from the setting sun floated in through the window and hallowed his body in gold, making him look like the preacher he claimed to be.

Angling his shoulders, Hayden stretched his back and gazed at his two friends. Though their skin was tanned a golden brown from hours in the sun, and dirt smudged their tattered clothes, both looked more robust and healthy than when he'd first met them on board the ship over four months ago. He wondered if the same were true for himself, for he'd never felt better, except for the sorrow welling in his gut at the thought of leaving them. His friends. He'd never really had friends before.

James stood. "You can't be serious. We are going to plant within the week. You've put so much work into this town."

Hayden stared at the ground. "It cannot be helped. I belong in a city, not a jungle," he lied. Truthfully, he had loved his time here in Brazil, away from the filth and crime that always encroached where large groups of humans inhabited, here out in the fresh air, perfumed with the sweet smells of the jungle, where fruit was plentiful and life was simple. Where everyone worked together—well, almost everyone—to build a new world. Where, for the first time in his life, he had put in a hard day's work and been rewarded for it. With muscle aches, yes. But aches he was proud of. Aches that came from honest work. Aches that caused a twinge of something foreign inside him, something he'd never expected to feel—self-respect. Not only that, but he had earned the respect of the two men who stood before him—men who wouldn't have given him a moment of their time back in the States. And that had been worth all the money he'd ever swindled.

But he couldn't stay. He had a man to find. A debt to pay. He'd promised his mother on her death bed.

Blake hobbled around the desk. His uneven gait from an old war wound did nothing to detract from his commanding presence, nor from the frustration masking his face. "I realize you were a stowaway on this journey, but you have fit in with the colony so nicely. You're a hard worker and an honorable man."

Hayden stifled the chuckle in his throat.

"And I've come to depend on you," Blake continued. "We all have."

"Indeed." The doctor's brow wrinkled. "You've taken on a leadership role among us. The town needs men like you."

Hayden crossed his arms over his chest and gazed out the window. He had expected opposition. He had expected frustration, even anger.

He hadn't expected to be cloaked in praise. Especially from the two men he admired most in the world. He cleared his throat. "I appreciate that. I truly do. But there is something I must do."

"Here in Brazil?" Blake asked.

"Perhaps. Perhaps not. But I must go to Rio to find out." Hayden silently chastised himself for saying far too much already, but the look of sorrow and concern in his friends' eyes was chipping away at his wall of resolve. "I cannot tell you any more than that."

Blake nodded and leaned back on his desk with a sigh. "It will be difficult without you."

James rubbed the scar angling down the side of his mouth. "Then there's a chance you will return?"

"A slight chance." Hayden shrugged. "Time will tell."

"When are you leaving?" Blake asked.

"Tomorrow."

"On foot?" James asked.

"Yes, Thiago gave me directions. It shouldn't take more than five days if I travel quickly."

"All alone in the jungle?" Blake asked.

"I can take care of myself."

Blake nodded. "Since you'll be in Rio, would you inform Mr. Santos that we've moved our location a mile west and that once we have planted our crops and started building the town, we will send Thiago back with the exact acreage we intend to purchase as stated on our provisional title?"

"Of course," Hayden said. He needed to speak to the immigration officer anyway.

Rising, Blake clutched Hayden's shoulders, his gray eyes pointed and somber. "We will miss you, Hayden. Be safe and God speed." He released him and sighed heavily.

Thankfully, before Hayden's eyes grew moist and he embarrassed himself.

"I will pray for you every day, my friend." James gave a sad smile. "And in particular that you will return to us soon. You always have a home in New Hope."

Hayden extended his hand to the doctor, but the man drew him into an embrace instead, slapping his back before releasing him and turning away.

Hayden shifted his face from their view. Clearing his throat, he nodded and grunted his thanks to both men before hurrying out the door. He'd never had a home. At least none he remembered with fondness. After his mother had been killed, he'd never had a family either. He'd been a gypsy, a drifter. He should be used to it. Then why was it so hard to leave this silly town?

Brushing aside leaves, Magnolia crept up to two men circling a fire just outside of town. Unable to sleep, she'd left her parents' hut, thinking some fresh air and listening to anything but her father's snoring would help settle her nerves. But the distant flicker of flames soon lured her to the outskirts of town. She wouldn't have ventured any farther except that she could make out Mr. Lewis's and Thiago's faces in the firelight. Harmless enough men. And she'd been meaning to speak to Mr. Lewis anyway. The friendly old carpenter, who reminded her of the bumbling overseer on their plantation back home, had a mind that dwarfed the size of his heart. All she had to do was smile and plant a kiss on his bristly cheek and he happily shared whatever spirits he had on his person.

And she sure could use a drink tonight.

So intent on whatever they were doing over the flames, the two men didn't hear her approach—didn't hear the leaves rustle or the twig snap beneath her boots. Didn't even turn until she said, "Whatever are you doing, gentlemen?" The teasing reprimand in her voice sent fear skittering across their faces.

"Oh, mercy me, don't trouble yourselves. Whatever it is, I won't tell a soul." She curled a hand on her hip. "As long as you let me in on it." Her grin disarmed them, and they both smiled in return.

Mr. Lewis returned his attention to the contraption sitting atop the flames, while Thiago rose to usher her close. "We make rum—Brazilian rum."

Delight filtered through her. "Oh, I knew I smelled something delicious." Adjusting her crinoline and multiple petticoats, she lowered herself onto a stump while Mr. Lewis checked a thermometer that was perched inside an iron pot hanging over the fire. Tubes sprang from holes in the container's sides and ran down to another kettle sitting in a bowl of water off to the side.

The old carpenter looked up, flames flickering over his pudgy face. "It's a distiller, miss."

"We distill sugarcane juice," Thiago added. "Make *pinga*, or rum. Very good." His handsome eyes sparkled as he took a seat beside her. Tall, lithe, tanned, with dark features, the interpreter's exotic looks were not without appeal, though he possessed a boyish impetuousness that prevented a more serious look. Besides, he had no wealth nor prominent position in Brazilian society.

"I should have known you'd be up to mischief, Mr. Lewis." She teased the old carpenter.

He chuckled. "Well, miss, our drinking supplies are rapidly shrinking. So when Thiago, here, informed me he knew how to make this pinga, so famous here in Brazil, what was a man to do?" He winked.

Thiago's brow wrinkled. "You will not tell anyone."

"She won't." Mr. Lewis answered with a sly smile. "Not if she wants us to share."

The fire crackled, shooting sparks into the air as the smell of smoke and night-blooming orchids battled for preeminence.

Magnolia placed a finger over her lips. "On my honor, my lips are sealed. Now"—she glanced around—"do you have any of this ping. . . pinga for sampling?"

"Ah, sim. . .yes." Thiago pulled a flask from his shirt pocket. "We made some last week." He uncorked it and handed it to her.

"Good thing 'cause I only have one more bottle of rum from the ship." Mr. Lewis scowled. "That is, unless Hayden can bring some back from Rio."

Hayden? Rio? Magnolia batted away a bug and took a sip. The pungent liquid stung her tongue, filling her mouth with a spicy orange taste. She coughed and struggled to breathe. "Mercy"—her voice sounded like an old woman's—"but this is strong."

Both men chuckled. The buzz of cicadas intensified around them, reminding Magnolia of the odd crackling she'd heard the other night. "But what is this about Hayden and Rio?"

"He leaves tomorrow." A breeze tossed Thiago's shoulder-length hair behind him as he stared at the fire. "I tell him best way to walk to Rio from here. I will miss him. We travel jungle together much."

"Tomorrow?" Magnolia took another sip of pinga, wondering why her heart suddenly cinched in her chest. "Why is he going? For supplies?"

"He say he not happy here. Did not find what he look for."

"He's not coming back?" Magnolia felt like she weighed a thousand pounds. She took another drink to ease the pain and was pleased when her mind began to numb.

That numbness, however, did not reach her heart. Not even after several more sips.

Three hours later, with valise stuffed and swung over her shoulder, Magnolia shoved aside the canvas door of Hayden's hut and entered the dark room. She had never been in a man's bedchamber before, and her heart did a hard tumble in her chest as she stood there frozen, focusing on the sound of male snoring, seeing nothing but shadows. She hated disturbing his sleep—had paced in front of his hut for hours—but she had no choice. What if he left before she'd had a chance to speak to him? Then she'd be stuck in this bug-infested jungle forever.

Hayden was her last chance.

She took a step toward his cot, the edge of which was visible now in a stream of moonlight drifting through the window. A dove cooed outside and somewhere in the distance a growl rumbled through the jungle, reminding her why she needed this man's protection on the way to Rio. If only he would agree to take her.

Another step and she could smell him. All musk and man. Not an offensive smell, but a scent that brought delight to her heart, much like the smell of peach pie brought a flood of good memories from her childhood. He stirred and shifted position, his arm landing in the moonlight. His hand—twice the size of hers—bore scrapes and calluses from his work in the fields. She hoped he wouldn't get the wrong idea upon finding her at his bedside in the middle of the night. But she was desperate. And desperate times called for desperate ways, or measures, or whatever it was they said.

She took another step and knelt beside his cot. His breathing was deep and rough like the man himself, and she wished she could see his face in the shadows. Now, how to wake the sleeping beast? A gentle touch, perhaps. That always worked with her father. She lifted her hand to lay it on his arm.

When his fingers gripped her wrist like iron shackles.

Before she could react, he leapt, flung her onto the cot, flipped her over, and pinned her arms down with his own. Magnolia would have screamed, but she didn't want to alert anyone. Instead, she struggled against his tight grip. "Get off of me this instant!"

He released her, disappearing into the shadows. A match struck and the flame sped through the air to light a candle, illuminating the petulant fiend.

"Magnolia?" Hayden blinked, trying to clear the sleepy haze from his eyes. "Zooks, Princess, what are you doing sneaking around my hut in the middle of the night?" He'd heard her—and smelled the alcohol on her breath—the moment she'd entered. He hadn't survived on the street for eight years without learning to sleep with one eye open. Of course, he hadn't known it was Magnolia. Or a lady, for that matter. Not until he'd tossed her, as light as a feather, onto the cot and felt her soft skin beneath his fingers—heard her quiet sob. Now as she sat up and rubbed her arms where he'd clutched them, guilt assailed him for hurting her.

"I came to speak to you. Why else would I be here?" She fixed him with a pointed gaze that dropped to his bare chest then quickly looked away.

He grinned. "In the middle of the night?" She looked delicious with her flaxen hair tumbling over her shoulders, cheeks flushed pink, and eyes sparking in anger. He licked his lips, wishing she had come here for a tryst, rather than for whatever reason put that scowl on her face.

"I heard you were leaving in the morning."

"Ah." He pressed a hand over his heart. "And overcome with sorrow, you came to tell me how much you're going to miss me."

"Don't be absurd!" Pressing down her billowing skirts, she struggled to rise, but instead plopped back hopelessly onto the cot with a growl. Hayden should help her, but he was rather enjoying watching her expression contort into cute little folds with the effort. Finally, she managed to stand. Stuffing strands of hair into their pins, she straightened her posture along with her skirts as if she hadn't just crawled off a man's bed. "Now, look what you've done to my hair."

"I've done?" Hayden snorted. "You're lucky that's *all* I did." Grabbing a shirt from the back of a chair, he tossed it over his head. "Do you always sneak up, besotted, on men in their beds? Not wise if you wish to keep your virtue, Princess."

"My name is Mag—" Her eyes speared him. "I am not besotted, and my virtue is none of your affair."

"And it won't be as long as you behave like a dissolute minx."

"Grrrrrr." She bared her teeth like a she-wolf. "How predictable that a man like you would have no care for a woman's virtue."

Hayden closed his eyes, trying to make sense of the woman's ramblings. An impossible feat, he finally decided. Sinking into a chair, he scrubbed his face with his hands. "What is it you want, Princess? I was rather enjoying my sleep." Only then did he see her valise lying on the floor with something lacy spilling onto the dirt.

She scrambled to retrieve it, stuffing the item back inside as a pink hue crept up her neck.

"Going on a trip?" he asked.

"Yes. With you." She lifted her pert nose in the air but then instantly lowered it, frowned, and formed a pout with those luscious lips. "Oh, please say you'll take me with you to Rio?"

Hayden would have laughed if he hadn't been so shocked. As it was, all he could do was stare at the candlelight flickering in her blue eyes. He searched those eyes that now looked at him with such innocence and pleading—searched for the shrew that had been there only moments before. But she hid the hellion well. When she wanted something. He raked a hand through his hair. "No."

"What do you mean, no?" Her tone was incredulous, as if no man had ever denied her request.

"I believe the word speaks for itself, Princess. I have business in Rio, and it's unclear whether I will return. The last thing I need is a woman, and a coddled one at that, to slow me down."

The corners of her mouth tightened. Her fists clenched. She seemed to be having difficulty restraining that inner hellion at the moment. Finally she said, "I will not slow you down, Hayden, you have my word. And once we get to Rio, you can wash your hands of me."

Hayden opened his mouth to respond, but she continued her tirade. "I only need an escort to Rio, where I intend to book passage on a ship back to Charleston. Then you'll never see me again. What is so difficult about that? Upon my word, I can keep up with you in the jungle. And you won't have to do anything for me except lead the way. In fact, you'll hardly notice me at all."

Hardly notice her? Hayden groaned inwardly. He'd have to be deaf not to hear the woman's interminable chattering and blind not to notice her stunning face and curvaceous figure. No, the woman would definitely be a distraction.

As well as a major aggravation.

"What of your parents?"

"They don't know. I'm twenty-three. I can take care of myself!" She patted her hair in place then took a step toward him. "I beg you, I can't stay in this savage backcountry another day. I'll simply go mad."

Hayden wasn't altogether sure that hadn't already occurred. After all, the woman had been hysterical over thinking she was bald just two days ago. "How will you afford to book passage on a ship?"

"I have money. You need not worry about me."

Of course he would worry about her. Was the woman daft? If she came with him, she would be under his protection. He would be responsible for her welfare and safety. And *that* he couldn't have.

He needed no complications, no obstacles, no temptations to keep him from his goal.

Temptations. . .ah, he knew just the way to be rid of her. Curling his lips in a sultry grin, he moved toward her, scanning her with his gaze. "What of your reputation? All alone in the jungle with a man for five days. And nights." He raised his brows. "What will people think?"

She looked away. Moonlight sprinkled glitter dust on her hair and cast shadowy arcs beneath her lashes. "No one need know. Especially not back home."

Hayden closed the gap between them. The scent of alcohol vied for dominion over her sweet, feminine scent—a scent that reminded him of citrus and cedar. He rubbed the stubble on his chin and drew a deep breath, leaning to whisper, "And would you risk arriving in Rio with your virtue shattered?"

Drawing a jagged breath, she retreated. Her leg struck the cot. She winced. "I assure you, there is no risk of that!"

He continued to stare at her.

Her eyes became flames. "You wouldn't dare!"

He fingered a lock of her hair. As soft as he'd expected. "You don't know what I would or wouldn't do, Princess." Of course he would never force himself on a woman, but she didn't need to know that. Besides, he quite enjoyed playing the cad. One of his many roles.

And a role that, apparently, she bought, lock, stock, and barrel. Eyes round, she swallowed hard and clutched her valise to her chest like a shield. "You are a vile toad, Mr. Hayden Gale!" she spat before storming out of the hut.

Hayden chuckled, a sudden emptiness settling on him at her departure. Perhaps he shouldn't have teased her so, but it was for the best. Releasing a heavy breath, he gathered his things as dawn's first glow slid over the wooden window frame. He should get going. The sooner he left, the better.

Chapter 7

With the tip of her parasol, Magnolia brushed aside a particularly slimy-looking vine upon which a family of monstrous beetles had taken residence. Not only residence, but they appeared to be procreating at lightning speed and in astounding numbers! She cringed as she held the vine out of her way and ducked beneath. Her parasol slipped. The vine descended like a dragon with gaping beetle jaws. It slapped her in the face, showering her with bugs.

She screamed. Then quickly slammed her palm over her mouth. Dropping her valise, she sprang back and furiously batted the foul creatures scrambling over her skirts and bodice. Her stomach leapt into her throat as she hopped about the clearing like a frog on hot coals, shaking out the folds of her gown. After several agonizing minutes—and when she could find no more of the black multilegged beasties—she drew a handkerchief from her pocket and fluttered it about her face, waiting for her heart to settle. Then, swearing under her breath, she grabbed her valise and forged ahead, scanning the endless canvas of green.

Mercy me, she'd lost Hayden again! Why did that infernal man have to walk so fast? Good thing he left boot prints in the mud large enough to belong to a bear as well as broken branches and leaves so she could follow his trail or she'd be hopelessly lost. She shivered at the thought and glanced around at the thousands of birds and insects abuzz in the tangled canopy. Chirping and croaking and warbling and hissing and droning. Could they never stop and give her a moment's peace? She would go mad with the incessant hum!

And the heat! Never should a lady perspire this much. With each step, her damp petticoats rubbed against her corset, which rubbed against her chemise, which of course was glued to her skin. Soon her petticoats would be stuck to her as well, and next her over-skirts and bodice, until finally she would be completely drenched.

And smelling nothing like a lady.

Her skirts caught on something. The sound of fabric tearing grated her ears before she had the good sense to stop and free herself. "Oh, bah!" She stared at the rent in her beautiful dimity gown as tears filled her eyes.

How was she to endure five days of this torture? Perhaps it hadn't been such a good idea to follow Hayden, after all. She had thought it wouldn't be too difficult to keep hidden among the brush of the jungle nor to follow the odious man's trail. After all, she'd gained some stamina these past months. She'd grown accustomed to the bugs and the heat and to walking more than usual. Hadn't she? Then why did she feel as though she slogged through molasses—hot, prickly molasses?

But what else was she to do when the man refused to escort her to Rio? And even if he had, after his provocative insinuations, she wasn't sure she trusted him. This way was better. He would lead her to Rio and never be the wiser. Of course, she hadn't thought what she would do at night. And for food beyond the fruit the jungle offered. But she couldn't think about that now.

Using her valise as a shield and her parasol as a sword, she forged ahead, searching the trail for boot prints. There. A huge one. And over there, another. My word, but the man had a hearty stride. Perspiration stung her eyes, and she swiped it away, looking for the next print. Nothing but mud and leaves met her gaze. Lowering her valise, she inched ahead, batting aside vines and scouring the ground in all directions. Nothing. No prints, no flattened leaves, no broken branches. It was as if he had been taken up by God on this very spot like Enoch or Elijah. But she knew that couldn't have happened to the stowaway rogue. How she remembered her Bible stories, she had no idea. She hadn't opened the book in years, nor had she truly listened to the sermons her parents had dragged her to each Sunday.

She swirled around, peering through the greenery, looking for a flash of his dark blue coat, a hint of his hair, the color of roasted almonds. But all she saw was a labyrinth of green spinning around and around until dizziness jumbled her thoughts and sent her breath huddling in her throat. Her heart seized. What would happen to her now?

"Looking for me?"

Magnolia shrieked as Hayden emerged from the jungle looking at her with that patronizing I'm-in-control-and-you're-a-dolt look.

"How dare you sneak up on me!" She poked him with her parasol.

Without even a flinch, Hayden snagged it and tossed it to the ground. "Me? Sneak up on you?" He snorted. "You're the one who's been following me."

"I have not. We just happen to be going in the same direction."

"Is that so? And what direction is that? North, south, east, or west? How can you tell when you can't see the sun?"

"How can *you* tell?" She placed a hand on her hip.

"Because I'm used to living on my own, finding my way, not relying on a footman and a carriage to take me wherever I want at the snap of my fingers."

Why was his voice so sharp with spite? And his eyes like green thorns? "It is not my fault that you were not born to privilege, Hayden."

He hung his head and sighed, his jaw bunching then expanding as if it were going to explode any minute. She took a step back, studying him: shirt plastered to his sculpted chest, coat in hand, tight trousers stuffed within boots. An extra belt was strapped around his waist that held a long knife, a pistol, and a canteen. Was that all he'd brought? Dark hair hung to his shoulders over a chin grizzled with stubble. When he lifted his gaze to hers, the look in his eyes sent an icicle down her spine. He wouldn't hurt her. . .would he?

"I heard you the minute you started following me, Princess. I figured if I gave you enough time, you'd quit and go home. This isn't exactly a stroll through Battery Park."

"Well, you're right about that. It's an absolute oven. Or hell. I can't decide which. A rather large insect has decided I'm his next meal"—she batted the air around her—"and, apparently, he's invited all his relatives to the feast. I have blisters on my feet." She pouted. "And my shoulders ache from carrying my valise and shoving aside these interminable leaves."

The right side of his lips quirked. "We've only been walking for an hour."

She frowned, withdrew a handkerchief, and dabbed at the perspiration on her neck. "An hour? Are you sure? It seems much longer. How can you tell the time when you can't even see the sky?" She glanced up. "I feel like I'm trapped in some maniacal green web. And no doubt the spider will return soon to devour me." She gave him a victorious grin. "And you, as well."

"No, just you." He crossed his arms over his chest. "Especially if you don't return to New Hope this minute." He jerked his head in the direction from which they'd come. "If you start now, you can reach camp before noon."

Magnolia gripped his arm, surprised at the rock-hard muscle twitching beneath her fingers. She offered him her most I'm-just-a-dainty-desperate-woman-who-needs-a-strong-man look—the one that always brought men to their knees. "Please take me with you, Hayden. I shan't be any trouble. I promise." She inched out her bottom lip and forced moisture into her eyes. There, that should do it. She'd lowered herself far enough in front of this plebian. In a matter of moments, even the hardened Mr. Hayden would crack beneath her feminine wiles and beg her to accompany him.

Instead he narrowed his eyes as if deciding what to do. "Nicely done, Princess." He pried her fingers from his arm. "A bit over the top for my tastes. But I'm still not taking you to Rio. Not now and not ever. I don't need a clingy, whiney female to take care of."

"Clingy?" She picked up her parasol and leveled it at him. "I cling to no man. And I don't whine either." She lifted her chin. "I softly protest."

He snorted and shook his head. "Run along, little one." He gestured toward the trail. "I haven't time for this foolishness."

"You would send me back alone?" She'd expected his defiance if he discovered her, but what man could resist a damsel in distress? "It's not safe."

"Then you shouldn't have followed me." He strode off. "Good day, Princess."

Magnolia started after him. "Why do you keep calling me that?"

"Because you behave as though your class and fortune make you queen of all." He waved a hand through the air in dismissal.

"I do no such thing!" She stomped her foot. "Come back here this instant. What sort of gentleman leaves a lady alone in the jungle? You will escort me to Rio at once, Hayden Gale."

He chuckled. "You prove my point, Princess. Now hurry along before it gets too late."

Fuming, Magnolia swatted a bug and watched as Hayden marched away with that swaggering gait of his.

She felt like screaming. She felt like crying. But she hadn't the energy for either.

At the sight of Thiago entering the hut, James punched to his feet, grabbed the letter off Blake's desk, and glanced at Magnolia's parents huddling in the corner. Finally they would get to the bottom of this. Mr. Scott's usual bombastic expression was absent, replaced by fear and shock as he held his sobbing wife by his side. Light from two lanterns attempted to wash away the early morning gloom that had saturated the town hall ever since the Scotts had dragged Colonel Blake and James from their beds just minutes before, waving a piece of foolscap through the air and rambling some nonsense about a kidnapping.

James rubbed his sleepy eyes and glanced out the window where the rising sun painted a verdant green over the dark canvas of the jungle. The scrape of the colonel's chair sounded, pulling James's attention back to the matter at hand. He cleared his throat. "What I'm about to say must remain within this group. Is that clear?"

Thiago raised his dark brows.

"It would seem that Miss Magnolia has run away."

Mrs. Scott burst into sobs.

"Apparently with Hayden Gale," Blake added.

Mr. Scott patted his wife's back in an attempt to calm the poor woman. "I am not convinced that she went willingly, I tell you! She loathed the scoundrel. Told me so herself on many occasions."

"But you can vouch this is her handwriting?" James asked, holding up the paper.

Mr. Scott nodded. "No doubt forged under duress."

"Perhaps," Blake said with a frown. "Yet I'm having a difficult time believing Hayden would kidnap Magnolia."

Mrs. Scott lifted moist, red-rimmed eyes. "Surely you remember that this man was a stowaway. He made advances on my precious girl before."

James tightened his jaw. Accusations that were never proven, but he wouldn't upset the poor woman further.

Releasing his wife, Mr. Scott thundered forward. "I demand you send out a search party at once."

Blake raised a hand. "Yet you do not want the lady's reputation besmirched, do you?"

"Yes, yes, that's right. Which is why we must tell everyone she has been kidnapped."

"I will not do that, sir," Blake said. "I will not ruin a man's reputation on pure speculation."

"But you'll ruin my daughter's on it?" Mr. Scott raised his voice, his jowls quivering.

"Not speculation. . .her own words," James said.

"Preposterous! She would never run away with a man." Mr. Scott's face reddened. "She's a good girl."

Not a girl at all, James thought. *A grown woman.* Even if it was the first kind word he'd heard Mr. Scott say about his daughter in all the time he'd known the man. Still, he doubted Hayden had anything to do with this. From what James could tell, the disdain between Hayden and Magnolia was mutual. The more likely scenario was that Magnolia had followed Hayden, hoping to get to Rio to make her escape. In fact, if James knew Hayden, the man was probably dragging her back to New Hope as they spoke.

"That charlatan has taken her. Kidnapped our baby!" Mrs. Scott wailed.

The colonel circled his desk. "Magnolia did not hide her hatred for Brazil or her desire to go home. Is it possible she saw this as her chance to do just that?"

"Alone with that. . .that rogue? No, no. Not my Magnolia." Mr. Scott gazed out the window where a breeze brought in the smell of rice cakes and mangos being prepared for breakfast. Yet something in his eyes, a flicker of apprehension, told James the man wasn't altogether sure of his statement.

"Hayden is no rogue," James said. "He has more than proven his good character over the past few months. Besides, I agree with Colonel Blake. Until we know the facts, we should stick to what we *do* know."

"Humph." Mr. Scott took up a pace across the hut. "Very well, then, at least send Thiago to bring her back." He waved at the Brazilian guide as if he were a fly on the wall. "He will suffice."

Blake's brow furrowed. "But a larger party would cover more territory, find her quicker. Surely that would be better if she is truly in danger."

Mrs. Scott slumped into a chair and dropped her head into her hands.

"No, I will not see our good name destroyed aga—" Mr. Scott halted midsentence, alarm rolling over his expression. "I will not risk her reputation."

"Very well." Colonel Blake faced Thiago. "Are you willing to go after the lady and ensure no foul play is afoot?"

"And bring her home." Mrs. Scott lifted her tear-filled gaze.

James raised a brow. "Only if she wishes."

Thiago stuffed hands in his pockets. "I cannot go, senhor. The emperor pays me to stay with colonists. I cannot abandon my work or there will be huge punishment. I will instruct someone else which way to go."

Blake faced the Scotts. "Will you compensate her rescuer? Offer some incentive?"

Mr. Scott's gaze skittered over the men in the room before he grabbed the lapels of his coat. "Whoever goes will have my undying gratitude, sir, as well as the satisfaction of saving my daughter's life."

James shook his head. Had Mr. Scott's grief, his desperation, of only a moment ago been merely an act? When the Scotts often bragged of their wealth, were they not willing to part with anything to see their daughter safely home?

Later that morning, James stood before the assembled colonists, open Bible in hand, ready to give the Sunday message—a sermon on love and self-sacrifice, a last-minute change in light of the Scotts' behavior toward their daughter. While the old carpenter, Mr. Lewis, played his fiddle and led them in the hymn, James tried to shake off the feeling of foreboding that had cloaked him since early that morning—since the middle of the night, in truth. Ever since he'd woken in a chilled sweat from a nightmare he couldn't remember. He only recalled that it was terrifying and grotesque, and that it had draped a heaviness on him that had been accentuated by Magnolia's foolish escapades. It was a heaviness he'd felt building ever since they'd arrived in this new land. Like an ominous cloud in the distance drifting ever nearer, blotting out the sun ray by ray by ray.

Gazing across the faces, he caught a glimpse of russet hair glowing like polished mahogany in the morning sun. *Angeline*. He shifted his stance for a better view of the petite woman who always seemed dwarfed by the other colonists. Of course, it didn't help that she'd sat all the way in the back, though he should be happy she'd accepted his invitation at all. If anything could improve his mood, it would be that charming lady. In fact, all the ladies of New Hope were present, Bibles in hand and faces alight with eager expectation of hearing God's Word. What a welcome change from the women he'd been accustomed to dealing with back in Knoxville, both in church and out. *As a jewel of gold in a swine's snout, so is a fair woman which is without discretion.* The verse from Proverbs rose in his mind, reminding him of women he'd known who had lured men to destruction. Who had lured him to destruction. He'd made it his life's goal not only to avoid such women but to clean the streets of them. Difficult to do in Knoxville, but much easier to accomplish in a new town, in a new utopia based on the Word of God.

Opening his Bible, James began reading from 1 Corinthians 13. He'd been officiating the services ever since Parson Bailey had run off with their money on Dominica. Yet he still felt unequal to the task. Worse, he felt like a hypocrite. He wondered if God looked down on him, shaking His head in disgust that James dared to preach after his many failings on both the battle and mission field.

His voice broke. Clearing his throat, he looked across the crowd. A shadow to the right caught his gaze. Dark mist rose on an empty stump like steam from a cauldron, spinning and curling and thickening until it took the form and shape of a soldier. A corporal, he could tell, from the two stripes on the arm of his coat. He looked familiar. That innocent face. That tawny mop of hair. Yes, James remembered him from a battle—the Seven Days Battle, if he wasn't mistaken. But the boy had been killed, hadn't he? Confusion twisted James's thoughts as he scanned the faces staring at him, waiting for him to continue. He shifted his gaze back to the corporal, who was really just a boy dressed like a soldier. So many of them had been.

A few colonists turned to see what he was looking at. Their brows furrowed and they shook their heads. Clearly they didn't see the young man.

The boy smiled at James, but his smile slowly faded as his eyes took on a vacant stare. Blood stains pooled on his gray coat, expanding in a circular death march. His uniform tore as if by an invisible blade. The boy's chest ripped open, riddled with bullets. Sunlight winked off specks of metal embedded in bloody flesh. Still he stared at James, not a shred of emotion on his pale, placid face.

"Why did you let me die, Doctor? Why?"

Chapter 8

Hayden poked the fire, urging the flames to rise, then threw another log on the embers. If he kept the coals hot enough and sat close enough, the mosquitoes kept their distance. There was a price, however—the sensation of roasting like a pig on a spit. Being eaten alive or roasted alive. Great choice. Something pricked the back of his neck. Swatting the offending insect, he eased up the collar of his coat, which only enhanced his discomfort. But at least his arms and chest were covered. More importantly, at least he suffered alone.

Retrieving a long strip of carne secca from his pocket, he shoved it into his mouth and tore off a bite as his thoughts drifted to Magnolia. He grinned. The audacity of that woman following him into the jungle! A bold move for the primped lady. She must have been desperate, indeed, to venture into such dangerous terrain without being assured of protection and proper escort. Desperate or stupid. Or brave. No matter. She could be whatever she wished as long as she did it somewhere else.

As tempting a morsel as she was, Hayden didn't need the extra trouble of forging through the jungle with a prima donna in tow, nor the trouble he would have facing her parents if he ever returned to camp. No doubt they would place the blame on him for their daughter's disappearance. Though he did feel a slight twinge of guilt for leaving her alone. He probably should have escorted her back to New Hope, but she'd been so close to town, and he'd wasted enough time in his life on empty-headed harridans.

He bit off another chunk of dried pork, savoring the spicy flavor. He'd only brought enough for two days. After that, he hoped fruit and small critters would suffice to keep him going until he arrived in Rio, where he was sure he could *convince* someone to offer him a meal or two and a change of clothes. Then he would proceed with his business—questioning the immigration officer about his father's whereabouts. If the man had changed locations, he would have to report his whereabouts to the proper authorities. Though the land was cheap at only twenty-two cents an acre, the Emperor certainly couldn't have immigrants swarming around, settling wherever they wished and on whatever sized plots they wished.

Reaching into his waistcoat pocket, Hayden pulled out a small leather-bound tintype. Flipping the latch with his thumb, he opened it and held it to the firelight, studying the photograph he'd stared at a thousand times. He'd memorized every feature of the man: his black hair, slicked back and curled at his collar; the cultured whiskers that covered his angular jaw; his gray satin waistcoat; the sparkling gem pinned to his tight cravat; the chain dangling from his pocket; the round-brimmed hat in one hand while the other rested arrogantly on his waist. But it was the man's eyes that drew Hayden. Always his eyes. Even in the fading picture, Hayden detected the smug gleam of a swindler.

Like father, like son.

The fire crackled and spit. Sparks danced like fireflies into the darkness. Around him, the jungle played a nightly orchestra that was so different from its daytime melody. More peaceful, secretive, almost sinister. Not a breeze stirred the leaves. Sweat dotted his forehead. A distant growl set his hairs on end. Whatever it was, it wouldn't come near the fire. He was safe for now. A twig snapped. Leaves rustled. Closing the tintype, he dropped it back into his pocket, grabbed his pistol, cocked it, and scanned the darkness as memories of his vision of Katherine Henley knotted his nerves.

Crackles that didn't come from the fire sizzled in the air, or was it merely the sound of crickets? Movement caught Hayden's eye. He slowly rose. Sweat slid down his back. A man formed out of the darkness, tall with stylish dark hair and cultured sideburns. Green eyes flashed at Hayden, followed by the hint of a sardonic smile.

Hayden's breath fled his lungs.

Father?

A woman shrieked, drawing his gaze. When he looked back, the man was gone.

Another scream.

Plucking a burning stick from the fire, Hayden darted into the brush, sweeping the torch before him, pistol at the ready. Something moved in the shrubbery. He leveled his weapon and thrust the flame forward to keep the creature at bay. A piece of torn lace flashed in his view. A glimmer of blond hair. His heart stopped. *Please, not another vision.* Another vision would only mean one thing—that he'd gone completely and utterly mad.

The lady whimpered. One hand emerged from the bush and flattened onto the dirt, followed by another. Then a face pushed through the leaves as terrified eyes glanced upward. Hayden swept the torch aside but before he took another step, the woman leapt to her feet and barreled into his chest.

"Oh, thank God, it's you, Hayden." Her breathless words escaped with a groan. "There were bats! Bats everywhere! Diving at me, attacking me! Trying to bite me and drain my blood."

Hayden couldn't help but chuckle as he braced one arm around the trembling lady.

"It was horrible! Just horrible! I thought they were. . ."—her grip on him loosened—"I thought I was. . ."—her voice faded—"done for." She went limp in his arms.

"Dash it!" Tossing the torch into a puddle, Hayden grabbed her before she fell. "Magnolia!" Her name shot from his lips with the hissing of the flame. Yes, it was her. He knew by the soft feel of her skin, the embellished hysterics in her voice. But not by her smell. The scent that filled his nose was most definitely not sweet citrus and cedar.

Releasing the hammer on his gun, he shoved it into his belt and hoisted her into his arms. Anger simmered the food in his gut. Anger followed by concern, for she felt as light as cotton and just as weak.

A dozen thoughts peppered his conscience. Was she injured? Had an animal bitten her? Had she encountered a poisonous snake or frog? He laid her down by the fire, tore off his coat, bunched it up, and placed it beneath her head. Whatever contraption women wore beneath their gowns made her skirts flare up like a balloon. Even so, with all her petticoats, he couldn't find her legs to inspect them for injuries. Not that he should be looking at her legs. Still, she bore no marks or bruises on her face, neck, and arms except scrapes from traversing the jungle and bites from insects. He poured water on his handkerchief and dabbed her face. She moaned. Ebony lashes fluttered over pearly cheeks.

"I thought I'd lost you," she whispered, her voice scratchy like wool.

"Are you injured?" Helping her to sit, Hayden dipped the canteen to her lips.

She gulped down the liquid as if she hadn't had a sip all day.

"Easy now." He withdrew while she caught her breath.

She pushed him away, her eyes regaining their clarity. "Injured? Of course I am." Her shrill voice returned, and he instantly regretted giving her the water. "My feet are covered in blisters, my arms with scratches"—she brushed fingers over her cheeks, horror claiming her features—"My face. Oh, my face. There are bites all over it. And my hair." Fingering errant strands, she attempted to tuck them into the rat's nest that used to be her coiffeur. "Everything aches and I'm dreadfully hungry. And frightened. And I was attacked by a flock of bats!" Her blue eyes became a misty sea.

And Hayden's anger returned. "A colony."

"What?" She sniffed.

"A colony of bats. Not a flock."

"Oh. Who cares?"

"I told you not to follow me." Hayden growled and rose to his feet, chastising himself for not hearing her behind him all day. For believing she'd obeyed him and relaxing his vigilance.

"I stayed farther behind this time." She gave him a satisfied smirk. "It's not easy to track a man from such a distance, you know. I did quite well. Well, except for this horrendous state I find myself in." Her gaze swept over her torn, stained gown, and misery shoved her pride aside once again.

Zooks, the woman's fickle moods! Hayden's jaw tightened to near bursting. "Too bad you wasted all that suffering. You are still not coming with me."

"You wouldn't leave me out here alone!" A look of innocent incredulity appeared on her face. "I'll never find my way back from this distance."

Hayden ran a hand through his hair and marched away from her lest he do something he regretted.

"I can pay you."

The words turned him around.

"My parents are wealthy."

"How wealthy?"

"We owned the largest cotton plantation in Roswell." Planting her hands on the ground, she struggled to rise, her skirts ballooning in her face. "Grr," she squealed in exasperation and flopped back down.

Despite his anger, Hayden took pity on her and extended his hand, helping her to her feet. "*Owned* does me no good. Especially since the North confiscated your land, did they not?"

She took a few tentative steps, her delicate features knotting in pain. Hayden kept his grip on her hand firm until she settled. "What pains you?"

"My feet. I can hardly walk."

"Yet you managed to follow me all day." He released her with a huff, refusing to fall for her charade. This coddled woman knew exactly how to get others to fawn over her every need.

Pressing down her skirts, she attempted to wipe dirt from the once pristine fabric, her brow and lips twisting into odd shapes in the process. Finally she gave up and turned her back to him in a swish of creamy cotton. "We sold everything as soon as those infuriating Yankees marched into town. That was long before the war ended, as you know." She affected a nearly believable sob. "We lived under occupation for months and months. It was simply"—she threw a hand to her chest and cast a despairing look at him over her shoulder—"well, it was simply unbearable."

Hayden snorted. Though he'd heard the news about Roswell, and it was quite possible her parents had cashed out what they could of their holdings in time, she was playing him. But for what? Sympathy?

Her chest rose and fell. "I believe I'm growing faint."

An owl hooted as if laughing at her declaration. Hayden folded his arms over his chest. "Then you'd better sit down."

Frowning, she fiddled with her skirts and lowered herself onto a tree stump. "Turn your face, I must remove my shoes."

For some reason he didn't feel safe turning his back on this vixen. Nor did he like being ordered about like some servant. "You may remove your shoes, Princess, but I'm not removing my eyes from you."

She scowled and began fumbling beneath her skirts. "How could I forget? You are no gentleman."

"Indeed. And now you have all but handed yourself to me on a platter." He'd intended his tone to be threatening, even sultry, but it came out laced with anger and disgust. Finally a breeze fluttered the leaves and cooled the sweat on Hayden's neck and arms. But it did nothing to cool his irritation.

She froze, her face paling. A growl in the distance drew her gaze and a visible tremble ran across her shoulders. Perhaps not everything was an act. Hayden took a step toward her. "You are safe by the fire."

She looked at him as if he'd been the one to just emit a feral growl.

"*And* with me." No sense in toying with the woman any further. As much as he hated to accept it, he was stuck with her.

She bit her lip and began fumbling for her shoes again but said nothing. A definite first for her. The fire crackled and spit. Turning, Hayden added another log and tried to shake off his anger. The prospect of being paid would certainly make the trouble of bringing her along worthwhile. "Do tell me of this vast estate." He snapped a branch with his boot and tossed it into the flames. Smoked curled into the darkness, biting his nose.

"It was to be my dowry," she said, her voice strained. "My parents sent it to my aunt and uncle in Ohio for safekeeping with the provision that upon my parents' death or my return to America, the money would be handed over to me at my wedding."

"And why didn't your parents simply bring the money along with them to Brazil?"

"As insurance. Provision for me in case something happened to them."

Hayden scratched his jaw. It sounded believable enough but something wasn't right. "Being the astute businessman your father claims to be, surely he would have preferred to invest that money here in Brazil and see a hearty return, rather than leave it so far out of reach languishing in a jar somewhere."

"There was no guarantee of any return here." Firelight etched lightning across her eyes. "We knew nothing about Brazil and saw no need to bring additional monies besides the amount required. As it turns out, it was a wise choice since the parson would be in possession of our fortune now." She gave him a smug look as her hands continued to grope beneath her skirts.

One muddy red shoe emerged from the flurry of soiled lace like a dragon from a cloud.

Plucking the pistol from his belt, Hayden laid it on the log and sat down. "So, you have a dowry. What is that to me? We are here and it is there." Zooks, he could have used that money. He needed supplies. Badly. And a tracker to find his father.

"You aren't going back to the States?"

"What I seek is in Brazil."

Another shoe emerged. Along with a wince and a frown. "Then, why are you going to Rio?"

He shuffled his boot in the dirt. "If you have no means to pay me, we have no deal." A final test to see if she had any money at all.

Cultured brows folded over eyes brimming with fear. "A gentleman requires no compensation to help a lady."

"Yet, we have already established I am no gentleman." He grinned, though his insides broiled at the predicament she placed him in. Of course he wouldn't leave her in the jungle.

A frog—no, more like a toad—hopped along the edge of the

small clearing. Magnolia gasped and drew her knees up to her chest, scouring the ground around her.

Hayden rose. "Why would I want to endure your feminine theatrics for four more days? Especially without payment."

"Feminine theatrics, mercy me!" She huffed. "Of course there are feminine theatrics. I'm a woman, after all."

She certainly was. Even covered in dirt and bug bites, she presented quite an alluring sight. One which he allowed his gaze to rove over at the moment. If only to taunt her.

"You are no better than that toad." She squinted and tilted her head toward the bush where the creature had disappeared.

"A toad who will take you back to New Hope tomorrow," he said. Perhaps Hayden should do just that. He hadn't been with a woman in over a year and this one was far too distracting. Far too distracting and far too infuriating.

"No, wait, please." Her voice pleaded. "I do have some money with me. I need some of it to purchase passage home, but you're certainly welcome to the rest. If that's not enough, I promise to send you more when I arrive at my aunt and uncle's."

"I thought the money would only be delivered upon your marriage."

"I have no doubt I'll be married soon enough. My fiancé waits for me even now."

A slight intonation, a slight hesitation in her voice, gave Hayden pause. She was lying about something. But was it the money, her fortune, or the fiancé? "So, where is this money of yours?"

Turning aside, she stretched out her legs until slender toes peeked out from beneath her skirts. Slender, blistered, bloody toes, laced in frayed stockings.

Hayden swallowed. Loathing the guilt that swamped him, he rose, tore off several leaves from a nearby plant and knelt before her. "May I?"

She hesitated, her eyes shifting between his. Finally she nodded and inched her skirts up to her ankles. Blisters and raw skin peered at him through what was left of her mangled stockings, and he cursed under his breath. Picking at the hose, he removed the silken scraps, grabbed his canteen, and poured water over her feet. She jerked but didn't cry out.

"All this from walking?"

"I suppose I'm not accustomed to being on my feet all day."

Hayden glanced at her ankle boots. Not really ankle boots but tall, fancy red-leather boots scrolled in velvet designs with silk ribbons and heels at least two inches high. "Not exactly the best choice of footwear for a long trek."

"I had nothing else."

He didn't doubt that. "Why didn't you tell me about your feet?" He poured more water on the wounds.

"I did." She pulled them back. "Wait, I brought some of Eliza's salve." Opening her valise, she waded through its disheveled belongings.

Hayden took the jar from her hand. Their fingers touched. Their gazes met. She was distracting him with those beguiling eyes. Eyes that shifted between his—unsure, fearful, needy. They did funny things to his stomach. And to his breath, which seemed to have vacated his lungs. He looked away, opened the jar, and began applying the ointment. He'd never seen such delicate feet. Nor such blisters. He concentrated on them, not on the creamy skin that wasn't marred, nor on the sweet puffs of her breath wafting over him as she tried not to cry out at his touch.

The jungle sang a chorus around them as a breeze spun a cluster of dried leaves across the clearing. The tattered lace at her hem stirred. There. There was her sweet scent beneath the sweat and mud, a scent unique to her, a scent that caused his pulse to rise. Especially now when she was so close. And so quiet. . .and vulnerable.

"Thank you, Hayden." For once her voice held no sarcasm or spite.

It weakened his resolve. And he couldn't have that. "And just how do you plan to walk tomorrow?" He kept his tone sharp.

"So, you *will* take me?"

Against his better judgment, yes. "First, show me this money you speak of." He finished applying the ointment and sat back, wondering at the sensation in his fingers where he'd touched her. The lady was comely, to be sure. More comely than most. Yet he'd never suffered a shortage of attention from alluring women. Why did this one affect him so?

Reaching once more into her valise, she sifted through the contents and pulled out a velvet drawstring bag. "Gold coins. At least three hundred dollars worth."

He shielded his excitement. Three hundred dollars would buy him a wagon full of supplies and a good tracker. Picking up the leaves he'd gathered, he pressed them onto her feet.

"All I need"—her voice came out shredded like her stockings as he continued wrapping her wounds—"all I need is enough to buy passage back home and then purchase conveyance to my aunt and uncle's and the rest is yours."

Searching the vines hanging from trees for the right size twine, he sliced a piece with his knife and tied the leaves in place around her feet. She thanked him again. He avoided her gaze. Avoided seeing the appreciation in her eyes that he heard in her voice. Avoided anything that would soften him toward her, make him weak. He took the bag, opened it, and held it to the firelight. Gold coins winked back at him. Gold that made his head spin with delight and his brows arch in surprise at her honesty. He bobbed it in his hands, measuring the weight.

She slapped a bug on her arm and glanced around the camp as if she weren't the least bit interested.

Tying the pouch, he handed it back to her as a wonderful idea formed in his mind. "You have a deal, Princess."

"So you'll escort me to Rio and see me safely on a ship back to America?" She eased her skirts down over her feet.

Hayden strangled a chuckle. Who was she fooling? She wouldn't make it alone on a ship to the States. Not surrounded by sailors who'd been out to sea for months. Not unless he could find a ship of monks! She would be a Magnolia blossom ripe for the picking. And he could never allow that to happen. He was a swindler, not a monster. "Yes, of course."

"A good ship with a good captain who will ensure my safety?"

He nodded. But he had other plans for the enchanting Southern belle. Plans that would aid him greatly in discovering the whereabouts of his father. For Hayden relied solely on the information provided by Brazil's immigration officer, Mr. Eduardo Santos. And the man was not forthcoming with information unless his palms were greased with gold. Gold Hayden needed for supplies and a tracker. Yet if there was one thing Hayden had noticed about the man—besides the fact that he was as crooked as a bent twig—it was that he had an eye for the ladies. And a woman of Magnolia's beauty and charm would have no trouble extracting the information Hayden needed. All she had to do was flutter her lashes, give him a coy smile, flatter him in that dainty, Southern, I'm-a-helpless-woman-in-need-of-a-real-man-accent, and Mr. Santos would tell her the location of Midas's treasure if he knew it. How did Hayden know? Because if he were not a stronger man, if he were not privy to feminine devices and the tricks of skullduggery, he would, no doubt, himself, be bewitched by the siren.

Besides, he wasn't being completely dishonest with her. If Mr. Santos informed Hayden that his father had left for the States, he would accompany Magnolia home. However, if not, he would return her to New Hope to her parents where she belonged. Maybe they would even offer him a reward. And, of course, he would keep the money she paid him to escort her. All in all, it promised to be a lucrative venture.

For him, that was.

He gestured toward her feet. "I won't carry you through the jungle."

Her satisfied smirk faded into anger. "I'll be quite all right in the morning. Besides, I can wear extra stockings." She glanced around. "Now, where can I freshen up before supper?"

Hayden rubbed the back of his neck. "Supper?" He chuckled. "I do apologize, Princess, but food was not part of our bargain."

"But. . ." Her brows crumpled. "What will I eat?"

"The jungle is teeming with edibles."

She scanned the dark, oscillating greenery as if expecting a platter of roast beef to emerge through the leaves. Hayden couldn't take his eyes off her. With her skin flushed and moist, her flaxen curls tumbling over her shoulders, her chest rising and falling beneath her bedraggled bodice, she'd never looked more beautiful.

She must have noticed the direction of his gaze for her breath heightened. "Food may not be part of our deal, sir, but my purity is. If you dare touch me, you will not see a single coin of my money."

He chuckled at the ridiculousness of her brazen demand, for they both knew he could take both whenever he pleased.

Chapter 9

The trail widened, giving Colonel Blake a chance to catch up to James on their way to the temple. "How are you faring today, Doc?"

"Well enough." James flicked a glance at him, hoping his friend would take the hint that he didn't feel like talking. In fact, he'd hardly spoken to anyone since his strange episode at the beginning of his sermon yesterday. Until he figured out what happened, he planned on keeping it to himself. He'd even skipped lunch and supper in order to avoid conversation with the colonists. Which didn't make him a very good spiritual mentor, but if he was going crazy, he wouldn't be much use in that area anyway.

Batting aside a huge fern, he trudged forward as the group followed Thiago to some strange temple the man kept going on about.

"What happened yesterday?" the colonel asked.

James ran a sleeve over his forehead. "Isn't it obvious? I made a fool of myself." Worse than a fool. He'd shouted and trembled like a leaf in the wind before he made his apologies and dashed from the dais.

"Not in my eyes, you didn't. Obviously, something upset you enough that you couldn't continue your sermon." Blake shrugged, rubbed the old war wound on his leg, and continued limping beside James. "You are human, not some supernatural creature, unscathed by life."

James ground his teeth. Wasn't it shameful enough his fear of blood prevented him from using his doctoring skills? Would God now send another unfounded fear to keep him from his spiritual duties as well? "As the town preacher, I should at least appear to have my emotions under control." But once again he'd let everyone down, including Miss Angeline, who had finally made an appearance at Sunday services. Most likely her last.

He gripped the musket so tightly his fingers ached as countless colorful birds flitted overhead, mocking his sullen mood. Stepping over a craggy root, he hoped Blake would continue on in silence as they made their way to this mysterious temple. Though Eliza, Miss Angeline, and some of the women had wanted to come along, the colonel forbade them. James agreed. No sense in putting the ladies in unnecessary danger. Hopefully, there would be no danger at all. Perhaps they would even find something useful for the colony.

Mr. Graves certainly seemed intrigued, for ever since he'd found the place, the man had spent all his waking hours in the ancient structure, or so Thiago had said. Yet for all Thiago's chattering about the place, once Blake decided to go, the Brazilian guide had warned them to stay away. And when Blake refused to listen, Thiago pleaded to remain at camp.

"You saw something. When you were starting your sermon." Blake's statement drew James out of his musing and back to a topic he didn't wish to discuss. He glanced over his shoulder at Dodd and a few other men following behind, and then forward to Thiago leading the way. "How did you know?"

Blake heaved a sigh. "What was it?"

"A boy I operated on at the battlefield. A young corporal." James swallowed. He squashed a bug on his arm and wished he could squash the memory as easily. "He died under my knife." His hand trembled, and he switched the musket to his other one.

"I saw my brother." Blake said the words so matter-of-factly, James thought he hadn't heard correctly. Blake's younger brother had died a vicious death at the battle of Antietam—a battle James had witnessed.

"When?"

"When we first arrived. I went into the jungle to sort things out about Eliza." He brushed aside a fern. "And there he stood, plain as these trees around us, in his private's uniform, staring at me."

James's mind spun, trying to make sense of the story.

"Then he took off," Blake said. "Darted into the jungle."

"What did you do?"

"I ran after him. Found him lying on the ground in a clearing, blood gurgling from his chest." The colonel's voice cracked.

James halted and stared at his friend. The others wove around them, casting curious glances their way.

"We'll catch up," Blake said before he faced James and whispered, "And Eliza saw her dead husband."

Heart tightening in his chest, James gazed up at the knotted canopy. "What is going on?"

"You're the preacher. I figured I'd ask you."

James wouldn't tell him he was no better preacher than he was a doctor. "You think this is something spiritual?"

"What else could it be?"

Planting the barrel of his musket in the dirt, James leaned on the butt. "When we stood on the beach right before we entered the jungle, you said you felt something strange. I've felt the same thing since we arrived. A heaviness. Something oppressive. . .dark."

"Indeed." The lines on Blake's forehead deepened as he squeezed the bridge of his nose. "And Eliza has sensed the same."

A lizard scrambled up a tree trunk. Sunlight shimmered a rainbow of colors on its slick skin as it stared at James with one eye. "Perhaps this ancient temple will give us some answers."

But all the temple did was cause James's stomach to convulse. While Thiago stood guard at the entrance, refusing to enter, and Dodd, with a glimmer in his eyes, went in search of gold, sounds from within the building drew Blake, James, and the rest up the stairs and through the front porch.

James covered his nose against an unidentifiable stench as they passed broken tables, chairs, pottery, and a steaming pool of water on their way to the back of the large open room. A glimmer drew his gaze to a golden crescent moon and stars embedded in the back wall above a stone altar. To their left, the sounds of digging and a man's grunt lured them through an opening into a tunnel that led downward to the distant flicker of a torch. Bracing against stone walls on either side, James groped his way over the uneven ground. By the grunts and moans coming from in front and behind, the others seemed to be having the same trouble keeping firm footing.

Finally they reached stairs that descended with ease to a place where the tunnel widened. Two lit torches hung on the wall. A pile of rocks and dirt sat off to the side.

Graves emerged from a hole to their left, a shovel full of pebbles in his hand. At least James thought it was Graves. His normally stylish shirt was torn. Sweat-caked mud splattered over his arms and face. Dust speckled his waistcoat and grayed his black hair, making him look older than his nearly thirty years. James had never seen the posh politician so out of sorts. Nor had he ever seen him smile.

"Ah, you've come to see for yourselves." Torchlight glimmered over rows of white teeth that stood out against his filthy face.

"See what? What are you doing down here?" James asked, wiping sweat from his neck. "It's hot as Hades."

"Digging." Tossing the pebbles onto a pile, Graves set down his shovel—the one that had been missing from camp for days.

"For what?" Mr. Lewis finally caught up to them, the smell of alcohol following the old carpenter in his wake. "Gold?"

Graves snorted and ran a finger over his once cultured mustache that now hung in muddy strands. "Nothing so meager. I assure you." He leaned toward them, his tone spiked with glee. "Can you feel it? Can you hear it?"

All James felt were a thousand invisible spiders crawling on his skin.

"I don't hear anything," the colonel said.

Graves gave an exaggerated sigh before his brows lifted and he held up a finger. "*Shh.*"

Nothing but the drip of water and the moan of wind sounded through the dank tunnel.

"There! Did you hear them?" Graves said.

James shook his head. Colonel Blake crossed his arms over his chest. They shared a look of agreement that the man had gone mad.

"You still can't hear them?" Disgust weighted his voice as Graves's thick eyebrows dipped together. "Of course not." He waved a grimy, bruised hand through the air. "Go back to your farming, gentleman. I will find them. I will dig them out. And then you will see."

"What are you talking about? Find who?"

"The glorious ones. They are trapped." Graves started back toward the opening.

"There's nothing here but ruins, Graves." Blake reached for the man. "Come back to New Hope. Help us build something new, not dig up something old."

Graves swung around and stared at the colonel as if he'd asked him to strip naked and dance a jig. "I want nothing to do with your New Hope. Now, leave me be."

James almost felt sorry for him. But hadn't they all thought his behavior on the journey to Brazil a bit strange? On board the ship, the politician had always kept to himself, more like an observer than a part of their group. He'd even seemed happy when misfortune after misfortune had befallen them. Now James worried how long he could stay at this ghastly temple without food and water. The colonel seemed to be of the same mind when they emerged onto the front courtyard, unable to convince Graves to return. "What are we to do with him? He's obviously lost his mind."

"It's so quiet." Removing his hat, the old carpenter wiped sweat from his brow and glanced up. Tufts of cotton-like clouds drifted across a cerulean sky they normally didn't see much of through the canopy. But it *was* quiet. Unusually quiet.

Eerily quiet.

James lowered his gaze to the haunting images on a nearby obelisk. Despite the sweat moistening his skin, a shiver coursed through him.

Mr. Dodd charged through the broken gate. "I found something you should see, Colonel."

Wondering what, besides gold, could have put the ex-lawman into such a dither, James and the rest of the men followed him back through the front entrance and then around the broken wall until they stopped behind the enclosed structure. A vast, open field stretched out from the temple. Huge black circles of what once must have been charred grass or shrubbery were scattered haphazardly across the brown—no, gray, deathly gray—terrain. Whatever had seared the ovals into the ground must have happened long ago, yet nothing grew at all in the wide space. No moss; no seedlings; no grass, trees, or bushes. Not a single speck of green. Heat waves spiraled from a ground that appeared as dry as bones—as dry as a grave.

"What happened here?" The colonel shifted weight off his bad leg.

"It looks like a battlefield." Dodd scratched his head. "Don't it?"

"Not like any I've ever seen," Lewis offered.

James swallowed down a burst of dread. He didn't know how he knew. But he knew. He could feel it in his gut. Sense it in his spirit. "Something horrible happened here. Something far worse than we could ever imagine."

Chapter 10

Magnolia folded the coverlet she'd slept on—or rather had lain awake on—and put it back into her valise. After they had forged their bargain last night, Hayden had begun to act strange, getting that look in his eye she'd seen among so many suitors back in Roswell—as if he were starving and she was a sweetmeat. She couldn't blame him, really. Even in her disheveled state, she was rather alluring. But really, the rogue! So, announcing her intention to retire for the evening, she waited for him to erect some sort of shelter or prepare a soft place for her to lay her head. Instead, he had shrugged, lain down on the ground by the fire, and promptly fallen asleep.

Of all the nerve! Did he actually expect her to sleep in the dirt with all the bugs and snakes and other mucus-oozing critters? And shouldn't he be keeping watch over her? Protecting her from beasts and intruders? But from the snores that soon filtered her way, she'd surmised that was the last thing on his mind. She'd been so furious, she considered sticking a hot coal inside his shirt or—she grinned at the thought—down his trousers, but thought better of it. No need to rouse his temper—or worse. And since she depended on him to get to Rio De Janeiro, she needed to stay in his good graces. If he even had any.

So, she'd done all she knew to do. She'd sat by the fire, huddled beneath her coverlet with a knife in hand should a predator happen by. And not just predators, but any of the innumerable crawly things that overran the jungle. One of them, a particularly gruesome beast of a spider had ventured within a few feet of her. Hairy and black and as large as a man's open hand, it had stared at her as if it intended to nibble her flesh. In her exhaustion, she'd thought she'd seen it lick its prickly lips. If spiders had lips. So, she did what she did best.

She screamed.

Hayden never stirred. She'd poked the ghastly creature with a burning stick. The spider, that was, not Hayden. Regardless, the entire incident had been far too much for a lady with such a delicate constitution! Though she'd hoped to ration herself, she'd even partaken of a few sips of the Brazilian rum she'd brought along for comfort. And comfort her it did. Sometime in the middle of the night, she must have fallen asleep for she woke up lying on her side, her cheek glued to the mud, and ants crawling on her nose.

The man in question, her supposed escort, her protector. . .was still fast asleep.

How could he sleep with the morning clamor blaring down at them from the canopy? An unholy cacophony that had begun before the first gray mist chased away the darkness and now continued in both intensity and volume as the heat rose with the sun. Plucking her French hand mirror from her valise, she eased her fingers over the elaborate gold gilding and smiled at the delicate violets painted on the back. A gift from her father on her fifteenth birthday. But like everything from her father, it came with an admonition. *Only the finest, fairest ladies in Paris have one of these, my dear. Keep it near to ensure you always look your best.* Magnolia could still feel the sense of unworthiness that flooded her at that moment, the fear of not being able to live up to her father's standard. A fear that had become her everyday reality since. Still, she had loved the mirror. And the ivory comb that came with it, which she now pulled from her valise and began sifting through the hopeless tangles in her hair, all the while keeping an eye on the sleeping hero.

"Humph." Some hero he was. What sort of man took payment to assist a helpless lady? What sort of man cared not a whit for that lady's comfort in the middle of the jungle? Her comb struck a particularly thick snarl, and she struggled to loosen it without breaking her hair. A man as stubborn and thickheaded and twisted as this knot, that's who!

Exasperated, she growled, and switched to another section of her hair, wishing Mable were here to make her presentable as the slave always did in the morning, but the girl would have just gotten in the way. Besides, Magnolia's mother needed her. All their other slaves had run off after the war, leaving Mable to be lady's maid to both Magnolia *and* her mother. The absolute shame.

She raised her mirror to examine her face and began to sob at the sight of dirt smudged on her cheek and bite marks rising like volcanoes across her creamy skin.

The hero moaned and turned on his side. Sculpted arms folded across his chest. Dark stubble peppered his chin and jaw, while equally dark hair dangled over his neck. Mercy me, but the man was handsome. When he was asleep. When he was awake, his brutish personality all but masked his natural good looks. Yet hadn't he displayed moments of kindness to her last night?

Lifting her skirts, she examined her leaf-covered feet, remembering his gentle touch as he'd applied the salve. So gentle for such a beast of a man. Equally confusing was the way his touch had made her feel. As if she were dancing in a field of flowers. But surely those sensations were merely a result of reaching the end of the most excruciating day of her life. Anyone's attentions would have caused the same reaction.

Having rid her hair of most of the snarls, she repinned it and returned her mirror and comb to her valise, then struggled to rise. An impossible feat when one wore a bird cage strapped to one's waist. Finally, she managed to lean forward on her knees, plant her hands in the mud—there was simply no way around that—and push herself to stand. Wincing at the pain burning across her feet, she made her way to Hayden.

"Wake up!" He didn't move. Searching the ground, she gathered a stick and poked him with it. "Wake up."

In one swift movement, he jerked upward, cocked a pistol, and swung its barrel at her chest. Magnolia screeched and leapt backward.

Hayden blinked several times, gaping at her, before he lowered his weapon and rubbed his eyes with a groan. "When are you going to learn it is dangerous to wake a man from his sleep?"

"I didn't realize you were such a grump in the morning."

"Well, now you do." He lay back down. "Leave me alone."

"Is there a creek nearby where I can wash and change my clothes?"

"You woke me to ask me that?" He growled.

"Yes I did. The sun is risen and we should not be dilly dallying."

Emitting a bestial sigh, Hayden sat up again, grabbed his canteen, and took a sip. "It's barely past dawn, Princess. I would have expected someone so accustomed to languid inactivity to sleep much longer."

"If you must know, I hardly slept at all. No thanks to you." She tossed the stick at him, missing him by an inch. He never flinched. Which only made her angrier. "I was assaulted all night long by feral insects and would have probably been eaten by a wolf if I hadn't stayed awake."

"I doubt your expert vigilance would have stopped a wolf." He handed her the canteen. "You get the last sip. We'll refill it when we find water."

Tipping it to her lips, she barely got enough of the precious liquid to wet her tongue. *No more water?* She stared in horror at her stained gown and the dirt smudges on her arms and hands. "But I simply must have my morning toilette." Besides, she was terribly sweaty, though it wouldn't be proper to mention that. "I've never slept in my clothing before and you have no idea how uncomfortable it is."

He didn't seem to be listening to her anymore as he stood, shoved the pistol into his belt, and retrieved his coat from the dirt. "Well, now that I'm awake, we shouldn't *dilly dally,* as you say."

"I'm a lady and I have certain needs." She hated the slight catch of desperation in her voice.

He turned to stare at her as if she'd dropped out of the sky.

"So, if you'll lead me to some water, *Hayden*"—she seethed out his name for effect—"I'd be most obliged." Better to establish who was in charge before things got out of hand.

"I am not God, Princess. I cannot produce water out of a rock no matter how much you demand it. However, if you need to relieve yourself, you may do so in the bushes. I will wait here."

Heat stormed up her face. "How dare you mention such a thing?"

He pinched the bridge of his nose as if he had a headache. "If we are going to be traveling together for four more days, I don't see how we can avoid such breeches of etiquette."

Magnolia flung her hands to her hips and tried to spit a retort, but only nonsensical stuttering emerged.

Hayden seemed to be trying to make sense of it but finally shook his head. "What about your feet?" He leaned over to examine her toes.

"I brought along a pair of satin dance slippers. Though this heinous wilderness will destroy them within hours, they will suffice for now."

He nodded his agreement then waved her off like a spoiled little child. "Run along. Take care of your business and be quick about it."

Magnolia's stomach growled, reminding her that she hadn't eaten anything since yesterday morning. "Aren't we going to eat breakfast?"

"We'll find some fruit along the way."

Magnolia had never met a more obnoxious brute of a man. As soon as she relieved herself, donned some new stockings, and slid her slippers over her bandaged feet, she returned to the clearing and handed him her valise.

His amused gaze shifted from the case back to her before one of his eyebrows lifted. "Why do I want this?"

"To carry, of course."

"You brought it. You carry it." He dropped it to the ground, then disappeared into the greenery.

Magnolia didn't have time to be angry. She didn't have time to pout or gather the tears that melted most men's resolve. No, it was all she could do to keep up with him or be lost in the jungle forever. She did have time, however, to pluck an orange from a passing tree and toss it at him. It would have struck him too, if he hadn't ducked. How he knew she'd thrown it, she had no idea, but his chuckle filtered in his wake like a slap to her face.

Several hours later, Magnolia wished she'd eaten the fruit instead. Not only was her stomach rasping out its final breaths, but she could no longer feel her feet. They'd gone from aching to burning to completely numb. She wished she could say the same about her arms. Pain stretched all the way from her fingers across her shoulders and down the other side as she shifted the valise—that had transformed into an anvil—to her other hand. It hadn't seemed so heavy the day before, but she hadn't been this tired, either. Her hair had loosened from its pins and hung in sweaty strands over her shoulders. The hem of her dress was so caked in mud, it felt like she'd sewn iron bars into it. Yet what worried her most was that her stomach had stopped complaining hours ago. She feared it had taken to eating her own flesh from the inside out, and if she ever had a chance to remove her clothing, she'd find her midsection completely gone.

Just when she thought about gulping down the rest of her pinga rum, Hayden stopped at a small creek to fill the canteen and eat some wild bananas he'd foraged along the way. But no sooner had she splashed water onto her face and arms and sat down to enjoy her fruit, than Hayden was ready to leave again. The man had the strength and stamina of a bull. And the personality to match. How could she have ever found him appealing enough to kiss?

A band of monkeys scampered on branches and swung on vines overhead, yapping and squealing—which was more than Hayden had said to her all day. More than once, she'd tried to engage the man in conversation, but all she'd gotten were grunts that sounded much like the monkeys above. Gazing up, she ducked to avoid any droppings that might further soil her gown and add to the putrid scent emanating from the stained fabric.

Trying not to think about her situation, Magnolia forced her thoughts to happier days back home in Roswell before the war, when her only concern had been what gown to wear and which social function to attend and with whom. Her parents had seemed happy then, hadn't they? That was before she'd made the fatal error that had cost them nearly everything. Then when the war took the rest, things had gone from bad to worse. Her parents had never treated her the same after that. Before Martin, she'd had freedom. Afterward, she was a prisoner. Before Martin, she'd been her father's princess. Now, he did nothing but scold her about everything from her attire, to her manners, to the way she wore her hair. Perhaps by regulating every detail of her life, he believed he could stop her from making another mistake, make her so perfect that she'd only attract the "right sort of gentleman." Of course, how he expected her to accomplish such a feat in the middle of the jungle, she had no idea.

"You owe your mother and me. You owe this family." She could still hear him say. "And by God, you're going to restore our family name and fortune or you'll be no daughter of mine. Do you hear me?"

Yes, she had heard him. And each time he'd said it since. Yet for all her trying, she still seemed to do nothing but disappoint him. Perhaps she would never be good enough. Batting aside a leaf the size of her body, Magnolia plodded ahead. Were her parents worried about her now or were they simply angry she'd left? Most likely the latter, for she had once again besmirched the Scott name.

Drawing a filthy handkerchief from her sleeve, she rubbed the perspiration from her neck and face, chuckling at what her father would say if he saw her now. Sunlight drew her gaze to her right where creeping plants, laden with clusters of pink flowers, circled a tree trunk in an arrangement too beautiful to describe. Stopping, she drew in a deep breath of mossy air, perfumed with orchids and a hint of the sea, and set down her valise. Just for a moment. She only needed a moment. Stretching her aching hand, she glanced at the luxuriance of tree ferns all around her, their massive leaves at least six feet long, in every shade from red to brown to green. A small bird with bright orange wings landed on a frond, studied her for a moment, and began to warble a tune. If she wasn't so miserable, she might say the jungle was stunning in all its dangerous beauty.

A shadow caught the edge of her eye. Turning she saw a man standing with his back to her, dressed in an elegant suit of fine poplin, complete with cane and silk top hat. A crackling sound filled the air. Magnolia froze. She rubbed her eyes. When she opened them again, the man glanced at her over his shoulder and winked. *Winked!* She'd know that wink anywhere, along with those green eyes, finely chiseled nose, and cultured whiskers. Martin? Martin Haley? Her blood ran cold. It couldn't be. He took off at a sprint.

"Martin!" Clutching her skirts, she tore after him, ignoring the pain shooting up her legs. She plunged through the foliage, shoving branches and vines aside, with one thought in mind. *Kill Martin Haley!* For what he'd done to her. What he'd done to her family. Her thoughts whirled. How could he be in Brazil? In the middle of the jungle? And dressed to the nines? No matter. She would kill him anyway. How, she didn't know and didn't care. She simply dashed ahead, blind with rage. Until he disappeared. Faded into the steam coming off the plants. Whirling around, she searched the trees, bamboo, vines, her breath heaving, her feet aching, her mind spinning. No sight of him.

Plopping to the ground in a puff of muddy skirts, she began to sob. Moments later, footsteps thudded, and she jerked her gaze up to see Hayden emerge from the leaves, fear rumbling across his face.

Was he afraid for her? Now, she *was* dreaming.

"What happened? Why did you run off?" He squatted and brushed a strand of hair from her face.

"It doesn't matter." She swiped her tears away and took the hand he offered. Once on her feet, she tugged from his grasp. "I can no longer feel my feet. I'm covered with bug bites and"—she hesitated—"sweat, if you must know. Yes, sweat."

The concern from his face vanished, replaced by his typical look of annoyance. "Forgive me if I don't have a carriage to convey your ladyship through the jungle. What did you think the journey would be like?"

"Must we walk so fast? And you don't listen to me. Or talk. And my arm hurts from carrying my valise." She glanced over the maze of green and brown. "And now I'm seeing things."

Hayden gave her a patronizing look. "Oh, do forgive me, Princess. I was under the impression you wished to get to Rio as soon as possible. Yet now I discover your real desire is to engage in idle chatter whilst we take a Sunday stroll through the jungle."

Magnolia would love to stroll over his face with her muddy feet at the moment. Instead she bent over, grabbed a handful of the black ooze, and swung her arm back to toss it at him.

He cocked his head, that devilish grin of his appearing on his lips. "Come now, are we reduced to such childish antics?"

"Apparently that's the only language you speak." She held the dripping mud up like a trebuchet about to release its fiery projectile. "I demand you give me the proper respect due a lady on this journey or you will not only be covered in mud, but you won't be paid."

He chuckled. "I will be paid, Princess. The deal was to get you to Rio. There was no mention of licking your boots along the way."

"In case you haven't noticed, I'm not wearing boots." She lifted her chin. "Why, you may ask? Because my feet are swollen to twice their normal size." Magnolia knew she was losing what was left of her sanity. She knew because she no longer cared *that* she knew. "I ache from head to toe. I can't feel my arm or my shoulders, and my stomach has shrunk to the size of a walnut. My body has become a buffet for a plethora of flesh-eating insects. And I'm in dire need of a bath."

At that moment, the sky split with a thunderous roar and a sudden deluge poured from the heavens. As if God tipped over an enormous pitcher, the liquid cascaded upon them, drenching everything in sight.

"Your wish is my command." Hayden grinned and swept an arm out in a royal bow. Then gazing up, he spread his arms wide, closed his eyes, and allowed the water to wash over him in sheets.

Water gushed over Magnolia, too, soaking her hair, streaming over her face, dripping from her chin, and flowing down her gown. Refreshing and cool. Puddles formed on the ground as water streamed off plants and leaves. She opened her palm, allowing the rain to wash away the mud. She felt like crying, like screaming. . .

Like dancing.

Thunder rumbled.

Their gazes met through the blur of rain. Water pooled on Hayden's dark lashes and glued his shirt to his muscled chest. He started to chuckle. Not a bombastic victor's chuckle, but the hearty, warm chuckle of friendship. He pointed at her as his chuckle transformed into laughter, deep rolling laughter, that caused him to bend over and hold his stomach.

An unavoidable giggle burst from Magnolia's lips. She glanced down at her saturated dress, then closed her eyes and lifted her face to the torrent, allowing her own laughter to ring free. When her glance took in Hayden again, looking like a drowned bear, her laughter grew louder, until she, too, spread out her arms and twirled around, basking in the refreshing rain.

Chapter 11

After several unsuccessful attempts, Hayden finally lit a fire with some sparse kindling and a few dry logs. The flames snapped and sparked. He blew on them, watching them rise to dance over the wood. Setting moist logs around the edge of the fire to dry, he stood, shook the water from his hair, and ran a hand through the saturated strands. The smell of spicy rain and musky forest filled his lungs.

Shivering, Magnolia inched to the fire, a dazed look in her eyes. Muddy water dripped from the hem of her gown. Sopping, flaxen curls hung down to her waist. Raindrops sparkled in her lashes like diamonds as she knelt by the warm flames and held out her hands. She looked like a forest sprite who'd tumbled over a waterfall. A delectable, delicious forest sprite. Hayden licked his lips.

A fine mist filtered through the canopy, coating everything in a silvery sheen as evening lowered its black shroud over the jungle. The scent of orchids and musky earth swirled about them. A hint of a breeze added the briny sting of the sea. Her lips trembled, and she hugged herself.

"You should change out of those clothes, Princess. Tending a sick woman is not part of the bargain."

She lifted her gaze to his. The numbness in her eyes transformed to ice. "What good will that do? It's still raining." She stared back at the fire. "I'm going to die out here in the middle of nowhere. I'm going to die in a puddle of mud and be eaten by worms and spiders and toads."

She slumped onto a carpet of wet leaves.

"Toads don't eat humans." Hayden could think of nothing else to say to such a ludicrous outburst. She lowered her head and let out an ear-piercing wail.

Splendid. He had no idea what to do with a blubbering female. He much preferred a shrew to this sobbing mass of dimity and lace. But she was right about one thing. The rain wasn't stopping, and although he would be quite comfortable curling up beneath a huge leaf somewhere, he could hardly expect her to do the same. Zooks! He'd known the woman would be more trouble than she was worth. Selecting one of the wet logs, he tossed it on the fire. The wood sizzled and hissed, sending smoke curling into the air.

With a grunt, Hayden shoved aside some hanging vines and headed into the jungle. Hopefully, he could find what he needed before the encroaching darkness stole everything from sight. After several minutes of stumbling around in the shadows, he followed the firelight back to the small clearing, bamboo, banana leaves, and palm fronds bundled in his arms. Magnolia looked up and wiped tears away as if she hadn't realized he'd been gone.

"What are you doing?" Her voice broke, reminding him of a little girl's, an innocent little girl who needed his help. Despite his best efforts, it touched a deep part of him that wanted to protect and provide.

"Making you a shelter." He set to task, hearing her sigh of relief even above the drone of the jungle. Choosing the largest tree trunk at the edge of the clearing, he began leaning the bamboo against it, tying the hollow stems together with twine and placing palm fronds and banana leaves on top. The rain turned from mist to drops that bounced off leaves and dirt, and he placed another log on the sputtering fire, hoping the flames wouldn't die out. Magnolia sat in the same spot, strands of hair glued to her cheeks, and eyes alight with disbelief.

"Where did you learn to do that?" she asked.

Hayden shrugged. "I slept in the woods outside Charleston when it became too dangerous in the city."

Her delicate brows dipped. "Outside? Why didn't you sleep in your bed?"

"I had none." Hayden returned to his task, stacking more leaves on top to form a watertight barrier, then tying more bamboo together to form a bed.

He heard her saturated skirts slosh as she struggled to rise, heard her unladylike curse and the slap of mud as she pushed herself up from her hands and knees. "Didn't have a bed? What of your parents?"

He clenched his jaw at her sympathetic tone, regretting his disclosure. He didn't want pity. Especially not from someone like her. Wealthy and pampered. The type of people who'd averted their eyes and held handkerchiefs to their noses when little Hayden had passed on the street, begging for food.

He slammed back into the jungle, returning within minutes with armfuls of dry leaves he'd found beneath an Inga tree. He laid them on the bamboo frame inside the shelter, ignoring those sapphire eyes of hers as they followed his every move. After a few more trips, he'd gathered enough to complete a bed for her to sleep on.

The rain lessened into a light drizzle as darkness took the final step onto the throne of night, issuing in the buzz and chirp of its evening subjects.

"Your shelter awaits, Princess." Hayden gave a mock bow with a sweep of his hand.

She eyed him with a mixture of gratitude and surprise. "I don't know what to say."

"Though I'm sure the words may feel foreign on your tongue, I believe thank you is in order."

Her lips drew into a tight line, and the harridan reappeared in her eyes. "Of course I know to say thank you, you untutored toad," she spat. But then her expression softened. "However I *do* thank you. Your kindness is most unexpected." She pressed down her sodden skirts with a ragged sigh as if saying the words had exhausted her.

Not sure whether he should be angry at being called a toad or appreciative of her first thank you, Hayden merely shrugged. "You should change into dry clothes and get into the shelter. I fear the rain may be with us for a while."

"And just where am I supposed to do that?" She gazed around

as suspicion tightened the lines on her face. Hayden smiled. Which caused her to lift a condescending brow—made all the more adorable because she looked like a drowned mermaid. If mermaids could even drown.

"Princess, I'm too tired and too wet to sneak a peek at your unclad body," he lied and gestured toward a clump of thick brush. "You may change behind that. I'll stay here and tend the fire." Which needed tending by the looks of the dying embers. Besides, the task would give him something to focus on. Anything but where his mind kept taking him—to the vision of her bare curves and silky skin, only enhanced by the tiny moans and whispery whines emanating from the bush as she struggled to disrobe. He shook the vision from his head, selected the least wet log, and placed it on the fire, suddenly feeling a bit aflame himself.

"Need any help?" He half-teased.

"You stay right where you are, Hayden Gale!"

Squatting by the flames, Hayden rubbed his stubbled jaw. The only women he'd known outside of those he'd swindled were the kind who had no compunction taking off their clothes in front of men. Some he'd befriended. Others he'd used. Most he'd forgotten. He had no idea how to treat a real lady, how to control urges he'd always satisfied on a whim. And despite her viper tongue, Magnolia was indeed a tempting morsel. Especially for a man who'd been hungry for a very long time.

A breeze blew against his wet clothes, etching a chill down his back. Perhaps if he stayed wet and cold all night, it would keep his thoughts in check. Either that or he'd catch his death. Which somehow seemed preferable over trying to resist the temptation that continued to grunt and groan from behind the thicket. Rising, Hayden searched for any remaining dry leaves to toss into the fire—

When Magnolia screamed.

Plucking a knife from his belt, he dashed toward the bushes, preparing to meet some wild beast or ferocious spider.

"Hayden!"

Diving through leaves, he grabbed Magnolia, shoved her behind him, and thrust out his blade to meet her attacker. Scattered firelight from the camp flickered over dark greenery that barely rustled beneath a weak breeze. Nothing was there.

"There it is! There it is!" Hoping over the dirt as if it were on fire, Magnolia let out another grating scream and pointed to the ground. The shadow of a snake—a rather large snake—slithered over the dirt, heading toward a curtain of vines. No doubt to escape the strident clamor.

Releasing Magnolia, Hayden dove and thrust his knife through its head. The thick body bounced and twitched for several seconds before finally stilling. After ensuring it was dead, Hayden reached for Magnolia, surprised when she folded against him, surprised even more by the soft press of her curves on his chest, the silky feel of her trembling body beneath her chemise. "Did it bite you?"

She shook her head.

Relieved, Hayden untangled himself from her arms and nudged her back. But the naïve temptress pressed against him again, sobbing hysterically. He groaned inwardly, keeping his hands at his side and clenching his jaw until it hurt, hoping the pain would help him focus. "Only a snake, Princess."

"But it's slimy and disgusting and it crawled on my leg." Her voice quavered.

Against his better judgment, Hayden folded his arms around her and rubbed her back. Her need for comfort oddly deflated his own needs at the moment. Besides, he might as well enjoy the feel of her while he could. Because he knew it wouldn't last.

"How dare you?" She stepped back and slapped him across the face.

Not long at all. He rubbed his cheek. "I was comforting you."

"You were taking liberties." Grabbing her wet skirts from the bush, she held them up to her chin. "In my frightened condition!"

Hayden huffed. "It was you who ran into *my* arms, Princess."

"You could have resisted me."

"You were hysterical. What was I supposed to do? Shove you aside and leave?"

"You should have noticed I wore nothing but my chemise and excused yourself."

"I had a snake to kill, if you remember."

She sniffed. "Well, after that, of course. Stop staring at me!"

Hayden was indeed staring at her, more from a stupefied confusion than any lewd intention. Besides, the darkness forbade him to make out the details he so desperately wished to see. And his desire to do so had vanished with her slap. Leaning over, he picked up his knife, still stuck in the snake's head and held up the beast.

Magnolia leapt back. "What are you going to do with that?"

Shoving aside the scraggly bush, Hayden headed back to camp. "Make dinner."

Lowering herself onto a rock, Angeline nuzzled her face against her cat, Stowy's, soft fur and stared across the dark water of the creek. Wisps of night mist danced atop ripples as they tumbled over boulders to form a dozen tiny crystalline waterfalls. She loved this time of night. When everyone had retired to their huts and she could steal away for a few moments alone. A time when she could dip in the creek and allow the warm waters to wash away the filth of the day and caress her skin—a time to reflect on her life and her future; on her uncanny attraction to the preacher, James; on what she could do about Dodd's constant attention; on how she ended up being a seamstress in a town without a single bolt of fabric, though there were plenty of repairs needed on the colonists' already-worn clothing. But most of all, she needed time to reflect on whether she'd been mistaken in hoping she could escape her past by hiding in the middle of the Brazilian jungle.

Stowy glanced up at her with a *merow* to complain that she'd stopped petting him. Smiling, she scratched his head then ran her fingers down his back as he rumbled out a loud purr. "You're such a good companion, little one." She set him down beside her. "Now, stay here while I bathe." The cat promptly plopped on the dirt and folded his legs beneath his chest, reminding Angeline she needn't worry about him. Ever since they'd come ashore, Stowy rarely left her side.

It was as if he sensed dangers in the jungle and decided it was best to stay close. Everyone in New Hope had predicted he'd be devoured by some predator within a week, but here he was three months later, fit and fine. What a wise cat. Much wiser than her it seemed, for she had not fared as well in the wilds of city life.

Angeline began unbuttoning her blouse as she gazed across the misty creek. One of the farmers' wives had come across this isolated stream last month, and after telling the other women, they had all been sworn to secrecy about its location. The reason why stared at Angeline from just a few feet away. A round, stone basin, formed out of a rock outcropping, lay perfectly positioned beneath a gentle waterfall. Constantly filled to overflowing with calm, fresh water and surrounded by enough leaves to provide sufficient privacy, it provided a warm bath in the middle of the jungle—pure heaven to all of the colony's ladies. Well, if one didn't mind the mud, insects, and fish.

Drawing off her blouse, Angeline untied her ankle boots, removed her shoes, and took a quick glance around. There was no one around except a bright yellow parrot, who stared at her from a tree branch, and a rather frumpy looking frog perched on a rock in the middle of the creek. After removing her stockings, skirts, petticoats, corset cover, and corset, only her thin chemise remained. Thank goodness she'd given up on her crinoline weeks ago. The darn thing was far too cumbersome to work in.

After laying her clothes on top of a shrub, she fingered the ring hanging on a chain around her neck—a sparkling ruby mounted in a gypsy setting. On either side of the ruby, two white topazes shimmered in the moonlight. It was her father's ring. He'd always told Angeline that she was the red ruby in the center while the topazes were he and her mother, always guarding and watching out for her. Sorrow caused her throat to clamp shut at the thought, and she glanced up into the star-sprinkled sky, wondering if they were looking out for her now. Even though her mother died in childbirth, Angeline had always felt her love from beyond the grave, as she did her father's, dead some four years now. She had pulled the ring off his cold finger, placed it around her neck, and had never taken it off since. Not even when. . .

But she couldn't think of that now. Didn't want to think of that now. . .

Or what her parents would think if they knew what she'd become.

"If only you hadn't died, Papa. If only you hadn't sent me to Uncle John's." Wiping away a tear, she kissed the ring and climbed to the rim of the basin. An unavoidable moan of pleasure escaped her lips as she slid into the warm water. The frog uttered a deep *ribbit*. She smiled at him, hoping he'd stay on his rock and wouldn't be tempted to join her. Floating her head back on the water, she stared through the canopy at the clusters of stars flung like pieces of glass across a velvet backdrop. She held her nose and dipped beneath the surface. The sounds of the jungle muted to gurgles and the heavy swish of liquid. So soothing—as if she were in another world. A world far away where there were no problems, no struggles, no heartache.

No past.

Her lungs ached and she broke the surface, back to reality, back to the hiss of wind and hum of the jungle and the crackle of a fire.

A fire? She scanned the clearing. A dark figure sat on the beach.

Covering herself, she shoved backward until stone struck her back. Water sloshed. A shriek stuck in her throat. A cloud shifted. Moonlight dappled the man in silver. He smiled, revealing a row of crooked, stained teeth. Brown hair as dull as paste hung limp to shoulders that sagged beneath a thick wool overcoat missing two buttons. Bushy, graying sideburns angled down his limpid jaw as he studied her and stretched out his booted legs. "How's about a little fun, missy?"

Blood raced from Angeline's heart, leaving her numb. *Joseph Gordon*. What was he doing in Brazil? "You can't be here." Surely she was going mad. The heat, the insects, the hard work, the fear of Dodd recognizing her from that one night in a tavern in Richmond. . . All of it had ruptured her reason, shredding it into nonsensical rubbish.

"Ah, but I *am* here." He chuckled and leaned forward on his knees, looking at her with that same wanton look he'd always worn during the six months she'd lived in Savannah. Before he and his inquisitive nature and constant beatings had forced her to move—yet again.

"How?. . . I don't. . . What do you want?" She finally said, eyeing her clothing on the bush. Out of reach.

"To tell you that you can't run from what you are, Clarissa. Not here in Brazil and not if you went to the farthest parts of the earth, nor to the bottom of the sea. No, no." He gave a feigned sigh of disappointment. "And you can't hide what you done neither."

Angeline swallowed, her heart sinking into the silt beneath her feet. It was all over. Old Joseph Gordan would have no compunction to sharing her dirty secret with everyone.

He grinned. "Yes indeedy, you and I are going to have barrels of fun getting reacquainted."

"What are you doing, Mr. Dodd?" Overcome at the shock of seeing the man in the jungle so late at night, Eliza's shout came out louder than she intended.

Dodd seemed equally startled as he leapt back from his position crouched behind a bush. Immediately, he regained his composure and smiled. "Why nothing at all, Mrs. Colonel. Nothing at all. Just searching for gold."

Eliza narrowed her eyes. The man only addressed her with her husband's military title when he was up to no good. Perhaps as a reminder to himself that she was married to the leader of the colony and he best behave. "Searching for gold in the dark?"

"I have eyes like a bat, madam. Eyes like a bat." He opened them wide as if trying to convince her.

Eliza moved her torch closer to study those eyes that now shifted away.

I bet you do, but not to see gold with. "And yet you have no shovel."

He frowned and stuffed his thumbs into his belt. "No sense in carrying around a shovel until I actually find treasure, now is there?"

Eliza groaned inwardly at the idiocy of his statement. But why argue with a fool?

"I assure you, your pirate gold is not at the women's bathing pool, Mr. Dodd." Angeline had told Eliza she was going for a dip, which was why Eliza was coming to join her. She could use a bath herself, and besides, it wasn't wise for any of the women to be out here alone.

"The women's bathin'. . . What are you talking about?" Mr. Dodd looked at her as if she'd told him he stood in the Sistine Chapel in Rome. "I had no idea Miss Angeline was at some bathing pool."

"I made no mention of Angeline, sir."

He rubbed his chin and gave a nervous laugh. "I just assumed since you two are friends and I hear she loves to bathe and she'd be the only woman to come out here alone without escort and disrobe in public. Not that I'm saying she did such a thing, but since you mentioned a bathing pool, I only assumed. . ." He shifted his stance and cleared his throat, still refusing to look at her.

The man was not only a greedy letch but a bad liar as well. "What exactly are you trying to say, Mr. Dodd?"

"Nothing. . .oh nothing. . ." He slapped his lips together and plucked a leaf from a nearby bush. "Never mind. It's late and my head is foggy. Good evening." And with that, he sauntered away, chuckling, as if she hadn't just caught him peering inappropriately at Angeline. Something she would definitely mention to her husband, Blake.

Shoving the foliage aside, Eliza's anger rose as she realized the ladies would have to find a new spot to bathe. But those thoughts were soon scattered when she saw Angeline standing on the shore, holding her loose petticoat up to her chest, her face as pale as the moon.

"Did you see. . ." She turned as Eliza approached and pointed a trembling finger to the sandy shore of the creek.

"See what?" Eliza scanned the clearing. No one was there except Stowy, who now circled his mistresses' ankles. "Come now, let's get you dried off. You're shivering."

She wrapped Angeline in a dry towel and led her to sit on a boulder. "Did Dodd bother you?"

"Dodd? No." Angeline's voice sounded hollow. "I saw someone. Someone I knew from Savannah." Stowy leapt into her lap.

Eliza's heart tightened as her thoughts drifted to the odd visions she and Blake—and now even James—had seen. "Who?"

Angeline's harried gaze skittered across the clearing. "When you emerged from the jungle, he simply vanished. Are you sure no one is here?"

"I don't see anyone." Eliza took Angeline's hand in hers, deciding it best not to tell her about Dodd. "Real people don't vanish. I'm sure it was just a bad dream. That's all." But she knew Angeline hadn't been asleep. None of them had been asleep when they'd seen their visions.

Dear Lord, what is going on?

Chapter 12

Holding her wet clothes over one arm and her valise in the other, Magnolia entered the clearing and made her way to the shelter. Setting her valise inside, she flung her wet garments over a nearby branch beneath the cover of a tree, doing her best to hide her personals. Just the thought of Hayden seeing them sent heat blossoming up her throat. Just like it had when he'd held her close with nothing between them but her chemise. The utter shame! Yes, she had screamed for his help. She'd been hysterical with fear. But any gentleman would have made a hasty retreat after killing the snake. Not taken her into his arms. Not rubbed her back and squeezed her tight. How could she possibly face him now?

More importantly, how could she deny the complete and utter pleasure she had felt in his embrace? Not just safe and secure, but on fire from the inside out. In a good way. A most pleasurable way. Mercy me, she'd kissed men before. She was well acquainted with the flutter in her belly upon such an action. But this, this sensation was beyond anything she had ever dreamed.

She needed a drink. She took in a deep breath, letting her nerves settle.

At least it had stopped raining. For now. Perhaps she should retire for the night and avoid looking at Hayden altogether. She heard him fiddling with the fire, could feel his eyes on her. Knew as soon as he looked at her, he'd see her embarrassment. No doubt he would utter some sarcastic quip, or worse, try to take further liberties. Reaching into her pocket, she pulled out her flask and took a sip, noting how dry it was in the shelter. She placed a hand on the bed of leaves. Thick and soft and raised off the ground to keep the ants and moisture away. An odd feeling warmed her belly—she wasn't used to being cared for. But no, she told herself, that must've been the pinga. She took another sip, wincing at the pungent taste when a most delectable scent caused her stomach to lurch.

Peering around the corner of her shelter, she saw Hayden holding a skinned snake over the fire. "Ready for supper?" he asked, his tone playful.

She crept toward him. Their eyes met. As she'd feared, heat swamped her, rising up her neck and face. The right side of his lips quirked. Magnolia stomped her foot. "Stop looking at me that way. You behaved the cad and now you remind me of it with your eyes." Jungle-green eyes that assessed her with impunity and something else that sent a tingle down to her wet toes. "You know I am at your complete mercy and yet you toy with me as an impudent boy would a poor little bird. Not that I'm as weak as a little bird, so don't get any thoughts in your bloated head—"

"Do you wish to eat or not?" He interrupted, one brow lifting.

She thrust out her chin. "I don't eat snake."

"Well, I have nothing else to offer, Princess." The snake flesh sizzled in the flames, sending up an aroma that caused Magnolia's mouth to water. She inched to the fire, saw that he'd dragged a log over for her to sit on and placed some dried leaves on top.

Hayden tore off a chunk of snake and popped it in his mouth, raising his brows at her as he moaned in delight. His wet shirt molded to his chest, carving lines around firm muscles. Damp almond-colored hair slicked back from a face that seemed more intense and angular in the shifting firelight.

Magnolia pulled out her flask and took another sip. What was wrong with her? She'd been courted by wealthy landowners, an English baron, even a governor's son, yet here she was ogling a man so far beneath her, the heel of her boot wouldn't touch his head.

An orphan. One of the many hapless street elves inhabiting Charleston, stealing and begging and causing mayhem.

"I'll have a sip of that," he held out his hand.

"*May I* have a sip, please?" she corrected him.

He cocked his head and studied her, his jaw tightening. "Thank you, Hayden, for saving my life from a snake," he taunted.

Magnolia fumed. "Did I not say thank you? Perhaps you were too busy fondling me to hear."

He laughed, a hearty laugh that echoed through the jungle. "How about an exchange then? I give you some food and you give me a drink." Rising, he approached and held out the stick of roasting snake flesh.

She gulped. "I couldn't possibly."

"Come now. It tastes like chicken. Besides, you must eat or you won't have strength to walk all day tomorrow."

Handing him the flask, Magnolia pulled off a chunk of meat. She closed her eyes, set it on her tongue, and forced herself to chew, trying not to gag at the thought of it. But Hayden was right. It did taste like chicken. Wonderfully delicious chicken. Her stomach welcomed it happily. She broke off another piece while Hayden sipped her pinga.

He lowered the flask and coughed, his face turning red. "What in the Sam Hill is this?"

"Brazilian rum. Thiago made it." She frowned and gestured for him to give it back. "And that's all I have for the journey." When he didn't return it, she tugged off another piece of meat and lowered herself with difficulty to the log. "But this snake is good. Very good. I'm going to think of it as chicken, however. How do you know it's not poisonous?" She stopped chewing and stared at him, fear trailing the last piece down her throat.

Hayden chuckled. Much to her dismay, he took another sip of rum before he handed the flask back to her. "Poisonous snakes are brightly colored. Besides, I cut off the head where the venom is stored."

Magnolia had no idea how he knew such a thing, nor did she want to know. She resumed chewing, finally feeling the effects of the pinga soften her frayed nerves. "So, you were an orphan in Charleston?"

Emboldened by the rum, she broached a subject that would be considered impolite to mention in society, but for some reason she was desperate to know more about this fierce, untamed man.

The fire cast a circle of light, skipping over the surrounding leaves and branches like a swarm of butterflies in a field of flowers. Pops and sizzles joined the drone of crickets and bullfrogs in a pleasant melody.

Sitting on a stump just a yard from hers, Hayden tore off another hunk of snake and stared at it for so long she thought he wouldn't answer her. "Eight years."

"What happened to your parents?"

"Father left when I was two. My mother was run over by a carriage when I was ten."

Magnolia's throat closed around a piece of meat. She coughed, struggling to breathe, and grabbed the flask for another sip. Her heart felt as thick and heavy as the air around her. What father would leave a wife and child? And his poor mother. . . "How horrible. Did you not have relatives, uncles, grandparents?"

He shook his head and tossed the snake into his mouth. His jaw rolled tight as he chewed. "No one."

Magnolia stared at the dirt. An ant scampered across the soil, forming a jagged path. First left then right, then left again as if it were lost and trying to find its way. Finally, it approached the fire then sped off in the other direction. All alone. Just like Hayden had been. While she'd slept in a feather bed, had a buffet of delicacies to choose from, and every luxury money could buy, he had been on the street, searching to find his way, scraping his sustenance from the dirt. "How did you survive?"

He grabbed a stick and poked the fire, sending sparks into the night. "I begged. Stole. Sometimes set traps and caught small animals, whatever I could."

His tone bore the nonchalance of a man who didn't want pity, yet pride and pain lingered in his expression. She wanted to touch him, to offer him comfort, but he seemed unsettled, like a powder keg about to explode. Besides, she didn't want to care for him. Caring meant risk. And risk meant pain. At least with men like him. Handsome, capable men with sultry smiles and mischievous eyes that made a woman's heart flutter, excitement and danger in their touch. She'd had her heart trampled by a man like that. But never again. They both sat silent for several minutes. Finally, he stood, strode to the edge of camp, and returned with two bananas. He handed her one.

"Yet you survived and obviously found a way to earn a living." She took the fruit, hoping to sweep away Hayden's somber mood with her compliment.

A breeze stirred the flames then spun around the camp, fluttering the surrounding leaves. Pinpricks of light flashed in the dark jungle. On and off. One there, and then another a few feet away. "Fireflies!" Shoving off the log, Magnolia jumped to her feet and twirled around, excited to see something so familiar. "Just like in Georgia! Do you see them? I've always loved fireflies ever since I was a little girl." Somehow it made her feel close to her homeland, as if it wasn't across an ocean, thousands of miles away.

Her eyes met his, and she found him smiling at her. Not a seductive sort of smile, but a smile of admiration. It did odd things to her insides, and she shifted her gaze away and sat back down. "What is it that you do, Hayden? To make a living, I mean."

This seemed to amuse him, though why she couldn't imagine. "You might say I'm a broker of sorts."

"A broker? And what does a broker do?"

He seemed to be pondering the answer as he tossed another log into the fire. "I arrange sales of properties and other investments." He smiled again, a smile of amusement, as if he'd just told her he was a clown with a traveling circus. At least that would be more interesting than being a broker from the sounds of it. In fact, it quite surprised her to learn that this uncultured man held such a professional job. Sailor, fisherman, blacksmith—those professions she could understand. But broker? "Sounds complicated," she said. "How did an orphan learn such a trade?"

He peeled his banana and took a bite. "One learns many things on the streets, Princess. You do what you must in order to survive."

Then why did his voice sting with guilt? Surely being a broker was an honorable pursuit. Perhaps not very lucrative, but honorable.

A monkey howled in the distance. Or was it something else? Something more menacing. Hayden didn't seem to notice as he stared at the fire, a pensive expression on his face.

Magnolia took another sip of pinga. My, but the man was acting strangely. Finally, after a quick glance her way, he rose and sat on a log on the other side of the fire, as if he couldn't stand to be near her.

She should be thrilled at his obvious disinterest. Relieved! Especially after their encounter in the bushes. Then why did the action disturb her so? She fingered a strand of moist hair lying in her lap and regretted not pinning it up appropriately. She must look a mess! Her father would be outraged. She could still hear him say:

"The Holy Scripture tells us that a woman's hair is her glory. Therefore, it must be properly combed and pinned up with modesty and decorum at all times. Otherwise you shame not only yourself, but your family and your God. Only women of tawdry morals wear their hair loose."

Corking the pinga, she slipped it in her pocket and retrieved her mirror from her valise. She barely recognized the woman staring back at her. Hair like coiled wet rope hugged the side of her face like a barnacle to a ship. Her lips were pale, her eyes dull, and red marks peppered her once porcelain skin. Retrieving her handkerchief, she quickly wiped the streak of dirt lining her forehead. How had she missed that before?

Perhaps her disheveled appearance was the reason for the look of disgust on Hayden's face, the reason he distanced himself from her. She ran fingers through the tangled strands of hair, shoved them away from her face, and held the mass of curls up behind her. She should pin it up. But she didn't feel like it tonight. Besides, who cared what Hayden thought? Letting her locks tumble down her back, she opened her flask and took another drink. Maybe she was worthless just like her father said. Especially without her beauty.

Firelight dappled leaves with golden light and flung sparks into the night. She glanced up to see stars winking at her through the canopy. She giggled at the sight and lowered her gaze. Things became blurry, distant. The pain throbbing in her heart numbed, and she tipped the flask to take another sip.

When Hayden plucked it from her grip.

"I think you've had enough, Princess." Hayden shoved the cork in the nozzle and slid the flask into his pocket. Though he'd love to take another drink himself, he was already having trouble keeping his wits about him with this capricious woman. Capricious and whimsical and oddly delightful. And beautiful. No one had ever asked him about his childhood before. Or his occupation. Nor had anyone seemed genuinely sorrowful at his woeful story. In fact, the last person he expected sympathy from was the spoiled daughter of a rich plantation owner.

Yet the concern and pain burning in those blue eyes of hers had nearly done him in, broken his resolve to allow no one into his heart. No one close enough to really know him. No one who could hurt him—abandon him. He'd told her more than he'd intended. And she was more beautiful to him for having drawn his sad tale out from hiding. But now, he must shove his past back into the cobwebbed recesses of his mind and close the door on further conversation.

At least about him.

"Here, have some more snake." He handed her the stick.

"I don't want snake. I want my rum back." She held out her hand.

He put a piece of snake in it instead.

Those eyes that had been so beautiful when they were filled with concern for him now flashed like lightning. He gave his gaze permission to rove over her curves, heating his body in remembrance of the feel of her. Zooks, but she was a delicious morsel. And now a besotted one as well. In her condition, he would have no trouble seducing her. Like he'd done with so many women before.

Which was why he mustn't take a drink. And why he must sit as far away from her as possible.

She tossed the snake into her mouth. "My rum, if you please?"

"Let's save it for tomorrow, shall we?" He returned to his seat and threw another log on the fire.

A frown on her face, she began peeling her banana. "You're a monster, Hayden Gale." She mumbled. "And no fun at all." She bit into the fruit and fumbled with her hair, trying to set it in place without pins. "No, you are worse than a monster. You're one of those giant toads down by the river. You know the ones that are big and fat and ugly and have all those hideous spots on them? Yes, you're one of those. Except there's not a libertine's chance in a convent that you'll ever turn into a handsome prince."

Hayden couldn't help but smile.

Until she began to sing.

"Open the door, my hinny, my heart,
Open the door, my own darling;
Remember the word you spoke to me
In the meadow by the well-spring."

Hayden must find a way to stop the irksome sound. "Tell me of this fiancé of yours."

She stopped and stared at him. "I've told you. His name is Samuel Wimberly, and he's a renowned solicitor." She sat taller as if trying to convince him of the man's worth. "He was an adviser to Jefferson Davis, you know."

"If he was such a great match, why are you here in Brazil and not playing the doting wife back home?"

She released a heavy sigh and gazed into the fire. "My parents didn't think Samuel was good enough for me. They wanted someone with more money and a better name to help our family recover from my—" She froze, her eyes widening.

"From your…?"

"From the war."

"From *your* war?" he teased.

"Don't be silly." She waved a hand through the air. "It doesn't matter. Anyway, Samuel must have gone into hiding after the war because we couldn't find him. And my parents got some harebrained idea of pawning me off on a wealthy Brazilian of royal blood or a rich American who came here to escape the war. Apparently many of both can be found in Rio."

"Then why didn't they stay in Rio with you when we first arrived?"

"Because. . ." She glanced at him and flattened her lips. "Because they want to get settled first, establish a presence, a name. . .to attract the right sorts. . .you know, appearances and all that."

"Hmm." Either the woman was lying or she and her parents had beans for brains. "Surely being part of the landed gentry, your parents could have found a suitable match for you in the States. Why come to an unknown country?"

Knowing how much she hated Brazil, Hayden expected her to agree vehemently. Instead a shadow rolled across her face as she fingered a wet strand of her hair.

"My father says a woman's appearance is all that matters. And because I was born beautiful, it is my duty to marry well. That's what beautiful daughters do, you know, they are useful for making alliances that help the entire family move up social and economic ladders." She wobbled on her stump then perched her chin in her hand. "Trouble is I can't seem to *keep* myself presentable enough for him."

A lump formed in Hayden's throat.

The shadows beneath her eyes deepened. "I can never seem to please him. I can't keep my hair in a proper coiffeur nor my skirts without wrinkle and stain. And I've tried so hard. So very hard. Which is why he dragged me to Brazil." She stared down at the strand of hair in her hand. "I owe it to him to form a good alliance. To pay off my debt. And now I've gone and run away. Ruined everything for him once again." Her voice caught, and she released a long sigh. "I simply can't stand another minute in this place, surely you understand? The jungle, the dirt, the bugs…and I love Samuel. And he loves me. How am I to find a proper man out here in this desolate cesspool? I want to help my father, I do, but I fear he's given up on finding me a match anyway, and I'm fast becoming an ugly old spinster." She dropped her head into her hands and began to sob.

Hayden ground his teeth together. He had never cared for Mr. Scott, but now he liked him even less. How dare any father treat his daughter like a commodity? Treat her beauty as if it was something to barter with, something with which to increase his own station in life?

Look what he had created. A miserable woman not only obsessed with her appearance but desperate for a father's love. Perhaps life behind the gilded doors of the pampered elite wasn't as merry as they pretended. Sympathy rose for the woman before him, and Hayden found himself longing to bring her comfort.

The fire spat and sizzled. A lizard sped across the clearing and disappeared into the darkness. "What could you possibly owe your father?" he asked.

She looked up, eyes swollen and face moist. She swayed to the left, blinked, and finally balanced herself on the stump. "I made a mistake. A big mistake. It cost my family dearly. And tore my heart in two." A flicker of awareness strengthened her glossy gaze. "But I can't tell you about it."

"It was a man, wasn't it?" It had to be. A suitor, perhaps, who took advantage of her innocence. "Someone close to you?"

"How did you know?" She snapped her gaze to his then shifted to stare at the fire. "An evil man. A trickster. A liar."

Hayden's stomach twisted. Like him.

Rising, she began to pace, her skirts floating over the dirt. She wobbled, held out her arms, then turned to go the other way.

He'd better settle her before she fell. Slowly, Hayden made his way to her. The last thing he needed was her darting off into the brush on a whim. Over the years, he'd seen alcohol cause people—especially distraught people—to do dangerous things. And he didn't relish the idea of traipsing after her through the jungle. Especially in the dark. She stumbled over a root and barreled into him. He steadied her. She smelled of sweet rain. "Regardless of what you feel you owe your father, you shouldn't have to sacrifice your life for it."

Her eyes wavered over his. A tiny furrow formed between her brows. Finally, she reached up and ran her fingers over his jaw. "I always wondered what that felt like. So rough and prickly." She scrunched her face and studied him. "You are quite handsome, Hayden Gale." She slammed a finger over her lips and grinned. "But I'll deny I said that tomorrow."

"And since I am not a gentleman, I will, of course, remind you."

Raising her nose, she jerked from his embrace and took up a pace again, charging straight into the stump she'd been sitting on. "Ouch!" She started to topple. Hayden caught her, hoisted her into his arms, and carried her to the shelter. Kneeling, he placed her inside. It was best that she got some sleep before she said something she'd regret. And before he *did* something he would definitely regret.

Lying down on the soft leaves, she threw a hand to her head. "Everything's spinning. Why is everything spinning? It's a fine shelter, Hayden, it truly is, but what of all the spiders and lizards, ants, and snakes!" She sat up and reached for him. "Don't leave me, Hayden. It's so frightening here in the jungle."

Hayden could only stare at her. Was she kidding? *God, if You're up there, this is far too much temptation for one man.* Especially a man like him. It was the first prayer he'd uttered since his mother's death fifteen years ago. That time, God had not answered him, why did Hayden think He would answer now? "The critters will leave you alone." For the most part. "Besides, I'll be right by the fire. You're safe."

"There's room for two." She lay back down and patted the leaves beside her. "You made the shelter—you should sleep in it."

She had a point. A very delectable point. Groaning, he forced himself to stand. "Good night, Princess. Sleep well." At least *she* would get some rest, for it would be a long time before he settled down enough to fall asleep. A long time, indeed.

During those hours, Hayden made a pact with himself. This woman not only stirred him physically, but she had begun to stir his heart. And that was far too dangerous. Dangerous for him and dangerous for her. He'd made a practice of never mixing business and pleasure, of never getting too close to one of his "clients." Which was why he must keep his distance from the lovely Magnolia for the rest of the trip. He was only flesh and blood, after all.

Chapter 13

Finally some level ground! Magnolia trudged after Hayden, every inch of her legs and feet aflame. For the past two and a half days they'd ascended one hill after another as they wove their way through a range of verdant mountains—through steamy jungles, up windswept crests, and even down to an occasional beach, so close were they to the sea. Hayden told her they traveled near the coast to avoid the larger mountains inland—a range of majestic peaks she could now see rising in the west like angry gods spying on intruders to their land. She half expected them to grow weary of holding their heads above the clouds and suddenly collapse, swallowing her and Hayden whole. Part of her wouldn't care if they did. At least she'd be able to rest. But the muted sounds of a large city kept her plodding forward. That and the glimpses of civilization they'd passed—if one could call them that—in the form of several small farms and mud homes abuzz with naked children like bees around a hive. The adults greeted them with unabashed friendship and grand enthusiasm, beckoning them to come and share a meal. At least that was what Magnolia surmised from their exaggerated gestures, once they realized she and Hayden didn't speak Portuguese.

But Hayden declined each time, trying to make them understand that he and Magnolia were in a hurry to get to the city. Unfazed by the refusal, they continued to smile and wave at them until they were out of sight. Magnolia couldn't help but remark at how friendly Brazilians seemed to be.

"Beware of smiling faces and beguiling invitations, Princess. Everyone has a motive."

Those were the first words he'd spoken to her in days, other than grunts and nods and an occasional "Hurry up." Magnolia couldn't imagine what she'd done to prick his ire. Yes, she'd overindulged in drink that one night, but she had no memory of saying anything untoward or rude. Like she usually did when besotted. All she remembered were the personal details they shared of their lives. Which should make people feel closer, not push them apart, shouldn't it? Yet, all their intimate conversation had done was erect an impenetrable wall around this man.

"So, you *can* speak" The path widened and she quickened her pace to slip beside him.

"Only when I have something important to say."

"What are you implying?" Magnolia snapped, shifting her valise to her other hand while she shook out her aching fingers. "That I don't speak of important matters?" She huffed. "Besides, what is so important about your cynical distrust of people?"

He halted. Green eyes assessed her as if she were one of the pesky butterflies that continually landed on them in the jungle. Then turning, he moved on without saying a word.

"You can't trust most people, Princess," he said after a few minutes. "Once you realize that, you'll be better off."

Magnolia drew a sleeve over the perspiration on her brow, having long since given up proper etiquette. Trust. Something she'd sworn to never give another man. Yet, here she was trusting this one to put her safely on a ship heading back home. "Can I trust *you*?"

When he didn't answer, she stopped. "I *can* trust you, can't I?" she called after him, but her voice blended with the annoying whine of insects darting around her head, and she wasn't sure he heard her. In fact, she wasn't sure she could take another step. Every inch of her body throbbed, from the pounding in her head to the crick in her neck from sleeping on the ground, to the strain across her shoulders, the gnawing hunger in her belly, the spasms in her arms and fingers, her sore calves, and blistered feet. And to make matters worse, she'd been shaking ever since she'd sucked down her last drop of rum over a day ago.

In fact, she was quite sure she'd walked across the entire country, hiking up craggy cliffs with deadly drop-offs, sliding down muddy trails with no end, tripping on massive roots that crisscrossed the ground, all the while being strangled by the web of vines dropping from the canopy like ropes from a castle wall. Only climbing these ropes wouldn't bring one to the safety of a fortress but to an entirely different world ruled by monkeys and bats and birds. And then there were the bugs. She'd thought Georgia's insects were hideous. If she ever made it back home, she'd never complain about them again.

She stared at Hayden, marching on his merry way, with that cocksure swagger of his, oblivious to her at-death's-door condition. As usual. Yet he *had* taken care of her. Good care. Especially at night when he erected a shelter for her and provided something for dinner. One night he'd even caught a couple fish. Magnolia was sure she'd never tasted anything so delicious. Though he'd ignored her many shrieks during the night at the bugs invading her shelter, he'd stretched out and slept across the entrance like a sentinel. His presence had brought her more comfort than she cared to admit. And aside from that evening when he'd held her in her chemise, he'd been the perfect gentleman, stunning her with behavior so contrary to her initial assessment of the man. Mercy me, he'd even given her back her flask, though it had been nearly empty.

Now, it *was* empty and she craved a drink. Picking up her valise, she forced her feet to move before Hayden disappeared from sight. Infuriating man! But they were almost in Rio, and she could rid herself of him soon enough. The sooner the better before he realized she'd lied to him about the money. She shuddered to think what he would do to her when he found out. Most likely take every last cent she owned before she could purchase a ticket home. Then, what would happen to her?

No, as soon as Hayden led her to the harbor, she would steal away and buy a ticket on the first ship heading back to the States. Even now as the chatter of people and clank of the tramway convinced her civilization was near, her heart lifted a little. She needed a bath. That and some warm food and a ticket home had been all that had kept her going these past five days. Home to America. To Samuel. To comfort and safety and love.

~

Grabbing Magnolia's elbow, Hayden escorted her into the throng amassing on the streets of Rio de Janeiro. Sweat streamed down his back as he ushered her through the wall of humanity lined up to see a religious parade coming down the road. He glanced at the brutal sun firing waves of heat upon the scene and wondered how these people could stand being outside. Or how they could stand the smell. Body odor and animal dung mixed with spices and overripe fruit formed an exotic yet putrid aroma that pinched his nose and he found himself longing for the shade and fresh air of the jungle.

Wealthy Brazilian ladies dressed in their finery stood at the windows of their homes where bright red curtains barely fluttered in the limpid breeze. Diamonds hung from their ears and necks, sparkling in the sun as they leaned on window sills, waving at the passing crowd. Odd music that sounded like a mix of an African chant and a French minuet flowed up the street. The mob shouted with glee as all turned to see a mannequin made of barbed iron sitting atop a horse leading the procession. "*São João*! *São João*!" the people yelled and prostrated themselves before the strange figure as it passed.

Magnolia stopped, awestruck at the sight. The impassioned throng bumped and jostled her on all sides, yet when Hayden tried to tug her away, she refused to budge. Her gaze was fixed on a troop of little girls following the freakish mannequin. No more than six years old, they wore short skirts embroidered in gold that were full and puffed out as if they wore hoops. Two large wings of gauze fastened to their backs, and on their heads a diadem of jewels glittered in the sunlight. They leaped and danced to the rhythm of the music while scattering rose petals from a basket over the dirty street.

The mob sang and swayed and worked themselves into a frenzy as they worshipped the figure on the horse and joined with the girls in dance. Finally, Hayden managed to drag Magnolia aside, away from the middle of the crowd. She leaned against him, weak and panting and looking like she was about to wilt. He must find shelter and food for her soon. She had endured far more than most ladies of her class ever would have been able to endure. More than *he* thought she would have. For a pampered sot, she had surprisingly kept up with his swift pace through the jungle. And aside from a few complaints here and there and some shrieking in the middle of the night due to bugs invading her bed, she'd stopped whining. One night, she'd even helped him gather firewood and palm fronds. He had wanted to thank her, wanted to tell her he was proud of her. But he thought better of it. No sense in teasing them both with a friendship that couldn't last. One that would be quickly severed when Hayden's deception came to light.

Pressed against the wall of a shop, Hayden slipped his hand into hers, lest he lose her in the mad crush. Much to his surprise, she gripped it willingly, desperately, and he hated the overwhelming need to protect her that welled inside of him. He'd never felt that way about a woman before, especially one he was about to swindle. Clamping down his jaw, he shoved through the crowd, focusing his mind on his plan, his goal, while squashing his emotions. Emotions made him weak, made him lose his edge. Any confidence man worth the money he swindled never allowed sentiment to interfere with a job.

Elaborate churches rose like guardians of light over the shadows of debauchery in the streets as the crowd drank and danced in celebration. The idol worship offended even Hayden's nonreligious sensibilities. Though he was sure they were shouting "Saint John! Saint John!" the entire festival seemed to have popped from the pages of some pagan ritual. Especially in light of the prostitutes lingering about. Large Negresses dressed in ruffles and lace, wearing high-heeled slippers, their necks and arms loaded with gold chains and ivory, and their heads adorned in colorful turbans, squatted before shops and dared to lounge even on church steps, baring bosoms to men who passed by.

Hoping to protect Magnolia from the sight, Hayden hurried her along, but her gasp and "Mercy me" told him he had failed. Rounding another corner, he led her away from the celebration, trying to recall the way to the immigration office. A donkey-led tramcar clanked along in front of them as dozens of mulattoes in every shade possible wove through the crowd, carrying sugarcane, bananas, oranges, prawns, and fish.

"Can you show me the way to the dock master? I need to see when the next ship leaves for the States." Magnolia finally released his hand and drew her parasol from her valise. "Perhaps there's one leaving tomorrow. I wouldn't want to miss it. Of course you don't have to accompany me. I could meet up with you later to say our good-byes."

Her voice sounded odd, hurried and clipped. When he glanced at her, she did not meet his gaze.

"They are closed in the afternoon," he said, not entirely sure of that fact, but it made for a good excuse to delay her plans. Besides, they'd passed several businesses and shops that had signs posted on their doors and no patrons within. Closed for the festival, no doubt. Which meant the immigration office might be locked up as well. Blast! He'd have to wait another day to find out about his father.

"Closed?" Her voice was so despondent, it nearly broke him.

"We'll go first thing in the morning." If—and only if—Hayden discovered his father had returned to America.

He turned down Rosario Street, where, if he remembered correctly, there was a hotel, Hotel d'Europe, which favored foreign guests. The least he could do before he swindled Magnolia out of most of her money—if it came to that—would be to provide her a decent room, a bath, and some food.

Shops lined the narrow street, their second stories housing for city dwellers. Carne secca and dried cod, along with bags of *feijjoes* and Minas cheeses sat in piles in front of the stores, emitting the most foul odor. Magnolia shifted her parasol and drew a hand to her nose, but her gaze soon found the bay and all discomfort vanished from her face.

"Look at the ships! Can you tell if any are American?" She halted, her eyes skittering over the water.

With the sun low in the sky behind them, the bay of Rio De Janeiro spread a panorama of glistening emerald across the horizon, dotted with boats, barges, and ships of all sizes: steamers, frigates, sloughs, brigs, and a Dutch trading ship, from what Hayden could tell. Large barks with high lateen sails, navigated by Negroes and laden with fruit, sped across the bay to the various pretty islets strewn like gems across the water.

"We'll check tomorrow. Come along." He offered his hand but she drew her valise to her chest and hugged it instead, giving him a look of suspicion. "Where are we going?"

"To get you a room for the night. You'd like a bath and a real bed, wouldn't you?"

Her face lit. Followed by a flash of her pretty white teeth. It was the first smile she had graced him with in several days. And he hated how good it made him feel. Like he was worthy. Like she trusted him. Like he'd do anything to keep that smile on her pink lips.

Even pay for the room at the Hotel d'Europe with his own money. Seven dollars. Good thing they accepted American money and didn't expect Reis, the local currency. Yet now Hayden had only five dollars left in his pockets. At least until tomorrow.

After unlocking the door to the room, Magnolia spun to face him, a look of horror on her face. "Where are *you* going to stay?"

Hayden rubbed the stubble on his chin and grinned. He'd love to tease her and insist they share the room, but she looked so pathetic and tired standing there in her stained, ripped gown and dirt-smudged skin, her hair all askew. "Is that an invitation?" All right, so he couldn't resist a little taunting.

"Of course not! How dare you insinuate—"

Hayden placed a finger on her lips. "Don't vex yourself, Princess, I can take care of myself."

At this, her eyes narrowed, and she swatted his hand away. "Very well." She set down her valise and started to close the door.

Hayden's boot halted its progress. "Why don't we settle accounts now?" He held out his hand. Something about the woman's demeanor pricked his suspicion. Surely she wasn't planning on running off before she paid him. She couldn't be that devious. Besides, she still needed him to escort her to the dock master tomorrow.

One brow lifted above eyes alight with enough mischief to confirm Hayden's suspicions.

"Do you take me for a complete fool?"

Hayden smiled. *Well...*

"Our bargain was that you'd bring me to the dock master. Besides, I won't know how much I have left over until I purchase my ticket." She pushed on the door then let out an exasperated sigh. "Now, if you'll please remove your mammoth boot, I'd like to rest."

Hayden studied her as she stared at the floor. Something wasn't right. But whether it was simply the woman's normal theatrics or something far more duplicitous he didn't know. He blew out a sigh. Magnolia was spoiled and pretentious and the most frustrating woman he'd ever met, but she wasn't shrewd. Especially not shrewd enough to trick the likes of him.

"If you try to run away with the money, Princess, I'll find you at the dock master's in the morning. There's only one in town."

Anger flared across her eyes, but only for a moment before she rubbed her forehead and leaned on the door as if she were going to faint. "I would never do such a thing. I'm just so tired, Hayden."

He shook his head, wondering whether to believe a word this woman said. "How about I return in a couple hours and escort you to dinner?"

She raised her eyes to his. Where moments before they'd spiked with annoyance, now they softened with what looked like sorrow. But that couldn't be.

"Thank you. That will be lovely," she said with a weak smile.

Hayden resisted the urge to run a finger over her cheek, to feel its softness, to see her response. Instead, he withdrew his boot. "Until then." He backed away from the door, expecting her to slam it on him. But she stared at him for another minute, her eyes becoming pools, before she closed it with a click that nipped his heart.

Reflecting on the woman's odd behavior, Hayden passed the time strolling the city streets, gazing at the oddities of this foreign place. Curiosity led him past the immigration office, just to see if it was open, and then inside when he found the door ajar. Though he'd wanted to have Magnolia—and her money—with him when he questioned Mr. Santos, he couldn't help himself from inquiring whether the man was there. A pudgy, grease-faced fellow wearing a suit that had gone out of fashion a decade ago informed Hayden, in rather broken English, that the immigration officer was away and wouldn't return until tomorrow. However, if the matter was urgent, Hayden might find him that evening at a party at the home of Adelino Manuel Guerra da Costa, one of the city's magistrates. The squirrely man even gave Hayden directions, but then quickly chastised himself with a chuckle saying that the party was by invitation only. His brandy-drenched belch a moment later confirmed Hayden's suspicions that the man would probably have given Hayden his mother as a gift if he had asked.

Regardless, Hayden emerged from the office into the heat of the languishing day with a huge smile on his face. He'd rather meet Santos with an advantage—a rather beautiful advantage carrying a pouch of gold. How could any man resist Magnolia? Within moments of lavishing him with her Southern charm, Mr. Santos would melt like warm butter in her hands. And Hayden would discover his father's whereabouts—if the swine had even returned to Rio. If not, perhaps he'd sent one of his colonists with information on a new location as Blake wanted Hayden to do. Hayden knew the immigration office kept updated records of each colony's precise acreage and position, and since his father was not where Mr. Santos had originally told Hayden he would be, he must have moved to a new area and reported the change. A huge gamble, but a reasonable one, and the only option Hayden had at the moment for finding the man. And finally ending his lifelong quest. Finally putting things right. For him. For his mother.

Alternatively, if his father had sailed back to America, Hayden would be able to escort Magnolia home and ensure her safety. He wouldn't have to swindle her, wouldn't have to betray her trust and return her to New Hope. For the first time in his life, the thought of not cheating someone pleased him immensely, along with the thought of spending more time with the lady.

He shook his head, wondering if he'd contracted some brain-eating jungle fever, for she'd done nothing but annoy him to distraction these past five days. No, that wasn't true. The lady had surprised him in more ways than one. The sad story of the debt she owed her father, how he used her for her beauty like some prize horse, how some swindler broke her heart, her concern over Hayden's unhappy past, her resilience these past few days—all had stirred something in his soul. Made him realize that, despite the wide gulf in their social standing, they weren't so different after all. Both of them wore masks to hide deep inner pain. And both were desperately searching for something to ease that pain.

Weaving around a Chinaman selling fish, Hayden shifted his thoughts to the immigration officer, Mr. Santos. A safer topic. If he waited until tomorrow to talk to the snake, he'd have to find a way to delay Magnolia from seeking passage on her ship. Besides, it had been awhile since he'd attended a party. He smiled. But how to sneak into the lavish affair without notice? And where to find some decent attire?

Preoccupied with his thoughts, he missed the turn and headed down a narrow avenue. Not until the clamor of voices, shouts of vendors, and bray of donkeys faded did he realize he was going in the wrong direction. Heat spiraled from the tiled roofs of houses lining the dirt road. He halted, spun around, and headed back, passing a group of abandoned buildings and a church that was no more than a mud hut with a raised tin roof and a brass crucifix affixed above the front door. The words "Igreja" were hand written on a sign tacked to the wall.

Wiping the sweat from the back of his neck, Hayden hurried past when the front door swung open and a thin man wearing a black priest's robe started toward Hayden. Ignoring him, Hayden continued walking. The last thing he needed was some castigating sermon. Yet, before he took two steps, the man touched his arm and spun him around.

"Portuguese?"

"Sorry." Hayden shook his head and continued onward.

"English then?" The priest followed him, a silly smile on his angular mouth.

"What can I do for you?" Hayden sighed and faced the man. An odd looking man for a priest. His slanted eyes, along with a long gray braid running down the back of his robe gave him a Far Eastern appearance. Yet his skin was brown, his body more reed-like than muscular.

The priest grew somber, his dark eyes studying Hayden as if searching for something. "You come from jungle, right? You part of colony from America, right?"

"Yes." Hayden's annoyance grew. All good guesses based on his appearance and accent. "I have no money, sir." He started walking again.

The man grabbed Hayden's arm. "Beware. Evil. Much evil there. Many men die. Many men disappear."

"What are you talking about?" Hayden wanted to call the man an old fool and walk away, but one didn't say that to a priest, even a crazy one. Sure, Hayden was probably going to hell—if there *was* such a place—but there was no sense in adding insulting a man of God to his list of crimes. But perhaps. . . "Do you know a man named Owen Godard?" Hayden spoke the alias his father had used on his journey to Brazil.

The priest shook his head and tightened his grip on Hayden's arm. "Many disappear."

"Did Mr. Godard disappear?"

"I do not know this man."

"Then who disappeared?"

"Other colonists like you. And men from Rio. Even priests who go to fight."

"Fight?" Hayden glanced down the street, anxious to leave.

"Fight the evil. From the *lagos incendito*." He folded his lips together and studied the ground as if expecting it to explode beneath his feet. Then he gripped Hayden's arm even tighter, his eyes flashing. "Fire lake beneath temple."

Hayden didn't know whether to laugh or feel sorry for the deranged man. Still, he hadn't time for this. He gently removed the man's boney fingers. "Fire lake, eh? Thank you for the warning. Now, if you'll excuse me." He turned and felt the claw-like grip on his arm once again.

"No. You listen. Much evil. Men not survive. Some tell of invisible beasts. See many visions. Some go mad."

Visions. Now the man had his attention. "How do you know about the visions? Where do they come from?"

"The beasts. They must be defeated."

"Beasts? Like wolves and jaguars?"

"No." He gripped Hayden's other arm, swerving him to face him. "Not natural. Not human. Only God can protect."

God again. How could a God who couldn't protect an orphan on the streets of Charleston possibly save them from these beasts?—if they even existed. No doubt the priest had seen some visions of his own.

Hayden placated him with a smile and a pat on his arm. "I promise to be careful." Tearing from his grip, Hayden stormed ahead. *I promise to not come down this street again!*

This time the man didn't follow him. But his authoritative voice did.

"Only one way to defeat. Only one way. You must go back. You are one of six. Consult the book. Only the six can defeat the evil."

Hayden wanted to ask him six what, but reason kept him moving. Evil, indeed. Outside of man's own selfishness, did evil even exist? Yet Hayden couldn't deny the heaviness that had weighed on him at the temple and the visions he'd seen—Katherine and the one of his father in the jungle.

Shaking the thoughts from his head, he reached the end of the street and started for the hotel. Just the ramblings of a crazy old priest. Or were they?

Chapter 14

In all her twenty-three years, Magnolia had never enjoyed a bath so much. Though the water was brown and had a coppery smell to it, and the tub itself was nothing but a sawed off ship's barrel, and the maids had dropped towels of questionable cleanliness on the dirty floor, Magnolia didn't care. She relished in the caress of warm water on her skin, washing away the grime and grit and filth of the past five days. If only she could wash away her fears for her future as well. Now, as she stood at the open window in her chemise, gazing at the ships teetering in the bay, and battling the hopeless tangles in her hair, those fears rose again like tenacious flood waters, threatening to drown her.

It was one thing to tromp through the jungle with Hayden protecting her, and quite another to face a journey on one of those ships with no one to stand up for her, no one to defend her should a sailor get the wrong idea about her traveling alone. And then, once in the States, she would have to find her way, unescorted, to her aunt and uncle's. Would they even take her in? Did they still live in the same home in Ohio? Since the war, they had not been on the best of terms with Magnolia's parents. Or perhaps it would be better to seek out Samuel in Atlanta. Surely he would provide for her until they could be married. Although the last time she'd seen him, he'd slammed out of their home in Roswell, leapt into his waiting carriage, and driven away in a rage.

"Humph!" Her father had joined her on their wide front porch. "It appears the man has a temper. I've done you a favor, Magnolia."

"Of course he was angry, Father. You broke off our engagement. Went back on your word as a gentleman. And for what?" She batted away her tears. "Because he doesn't make enough money? Isn't high enough on the social ladder? It isn't fair!" She'd rarely spoken to her father in that tone, but as she'd continued to gaze at Samuel's carriage rumbling away, she saw her future rumble away with him.

Her father swung to face her, his jaw tight. "If you hadn't played the fool and lost the family fortune, I wouldn't be forced to make such hard choices." Indignation puffed out his cheeks even as his eyes grew narrow and cold. "Thank God we still have a sliver of our good name. Something, along with your beauty, that should lure a better positioned and wealthier prospect."

Magnolia wilted beneath his fury and gazed down at her pink, tasseled shoes, lest he see her cry again.

"You have no right to speak to me of what is fair," he continued, his voice thundering. "You have ruined us and you will unruin us. Or by God you'll put me in an early grave!"

At that moment Magnolia finally realized she would forever be under her father's thumb. Like their few remaining house slaves, her life was his. He owned her, and he would never let her forget.

Of course she and Samuel had continued secretly corresponding. He still loved her and wished to marry her. And she, him. But no amount of convincing, cajoling, or crying had changed her father's mind. And after multiple attempts to wed her off to what remained of the landed gentry, wealthy politicians, and elite families in Georgia, he'd given up, sold what little they owned, and booked passage to Brazil. Apparently, the news of Magnolia's scandal had swept through Georgia like wildfire, and no decent gentleman with a reputation to uphold would consider joining himself with their family. But in Brazil "the slate would be wiped clean and no one would be the wiser," her father had said when he announced his decision. "And Brazil boasts of many wealthy land owners as well as those of royal descent with whom we can align ourselves."

Magnolia only had time to send a quick dispatch to Samuel, informing him of her father's plans. But word was he had gone into hiding after the war, and she had no idea if he'd received it or if he still loved her.

And, of course, now that she'd run away, she would never pay her debt to her father. She was a horrible, disrespectful daughter who only thought of herself. He'd told her that on so many occasions, she'd begun to believe it. Perhaps it was true, after all.

She combed through the last tangle and watched as a mulatto woman, four children in tow, walked past the hotel, each with baskets of fruit on their heads. The briny scent of the bay drifted in with the wind, floating atop the sickly sweet smell of decaying fruit. It was a peculiar city. A peculiar, beautiful city. A city filled with the most unusual, exotic people.

And yet she felt more alone in the world than she ever had. Would Hayden even come back? The way she'd treated him, she wouldn't blame him if he abandoned her to begin his search for whomever or whatever he was looking for. But then again, he would want his money, wouldn't he? Her chest tightened. If only the dock master was open, she'd be long gone. As it was, she'd have to find a way to run away in the morning, purchase a ticket, and board a ship without Hayden's knowledge.

Her hands shook and she clasped them together. Nearly two days without a drink had taken its toll on her body. Perhaps that was why her thoughts spun in such a whirlwind.

A knock on the door startled her and Hayden's voice on the other side caused an unavoidable smile to form on her lips. Coughing it away, she forced the traitorous glee from her voice and replaced it with petulance. "I'm not ready yet, Hayden. What do you want?"

"How would you like to go shopping, Princess?"

Shopping? She could almost see that pleased-with-himself grin of his through the door. "Shopping for what?"

"For a new gown."

Regardless of how nonsensical his answer was, how ludicrous the notion, she yelped her "Yes" and then dashed through dressing. Aside from a few moans, groans, and unladylike curses at the difficulty of putting her clothing on without her lady's maid, she managed to don her least filthy blouse and skirts and pin up her damp hair as best she could. By the time she opened the door, Hayden was leaning his head against the post, pretending to be asleep.

Pretending, she knew, because he usually didn't wear a playful smirk in his sleep.

"Oh, mercy me." She slapped him with her fan. "I didn't take that long."

He opened one eye, one devilishly green eye, and grinned, sending a thrill through her.

"You tease me, sir. But you have no idea of the complexity of a lady's attire. Without my maid, I must tighten my corset behind me and then tie on my crinolette. . ."—he was still grinning. Rather mischievously, in fact—"Well, never mind. Let's just say there are far too many things a lady must put on."

His brow cocked. "You need not wear them all on my account."

Heat sped up her back. "You are indeed a toad, Hayden. And why are you being so nice to me all of a sudden?"

He didn't answer. Instead he gestured toward her valise sitting on the floor. "We will need your money."

"*My* money?" Magnolia snapped. "But I don't know if I have enough. I mean. . ."—she fumbled with her fan—"For the ticket, of course, and then to pay you as well."

"Then we'll take it out of my share."

This confused her further. Surely a man who would only escort and protect a lady for a fee wouldn't so willingly purchase her a gown. Besides, unbeknownst to him, it would still come out of *her* money.

Magnolia bit her lip and looked down at her stained skirts and the tattered fringe drooping from the hem. She supposed she did have enough for traveling *and* a new gown. Besides, she couldn't very well allow Samuel to see her in these rags. He might mistake her for a street urchin and send her away!

"Very well." She plucked her purse from inside her valise and met him in the hall. "What is the gown for?"

"For tonight, Princess." He extended his arm. "We are going to a ball."

The oddest thing happened to Hayden. He actually enjoyed shopping with Magnolia. It was odd for a number of reasons. One, he had about as much interest in women's clothing and fripperies as—to use her analogy—a toad had for fine literature. Two, her spoiled coquettish ways normally caused his blood to boil. Yet today, strolling about Rio, seeing the way her eyes lit up at all the fanciful items being sold at market, watching her caress the silk scarves from India, bite into a fresh mango till juice slid down her chin, giggle at the colorful parrots and chattering monkeys hopping along the roofs, and successfully haggle with a woman for a beaded bracelet, Hayden found himself utterly enamored. She may be spoiled and a bit self-centered, but she was the epitome of femininity. All lace and fluff and softness.

She seemed to grow more beautiful with each passing moment. Her sun-kissed hair, dried by the gentle breeze, dangled from her chignon in golden ringlets. Roses blossomed on her cheeks. Even the sheen of perspiration on her face and neck made her glow like an angel. Hayden swallowed and tried to avoid staring at her as they turned down *Ruo do Ouvidor* and found a drapers as fine as any in Charleston. Bolts of taffeta, calicos, and gingham filled the room that smelled of French perfume and musty cloth. Neither the language nor monetary differences impeded Magnolia from bartering for a ready-made blue gown that hung in the back. Apparently a return from an unhappy customer who thought the needlework subpar.

So, with wrapped gown flung over her arm, Hayden escorted her back to the hotel with a promise to return after sunset. Of course he had nothing to wear himself besides the disheveled, torn suit he had on. But finding something suitable had never been a problem before.

So, it was with a jump in his step that he returned to fetch Magnolia promptly at 8:00 p.m. He attributed his exuberant mood to his upcoming chat with Mr. Eduardo Santos and the possibility of discovering the whereabouts of his father. Hayden was tired of chasing the man all over the world, putting his own hopes and dreams on hold. Once justice was served, Hayden could get on with his life, perhaps learn a trade, become a sailor, or help out in his friend's furniture shop in Savannah.

Entering the hotel, he tipped his hat at an attractive lady in the lobby and mounted the steps. He might even get married, have children. His conscience rose to chastise him for the ridiculous notion. No decent woman would marry a confidence man—a swindler who had ruined so many lives.

Magnolia opened the door to his knock and widened her eyes when she saw his gray cotton suit with black velvet trim and double-breasted cutaway coat. "Where on earth did you get that?"

No decent woman would marry a thief, either.

But that thought quickly dissipated at the sight of her. Her flaxen hair, adorned with sparkling beads, was swept back in a bun from which golden swirls fell across her neck. The shimmering blue of her gown only enhanced the color of her eyes. Ruffles bubbled like foam from her bell-shaped sleeves, while the lace embellishing her low neckline drew his unbridled gaze. He gulped and prayed for a breeze to drift down the hall and cool the heat swirling in his belly. The victorious sparkle of delight in her eyes told him she'd noticed his approval. But then she was accustomed to men fawning over her, wasn't she?

"So?" She tapped him with her fan as her eyes took him in. "How did you purchase such a fine suit?" Now it was his turn to be delighted for he could see the appreciation in her eyes as she scanned him from head to toe.

"I borrowed it." He winked and offered his elbow. Giving him a suspicious look, she gripped it and allowed him to lead her down the streets of Rio. With every step they took, every street corner they turned, they drew appreciative glances. Hayden's shoulders rose a bit higher, and for the first time he no longer felt like a thief and a rogue. For the first time in his life, with Magnolia on his arm, he felt like a gentleman. Not just pretending to be one. But a real gentleman. Strangely, it made him want to become one.

That illusion, however, slipped away once they reached the estate of Adelino Manuel Guerra da Costa. Though music and laughter spilled from the windows of the palatial two-story home onto the manicured lawn, sprinkled with flowering bushes and majestic palms, Hayden was forced to tug Magnolia to the side and head down the fenced outskirts of the property like the uninvited guests they were. She glanced back at the open front doors and the guests being greeted by their host and hostess and gave an adorable little chirp signifying her dismay.

"Where are you taking me?" Her voice turned shrewish.

Ignoring her, Hayden peered into the darkness, finally finding what he sought. "We can slip in through here." He gestured toward a broken spoke in the fence that created a two-foot gap.

"I thought you said we were invited."

"I said we were attending. I said nothing about being invited."

"Well, I shan't sneak in the back like common riffraff." Clutching her skirts, she flounced away.

Silently growling, Hayden caught up to her and spun her around. "There's no other way. Either we go in through here or we don't attend at all."

"Then we don't attend. Barging into parties uninvited is for uncultured plebeians, not someone of my station." She turned to leave.

He wouldn't release her arm. "Then I won't help you book passage tomorrow."

He couldn't quite make out her expression in the darkness but he was pretty sure she bared her teeth like a tigress. "Who says I need your help?"

Hayden ran a hand through his hair. "Listen, Princess. There's someone at that party I need to speak with. It's quite possible the information he has will lead me back to the States. In which case, I can give you a proper escort all the way home." He felt her relax. He released his grip on her arm. Zooks, but it felt good to speak the truth. For once.

"This man. . .he can help you find what you're looking for?"

"Yes."

"Then go speak to him. I'll wait here."

Hayden sighed, hating his next words. "I need you with me."

"How can *I* possibly assist?"

"This man is a scoundrel of the worst kind. He refuses to give away any information unless his pockets are lined. And believe me, even with the money you are paying me, I won't have enough. But he's soft on the ladies and—"

"So you're using me," she snapped. "It's why you bought me this gown, asked me to the ball. You planned this all along. In addition to taking my money." Her voice stung with pain.

Guilt sat heavy on his shoulders. She was right, of course. But he couldn't let his feelings for her or his own shame dissuade him from his mission. He forced desperation and remorse from his tone and replaced it with silky charm. "After all we've been through, would you please do me this one small favor?"

"All we've been through? You mean all you've put me through!"

Zooks, the woman aggravated him! Hayden clamped his jaw until it hurt. Music floated atop the scent of savory spices, giving him a grand idea. "There will be good food and plenty of spirits inside." Totally unfair of him to mention the alcohol, of course.

But it did the trick. He sensed her weakening.

She stepped away from him. "Very well." But her tone carried none of joy it had held just minutes before.

Hayden hated being the one who'd swept it away.

However, her blasted hoops wouldn't fit through the fence opening. His suggestion for her to remove them didn't fair too well. In fact, they unleashed a series of gasps and "I never" and "How dare you?" until finally she settled with a childish pout and a firm chin, demanding they leave at once.

Desperate, Hayden searched the area, found a stack of bricks, and formed a step for her to stand on. Then squeezing through the opening in the fence, he dragged over an old wooden bucket, leapt on top, and reached his arms above the railing. "Step on the bricks, and I'll grab your waist and hoist you over."

"You can't be serious."

"I am quite serious. Come now, it will be an adventure. Something to laugh about in years to come."

She said nothing.

"Nothing to fear—I'm right here." He moved his hands above the fence for her to see. "I'll catch you."

"You are a toad, you know."

"As you have informed me."

Her skirts swished. "I can't believe I'm doing this," she grumbled. "And as a favor to you!"

Their hands locked and Hayden hoisted himself onto the top of the fence. "Grab onto my neck." She did. It felt good. He found her waist. Straining, he lifted her to sit beside him. Thankfully the top of the fence was at least a foot wide. Still, she teetered. He jumped down to the bucket then turned to place his hands firmly on her hips. "Now, swing your legs over."

"Close your eyes."

"For the love of. . ." he ground out. "Very well." Lace and silk swished. The bucket beneath him wobbled. He grew dizzy. . .lost his bearings. He opened his eyes to a heeled boot slamming his chest. Groaning, he tightened his grip on her waist. The bucket teetered. Hayden lost his balance. The world spun and he toppled backward to the ground, dragging Magnolia on top of him. The air fled his lungs with a mighty squish. Neither said anything. The hem of her skirt circled her shoulders as her sweet breath puffed over his face. Her warm curves molded against him. Her lips were but inches from his.

And he did the only thing he thought to do.

He kissed her.

Chapter 15

The kiss sent a sultry ripple through Magnolia, ushering out her anger and embarrassment and inviting in an ecstasy she'd never known existed. She knew her gown had flown up around her face, could feel the braided hem of her skirts on her cheek. But lying atop Hayden's warm, steel-like body, she found she didn't care. Nothing mattered but the touch of his lips, the thrill spiraling through her. The way he cupped her head in his hands and drank her in as if he were a man deprived of drink for decades. Until a small flicker of reason invaded the pleasurable fog in her mind—a tiny shred of reason that forced her to remember who she was and what she was doing. And how another man, equally as charming as Hayden, had torn her heart in two.

She shoved from his chest. "Get off of me!"

"I believe it is *you* who are on me, Princess."

"Oooh!" Realizing in a flush of heat that she still straddled him, she flipped back her skirts then vaulted onto the grass. Crinoline flailing, she attempted to rise amid a flurry of unladylike grunts. Finally, rolling onto her hands and knees, she managed to stand. "How dare you take advantage of me—yet again!"

"If you hadn't forced me to close my eyes, I wouldn't have lost my balance." Hayden leapt to his feet, his voice raspy with desire. He turned his back to her as if trying to collect himself.

"It's a simple task to stand steady on a"—she glanced at the overturned pail—"bucket. I should have known not to trust you.

Now, look what you've done to my new gown." She swatted the twigs and grass from her skirts. "Could you not have allowed it to remain unstained for one evening?" An evening, that if she admitted, she'd been rather excited about. Hopeful, even, that beneath Hayden's rugged, raffish exterior, he was an honorable man, a man who might actually care for. . .oh what did it matter? He'd not invited her to a ball because he enjoyed her company or because he wanted to become better acquainted with her or treat her like a lady. No, he'd simply been using her. For her beauty. Like her father. Like everyone else.

Finally, he swung about and brushed grass from his coat. "Perhaps it was being so near to you that made me dizzy." Despite being unable to see his face in the shadows, she sensed a smile. He held out his hand. "Now, if you're quite done yammering, shall we go enjoy the party?"

Yam. . . Magnolia knew the daggers in her eyes were lost to him in the darkness, but it felt good to fire them at him anyway. "So much for the toad ever becoming a prince."

"Ah, but the evening is still young."

Though he tried to hide behind sarcasm, passion still dripped like dark molasses from his voice. And if Magnolia were honest, it tingled through her as well. But she no longer wanted to attend the ball. She didn't want to be used. She wanted to be loved. Wanted to be special. She wanted to have value beyond her appearance. Her vision grew hazy as tears filled her eyes.

Oh my, but she could use a drink!

Which was the only reason she now followed the rogue through the back entrance, past the kitchen, and into the warming room, where he waved off the servants' curious gazes with the excuse of getting lost.

The sound of an orchestra and the hum of chatter and laughter bubbled over Magnolia as Hayden led her upstairs to the main ballroom, where they joined the glittering throng. Dipping his head in greeting, he smiled at everyone as if he'd known them all his life. Most smiled in return, mainly the ladies, whose appreciative gazes drank him in as if they were parched and he were an oasis. Yet, not a single suspicious brow rose as they wove through the crowd. The ease with which this ruffian slipped into the role of an aristocrat astonished

Magnolia. From the stretch of his shoulders, the lift of his chin, and the swaggering confidence with which he strode through the room, people no doubt guessed he was a gentleman born and bred into luxury and privilege, not an orphan who grew up without benefit of home, food, and education. In fact, she'd met sons of earls who held themselves with less dignity. Strangely, the thought unsettled her.

He led her to a table laden with delicacies she could not name, an ivory-colored pudding, a bowl of creamy paste with a cocoa nut on top, and other assorted cakes. But it was the *vinho virgem*—French red wine—that drew her gaze. Hayden poured a glass and handed it to her. The sweet yet pungent taste lingered on her tongue and sped a heavenly trail down her throat. Ah sweet, sweet nectar! But when she raised her gaze to Hayden's devilish wink, she couldn't be sure if it was the wine or the way he looked at her that caused her blood to suddenly heat.

Clearing her throat, she glanced up at sputtering chandeliers that dappled light upon a fresco of orchids and ferns painted on the tall ceilings. Below, framing the room, high-backed chairs stood alongside gilded card tables while great oval mirrors with tawdry decorations hung on the wall. Young mulatto boys, dressed all in white, wove barefooted through the crowd, hoisting trays of drinks and cakes.

She took another sip while Hayden fetched his own drink and then led her through the maze of ladies and gentleman, their skin in every shade from dark as night to snowy white, all decked in silks and brocades as colorful as spring flowers in an open field. Magnolia could not keep from staring. She'd never seen a Negress wearing a gown that could be found in a ballroom in Paris, nor speaking with the confidence and education of any genteel woman back home. Men, bearing the blended features of both Europeans and Africans, sauntered through the crowd, women on each arm while their wives stood in corners, ignored. Even the priests partook of drink and engaged in playful dalliances.

In the center of the room, couples spun and bobbed as they floated across the floor like lilies on a pond. Portuguese thickened the air as the scent of orange blossoms and salt swept in through open windows, masking the miasma of perfume and alcohol.

Despite her sore legs and blistered feet, Magnolia found herself swaying to the music, wishing more than anything that Hayden would sweep her onto the dance floor and she could spend one night—just one night—forgetting that she was all alone in the world without a penny to her name and without anything to offer but her beauty.

But instead, the toad popped a sweet cake into his mouth and gestured with his drink to a man on the other side of the room.

"There he is. Mr. Eduardo Santos. The petulant squab speaking with the tall gentleman in the blue suit."

Magnolia stared at the man she was supposed to charm. Short in stature and as wide as he was tall, he reminded her of the toad she so often called Hayden. Thin, greasy hair crossed the top of his head in perfect rows as if he had plowed furrows in his scalp. His posh broadcloth coat with satin lining did nothing to enhance his boorish mien or the aura of base ignorance surrounding him.

She cringed and looked away. Right into Hayden's anxious green eyes.

"He's despicable," she said.

"You think so? Wait until you meet him." He chuckled and sipped his wine.

"Who is he, anyway?"

"The immigration officer."

The dance ended, and a flood of people cascaded to the refreshment table. Taking her arm, Hayden led her aside, whispering in her ear. "Take my lead, Princess, and use that seductive charm of yours."

"All of a sudden, I'm seductive and charming, is it? I seem to recall other names flung my way in the jungle. Shrew. Spoiled. Harridan." They twisted through the crowd as the scent of cheap perfume and cedar oil threatened to strangle her.

"I admit you are a woman of many talents."

Before she could come up with a witty retort, Magnolia stood before Mr. Santos. The taller man he spoke with excused himself and the immigration officer faced them, his dark eyes flitting over Hayden in brief recognition before landing on Magnolia like a bird of prey.

Delight, followed by desire, strolled across them as a feline smile lit his face.

"Mr. Santos." Hayden dipped his head. "What a pleasure to see you again."

The man seemed reluctant to draw his gaze from Magnolia. Though she did nothing to hide her disinterest. Finally he glanced at Hayden. "Yes, indeed. Mr. . . .Mr. . . ."

"Gale."

"Gale. Ah, yes." He cocked his head. "I thought you would have joined your American colony by now."

Despite his strong accent, Magnolia was impressed with the man's English.

"I did. But Owen Godard was not where you said he would be."

"Owen Godard." The man ran a finger over the thin hair on his forehead, his bulbous nose pinching. "Ah yes. I remember. Older gentleman. Small group of Americans. But I told you where he settled."

"He wasn't there," Hayden repeated.

The orchestra began playing a waltz.

Mr. Santos sipped his drink, staring at Magnolia over the rim of his glass. "But where are your manners, senhor? I must be introduced to this lovely creature."

Hayden's jaw tightened beneath a forced smile. "My apologies. This is Miss—my wife, Magnolia Gale." He placed a possessive arm across her back.

Under any other circumstances she would have enjoyed the protective action, but instead she stiffened and stifled a gasp. With great difficulty, she extended her gloved hand. "A pleasure, sir."

Mr. Santos ran his thumb over her fingers, fondling them as if he'd never touched a woman before. She tugged away before he could raise her hand to his lips and cause the wine to curdle in her stomach.

Hayden gave her a sideways glance, frowning as if displeased with the action. Which only made her angry. Just like her father, just like every man she'd ever met, Hayden used her like some pretty puppet to achieve his ends. Forcing down the agony burning in her throat, she looked toward the door. She should leave. She wanted to leave. But

Hayden said this man's information might make it possible for him to accompany her on the voyage home. And she was so very frightened of traveling alone. The thought of being safely escorted back to the States, even the slight possibility of it, kept her feet in place. Kept her willing to help Hayden.

Mr. Santos sipped his drink. "I had no idea you were married to such a beauty."

"My wife and I have returned to Rio in the hopes that Mr. Godard may have also returned recently," Hayden said. "Perhaps for supplies? Or to submit the appropriate paperwork to settle on a different plot of land?"

Impressed with Hayden's ability to lie without blinking, Magnolia wondered who this Godard man was and why he was so important to Hayden.

Wrinkles formed on Mr. Santos's forehead as if the attempt to recollect such a transaction taxed his tiny brain. "Hmm. Maybe he returned. Maybe not. I cannot remember, Mr. Gale. Perhaps"—the gleam in his eye turned greedy—"you have something to help me recall?"

Hayden released Magnolia, a tiny twitch in his jaw the only indication of his vexation. "I'm afraid I haven't any more money to give you, sir. I appeal to your generosity."

Mr. Santos frowned and slammed the rest of his drink to the back of his throat.

Magnolia rolled her eyes. *Yes, you supercilious buffoon, please do be generous.* Just the thought of getting any closer to this man made her insides squirm.

But she could tell from his rigid stance and the indulgent hunger in his eyes that he hadn't a generous bone in his body.

"What you can count on, senhor, is that I am not without honor. Mr. Godard's affairs are Mr. Godard's affairs, not yours. However with a bit of persuasion. . ." He assessed Magnolia as if she were a gift at Christmas.

Hayden shifted his stance and gazed across the room. Magnolia bit her lip. If he had a speck of decency, if he had a speck of chivalry within him, he wouldn't leave her alone with this wolf. Finally he faced

Mr. Santos and took his empty glass. "Allow me to get you another drink. And you as well, my dear." He winked at her. "While you two become better acquainted."

Magnolia growled inside. The man was a cad through and through.

Hayden had never hated himself more than he did at that moment. The look of spite in Magnolia's eyes as he left her with Mr. Santos shot a gaping hole in his heart. Gaping and vacant and empty—like his soul. Hayden used people for a living. He made money off of people's pain. Zooks, he'd certainly done far worse than leaving a lady with a lecherous fool. Then why did he feel like such a louse for asking her to do something that came natural to her? Innocent flirting. That was all. No harm done. Besides, what choice did he have? He must find out where his father had gone. He must put an end to this mad quest or he would surely go mad himself.

Yet everything within him wanted to whisk Magnolia away to safety—away from scum like Mr. Santos and anyone who could hurt her. He'd never felt protective toward anyone in his life, and he certainly didn't want to start now. It made him vulnerable. It made him lose focus on the task at hand. And he couldn't have that. Not that her kiss hadn't already distracted him beyond measure. The soft feel of her atop him, the passionate way she'd embraced him, caressed his lips. She'd stirred his passions into such a frenzy it had taken several minutes to regain his composure. So unlike him. He'd always been in control. In control of himself, his emotions. Of everyone around him. And if he was to succeed in serving justice to his father, he must stay in control.

Ignoring the coquettish glances from several women, he made his way to the refreshment table and grabbed a glass of punch. Tossing it to the back of his throat, he yearned for it to soothe his nerves. He would delay returning with fresh drinks—give Magnolia time to perform her magic. In the meantime, he could at least keep an eye on them should Mr. Santos cross the boundary of propriety. Hayden spun around to do just that.

But Magnolia and Mr. Santos were no longer there.

Chapter 16

When the pernicious fatwit suggested they take a stroll in the garden, Magnolia almost lost the wine she'd consumed. She'd wanted to say that she'd rather sit in a dung heap, but instead, she smiled and looped her arm through his as he escorted her from the room. She could do this. She knew she could do this. It would only take a few minutes of her bewitching charm to extract the information Hayden needed from this man. How many times had she done the very same thing back home in Roswell whenever she'd wanted a particular favor from a particular gentleman?

Except those particular gentlemen hadn't smelled like sour cheese, nor made her insides stir into a putrid brew. But no matter.

She tried to get Hayden's attention as they passed the refreshment table, but he seemed deep in thought. Mercy me, another drink would certainly make her task easier. Besides, she wanted him to see where they were going just in case Mr. Santos attempted liberties which weren't his to take. Certainly Hayden would come looking for her. Wouldn't he?

Glancing over her shoulder, she allowed Mr. Santos to lead her outside through a line of orange trees and cultured palms, framed by resplendent crotons and bamboo. Castor oil lamps hung from tree branches, flinging lacy ribbons of light on the grass below. He gestured toward a secluded spot at the far end of the garden where a stone bench edged a pond.

"We do not see—how do you say, much or often?—such lovely, cultured ladies in Rio," Mr. Santos said, gesturing toward the bench. Releasing his arm, Magnolia slid onto the hard stone as he took a seat beside her. Far too close.

"You are too kind, Mr. Santos." She inched away and tugged her fan from her sleeve—if only to use as a weapon.

"And your accent. I hear it from many new colonists but it makes music on your lips." He took her hand in his.

Something sour and thick rose in her throat.

"Mr. Santos, as you know, my husband is most desperate to find"—oh, what was that name again? How could Hayden leave her like this? Ah yes—"Mr. Godard. Any information you have would be greatly appreciated." She forced a smile that nearly caused her to choke as the man leaned even closer.

"*How* appreciated?" His breath smelled of wine and curdled milk.

"You would have our. . .*my* undying gratitude, sir. Wouldn't that be enough? Helping out a lady in distress. Why, you would be my true hero." She fluttered her fan about her face. "I just knew you were a gentleman when I first laid eyes on you. Why, I wager you are quite the ladies' man. Aren't you, Mr. Santos?" She tapped his chest with the tip of her fan and smiled.

He shrugged and pressed back the oily hair at his temples. "*Sim*, yes, I do have a reputation."

Magnolia could only imagine. She giggled playfully. Which apparently was all the enticement the man needed to lean in and nibble on her neck. "Why, sir, you forget yourself." She pushed him back, all the while giving him her most alluring smile. "I cannot possibly enjoy myself when my husband suffers so miserably from lack of information."

A breeze fluttered the palm fronds overhead and sent a ripple across the inky waters of the pond, stirring the cattails lingering at its edge. Distant orchestra music drifted atop the chirp of crickets in a pleasing melody that would have been peaceful except for the brute beside her.

That brute seemed to be pondering what to do. He finally flattened his surly lips. "Yes. I saw this Mr. Godard. He came back with a crazy tale about the land being bad. Cursed, sim, cursed is what he said. He moved his expedition west." He leaned in to kiss her.

Magnolia turned her cheek to him. "How far west?"

"Twenty of what you call miles, I believe." A groan of delight erupted in his throat as his lips seared her skin. "I have paperwork in my office with the exact location." He trailed slobbering kisses down her neck. "We can go there and I show you."

Magnolia would rather leap into a volcano. In fact, at the moment her skin felt as though a thousand lizards scampered over it. And her stomach wasn't doing much better. She pushed Mr. Santos away yet again, her heart plummeting like a stone in a pond. The information would take Hayden from her and send him back to New Hope. Leaving her to travel all alone. Yet, at the moment, she was preoccupied with preventing Mr. Santos from tossing her to the grass and having his way with her. Surely she'd learned enough about Mr. Godard to suit Hayden's purposes, for Magnolia could hardly stand another moment with this snobcock.

A snobcock who dove in for the kill. He nibbled on her earlobe, grunting like the swine he was. Shooting off the bench, Magnolia cast a quick glance around to see whether anyone was near to assist her. "Sir, you do yourself no credit with such beastly behavior." She kept her voice playful, not wanting to prick his ire in such isolated circumstances. Could she make a run for it? Surely a man as pudgy as Mr. Santos would not be able to catch her. "I bid you goodnight, sir."

She turned to leave.

He clutched her arm. "Where is my kiss?"

"A kiss was not part of our bargain, Mr. Santos. You have had your fun. Now, release me at once!" She struggled in his grip.

Leaves fluttered and a footstep sounded behind her, but Magnolia hadn't time to look before Mr. Santos said something about her paying him his due and shoved his mouth onto hers. She squirmed, causing his slobbering lips to slide over her cheeks and chin. More disgusted than afraid, she placed both palms on his chest and pushed him. Tripping on an uneven cobblestone, he stumbled backward toward the pond, arms flailing and curses flying, as he attempted to right himself. Before he did, Magnolia stormed toward him and gave him one final shove into the water. The immensity of his frame caused an enormous splash, which would have soaked her if she hadn't leapt out of the way.

Flopping like a fish in the shallows, he finally managed to sit in the silt near the shore. Water dripped from threads of hair hanging in his face. He sputtered and moaned and cursed her—*and her mother!*—to some hideous fate, which she dared not repeat.

Laughter rumbled behind her.

Spinning around, she barreled into a tree trunk that smelled like Hayden. Wait, it *was* Hayden. All six foot one of his sturdy frame. He held a glass of wine. Her nerves unwound at his presence. Or maybe it was at the sight of the wine. Either way, they quickly knotted again in anger. "You left me with that leech!" She punched his chest.

Which loosened a chuckle from his throat.

Mr. Santos attempted to rise from the pond, but slipped and splashed back in the water with a loud curse.

Grinning, Hayden led her back toward the house. "I was here the entire time. If things had gotten out of hand, I would have stepped in." He handed her the glass.

She gulped down the wine. "You waited long enough. The man was about to accost me. He *did* accost me, in fact."

"You seemed to have things in hand, Princess." Hayden winked and slid his hand into her free one. "In fact, I thought you handled yourself quite well."

He led her into the ballroom again. Magnolia blinked at the bright lights as music and the prattling of guests assailed her. She tugged from Hayden's grip and finished her drink. The comfort of his large hand around hers drained away her anger, bit by bit. And she wanted it to remain. At least for a while.

Returning the smile of a rather handsome Brazilian gentleman, Magnolia set down her empty glass and gathered a full one from the table. Hayden stole it from her hand. "Perhaps you've had enough."

"You are not my father. Besides, I deserve a reward for enduring that oaf slobbering all over me."

He held the glass out of reach. "And, pray tell, what did that slobbering oaf tell you about Mr. Godard?"

She studied him, wishing the wine in her belly would hurry and numb her conscience. All she had to do was utter one lie. One tiny lie and Hayden would escort her home. One tiny lie and all her fears of traveling alone would dissipate. One tiny lie and she could spend more time getting to know this mysterious man as she longed to do. One tiny lie. He certainly deserved it and worse after using her to get what he wanted. But the desperation in his eyes undid her. Whoever this Godard was, it meant everything to Hayden to find him. And she couldn't be the one to deny him that.

"Your precious Mr. Godard has moved twenty miles to the west. Isn't that what you wanted to know?" She speared him with a gaze.

"He is anything but precious." His tone was shattered glass. "But I do thank you for finding that out." The corner of his mouth twitched as he gazed absently into the room.

"So who is this Mr. Godard, and what did he do to invoke the wrath of Hayden Gale?"

The twitch intensified. "Let's just say he stole everything from me."

"Ah, now *that* I can relate to."

Hayden studied her. "You speak of this huge mistake you made... of your debt to your father?"

"I was taken in by a charlatan." But she had said too much already. "Perhaps he is the same man as your Mr. Godard?" She teased, trying to change the topic back to him.

Hayden laughed. "If you had crossed paths with my...Mr. Godard, I doubt you would be in Brazil. He rarely leaves his victims with enough to live on, let alone to travel."

"So it was money he stole?" Magnolia pressed, desperate to understand this man before her.

"No. Something far more precious." His vacant stare took in the room as sorrow stole over his features. Perhaps they had more in common than she first realized. She was about to inquire what exactly the man had taken from him when a commotion drew everyone's gaze to the veranda. Poor Mr. Santos hobbled into the room, scattering droplets on the tile floor and firing an angry glare over the assembly.

Ushering Magnolia aside, Hayden ducked behind a cluster of people as the man let out a frustrated growl and stormed out the other side of the room, demanding the servant retrieve his coat. A moment later the front door slammed, and Magnolia could only assume he'd left since the room suddenly burst with mocking laughter.

Hayden handed her the wine, his smile returning. "I suppose you *do* deserve this." The hint of adoration in those jungle green eyes made her want to do more for this man, anything he asked—just to keep him looking at her like that a little longer.

She sipped the wine, keeping her eyes trained on his. A grin lifted one side of his lips as he continued to stare at her, seemingly looking past the silk and lace, past the beads and fripperies, into her very soul, absorbing her with the delight of a man who'd found a priceless jewel. But that couldn't be right. She was no jewel. Her throat went dry and she looked away. She had to keep her focus. She couldn't allow this man to charm his way into her heart, for in the morning she had to leave him—buy a ticket and get on a ship and never see him again. An ache radiated through her at the thought. If only Mr. Godard had gone back to America. Then she wouldn't have to travel alone. And this wouldn't be her last night with Hayden.

But it *was* her last night with him. And despite the threat to her heart, she wanted to make it a night to remember.

He was still staring at her, an unreadable expression on his face. Was her hair out of place? Suddenly self-conscious, she began stuffing loose strands into her bun. But a gentle touch to her hand halted her, charmed her into saying, "I do have a favor to ask of you, Hayden."

"And what is that, Princess?"

"Would you dance with me?"

Was the princess flirting with him? By her coquettish grin and the way she lowered her lashes innocently, Hayden could come to no other conclusion. After he'd forced her to welcome that foppish squab's attentions, he wouldn't blame her if she poured her drink on his head and stomped off. Instead, she asked him to dance!

He cocked his head. She was up to something. But what? Perhaps she hoped to convince him to escort her to the States. Which—no matter how much he wanted to—he couldn't do. Perhaps she hoped to lessen the amount she owed him. Which now he needed more than ever if he was going to find his father. He glanced at the couples floating across the floor in a country dance. Whatever her reasons, the lady did have a point. Since they were here in the midst of this elaborate party, why not enjoy it?

He offered his arm. "I'd love to."

Delight brightened her smile as he led her onto the floor, took her hand, and joined the other couples bobbing and gliding to the music.

"Why did you tell Mr. Santos I was your wife?" Magnolia asked as they bowed to each other.

"I thought it might temper the man's passions." Hayden took her hand and together they strolled down the line of couples.

"Why temper them if their very existence brought you the information you sought?" Her voice was sharp, her chin lifted.

"If you're asking whether there was a limit to the price I would see you pay, there was." He took both her hands and spun her around. "And Mr. Santos had reached that limit when you shoved him into the pond."

At this she giggled, though an odd pain lingered behind her eyes.

"Besides, I knew he could not resist your charms for long."

She gave him a disbelieving look, but for once, Hayden spoke the truth, for he was having trouble resisting her himself. The way little wisps of her flaxen hair bobbed about her neck as she danced, the delicate curve of her jaw, her high cheeks flushed with excitement, and her lips swollen and pink. The gossamer lace edging her low neckline rose and fell with each breath, drawing his gaze, though he tried not to look. Save for a few beads in her hair, she wore no jewels or baubles, no silver combs or satin sashes, yet she outshone every woman there. And those eyes—blue as sapphires—flashing like lightning. And just like lightning, they were electric and powerful. Especially when they looked at him as she was looking at him now.

They finished the dance, but at her request, they stayed on the floor and continued with a Scottish Reel. And then another dance and another, stopping only for refreshments and a stroll in the garden. Her laughter became his healing elixir, her smile his hope. Hours sped by like minutes, and for the first time in his life, Hayden found he was enjoying himself. Immensely. All because of Magnolia. Her coy glances, her witty repartee, the way she looked at him as though she saw a prince instead of a toad.

He knew she could have her choice of any gentleman present, most of whom bore the noble posture of gentility and wealth, not the stink of an impoverished orphan. Instead, she seemed to barely notice the men who looked her way, her attention fixed on him alone. She was his for tonight. The realization made his chest swell. He felt as though someone had placed a precious gem in his hand and charged him with its care. Instead of dodging the assignment, he cherished it.

Zooks, what was happening to him? No doubt it was the wine, the rich food, the music and opulence. It combined to spin a magical web, deluding him into believing that he was not a thief and an orphan and she was not a stunning patrician. And that perhaps they might have a chance together.

He brought her a glass of lemonade, ignoring her look of disappointment at the drink. But he'd had a hard time resisting her in the jungle when she'd been inebriated. He doubted he could summon enough self-control in this magical place.

"You dance marvelously," she commented.

"That surprises you?"

"Yes." She looked at him but there was no condescension in her eyes. "Where did you learn?"

Hayden grinned. "Here and there."

"Ah yes, I've seen your skill at sneaking into parties uninvited."

"It does come in handy. I will teach you some time."

She lowered her gaze as if a sudden sadness stole her joy.

He determined to gain it back. "You look lovely tonight."

She raised sparkling eyes to his. "Ah, a compliment. The first one you've paid me." She began fiddling with her hair.

He stayed her hand. "Your hair is perfect." He brought her hand to his lips and kissed it. The music, the laughter, the exotic sound of Portuguese, all faded around them as their eyes locked together. Time floated on a whisper—a whisper that held all his dreams in its breath. A whisper that danced around them, between them, caressing her face, stirring her curls, filling him with her scent, with a hope that dangled within reach. Her eyes shifted between his as if seeking an answer.

But what was the question? Was it the same one that burned on his heart?

Could a pampered rich plantation owner's daughter love a baseborn swindler?

But he already knew the answer.

Not in the real world.

Tonight was a fantasy, a dream. And it would soon come to an end. Especially when the sun rose in the morning and she found out the truth.

Chapter 17

Darkness cloaked the stairs leading up to Magnolia's hotel room. She tripped on one of the treads and Hayden's arm swung around her waist.

"I told you to stop drinking wine," he said.

"I didn't have too much," she shot back. "I simply can't see the steps." The only light came from a sputtering lantern on the landing above them. Not that she minded Hayden's arm around her. She'd felt his touch quite often during the night. With each possessive press on her back, each grip on her elbow, each squeeze of her hand, he'd been staking claim on her, making her feel cared for and protected for the first time in her life.

The steps creaked. Her skirts swished. The rhythmic tick of a clock joined the distant pattering of a mouse as they reached the top. The hallway spun and she leaned on Hayden. Perhaps she *had* overindulged just a bit.

What a wonderful evening! Dancing, the orchestra, the wine and delicacies. And Hayden looking so dashingly handsome. The way he'd swept her across the dance floor with the style and grace of any aristocrat while a multitude of envious eyes followed them. It was a dream, an incredible, magical dream. Yet now her feet felt as heavy as cannon balls.

Hayden was silent beside her. Was he distraught at their parting? Halting before her door, she spun to face him. Lantern light rippled over the firm lines of his jaw, his cheeks, and over the speck of sorrow in his green eyes. He stared at her lips and licked his own. For a brief, exhilarating moment, she thought he might kiss her again.

Instead he swallowed, shifted his stance, and leaned in to whisper, "I had a wonderful time tonight." His warm breath fondled her neck and spiraled a pleasurable shiver down her back. She gripped the door handle behind her. Anything to keep from throwing herself in his arms. From begging him to come with her to the States. From telling him that she'd never felt this way about any man before. Not even Samuel. Or it had been so long since she'd seen her fiancé that she'd simply forgotten? Regardless, she should say goodnight, slip inside her room, and close the door before she did something only an unchaste woman would do.

"I enjoyed myself as well," she replied, soaking in every detail of his face, his strong Roman nose, sculpted cheeks, thick brows and lashes that matched his dark hair, and the stubble that circled his mouth and trailed his jaw. She never wanted to forget him.

Hayden scratched that stubble now and met her gaze. The *tick-tock tick-tock* of a clock down in the lobby counted out their final moments together. Final moments only she knew about. For he no doubt assumed he'd be escorting her to the dock master come morning. Snoring rumbled down the hall. Hayden's breathing grew deep. He seemed as unwilling to leave her as she was him. Finally, he grinned. "So you didn't mind spending an evening with a toad?"

"I make concessions for toads who know how to dance."

"But you would prefer a prince?" He eased a lock of her hair behind her ear, suddenly serious.

The intimate gesture nearly caused her to blurt out *No! I much prefer the toad!* But instead she lifted her chin and said, "Of course. What princess wouldn't?"

He frowned. Good. She must stop this dangerous dalliance or she'd be done for. She forced her thoughts to what she must do in the morning—escape this man, leave him behind.

"Where will you stay tonight?" she asked.

"I'll find somewhere. I'm used to being on the streets, remember?"

Yes, she did. And it endeared him to her all the more. She'd never met a man like him. He'd suffered so much, grown up without a single advantage, yet he was more competent than any man she'd known. Even Samuel, who although he was a successful solicitor, could barely start a fire without a servant's help.

Hayden studied her, a sudden twinkle in his eyes. "Hmm. I do recall, however, that in your *Maiden and the Frog* story, the young lady made a bargain with the toad that allowed him to share her bed for two nights."

Magnolia would have slapped any other man for such an insinuation, or at least slammed the door in his face, but she knew Hayden, could hear the teasing in his voice. "You remember correctly, sir. But I believe he gave her something first, something invaluable to her survival."

"Alas, I have brought you to Rio, my princess."

"And you will be paid," she lied.

He sighed and loosened his string tie. "Very well. If you don't wish to see the toad transformed into a prince..."

Magnolia wouldn't tell him that he had already made the transformation. "But you forget the end of the story. After the toad spent two nights with the maiden, she had to chop off his head in order for him to turn into a prince."

Hayden rubbed his throat, his brow crinkling. "On second thought, I believe I'll remain a toad." He grinned, leaned over, and kissed her cheek. "Sweet dreams to you, fair maiden." Then with a wink, he turned and disappeared into the shadows.

Chirp, tweet, chirp, tweet, the shrill clamor pierced Magnolia's ears and penetrated her blissful slumber. She groaned and tossed the quilt over her head. Mercy me, why did the jungle always have to wake up so early? *Wait*. She wasn't in the jungle. Moving her hands, she felt the scratchy fabric of the bed sheets. She wasn't in a hammock on a ship or on her feather bed in Roswell either. Or even on a bamboo cot in New Hope. Her mind snapped to attention. She was in some shamble of a hotel in Rio de Janeiro. But she wasn't complaining. It was the first night she'd slept on a mattress in nearly five months. *Chirp, chirp.* Drawing the cover from her head, Magnolia pried one eye open to find a small, plump, and very colorful bird sitting on her window ledge. Behind the winged annoyance, a pinkish-gray glow chased away the night.

"Shoo! Go away!" She swatted the air and closed her eye again. An unavoidable smile curved her lips as memories from last night came out from hiding. The ball, the music, dancing, Hayden. . .

She let out a satisfied moan and stretched across the lumpy mattress that was, no doubt, home to a myriad of tiny beasties. But what did it matter? She'd had such a marvelous evening—a fairy tale evening, an evening she wished had never come to an end. But it had. . .and today. . .

She shot up in bed, rubbed her eyes, and glanced once more at the window. Dawn. She must leave before Hayden arrived! The bird cocked his red-feathered head and stared at her curiously.

"I suppose I should thank you for waking me, little one."

Leaping from the bed, she made quick work of her morning toilette, all the while ignoring the pain lancing through her heart. Pain at leaving Hayden. Wasn't this what she wanted? To go back home, find Samuel, and get married? She shook her head as she made her way to the wardrobe, trying to break the spell Hayden had cast on her. Last night was a fantasy. Today, she was back to reality. Today she would begin her journey home.

After dressing, she packed everything in her valise and checked herself in the mirror, pleased she'd been able to pin up her hair in a fashionable coiffure all by herself. Removing a slip of paper and a pen and ink from her case, she scribbled out a note.

Hayden,

I'm sorry. Hope you can forgive me someday. . .Yours affectionately,

Magnolia

Short and to the point. No sentimentality. He would appreciate that. No doubt he was still fast asleep somewhere and wouldn't see this for hours. And she'd be long gone. She hoped. For she didn't think she could handle saying good-bye to him again.

Releasing a heavy sigh, she cast one final glance at the bird who still stared at her from the window before she grabbed the door latch and swung it open.

To find Hayden sound asleep on the bench across the hallway.

Hayden peeled his eyes open and was rewarded with a vision of loveliness tiptoeing past him. Lovely until she saw him looking at her and her expression crumpled. She halted with a huff. "What on earth are you doing here, Hayden?" Her shrill voice bore no resemblance to the soft, enchanting cadence of last night. Had the princess turned into a pumpkin while she slept? All the better. For it would make his task today much easier.

Rubbing his aching eyes, he sat, leaned forward, and placed his elbows on his knees. "I was protecting you." *And keeping you from leaving without me.* He wouldn't tell her that he'd sensed something in her last night, something secretive, duplicitous.

"Protecting me?" The hard edge to her voice softened.

Hayden raked his hair back and gazed up at her. "Rio's not the safest town, nor are we in the safest location down here by the docks."

Her delicate eyebrows folded together, and she glanced toward the stairs as if she wished to escape. "How very chivalrous of you," she mumbled. Then why did she seem so troubled and distant?

She faced him, her smile tight as a stretched bow. "You must not have slept at all on that hard bench. Why don't you go lie on the bed? I believe we have the room until noon, do we not? In the meantime, I will go see about some food and perhaps stop by the dock master's." She batted the air around her face, her gaze skittering about. "After the news about this Godard fellow, I assume you aren't going back to the States with me. So, after I book passage, I'll return to say good-bye."

Uneasy at her nervous chattering, Hayden rose and cocked a brow. "And pay me."

"Of course." She gave an exaggerated giggle. "Well then, I shall see you in an hour or so. Do get some rest, Hayden. You look an absolute fright." Sorrow cracked her voice, and he thought he saw moisture cover her eyes before she turned to leave.

Hayden caught her arm. She didn't turn around.

"I've no need for further rest, Princess, though I'm thrilled by your concern." Why was she behaving so strangely? "Perhaps it's best you pay me now."

She tugged from his grip and took a step back, her gaze lowering to the stained and marred floorboards. A man emerged from the room next door, assessed them for a moment, then tipped his hat and headed downstairs.

Magnolia's jaw tightened. "I'm not sure how much my ticket will be."

"Then I will accompany you."

Speechless—for once—she stared at him. Or more like *through* him as alarm screamed in her eyes. Yes, indeed, there was definitely some tomfoolery afoot. Foolish girl! She obviously had no idea who she was dealing with.

After a vain attempt to press the wrinkles from his coat and trousers, Hayden escorted her from the hotel. Better to tell her the truth away from prying eyes and ears, away from people who might wish to intervene in the ensuing confrontation. And what a confrontation it would be when he told her he had no intention of allowing her to put her life at risk by traveling back to the States alone.

Except for a few people, wagons, and chickens milling about, the street was refreshingly empty. Bright fingers of sunlight curled over the edge of the water, spreading a coral ribbon across the horizon and splashing violet on the underbellies of clouds. Sugar Loaf, the peak guarding the bay, rose like a dark thumb imprinted onto the majestic painting. The smell of fish, salt, bananas, and mangoes swirled about Hayden as he battled a myriad of conflicting emotions.

Magnolia hurried along, head down, and valise pressed to her heaving chest. Perhaps she was simply nervous about her upcoming voyage. But soon enough, she would be relieved of such fears.

Of course, he had to get his money from her first. Before she got to the dock master and bought a useless ticket. Turning, he scanned the street, seeking a coffee shop or fruit stand where he could entice her to stop for a moment. Nothing but houses and hotels and a gaudy French theater lined the avenue. Dread clenching his stomach, he faced forward again.

Magnolia was gone.

His heart lurched. He scanned the sparse crowd for a flash of flaxen hair and blue skirts. There, darting down a narrow passage between a cigar shop and a stall selling fine silks. Cursing himself for his stupidity, he tore after her, down the alleyway, out onto a main street bustling with activity. Good thing he was taller than most for he had a clear view of her light hair threading the crowd like a needle through canvas.

So, she intended not to pay him, to go back on her word. Perhaps that had been her intention all along. His blood boiled. How dare she try to swindle him! The best confidence man in the Confederacy.

It didn't take long to catch her. In fact, he considered delaying the chase to grant her a few extra moments of hope. But sweat began to bead on his chest and neck, and his breath grew heavy, so he lengthened his stride, grabbed her elbow, and dragged her off the street into an alleyway.

Forcing her against the brick wall, he imprisoned her with his arms. "What in the Sam Hill are you doing, Princess?" His breath came out in heated bursts, filling the air between them.

Her chest heaved in time with his. Waves of freed hair tumbled down her shoulders. Perspiration shone on her face and neck. But her eyes were ice. "I hate good-byes."

"And I assume you hate parting with your money as well."

She ducked beneath his arm and darted to the left, but he snagged her and brought her back. "Ah, ah, ah, Princess. Not until you pay me my due." Not ever, actually. But he wouldn't tell her that until he got his money—money he desperately needed to purchase supplies and a scout to locate his father.

"It's always been about the money, hasn't it?" Spite hissed in her voice. "Not about helping a lady in distress. Even last night. You were playing a part, being kind just to get the money, weren't you?" The ice melted in her eyes, and he couldn't tell whether the tears were an act or real. *Baffling woman!*

He pushed off the wall and held out his open palm. "Nevertheless, we had a deal."

She swallowed hard, her gaze flitting from him to the street and back again. Finally, she sighed, retrieved the pouch from her valise, and slammed it into his hand.

The sheer weight of it delighted Hayden.

"You're welcome to what's left after you purchase my passage home. In fact"—she picked up her valise and started down the alleyway—"why don't we go buy a ticket now? Then I'll board the ship and you'll be free of me."

Hayden leapt in front of her. A breeze sifted through the passageway, cooling the sweat on his neck. He snapped hair from his face, studying her. She wouldn't meet his gaze. "I have a better idea. How about we count it first? Three hundred dollars worth of gold coins, if I recall?"

Her face blanched. She seemed to be having trouble breathing. She set down her valise and leaned against the brick wall with a huff of resignation. "Very well."

Tipping her valise on its side, Hayden poured the contents of the pouch onto the patterned fabric. A few gold coins sifted out from the top, but they were soon smothered beneath a massive pile of copper pennies.

Chapter 18

Magnolia gripped the wall behind her, snagging her last pair of good gloves, wishing she could melt into the bricks and disappear. The look of shock in Hayden's green eyes transformed into fury as hard as emerald. He clutched a handful of pennies and rose, thrusting them in her face. "You tricked me!" Nostrils flaring, his jaw reddened beneath dark stubble like embers beneath coal. "You lied to me!"

Magnolia's breath fled her lungs. A squeak emerged from her lips.

He flung the coins on the ground by her feet. Some struck her hem and landed on her shoes. Others crashed to the stone walkway, their *clanks* and *clinks* sounding hollow in her ears—hollow like her promise to Hayden. She couldn't blame him for his anger. She'd tried to avoid it. But now as he took up a pace before her like a raging bull about to charge, she grew concerned at what he might do.

He kicked the pennies down the street, growling. "I counted on that money. I trusted you."

Halting, he slammed his palms on the brick on either side of her and pinned her to the wall once again. The man could start a fire with that look in his eyes. As it was, Magnolia felt her heart sear beneath his stare. He tried to say something, bared his teeth, but only a groan emerged as he pushed off the wall and backed away.

Finally, she found her voice, shaky as it was. "I only had enough for my passage, Hayden. I didn't know what else to do. You wouldn't have taken me along without being paid."

"No, I wouldn't have." Clenching his fists, he crossed his arms over his chest.

"You left me no choice." Tears blurred her vision.

A flash of understanding lit his eyes before he narrowed them. "You prepared the trap before you even knew I would deny your request. You intended to trick me all along."

Unable to bear the pain in his eyes, she lowered her gaze. "I suspected money might influence you, yes. I'm sorry, Hayden. I hated lying to you." A bell rang from the harbor. She bit her lip and watched a woman pass by with a basket of fruit on her head. "Please let me use what little gold I have to buy my passage. As soon as I get home and marry Samuel, I'll send you ten times that amount."

He gave a cynical chuckle. "Fool me once, Princess." He shoved a finger at her and shook his head. Then kneeling, he gathered the gold coins and slid them into his pocket—seven coins that would amount to no more than forty dollars. Just enough to pay for her passage home and perhaps conveyance to her aunt and uncle's in Ohio. But now they were in the possession of this angry bull before her.

Angry and wounded and possessing a crazed look akin to a feral wolf. Oh, how she wished the ardor of the prior night would return, but she'd never see that again. She'd ruined that possibility with her lie. Ruined any affection that had grown between them. And now, there was truly nothing left for her in Brazil. Despite the heaviness in her heart, she put on her most charming smile and inched toward him. "I know I lied to you, Hayden, but I promise I will send you money. As much as you need." Self-loathing curdled in her belly at another possible deception. But how else was she to get home?

A breeze snaked an eerie whistle through the alleyway, flapping Hayden's dark hair across his collar. He shook his head and snorted. "Your pardon, Princess, if I no longer believe you. Besides, you're coming back to New Hope with me."

"What?" Magnolia screeched. "I will do no such thing!" She backed away. "I didn't come all this way, suffer all I have, to return to that barbaric place. Give me back my money this instant!" She gestured toward his pocket.

"Your money?" He snorted. "You mean my payment for escorting you to Rio." He grumbled out a curse. "Or at least my partial payment."

"The bargain was to buy my passage home and the rest would be yours."

"The rest of"—he glanced at the pennies strewn across the ground, his voice coming out strangled—"nothing is nothing!" Growling, he raked a hand through his hair, took up a pace, then stopped and collected himself. "Besides, it's not safe for you to travel alone. You'll be ravished or robbed. Or both."

Steam rose up Magnolia's back. Hot, furious steam. "I have nothing for anyone to steal."

"Then just ravished." He pointed toward the pennies. "If you want those, you best pick them up."

Grinding her teeth, Magnolia glanced toward the street, now bustling with people, wagons, and donkeys. A monkey skittered past the alley, stopped, cocked his head curiously at them, and then jabbered something that sounded like a rebuke before he darted away. She closed her eyes as a groan erupted in her throat. She must leave this savage country! She simply couldn't bear another five days traipsing through the jungle, dealing with insects as big as cats and snakes as long and thick as ship's ropes. Nor could she face her father again. If he didn't kill her for leaving, his continual berating would drive her to suicide.

She gazed at the coins scattered over the moist ground. Scattered and worthless just like her dreams, her hopes. Just like her. Yet something Hayden said haunted her dismal thoughts.

"You were never planning on putting me on a ship, were you? You merely told me that so I'd help you with that repulsive immigration officer."

He didn't need to answer. She saw the answer shouting from behind those green eyes of his.

He sighed and rubbed the back of his neck. "I fully intended to escort you home if Mr. Santos had informed me that Godard had gone back to the States."

"And if not?"

He shrugged. "Like I said, you wouldn't survive alone on a ship."

"What is that to you?" Blood surged through her veins, thick and scorching. "You lie to me, cheat me, use me. Why do you care if I survive the trip or not?"

He raised his brows. "I am not a complete monster, Princess."

"No, you are worse than a monster! You are a heartless beast, a cruel, heartless beast who preys on innocent women."

She must have struck a nerve for a hint of remorse shoved the pompous fury from his face.

"Listen, Princess," he began, hands raised in a truce.

But Magnolia couldn't hear him anymore. Rage seared through her, befuddling all rational thought. Lifting her foot, she kicked him as hard as she could.

She aimed for his thigh, hoping to knock him to the ground, but she must have struck a more sensitive area, for he toppled over with an agonizing groan.

A moment's consideration told her she didn't stand a chance of retrieving her money from his pocket so instead, she grabbed her valise and darted into the street. Tears mottled everything into a kaleidoscope of colors as she twined her way through the swarm of beasts and humanity. Creaking wagons, shouting vendors, and squawking birds blended in a perverted, dismal hum. She had no idea where she was going. She had no money, knew not a soul, and didn't speak the language. But what else could she do? She'd rather die alone in Rio than go back to New Hope. Besides, she was a capable woman. She would think of something, wouldn't she?

Her mind and heart a jumble of fear and panic, she clutched her valise to her chest and rushed forward, stumbling over the uneven cobblestones. She turned down a familiar-looking street and hurried past a huge church with white columns, lofty spires, and a scrolled bell tower. Halting to catch her breath, she studied the way the rising sun reflected off the stained-glass window, enhancing a portrait of Jesus on the cross. A young boy sat on a bench out front. A beggar? No. His clean, stylish attire and well-groomed hair spoke otherwise. He smiled at her, flashing a rank of snowy teeth before he went back to weaving a basket. Sniffing, Magnolia wiped her face and started up the pathway.

A church would be the perfect place to hide, to think, to decide what she should do next.

She pushed against one of the large, heavy doors. The aged wood creaked as it opened to darkness and a blast of cool, musty air. Stepping inside, scents of candle wax and incense wafted around her—pleasant smells that seemed to leech the worry from her pores. She would be safe here. A man like Hayden would never set foot in a church. Nor, she supposed, would he think she would either. Sliding into one of the pews, she set down her valise as her eyes grew accustomed to the dim lighting. Rows of empty wooden benches stretched to an altar laden with white linen, lit candles, and silver bowls. Beyond the altar and above the chancel hung a carved figure of Jesus on the cross. Golden angels with trumpets to their lips perched on either side of him. Of course Magnolia knew the story of the Son of God, who died to save mankind from their sins. She'd heard it preached repeatedly in her childhood. And while it made for an interesting tale, she'd never seen how it applied to her. Perhaps this Jesus *was* the Son of God. Perhaps He did die for her. But where was He now? Why didn't He show Himself? Talk to her? Help her figure out her disaster of a life? No, God had always seemed so far away, so unreachable.

Leaning back on the hard pew, she plucked her mirror from her valise and attempted to stuff her wayward hair back into her bun. How her father would scold her for entering a church in such disarray. Not only was her hair a mess, but perspiration covered her face and neck. Grabbing a handkerchief, she dabbed the offending moisture, all the while wondering, if God did exist, why He cared so much about appearances. Was He just like her father—always expecting perfection? If so, she wanted nothing to do with Him. Lowering her mirror, she dropped it back into her valise.

A gust of wind blasted over her, warm and scented with roses and vanilla, and so strong it loosened her hair once again from her pins. Magnolia turned to see where it came from when a voice sent her heart into her throat.

"Well, hello, dearest."

An old woman sat beside her. A very old woman. A stained, torn dress covered her from neck to ankles, divided by an old tattered rope tied around her waist. Furrowed skin hung from a skeletal face framed by shriveled sprigs of gray hair. Where had she come from?

"I didn't mean to startle you, dearest." Her voice cracked with age, but her eyes were bright and clear, and the light that shone from within them put Magnolia immediately at ease.

"My apologies. I didn't see you come in," Magnolia said. In fact, she hadn't heard a thing. Odd since every sound seemed to magnify through the hollow, high ceilings of the church.

The lady smiled, revealing a scattering of dull teeth over fleshy gums. Magnolia's annoyance rose. Of all the places to sit in the vacant church, why did the old woman sit beside her? Especially when Magnolia wished to be alone, to think, to figure how to get herself out of her predicament. The smell of sweat and age and foul breath curled her nose, and she turned to gaze up at the crucifix. "Forgive me, madam, but I would prefer to be alone to pray."

The woman chuckled. "Is that what you were doing?"

The sarcasm in her tone sent anger through Magnolia. "Yes, it was. Now if you please." She scooted away, wondering why the woman spoke fluent English with no accent.

She shifted even closer to Magnolia.

With a huff, Magnolia shoved her ever-rebellious hair into her bun and patted it in place. Then rising to her feet, she pressed the wrinkles from her skirts and grabbed her valise, intending to bid the woman good day. But a bony hand reached out and stayed her.

"You concern yourself far too much about your appearance, dearest Magnolia—far too much about your outside, when it is your inside that needs attention."

The words turned nonsensical in Magnolia's mind. She jerked from her touch. "How do you know my name?"

Again that smile, filled with such peace. "I know much about you, dearest."

Magnolia's legs wobbled, and she sank back into the pew, studying every line and crevice in the woman's face, trying to determine if she'd met her before. But no, she would remember someone this bent and wrinkled with age.

"You find me ugly, don't you?" the woman asked.

Magnolia lowered her gaze, unsure of what to say and yet somehow knowing this woman would see through vain flatteries. "No. . .yes. . . but you are old. It is to be expected."

"Old, indeed, dearest. If you only knew." She chuckled. "But this body is merely a covering, a used garment that one day will be shed. True and lasting beauty comes from within."

Sunlight shone through the stained glass, sending a rainbow of dusty spears through the church and haloing the figure of Jesus with brilliant light. The old woman gazed up at Him as if she knew Him, as if He were a dear loved one. "God cares not for the outside. His concern is the heart. He sees only the heart."

Pondering the woman's statement, Magnolia suddenly wondered at the condition of her own heart. Surely it was clean and good. She hadn't told too many lies, hadn't stolen from others. She'd been chaste and moral. She hadn't hurt anyone purposely, had she? Certainly not like many of her prudish friends back home.

The woman touched her again, and Magnolia felt a spark shoot through her. "Here and henceforth," the woman began, "your reflection will reveal the true beauty of your heart, the way you appear to those who inhabit eternity. Take care to adorn yourself with jewels that last forever."

Her words floated through Magnolia's mind, forming a tangled thread of nonsense. She was still staring at the woman when the old lady gripped the pew back in front of her and pulled herself to stand. With body curled and bent, she waved a bony hand above her head. A bright light flashed. Magnolia blinked. The woman's body unfurled like a new flower in spring. Her back straightened. Her shoulders stretched. Her withered gray hair plumped and lengthened into gold, silky strands. Creases on her skin faded and tightened, leaving a complexion that glowed. Her eyes sparkled, her lips grew rosy. Her rags transformed into white robes trimmed in silvery glitter.

Magnolia's heart stopped.

The woman smiled again. "This is how I look on the inside." Even her gruff voice had transformed into music.

The foyer door squealed. Magnolia turned to see a man enter. A gust of wind struck her with the scent of sweet roses. When she turned back around, the woman was gone.

Chapter 19

A church was the last place Hayden expected to find Magnolia. It was the last place he expected to find himself. Still throbbing from her assault, he approached her with caution, lest the wildcat reveal her claws again. But when he grew close, she made no move to run, made no move to fight. Instead she remained in the pew, her face a white sheet, her eyes stark and skittering. Finally she gazed up at him, her befuddled expression transforming into recognition, followed by fear, then resignation.

"I see you found me," she said.

"Perceptive as always, Princess."

She rose, teetered, and grabbed the pew back for support, the fight gone out of her. So easily, or did something happen? Hayden glanced through the church but no one was in sight. Just the crucified Jesus staring down at Hayden as if he weren't worthy to be in such a holy place.

A shiver etched between his shoulders.

Magnolia grabbed her valise. "I take it I am now your prisoner."

"Call it what you may, I will not allow you to put your life and your purity at risk."

She stepped into the aisle, raised a hand to her head and swayed. An act? No, not by the way she gasped as if all air had evacuated the church. Hayden grabbed her elbow, and she all but fell against him. Despite his anger, he wrapped an arm around her waist and felt her tremble. "What happened? Are you all right?"

She sniffed and shook her head, but said nothing. Hayden found he quite enjoyed the pussy cat over the tigress. Besides, he could not deny his relief at finding her. At first, as he folded in agony from her kick, unable to move or even breathe, his anger told him to just let her go, just let her be. After all, he had what little money she possessed. If the shrew wanted to be on her own, what was that to him? But he couldn't do it. Couldn't even think clearly while she was wandering the streets alone. And in far more danger than her innocence realized.

Taking her valise, he ushered her to the door. No sooner did they step out into the blaring sun than the tigress reappeared. Tearing from his embrace, she shoved him aside, nearly knocking him down the steps. "You deceived me!"

He turned his body, shielding himself from another kick, and clutched her arm lest she try to run again. "*You* deceived me, Princess." He still couldn't believe that she'd swindled him so effectively, that she'd charmed her way into his heart with lies and promises. The notorious confidence man, Hayden Gale! It was not only unheard of, it was infuriating, and even worse, it was humiliating beyond all measure.

Halting at the bottom of the stairs, she snapped from his grip and faced him. "So, we lied to each other. Used each other. We are even." Squinting against the bright sunlight, she scanned the street. "How on earth did you find me?"

"The boy." Hayden gestured toward the bench, but it was empty now. He scratched his chin. "There was a boy. He called to me while I sped past. Told me an American lady was in the church."

Magnolia frowned and marched onto the muddy street, nearly bumping into a man who was being carried in a chair by four dark mulattoes. Thunder bellowed in the distance. She slowed and faced Hayden, her anger gone, her eyes soft wisps of sapphire. "Why don't we go home, Hayden? Back to the States. Just you and me." Her voice was honey. "I'm sure we have enough for two tickets. Let's leave this horrid place, return to the familiar comforts of home. Please?" Was it his imagination or did her bottom lip suddenly plump like the inviting cushion of a divan? One he normally would long to lounge upon. If he weren't so furious. Lashes lowering to her cheeks, she played with the lapel of his coat.

For a moment, he felt his anger receding beneath her feminine charms. Oh, but she was good. She was very good. He could see why most men melted at her feet. He'd never met a woman—or a man, for that matter—who possessed the same innate skill as he did to charm a piece of meat from a starving man. Together they could have amassed a fortune back home.

But he wouldn't fall for her schemes again. He shifted his gaze away.

She placed a hand on his arm. "If you escort me safely to my aunt and uncle's estate, I'll give you my entire dowry."

Hayden snorted. "Why do I find it hard to believe that such a dowry even exists?"

"Of course it does. Please, Hayden. This Mr. Godard is no doubt long gone by now. I know you say he stole everything from you, but you are here and alive and we both have a chance at getting out of this savage country. I can tell you don't wish to stay in New Hope, so why delay—"

But Hayden wasn't listening anymore. Just the mention of his father's alias sent renewed zeal through him. And as tempting as it was to run away with this beautiful, unpredictable, spitfire, he had a promise to keep to his mother. "I can't."

"Of course you can."

"No." Taking her arm, he started walking.

"Then leave me here. I can't bear to go back to New Hope." Her voice degraded to a sob.

"It isn't safe."

"What is that to you?"

Hayden wouldn't tell her that, much to his chagrin, and even after her deception, he cared very much what happened to her. "Perhaps your parents will offer me a reward for bringing you back."

He could hear the pain in her long, ragged sigh. Felt the ache in his own heart. She yanked her valise from his grip. "I assure you, sir, they will not. You are wasting your time."

Seconds passed in silence as she trudged beside him before blowing out a huff of surrender. "Well, if you insist on dragging me through the jungle again, can we at least stop and purchase some rum?"

Setting down his shovel, Wiley Dodd wiped sweat from his brow, plucked a map from his pocket, and spread the crinkled paper over the stump of a felled tree. A spindly insect dove at him. He swatted it away as sweat stung his eyes, blurring the lines on the map. He rubbed them and tried to focus despite the heat that spiraled down from the sun, making everything look like a mirage. But the hard, rocky ground was no mirage. His aching muscles attested to that. He'd been digging for days in the exact spot indicated on the map, but all he'd gotten for his trouble was a ten-foot-deep hole, a mound of dirt and pebbles, raw blisters on his hands, and a mood so foul it scared even the monkeys away.

He ran a finger over the points on the treasure map. He'd found the purple boulder shaped like a turtle fifty paces from the spot where the river split. He'd followed the edge of the shallow ravine in a semicircle to find the old cassia tree with the carved hole in the center. Inside, he'd gathered the twelve stones, along with several surly spiders, which he'd shaken off before they bit him. Upon each stone two numbers were etched. According to the map, the first, a number between one and four, indicated the direction—north, south, east, or west—and the other was the number of paces in that direction. Just finding the stones where the map said they would be, had caused him to yelp and leap like a man whose britches were on fire. It was proof that he wasn't mad after all. How he'd love to tell the other colonists, to show to them he'd been right, that there must be gold here in the Brazilian jungle, but they'd probably want in on the treasure.

And he couldn't have that. He'd worked too hard for too many years. First as a boy in a sailmaker's shop, sweeping the floors of scrap canvas and cordage, and stirring the kettle of tallow—doing whatever he could to support his mother and two sisters. Then as a sheriff, first in Norfolk and then in Richmond, sweeping the streets of equally useless scraps of humanity. Hard, dangerous work for so little pay. Now, it was fortune's turn to smile upon him—for once.

A drop of sweat landed on the map, and he brushed it away. He'd followed the directions on the stones to the waterfall. Or at least he hoped it was the same waterfall drawn on the map. Ten paces off, he'd found the group of larger rocks piled in the shape of a pyramid. And beyond them, a circle of mango trees, in the center of which stood the treasure. At least that was how it appeared on the map—a chest filled with gold. In reality, there was nothing but leaf-strewn, hard-packed dirt. And so he had dug. And dug. And dug and dug.

Scratching the back of his neck, he stretched his shoulders. Where had he gone wrong? He carefully folded the map and stuffed it into his pocket. After gulping down water from his canteen, he grabbed the shovel, leapt into the hole, and started digging again. His sweat soon returned, along with the mind-numbing thrum of insects and birds above. But when his shovel struck something hard, he no longer cared. The sweet chink of metal on metal brought a huge smile to his cracked lips.

Magnolia couldn't believe she was in the middle of the jungle again. After she had endured so much discomfort in order to get to Rio. After she could see the ships in the bay preparing to sail for home...

If not for the lying, thieving barbarian sitting across the crackling fire from her, she would have made it home, too. Somehow or another. She would have found a way. But instead, he had made her his prisoner—forced her to walk in front of him, never taking his eyes off her, so she "wouldn't get any fool notions about running back to Rio," he had said.

Many such notions had crossed her mind during the long day, but they now faded with the last vestiges of sunlight angling through the trees. She was too far enmeshed in the steamy web to ever find her way back. The brute obviously knew that too, for he sat on a log whittling a piece of wood, completely ignoring her. Beside him sat a knapsack filled with supplies he'd purchased with her money. *Her money!*

Leaning over, she unlaced the new shoes they'd also bought in Rio, a pair of black kids with shiny buckles. Plain, yet practical. Of course, after a day of traipsing through the jungle, they were already ruined. She rubbed her toes through her stockings, feeling the hardened skin of old blisters and hoping her feet wouldn't grow large and callused like some women's. She'd always prided herself on her petite, flawless feet.

"What are we going to eat?" she asked.

Without looking up, Hayden gestured to a pile of fruit he'd gathered earlier.

"But what about the dried pork you purchased in Rio?"

"That's for my search after we return."

"But it was *my* money. I should have some of it."

Finally he looked up, eyes darkening like the growing shadows of the jungle. "It was *my* payment."

"But the bargain was not completed. You did not see me safely on a ship to America."

He went back to whittling. Dark hair the color of almonds grazed his shoulders, stirred by a welcome breeze that whistled through the leaves. He shifted his boots over the dirt, clearly avoiding the discussion.

Magnolia felt like growling, but that wouldn't be very ladylike. Did the man have any idea what eating only fruit did to her delicate digestion? She dropped her chin into her palm, putting on her most adorable pout. Though why she bothered, she had no idea. It never worked on him.

He ignored her.

How rude! Especially when she had far more reason to be angry at him than he did her. What did it matter if he didn't have as much money as he'd hoped? He could still search for this Godard fellow. While she, on the other hand, had to face the wrath of her father for her betrayal, a lifetime of his criticisms, and a hopeless future in the primordial sludge of Brazil. Not to mention, her father would probably marry her off to some dowdy, feeble-minded Brazilian. A sour taste rose in her throat and she released a wilted sigh—a sigh that begged for Hayden's help.

Still, he ignored her.

And to think that only last night she'd thought she might be developing affections for him. There. She admitted it. Yes, she had felt something. Most likely just cheap wine. But he'd been so gallant at the ball. Such a gentleman. So handsome and charming and entertaining and clever. She'd had fun. For the first time in her recollection, she'd truly enjoyed herself at a party.

Now, that same man had transformed back into a toad—all angry and somber—dressed once again in his stained white shirt and black trousers tucked within muddy boots. And search as she might, she could find no resemblance between him and the man she'd been with last night. Perhaps it had all been an act. Hayden was just like all the other men in her life. He had used her for her beauty then used her for her money. And now, he was using her for a possible reward from her father. Pain lanced her heart, the blade turning and twisting until tears filled her eyes. Maybe that was all she was good for. Beauty and money.

She ripped a banana from a bunch and started to peel it as a chorus of katydids began their nightly orchestra. Fireflies flickered in the darkness, matched by stars beginning to twinkle through the canopy. She shoved away her sorrow. It did her no good. Besides, she was lonely and frightened and talking helped soothe her nerves. Even if the only person she could converse with was the man who had put her in this predicament.

"Who is this Godard anyway?"

He blew out a sigh. Was it her imagination or did his knife cut a little deeper into the wood? "I told you. Just someone I need to find." Setting down his carving, he tossed another log onto the fire, the flames reflecting red in his hard eyes. Magnolia swallowed at the fury she saw within them. Surely, that wasn't *all* directed at her.

"I have a right to know who he is," she said, "since it is on his account you are dragging me back to a father who will punish me to the end of my days for running away." Something flapped across the clearing, disappearing into the leaves. Magnolia hoped it wasn't a bat. She hated bats.

The tight lines on Hayden's face seemed to soften. He picked up his whittling again. "I am truly sorry about your father."

His tone carried remorse, but she wasn't buying it. "If you are truly sorry, you'd take me back to Rio and put me on a ship." She bit into her banana, the sweet taste flooding her mouth.

"Trust me. I'm doing what's best for you." His shirt sleeves were rolled up, drawing her gaze to the muscles flexing in his thick arms with each dig of the knife into wood.

"You are a toad, Hayden Gale."

He smiled.

Did the man truly care what happened to her on the ship? Or did he simply not wish to part with any of his—*her*—money? The thought that he might actually care brought a measure of comfort to her otherwise aggravated heart. Magnolia focused on a trail of ants edging the clearing. A monkey howled in the distance. "So this Mr. Godard, did he steal your lady, kill your dog? Ah, I know"—she nodded, studying him—"He lied to you. Deceived you like I did. But for something besides money. Hmm. . ."—she tapped her chin—"That would explain why you are so furious with me. You hate being tricked, outwitted. That's it. He made you out to be a fool, didn't he?" Like Martin had done to her. If so, she could well understand Hayden's need for revenge. She could even understand why he'd traveled all the way from Charleston to Brazil in search of the man, for she would do the same thing if she knew where Martin was. If she ever saw that fiend again, he would regret the day he laid eyes on her.

"Let it alone, Princess." Hayden's jaw tightened even further as his tone brooked no further discussion.

Tossing the empty banana peel, Magnolia plucked an orange from the pile, tore off the skin, and plopped a piece into her mouth. Sweet juice dribbled down her chin. Thankfully Hayden didn't see it before she wiped it away. Not that she cared what he thought of her. He was the worst sort of cad. The opposite of Samuel. Perhaps Samuel couldn't start a fire or build a shelter or catch fish. Maybe he couldn't find his way through the jungles of Brazil, but he knew how to treat a lady. He was cultured and well mannered and could converse on any number of topics—though most of them bored Magnolia. But that didn't matter.

He was courteous and kind and chivalrous, a true gentleman. And he would never lie to Magnolia. Or use her. Nor would he be churlish when she depended on him for survival.

"If you are intent on ignoring me, might I at least have some rum?" She'd seen Hayden purchase a flask in Rio, and the liquor would do much to relieve her tension.

He studied her, assessing her like a schoolmaster assessing a child. Finally he reached into his knapsack and handed her the flask. "Just a few sips."

"Am I to be rationed as well?"

"Until you learn to control your drinking, yes. I'll not have a besotted nymph running around the jungle."

"Nym. . .I do not overdrink!"

He snorted out a chuckle.

She frowned. "Then, why did you purchase it?"

"To control your shakes," he said. "And yes, I noticed."

Heat stormed up her neck as she uncorked the flask and tipped it to her mouth. Spice and fire slid down her throat and warmed her belly. Now, if it would only make the toad disappear. She took another sip.

"Easy now, Princess. Ladies don't gulp."

"How dare you!" Magnolia seethed. She attempted to rise but her insufferable crinoline pushed her back down. Carefully setting down the rum, she dropped to her knees, planted both hands in the dirt, and shoved herself up with a groan that she was sure would also be dubbed indelicate. "I am not a lush." She plucked the flask from the ground.

"When are you going to get rid of that cage you wear under your skirts?" He pointed his knife at her gown.

"Of all the. . .I. . ." She inhaled a breath. "What is under my skirts is none of your affair!" Mercy me, what had she just said? A tidal wave doused her in heat. She pressed a hand to her cheeks, certain that they were as red as pomegranates.

He grinned and continued whittling.

She sipped the rum, praying it would loosen the tight noose around her nerves. "What do you know about ladylike behavior, anyway? I imagine the only ladies you associate with are those who make taverns their home."

He chuckled. "In which case, I should not consider your behavior out of the ordinary with all the spirits you consume and the way you kiss a man without provocation."

"Without prov...kiss!" Rage strangled her. Followed by humiliation as the truth of his words struck home. Was she nothing but a common hussy? Had it been her lack of moral character that had caused her to fall for Martin's lies? Was that the reason her father constantly reprimanded her about her appearance? To hide her wench's heart? The old woman's words blared like a trumpet in her mind. *Here and henceforth your reflection will reveal the true beauty of your heart, the way you appear to those who inhabit eternity.*

Dropping to her knees, she set down the flask, opened her valise, and yanked out her gilded mirror. Eyes blurry with tears, she slowly raised it to view her reflection. Gray hair, frizzled and scorched, circled a face furrowed with lines and marred with dark spots. Her thin, leaden lips were drawn and cracked. Dark wells tugged at the skin beneath her eyes as hooded lids slanted over her once luminous eyes.

Magnolia screamed.

Chapter 20

Magnolia's scream sent Hayden leaping over the fire, knife drawn, ready to defend her against some reptilian, multilegged invader. But when he landed beside her, no such creature was to be found either on the mirror she continued to hold up to her face, or on her arm, her skirts, or anywhere around her. Her screaming reduced to sobs as she continued to stare at her reflection, gingerly touching her cheeks.

"What is it?" He nudged her hand and the mirror away, grabbed her shoulders, and forced her to look at him. Tears streamed from blue eyes as liquid as the sea. "She was right. She was right. The old lady was right," she kept repeating.

"Who was right? About what?"

"How can you look at me?" Jerking from his grasp, she turned her back to him. "I'm grotesque."

Hayden could make no sense of her ramblings. It couldn't be the rum. She'd only had a few sips. "You're anything but grotesque, Magnolia. You know that." He touched her shoulder but she moved out of reach. "Why all the theatrics?"

"You used my common name." She sniffed. "Not Princess." Her shoulders rose and fell upon a sob that seemed to calm her until she glanced in the mirror and started wailing again.

"By all that is holy, what is wrong?" Hayden's patience was fast coming to an end.

"Can't you see? Look." With her back still to him, she held the mirror up and gazed at him through the reflection. Nothing but her beautiful tear-streaked face stared back at him. Her eyes assessed him, the terror within them fading into confusion.

"Don't you see me?" she finally asked.

"Of course I see you. Lovely, alluring you."

"I look the same to you in the mirror?"

He studied her reflection again. "Except for your red, swollen eyes."

Leaning over, he picked up the flask, suddenly needing a drink himself. The pungent liquor warmed his throat. And heated his suspicions. "You did all this, behaved like a rattlebrain, just to lure a compliment from me?" He shook his head. "Of all the conceited, egotistical, selfish—"

"I did no such thing!" Stomping to her valise, she tossed her mirror in and slowly turned to face him, studying him as if gauging his reaction. Finally she planted her fists at her waist. "How could you think something like that? Do you find me so shallow?" Her eyes flashed like lightning, but then the anger faded, and she lowered herself onto a log, skirts puffing about her. Caked mud covered the hem from their long trek through the jungle, her new gown already ruined. But she didn't seem to care.

Instead, she stared at the fire as if in a daze, her tears drying on her cheeks. Hayden had no idea what to do. The great confidence man who could see past any facade, who could read people and match his own behavior to theirs in order to achieve his goals, now found himself at a complete loss.

Yes, he'd been furious at her for tricking him, for being the only one who had ever managed to swindle the infamous swindler. But perhaps that was just his pride. Besides, how could he blame her for doing something he did for a living? They both had good reasons for their deceptions. She to escape her father's tyranny, and he, of course, to finally end his quest for the man who had killed his mother and ruined his life.

The croak of a frog joined an owl's hoot in the distance as a breeze stirred the leaves into a crescendo of laughter. Laughing at him, no doubt. At his weakness for this Southern sprite. Slipping the flask inside his pocket, he squatted and poked the fire, sending sparks into the dark sky. Still, Magnolia didn't move. Hayden had been outwitted by a conceited debutante. But what bothered him more than her lie was the pain he'd felt when he discovered it—the agonizing pain of betrayal by someone he trusted. Sure, he had his suspicions. In his profession, he'd learned to be leery of most people. But deep down he supposed he had truly believed Magnolia. Otherwise, why would he feel such a palatable ache deep in his heart?

Something bit his neck and he slapped away the offending varmint. Had any of his victims felt this gut-wrenching pain? Memories of his vision of Katherine pricked his conscience. She'd seemed so upset, so tormented. But that hadn't been real, had it? In truth, he had no idea what her reaction had been. He'd never stuck around to witness the trail of destruction he'd left behind. By the time his targets discovered they'd been swindled, he was long gone. He'd always imagined their fury, their rage, but he'd never thought about their heartache.

Not until now.

Magnolia began mumbling something about being ugly inside and some old woman in a church, but Hayden couldn't make sense of it. Zooks, was the woman going mad now on top of everything else? He pictured himself hoisting a foaming-at-the-mouth lunatic over his shoulder and attempting to carry her through the jungle. The idea held no appeal. Finally, he suggested she retire, and much to his surprise she nodded and crawled into her shelter.

Two hours later, her deep breathing assured him she was asleep. Squatting by the opening of the shelter, he stared within, cursing himself for making the frond roof so snug that not a sliver of moonlight gave him a view of her face. What was it about this woman that had him so bewitched? She was spoiled, pompous, self-centered, and whiny. Besides, she hailed from a class of landed gentry that was as far from his own heritage as Queen Victoria was from a chimney sweep. To make matters worse, she had a viper's tongue in that sweet little mouth of hers. Sweet indeed! He rubbed his lips, remembering her taste. Honey and spice and passion. His body reacted, and he shifted his stance.

But she was also witty and smart and charming and feminine and passionate, and deep down she cared for others. And much like him, she'd also been given a rough start in life. Maybe she hadn't grown up a destitute orphan, but she'd grown up equally unloved by a critical, demanding father who valued her only for her beauty and held her captive to a mysterious debt she couldn't pay. It was no wonder she behaved the way she did.

Hayden sighed and rubbed his chin, studying the edge of her lacy petticoat peeking from beneath her skirts and the way her stockinged feet curled at her side. When he found his father and completed his mission, he would take Magnolia back to the States with him. He would hand her over to her fiancé, this solicitor Samuel Wimper. . . Wimperly or whoever he was. Just the sound of his name created an image of a spare, lanky man with greased hair, spectacles perched on his nose, and wearing a fancy frock coat.

But she obviously loved him or she wouldn't have gone to such trouble to find her way back to him. Hayden rose and circled the fire, hating the sudden pain that made his heart feel like an anchor. Hating it because he didn't understand it. Because he'd never felt it before. And because the woman who had caused it was forever outside his reach.

James emerged onto the sandy bank to find Miss Angeline, her skirts hiked up to her knees, standing in the river, slapping clothes against a rock. On the shore, Stowy, her inseparable cat, pounced on leaves and frogs and anything that dared move. Sunlight set Angeline's hair aglow in spirals of glittering amber trickling over her elegant neck. James had never seen a more beautiful sight.

Despite the rushing river and the warble of birds, she must have heard his boot's tread, for a pistol appeared in her hands so fast, he hadn't seen her draw it or from whence it had come.

He raised his hands, taken aback at the familiar way she held the weapon. Not with the hands of a seamstress, but with the hands of one accustomed to handling a gun. "I surrender."

Her eyes sparkled, and her shoulders lowered...along with the gun. "Do forgive me, Doctor. I've been a bit skittish lately."

"No need. I'm glad for it. It isn't safe for you to be out here alone." Which was why he had come in the first place. He'd seen the other women leaving with basketfuls of wet laundry, but not Angeline. Though James hadn't spoken to her since he'd made a fool of himself and run off during his sermon at church, he'd kept his eye on her. Especially after Eliza had told him about Dodd's propensity for peeping at the women.

James approached, sweeping a cautious glance over the clearing, then to the bank on the other side of the river. Afternoon sunlight rippled in silver ribbons across water that stretched at least forty yards before thick jungle kept it at bay. No sign of intruders or Peeping Toms. "You should always have at least one other person with you."

Stuffing the gun into her belt, she waded to shore, but then glanced down at her raised skirts and lowered them immediately, face reddening. James smiled. How refreshing to find such a modest woman. In fact, all of the women in the colony seemed in possession of the highest morals. And if James had his way, he intended to keep it that way. He'd had his fill of unscrupulous women.

"To deliver thee from the strange woman, even from the stranger which flattereth with her words. . . For her house inclineth unto death, and her paths unto the dead. None that go unto her return again, neither take they hold of the paths of life."

The words of Proverbs, words he had memorized and recited each day, stood to attention in his mind.

"I'm nearly done here." Angeline's voice snapped him from his musings. "And though I appreciate your concern, Doctor, I can take care of myself." She scooped up Stowy and stroked his fur, eyeing James with those exquisite violet eyes of hers. "Is there something I can do for you?"

He shifted his boots in the sand, wondering why the lady always turned his insides to porridge. "I'm checking with all the women to make sure they feel safe in the colony and aren't being bothered by any of the men." He invented a half-truth, ignoring the twinge of guilt that came with it. He'd fully intended to talk to Angeline after Eliza told him about Dodd, but he hadn't gotten around to it yet.

Her brow furrowed. A breeze stirred a pile of leaves, and Stowy leapt from her arms onto the pesky foliage. "Are you applying to be our town's constable as well, Doctor?" She smiled.

He suddenly felt rather silly, like an awkward schoolboy with his first infatuation. "No, I believe being preacher keeps me busy enough." He slanted his lips, wondering how to explain his concern without seeming like a lovesick fool. "The colonel and I want to keep an eye on all the single ladies in New Hope." Truss it, that didn't sound right either. "I mean we. . .well, in the absence of a lawman, we feel responsible for the ladies who live alone."

A tiny line formed between her brows. She studied him as if he were an oddity. James swallowed. Splendid. If running from the pulpit at church hadn't convinced her he was utterly mad, surely his present ramblings were proof enough.

A fish leapt from the lake, drawing Stowy to the edge. Was it overly hot today? Sweat moistened James's neck and arms, and he had a sudden desire to jump into the water. Even better, jump in with Angeline. The thought did nothing to cool him off.

She approached, the hem of her skirts scraping over hot sand. "I assume Eliza told you about Mr. Dodd." She raised a hand, shielding her face from the sun and darkening her eyes to deep lavender. Soothing, entrancing lavender.

"He hasn't done anything except stare at me and make me uncomfortable," she continued. "Let's hope his hunt for gold keeps him otherwise occupied."

"Indeed."

"But I thank you for your concern, Doctor."

She was so close he could smell the lye soap from washing clothes and her own sweet scent that reminded him of coconut. He cleared his throat, trying to clear his head as well.

"I do see that perhaps my concern for your safety has been exaggerated." He pointed toward the pistol stuffed in her belt. "I've never seen a lady draw a weapon so quickly. Where did the daughter of a shipwright learn such a skill?"

Angeline couldn't tell James that she'd learned how to load and shoot a pistol the hard way. That she'd had to defend herself against the worst possible monster. After that, it had been a matter of survival. "Oh, here and there." She offered him a coy smile, hoping he'd let the topic drop. Stowy jumped onto a rock at the edge of the lake and began swatting at fish swimming beneath the water.

"I also understand you had a disturbing vision," the doctor said, drawing her gaze back to him.

Those eyes, such a magnificent shade of bronze, exuded a strength equal to the metal itself. Somehow that made her feel safe in his presence. That and the way thick muscles in his chest flexed beneath his gray shirt. Power and strength that could subdue any villain. Power and strength she could have used three years ago. Power and strength coupled with the concern pouring from his expression that could have saved her a lifetime of misery.

Her pulse raced. She forced it to slow. James was not who he seemed. She must remember that.

"The vision, Miss Angeline?" He lowered his gaze to hers and stared at her quizzically.

"Yes. Forgive me. I did see something. But it was dark and late and I was very tired."

"Would it surprise you to know that I, too, saw a vision? That morning a week ago when I ran out on my sermon."

So that would explain his odd behavior. At the time she'd thought he'd become ill. "I couldn't imagine what had gone wrong."

"You haven't been back to church since. I feared I frightened you away." A burst of wind tossed a strand of his wheat-colored hair into his face. She longed to reach up and ease it aside.

"I told you I'm not much for religion." She lowered her gaze and saw the pink scar on her arm. Horrified, she unrolled her sleeves to cover it before James noticed. She didn't need any more questions she couldn't answer without lying.

But he must have seen it for he rubbed his own scar—the one on his cheek that angled down the side of his mouth like an oversized dimple. "Do say you'll come back to church. I promise not to become a babbling fool again."

How could she resist such a boyish smile? "I will make an attempt." She straightened the cuffs of her sleeves, wanting to know more about this man. Wanting to know why he was so different from the man she'd met a year ago. "May I ask what you saw in *your* vision?"

James turned and stepped toward the river. The mad rush of water surrounded them, drowning out the ever present buzz of the jungle. Sorrow darkened his eyes and formed tiny lines at the edges. Finally he answered, "It was a young corporal who died on my operating table during the war."

Angeline's stomach tightened. She had seen someone from her past as well. And so had Eliza. "From the ship before we even arrived, Eliza saw her dead husband standing on shore."

James faced her. "And Blake has seen someone too."

"Perhaps it is just the strain of moving to a different country, eating unfamiliar food, starting a new colony." Angeline would not allow for any other possibility. She couldn't. New Hope was her last chance at a normal life.

A cloud swallowed up the sun. "Being the preacher, I feel responsible for the emotional wellbeing of the townspeople. And these odd visions reek of something amiss in the spiritual realm."

Angeline stifled her laughter. Not at the man himself. No, James was nothing to laugh at. He was all man and strength and wisdom. It was his insistence on being a spiritual leader that gave her pause. She stared into those bronze eyes, so clear now. Yet only a year ago, those same eyes had stared at her, glazed and murky, as she'd led him upstairs to her room.

Taking a step back from him, she fingered the ring dangling on a chain around her neck—her father's ring. The only man she had ever trusted.

If James had truly changed and become a godly man, he wouldn't want to associate with the likes of her.

And if he hadn't, Angeline had had enough of lying, hypocritical men to last a lifetime.

Chapter 21

A rather obtuse insect of epic proportions and sporting a pair of orange wings had decided he loved Magnolia more than any creature in the jungle. He'd been following her for hours, buzzing about her face, trying to get her attention, looking for a place to land where he could shower her with his affections which, no doubt, would be in the form of some vile bug ooze. Which, of course, she couldn't possibly allow. So, she'd been swatting at him all day, and trying to stab him with the tip of her parasol, until her arms ached and her frustration was about to burst.

Hayden had reverted into being a toad again. For two days he'd barely said the same number of words to her. He'd been polite. He had provided for her. Mercy me, he'd even carried her valise, but whenever she tried to engage him in conversation, he replied with nonsensical grunts and groans. Did all men revert to barbarians when living in the wild?

She swung her closed parasol at the fawning bug again just as Hayden, marching in front of her, shoved aside a large leaf and released it. The green monster descended on her as if the sky had changed from blue to jade and was crashing to earth. It slapped her face and swaddled her in suffocating foliage.

Sputtering, she coughed and thrust it away, her insides seething. "How kind of you."

He grunted.

The only reason she could find for his rude behavior was that he'd seen her horrifying reflection in the mirror and was completely repulsed. Yet he'd claimed she looked the same. Perhaps he was lying, though she couldn't think of a single reason for that. Fine, if he wanted to be so shallow as to not even talk to her because of her appearance, then she didn't want to talk to him either. Oh, mercy me, was she truly old and ugly? She hadn't looked in the mirror since that night. Didn't want to see. Didn't want to know. She hoped it was just a bad dream—a delusion her mind had conjured from what that demented, shriveled-up woman had said. Surely that was it. But if so, what was wrong with Hayden? Magnolia knew she wasn't useful around camp. She couldn't even light a fire or catch a fish or build a shelter. She was worthless. As usual. And now, without her beauty, what good was she? That had to be the reason for his disdain. He couldn't still be angry about the money. After all, he'd lied to her as well! If not for him, she'd be on a ship right now enjoying the fresh ocean breezes, not being smothered by air as thick as syrup.

Wiping perspiration from her neck, she gazed up at the canopy, a lattice of vines and branches and leaves over which skittered hundreds of birds, monkeys, and crawly things that she preferred would stay above. A swarm of white butterflies flitted among the foliage like a band of tiny angels sent to keep watch on God's creation. She wished that were so, for at least then someone would know how miserable she was.

Hayden tromped in front of her, his hair tied behind him. The sound of his boots crunching on dry leaves rose in a steady, soothing cadence. His damp shirt clung to muscles that rippled across his shoulder and down his back with each graceful move. Unfortunately, being right behind him, Magnolia could hardly avoid such an alluring sight—alluring and hypnotizing and warming down to her toes. She realized she felt safe with this man—a man who was nothing at all like her Samuel. Samuel, who always dressed in the latest fashion from the heels of his leather Congress shoes to the top of his silk hat. His short-cropped hair was never out of place, his face always stubble-free, his movements so refined they could be considered dandyish.

Completely opposite from the wolfish gait of the man before her.

She drew in a breath of sweet jungle air, remembering Samuel's impeccable manners and how he always smelled of cedar oil and cigars.

The pesky bug swooped down upon her again. She shrieked.

In a move so quick she had no time to react, Hayden spun around, gun in hand, cocked it, and fired.

Magnolia squeezed her eyes shut, her one thought being that perhaps she'd been premature in her feelings that she was safe with this man.

Shock buzzed through her as the smell of gunpowder stung her nose. No pain seared her body. Her head felt intact. Her heart still beat. Slowly, she opened her eyes to see Hayden shoving the gun into his belt. He gave a wink before he continued onward.

"You"—she struggled to find a voice but it felt as if it had been shot clean through—"could have killed me."

"I didn't."

"Why did you do that?" She stumbled after him, glancing around for the bug that, no doubt, had been blown to pieces.

"I was tired of hearing you moan and groan every few minutes."

"Well, mercy me, I'm sorry to have disturbed you, but since you make me keep up with your impossible pace and won't give me a moment's rest to catch my breath or take a drink, you are bound to hear a little moaning from time to time." She swept a large vine aside with her parasol, shrinking back at the colorful lizard scampering up it. "I'm doing the best any lady could do under the circumstances."

He continued onward. "Perhaps if you remove that cage you wear under your skirts, your gown won't scrape against the branches as much."

Ugh. She wanted to swat him with her parasol. Instead, she burst into tears. "And you won't even speak to—" She barreled into him, realizing he'd stopped.

His hand was raised; his dark brows dipped. Only then did she notice the normal hum of the jungle had quieted, replaced by a crackling sound. It sizzled all around them yet seemed to come from nowhere. "What—?" Hayden laid a finger on her lips, silencing her. His body stiffened. He scanned the tangle of green. His gaze froze while his chest rose and fell like a ship in stormy seas. "Did you see that?" he whispered.

"No. What?"

"Not what, who," he mumbled before rubbing his eyes and starting forward again, his steps cautious. After a few minutes the crackling ceased and the thrum of the jungle returned. Tension spilled from Magnolia's shoulders. The last time she'd heard that sound, Martin—the fiend who'd destroyed her life—had appeared out of nowhere. And she was in no mood to deal with him.

Within an hour, the sound of rushing water drew them to a stream cutting through a narrow gorge. Steep, moss-covered cliffs rose on two sides where cascades of water plunged some sixty feet over bare rocks, splashing into deep pools at the base. With no more than a "stay here," Hayden went off in search of fruit, leaving Magnolia to stare at the refreshing pond. She longed to disrobe and plunge beneath its swirling waters, but Hayden could return at any moment. Instead, she settled for removing her stockings and shoes and dipping her feet in the cool liquid. The reflection of her legs bounced off the water in squiggly lines and a frightening idea occurred to her. If she hung her head over the water, what would her face look like now? Had she simply been delirious with exhaustion two nights ago? After one quick glance over her shoulder, she leaned over the calm pool.

Hayden plucked a ripe mango and scanned the tree looking for another one, wondering if he'd lost his mind. Perhaps the assault of insects, the stifling heat, and the overwhelming temptation of Magnolia had finally sizzled away all his reason. Or at least his eyesight. For he was sure he had seen old Mr. Carson sauntering through the jungle as if he were walking down East Plume Street in Norfolk. But of course, that couldn't be. Unless the man had immigrated to Brazil, which would be totally out of character for the timid, weak-minded goosewit. Besides, what would he be doing alone in the middle of the jungle?

Shoving the impossibility aside, Hayden spotted a banana tree and headed in that direction, thankful for a moment's reprieve from

Magnolia. Not because she annoyed him. Quite the opposite, in fact. Though he'd maintained a rapid stride the past two days, she'd kept pace with him, offering nary a complaint. An occasional moan and hapless sigh, yes, but no complaint. At night, she'd helped gather firewood and ate what he provided without a single grumble. Not one—even though he knew her feet ached and she was hot and weary and covered in bug bites. Even though he was returning her to an abusive father and keeping her from a fiancé she loved. He found her resilience admirable, her forgiveness commendable, her company, dare he admit, pleasurable.

In fact, he felt a strange urge to provide for her, to protect her, if only to draw an adoring look from those sapphire eyes. But that would make him like all the other men who fawned at her feet, begging for one favorable glance, one cherished kiss. And he hated himself for it. He wouldn't allow himself the indignity. Not the great confidence man, Hayden Gale. So, what else could he do but try to ignore her as best he could? A task made all the more difficult when, even covered in filth and bug bites, she glowed like a lantern on a dark night. No wonder insects surrounded her. If Hayden could fly, he'd hover around her too, just for the chance to land on those luscious lips.

Slapping a mosquito on his arm, he reached for a bunch of bananas when sizzling filled the air. A chill iced down his spine. He scanned the jungle. Nothing out of the ordinary. Snapping off the bananas, he headed back to the waterfall, determined to ignore the puzzling sound. Just his imagination. Or perhaps merely a swarm of insects in the canopy. Though the sound didn't come from above. He batted aside a leaf and froze.

Mr. Carson sat on a tree stump.

Hayden closed his eyes and drew a deep breath. When he opened them Mr. Carson was staring at him inquisitively.

"You aren't real," Hayden said.

The man flinched then glanced over his body. "I assure you, sir, I am as real as you."

"What are you doing here, Mr. Carson? Did you move to Brazil?"

"Brazil?" He glanced over the jungle as if seeing it for the first time. "What does it matter where I am, Mr. Grenville, or whatever your name is?" Steel eyes speared Hayden.

He swallowed and began to circle the man, remembering the vision of Katherine that had seemed so real in the temple. But she hadn't been there. And neither was this man here now.

"You sold me a shipyard that wasn't yours to sell." Mr. Carson released a heavy sigh, following Hayden with his eyes. "Turns out it belonged to a shipwright named Paine. But you knew that, didn't you?"

Hayden stopped a few yards from the man, resisting the temptation to pounce on him to see if he was flesh and bone. "What do you want? If it's your money back, I don't have it."

The man's gaze grew distant, his face folding in sorrow as if he remembered something dreadful. "I trusted you."

For being only a vision, Mr. Carson sure was causing a rush of guilt to burn in Hayden's throat.

"I lost everything. My wife left me. Took the children and went back to her father's farm."

Hayden had no words to say. What could he say? Mr. Carson was a gentle man with a limited mind—the perfect target. He'd wanted to be a shipwright. And Hayden had found an empty shipyard that had recently been sold to another man. It had been easy to forge the necessary papers.

"I killed a man," Mr. Carson said. "Mr. Paine, in fact. When he came to claim his property." He swallowed and looked down. "I thought he was trying to steal from me. We fought. I pushed him." He thumbed a tear from beneath his eye. "I didn't mean to shove him so hard. He fell out a window to his death."

Hayden's heart crumpled like old vellum—old and stained with guilt. The vision of Katherine rose fresh in his mind as well as the other dozen or so people he'd cheated. And for the first time in his life, he felt like sinking into the mud beneath his feet—deserved to sink into the mud and be buried like the scoundrel he was.

"I'm sorry." The words echoed hollow and heavy in the humid air. "I'm truly sorry."

Mr. Carson only stared at him, his eyes now blank and lifeless.

A woman's shriek drew Hayden's gaze over his shoulder. *Magnolia!* When he looked back, Mr. Carson was gone. Shaking the vision from his mind, Hayden wheeled about and dashed through the jungle, plowing a trail of scattered leaves and branches. He found her sitting near the creek, face in her hands, sobbing and muttering something about being grotesque and repugnant. His anger sparked. But her wails continued, long and painful. This was no act. Dropping beside her, Hayden took her hands. They trembled just like his. Something horrible was happening to them both, and the sooner they got out of this jungle, the better.

Magnolia studied Hayden as he scoured the jungle for wood. She rubbed the aches from her stockinged feet, proof that they'd walked much longer today than usual. No doubt Hayden wished to get back to New Hope as soon as possible and rid himself of her. Though she'd really been trying to be less whiny and annoying and not cry all the time. But when she'd seen her aged face in the pond earlier that day, she'd been unable to stop the tears.

Of course Hayden had pretended not to be annoyed, had tried to console her, but she could see the frustration on his face. Or had it been fear? Regardless, since then he'd seemed preoccupied and had hardly spoken a word to her. As usual.

And she was still old and ugly. Was this to be her curse? Never to see her reflection as it truly was? Only to see how she would look in sixty years or longer? Never to see if she had a hair out of place or a smudge on her cheek. Never to see when she truly aged.

What had the old woman said? That Magnolia's reflection was a picture of her insides. But how could her insides be *that* ugly? She was a nice person, wasn't she? Even after Hayden had dragged her back into the jungle, she'd tried hard not to complain. She'd even thanked him for taking care of her. Why, she hadn't even mentioned the blisters on her feet! Perhaps if she tried even harder to be kind, to think of others, then that gruesome reflection would disappear. Oh, how she wanted it to disappear.

Hayden tossed another log into the fire, took a seat, and picked up the chunk of wood he'd been whittling. Strands of dark hair hung over his jaw and jerked with each strike of his knife. Magnolia reached for another piece of turtle meat and plopped it into her mouth. "Um." She hoped to draw those magnificent jungle-green eyes to hers, but he remained focused on his wood. She swallowed the turtle. It was actually quite delicious. At first she'd been hesitant to try it, but after all the effort Hayden put forth—not to mention skill—to catch the thing and then break the shell and roast the meat, it would have been rude to refuse. Besides, she was so weary of fruit.

As darkness fell, shadows crept out from the jungle like unholy specters. Frogs began to croak. Crickets chirped. Somewhere in the distance an animal howled. She hugged herself, longing for conversation, companionship, anything to get her mind off the dangers surrounding them. As well as the ones she'd face when they returned to camp.

"You must think me mad," she said, "crying like a fool by the pond."

"No. I think you have an unnatural obsession with your appearance that is making you see things."

The sentence contained more words than he'd spoken to her in three days. She was so thankful to hear his voice, she didn't even mind the insult. Well, not entirely. It *was* quite loutish of him to say. Nevertheless, she'd just promised herself to be kinder to others and kinder she would be. As a start, she would forgive his affront. There. That was easy. Yet as she watched him stare at the flames and sensed a deep sorrow cloaking him, her chest suddenly felt heavy. She tried to force herself to not care, to still be angry at his deception, but found the task fruitless. Something bad had happened to Hayden, aside from his being an orphan and having to struggle to survive. And it had to do with this Mr. Godard. She wanted to know. And baffling as it was, she wanted to take his pain away.

"Is there something bothering you, Hayden? Do you wish to talk about it? Perhaps it will make you feel better. My mother always said that keeping problems to yourself makes you old before your time."

The flicker of surprise in his green eyes quickly faded. At least he looked up at her. "It's nothing," he said, returning to his work.

Oh, mercy me, this wasn't going well. "It's me, isn't it? My whining?" Though she'd been so well behaved, she doubted that was the case.

"Not everything is about you, Princess."

Magnolia blew out a sigh. She took another bite of turtle, desperate to draw out Hayden's sad tale, but not wanting to anger him or, worse, push him away. Perhaps a change of topic. Her thoughts drifted to the old woman in the church, the way she had gazed at the figure of Jesus with such love, such complete devotion, as if that immovable sculpture actually loved her in return. Was it possible to love and be loved by a God she couldn't see or hear?

"Do you believe in God?" she asked.

"Not sure." He stomped his boot on a spider crawling in front of him as a low growl rumbled through the trees. Drawing his pistol, he laid it beside him on a rock.

"Do you suppose God cares what we do? I mean, do you think He watches us?"

Hayden shrugged. "If He exists, I'm sure He has better things to do than look after us."

Though Magnolia hadn't thought much about God, Hayden's statement saddened her. "Our reverend back home said that God loves all of us, that He is always with us to help us."

Hayden chuckled. "If your reverend is anything like Parson Bailey, I wouldn't put too much credence on his words."

"Well of course he isn't! He doesn't steal from people." Magnolia bit her lip as her stomach churned with frustration. She reached for the flask sitting on the ground between them and tipped it to her lips. Hayden only allowed her a few sips each night and she hated to use them up so early, but the man was beyond infuriating. He eyed her, one brow raised. She corked it and set it down.

"When will we arrive in New Hope?"

He returned to his whittling. "If we get an early start, we should be there tomorrow evening."

Magnolia's insides shriveled. Then she would have to face her father's wrath. And her time alone with Hayden would come to an end.

"When will you leave to search for Mr. Godard?"

"Soon."

"You never told me exactly what he did to you."

"You ask too many questions."

"Perhaps it's because I care, you big oaf." She huffed. "You're always telling me I'm self-centered and now that I'm asking questions, I'm too meddlesome."

She received the first smile from him in days.

Prompting her to ask one more question. "How long will you be gone?"

His smile faded. "If I had been able to purchase a guide, I wouldn't be gone long at all, but as it is, it could be weeks." He scraped his knife over wood, flinging shavings into the air.

"I suppose you blame *me* for that."

"Do you see someone else here who robbed me of money that was my due?" He glanced around.

She jumped to her feet, instantly regretting the movement for the pain in her tired legs. "Of all the nerve. Your lie was far larger than mine. Besides, at least you got something out of the deal. All I'm getting are blisters and bug bites."

He grinned. "And a trip to Rio de Janeiro like I promised."

"Oooh." She fisted her hands, regretting that she'd ever felt sorry for the rogue or wanted to ease his pain. "I cannot wait to be rid of you. Bedeviled, odious toad!"

"Ah, but according to the story, us toads are only princes in disguise." His tone taunted her.

"Even if I could chop off your head in the morning, you'd never turn into a prince."

"Just a headless toad." He dug his knife into the wood. "And then you'd be lost and all alone in the jungle."

"Quit patronizing me."

"Quit behaving like a minx." His eyes glinted with amusement.

Something moved behind Hayden. The fire crackled. Leaves fluttered. A man materialized from the jungle, tipped his hat at Magnolia, then dashed away. "Martin!" Clutching her skirts she darted after him, ignoring Hayden's call to stop. Smacking leaves and vines aside, she caught sight of his suit up ahead, a gray mist floating through the darkness. "Come back here this minute!" The charlatan was obviously following her around Brazil. To taunt her, no doubt—to flaunt the fact that he'd ruined her and her family. Ruined Magnolia's prospects and chained her to a debt she could never repay.

He stopped and glanced over his shoulder. A shimmer of moonlight caught his smile. She knew that devious grin anywhere. He took off in a sprint. She tore after him. What she would do with him when she caught him, she had no idea. Kick him, for one thing, give him a tongue lashing for another. Tie him to a tree and leave him to rot would be her preference.

She raced ahead, leaves and branches assaulting her as she went. Dashing into a clearing, she scanned the shadows, her chest heaving. Martin was nowhere in sight.

A low growl stiffened the hairs on her arms. She slowly turned around.

A pair of golden eyes gleamed hungrily from within the shadows. The creature stepped toward her, fangs bared.

Chapter 22

James eased aside the rotted doors of the ancient temple, trying to shrug off the morbid foreboding that had smothered him before they'd even spotted the dilapidated structure. What made the feeling worse was that Eliza had insisted on joining the expedition. Her smile as she passed him now and entered the courtyard did nothing to assuage his unease. He hadn't wanted any of the women to witness the horror of this place. He hadn't wanted them to feel the terror and grief of the hundreds, perhaps thousands, who had been tortured to death within its walls; but once Eliza got something in her mind, it took a battalion to defeat that will of hers. Not even her husband, Blake, seemed able to control her. And he was the leader of the entire colony!

"Besides," she had said, "perhaps Mr. Graves is injured and is in need of medical attention." Though she hadn't meant it, the statement stabbed James like a knife. She was right. His fear of blood made his doctoring skills useless.

Blake went in behind her, then Dodd, running a hand through his mop of light hair, and finally Mr. Lewis, the old carpenter, whose wary eyes shifted back and forth over the scene. Begging off with an excuse of illness, Thiago had remained at New Hope. But James knew it was fear that kept the Brazilian guide away. Even Eliza seemed out of breath as she gazed at the courtyard: the ancient roasting pit, the obelisks carved with the silent screams of victims. "This place." She lifted a hand to her mouth. "I can *feel* the evil."

"Don't say I didn't warn you." Blake circled an arm around her waist as James shifted his own shoulders against an uncontrollable shudder.

He'd seen something on the way there, a vision perhaps, a memory maybe, or more likely an invention of his overheated mind: his father pacing through the jungle, head bent over a Bible clutched in his hands, muttering to himself as he'd always done every Sunday before giving his sermons. The sight tore open a wound in James's heart he'd thought long since healed. Then his father was gone, like a puff of smoke dissipated by the wind. Just like he had vanished from James's life that fateful night over a year ago.

The ground shook, jerking him to the present and shifting pebbles over the hard earth. Rocks tumbled off the temple's roof and peppered the cracked stairs like hail. An eerie *caw caw* lifted their gazes to a massive black bird soaring overhead.

Mr. Lewis plucked a flask from within his vest and took a sip, his ruddy face paling. James had wanted to bring Moses—sturdy, dependable, godly Moses—just in case they ran into trouble, but the poor man's eyes had grown so wide at the mention of the temple James hadn't the heart to insist. So, they were stuck with Lewis and of course Mr. Dodd, who had jumped at the chance, greed sparkling in his blue eyes. Which meant he hadn't found his pirate's gold yet. If he had, he'd be long gone to Rio and back to the States.

James hoisted the knapsack over his shoulder. "Let's find Graves, give him these supplies, and get out of here."

The group headed for the building and mounted the chipped, moss-laden steps.

Stopping at the top, Blake faced Eliza. "There's no need for you to go any farther, dear. If Graves is hurt, I'll bring him to you."

"Quit fussing over me, I'll be all right." Carrying her medical bag in one hand, she squeezed her husband's arm with the other and gave him one of her knowing smiles. "If he's too badly hurt, you won't be able to move him."

With a sigh of frustration, Blake took her hand in his and led the group into the inner sanctuary. Mr. Lewis nursed his flask of liquor, jumping at every shadow while Dodd dashed about excitedly, examining the ancient writing on the walls, peering beneath bits of broken furniture and pottery, even inspecting the steaming spring. James, however, made a beeline toward the back where a flaming fire kept guard over the entrance to the tunnels. The tended fire, along with the flickering light from deep within the tunnel, gave him hope that Mr. Graves was still alive.

"Mr. Graves!" James's shout echoed over the walls, hollow and metallic as if it weren't human.

Plucking one of the unlit torches from a pile on the floor, Blake dipped it in the fire and swept the flame over the dark opening. "Graves!"

A stench reminiscent of spoiled eggs wafted from the hole. Eliza covered her nose.

"Gold!" Dodd exclaimed as he climbed the stone altar and pointed to a large moon and stars embedded in the wall. "They are made of gold! Why didn't you tell me there was gold here?" Flames flickered excitement in his eyes.

"They aren't yours," James said. "Leave them be."

"Whose are they, then? No one owns this place." Plucking out a knife, Dodd dug around one of the stars, scattering dirt onto the altar. "I'm staking my claim first. You are my witnesses."

A low rumble sounded, much like a distant train. The ground shook. Dust showered them from above. Screeches preceded flapping as a group of bats took flight.

Eliza gasped and gripped her husband's arm.

Dodd stopped digging and leapt from the altar.

"Perhaps someone or something has already staked a claim, Dodd," Blake teased.

"I'm going down." James gathered a torch and lit it in the flames.

"I'll stay here and guard." Mr. Lewis clung to his flask as if it and it alone could save him from whatever lurked in the tunnels.

Blake nodded, took his wife's hand, and followed James into the tunnel, Dodd on their heels.

Jagged rock formed the walls of the oval passageway, twisting the torch's glow into angular patches of light and dark. Foreign letters scribbled atop ancient paintings passed in James's vision: pictures of people in various poses of work and play, some so faded he could barely make them out. Figures hunting, fishing, playing, and dancing leapt out at him as his flame brushed over the moist walls. Most likely etched there by the cannibals who built the temple long ago. Eliza ran her hands over the scribblings as they went along. "They're beautiful."

As if in defiance of her words, the pictures suddenly became gruesome: men with knives raised over animals, blood dripping from their blades, others stabbing victims laid out on slabs, fires blazing, faces twisted in agony. But what drew James's attention were the paintings of enormous winged beings carrying staffs with lightning bolts firing from their tips. He tripped over something and stumbled forward, his torch revealing piles of rock and dirt that, no doubt, marked Grave's progress.

Hot waves as thick as boiling molasses rolled up from below, dousing them in sweltering heat. Eliza visibly struggled to breathe, but still refused her husband's suggestion to go back.

Around a corner, a lit torch hanging on the wall revealed a set of stairs leading downward—downward into the pit of hell, it seemed. Rocks and dirt littered each step, and James braced against the walls to keep from slipping. Behind them, Dodd moaned his displeasure, mumbling something about wishing he'd stayed with the gold.

At the bottom of the stairs, they found another turn, another torch, and ground that angled ever more sharply down into the bowels of the earth. An odor akin to rancid meat curled around them.

The ground trembled again. A low rumble that was more like an agonized groan rolled through the small tunnel. James's spine stiffened. Pebbles flew at them from all around. Ducking, Blake covered Eliza with his body. A small rock struck James's neck and tumbled down his back. He shrugged off the pain and pressed onward.

"That's enough. I'm taking you back." Blake tugged on his wife, ignoring her complaints, pushing past Dodd, and starting upward when James's torch revealed a jagged opening in the tunnel wall. "Here! Over here!" he called.

Shoving the flame first, James stepped through the hole, hearing Blake retrace his steps behind him. At least ten torches flamed from hooks on the walls of a large cave, their flickering light transforming the stalactites hanging from the ceiling into shadowy fangs. Two circular alcoves were hewn out of solid rock on the wall to their left. Within each one, a giant pole, made from some type of metal, ran from ceiling to floor where massive iron shackles lay broken. Above the alcoves, something was written in what appeared to be Latin over a single Hebrew word.

Blake squeezed in behind him, followed by Eliza and Dodd.

"By all that is holy. . ." James finally said. "What is this place? And why is it so hot?" Sweat sucked his shirt to his skin.

"I don't think holy has anything to do with it," Eliza remarked, her voice unusually timid.

Scuffling sounds drew their gazes to a small opening on their left. Blake and James pulled their pistols and leveled them at the spot just as Mr. Graves emerged. Or at least James thought it was the crazy politician.

He gave them a cursory glance before carrying the large rock he was holding across the room and dropping it onto a pile with a loud *thunk*! Spinning to face them, he withdrew a soiled handkerchief and wiped his face, managing to smear the black smudges into streaks. Stripped down to a once-white shirt that was now blotched in mud and a pair of torn trousers, and with his black hair matted to his head and his cultured goatee growing like wild brush, he resembled nothing of the polished, sophisticated senator's son from Maryland.

James almost felt sorry for him. Would have felt sorry for him if he wasn't burning alive and enduring the worst stench of his life. He shoved his pistol into his belt and coughed, trying to expel the fumes from his lungs.

"I knew it was you," Graves said, his tone hurried and annoyed. "Knew you were here. They are agitated because you are here."

Lowering his weapon, Blake swiped a sleeve over his forehead. "Blast it, what are you talking about, Graves?"

But Graves didn't seem to hear the colonel. Instead, his dark, bloodshot eyes skittered over them as if trying to solve a puzzle. "But there are only three. There cannot be six. Six would ruin it."

Grabbing the knapsack, Eliza started toward the madman. "When was the last time you ate, Mr. Graves? Or got any sleep?"

Blake leapt in front of his wife and snagged the satchel from her hands.

She peered around him. "Are you injured, Mr. Graves? Give him some water, Blake, please."

"Would ruin what?" Dodd fingered his pointed chin, fixated on what Graves had said earlier. "You aren't talking about gold, are you?"

"Everything. Why the six would ruin everything, my friend! That's what they told me."

Friend? When had Graves ever called anyone *friend*? Or been this excited about anything? James handed his canteen to Graves. "And just who are *they*?" he asked.

"The rulers of course. The glorious ones. I'm helping them." Graves scratched the top of his head, making his filthy hair stand on end. Grabbing the canteen, he glanced to where he'd entered the room as if someone were waiting for him below.

"Helping them do what?" James fingered the handle of his pistol.

"They call to me, you know. They need me." He tipped the canteen to his mouth. Water dribbled trails of gray mud across his beard before splattering on his shirt. "There is power here. Power for the taking."

Dodd's brows shot up. "Do they have any more gold like I saw above in the temple?"

"Better than gold, my friend. Better than gold."

Dodd frowned as if there was no such thing.

Moving to the first alcove, James knelt to examine the broken irons lying at the bottom of the pole. "Who was locked up here?"

"They were, of course." Graves huffed his impatience.

"We brought you some food." Eliza elbowed Blake.

Reaching in the knapsack he pulled out an orange and handed it to Graves.

"You really should come back to New Hope," Eliza said. "It isn't safe here, and your hands. . ." She pointed at the cuts and scrapes all over his once soft, uncallused hands. "I need to look at those."

"No time. No time." Refusing the orange, Graves dropped the canteen to the ground and darted back the way he'd come, disappearing inside the hole.

Dabbing the sweat from her neck, Eliza gazed after him. "We can't leave him. He'll die here alone."

"What do you suggest we do with him?" Blake shook his head. "I have nowhere to restrain him."

"He's right." James dropped the irons, stood, and gazed curiously up the long pole. "We aren't equipped to care for the insane. We can't even lock up criminals."

"I agree." Dodd opened his watch and looked at the time as if he had an appointment. "Leave him here. He's harmless."

Blake gave Eliza a reassuring smile. "I promise we will bring him food and water every week. At least until we can provide a safe place to keep him while his mind recovers."

Graves returned with another rock and tossed it onto the pile, slapping his hands together.

"These writings." James pointed above the alcoves. "Rather curious. A Latin phrase above Hebrew. This one says "Deception and"—he gestured toward the other. "That one Delusion."

"You know what they say?" Graves's voice quivered with excitement. Grabbing a torch, he scrambled across the cave, leaping over rocks and stalagmites with the expertise of a bobcat through a field of thorns. Deep into the shadows, his light revealed a shelf carved out of the rock. He took something from it and darted back, hefting a thick leather-bound book at James. Odd thing for cannibals to have, James thought. Hebrew lettering lined the left side of the cover while a crescent moon and cluster of stars were engraved on the right.

"What does it say?" Mr. Graves pointed to the words as he leapt up and down with the giddiness of a child getting a gift. "What does it say?"

James ran his hand over the ancient Hebrew. "It says, *The Judgment of the Four.*"

Chapter 23

Magnolia's blood turned to ice. She couldn't breathe. She couldn't move. She couldn't think. The wolf's golden eyes locked on her, no doubt assessing her ability to resist her tastiness as a meal. The beast growled again, malevolence dripping from rows of sharp fangs. And Magnolia knew it was all over. She would die here, her flesh ripped apart and devoured by this monster. Foolish, foolish girl. Why hadn't she stayed with Hayden by the fire?

She flashed to her parents. Would they mourn her? Would Hayden?

Ever so slowly, she retreated a step. The wolf drew back on his haunches. Magnolia's heart stopped. She closed her eyes and prayed, *God if You're there, help!*

Footsteps thundered. Leaves crackled. The wolf roared. Magnolia dropped to the ground and covered her head with her arms. She sensed the wolf leaping, felt his hot breath on her skin, his ravenous spittle on her hair. Then another growl shook the ground. This one human. Someone shoved her back. She landed in a tangle of shrubs and vines and opened her eyes. A shadow, a man—no, Hayden—had the wolf in a stranglehold, the fiend's barbed teeth just inches from his neck.

Untangling herself from the vines, Magnolia leapt to her feet. Hayden and the wolf tumbled over dry leaves. Moonlight glinted off the knife in Hayden's hand as he strained to keep the wolf's fangs at bay.

"Oh, God, no. God, please no." Dropping to her knees, Magnolia groped for a sharp stick, a rock, anything to use against the ferocious animal.

Man and beast fought, growling, tumbling, rolling over the ground like storm clouds on the horizon. Her fingers clamped around a rock. The wolf was on top of Hayden again. Magnolia could smell its foul breath, his animal smell, raw and primitive. She also smelled blood. But whose? Hayden's heavy breath filled the air. Along with his agonizing moans and grunts as muscles strained to exhaustion. She hoisted the rock, aimed for the wolf, but he twisted and dug his fangs into Hayden's arm.

Hayden roared in agony. Magnolia lunged for the beast and slammed the rock at his head. Yelping, the wolf released his hold. Golden malevolent eyes swung her way. Magnolia's blood turned to ice. She tried to scoot back over the ground. He leapt for her. His razor-sharp teeth filled her vision. But then he let out a tormented shriek and fell to the ground at her feet. Hayden's knife stuck in his side. With a howl of his own that was almost beastlike, Hayden pulled it out. The wolf gave a painful wail and limped away. Within moments, the jungle swallowed him up as if he'd never been there.

Dropping to his knees, Hayden gripped his arm. His breath exploded into the humid night, his knife pointed at the place the wolf disappeared. Magnolia crawled toward him, every inch of her trembling. He turned and gathered her close, pressed her tightly against him, his muscles still twitching from battle. No words were said, just their heaving breath mingling in the air between them, their hearts pounding against each other's through flesh and bone, their minds reeling in shock. Finally Hayden rubbed Magnolia's back and kissed her forehead. The metallic smell of blood jarred her senses.

"He bit you!" She backed away, trying to see his arm in the darkness. But she didn't need to see. She could hear the blood dripping onto the dry leaves. *Plop, plop, plop.*

"Just a scratch." Hayden's chuckle sounded weak.

"Let's get back to camp." She stood, forced strength into her wobbling legs, and tugged on his good arm. Sheathing his knife, Hayden rose, wrapped an arm around her, and started through the greenery. "You're still trembling," he said.

"I don't think I'll ever stop."

Back by the fire, she grabbed the canteen and an old petticoat and sat beside Hayden, preparing herself for the sight that would meet her eyes, trying to settle her nerves. Blood seeped between his fingers and trickled onto the ground below. But his eyes were on her, an intensity in their green depths she'd not seen before. Despite her fear, his gaze sent a flutter through her heart. Without asking permission, she grabbed the knife from his belt, ignoring the wolf's blood splattered over the blade, and ripped her petticoat into thick strips. Then turning toward him, she tore his sleeve from shoulder to wrist and pried back the torn fabric.

Blood dribbled down biceps bulging and bunching from exertion.

Bracing herself, she peeled his hand from the wound. Punctures littered his skin like bubbling wells. His flesh hung open, revealing muscle and bone. Magnolia gasped, groaned, looked away. Her head swam.

"That bad, huh?"

"No. . .yes. . ." She pressed a cloth over the wounds, wondering how he could even talk, let alone joke, with the pain he must be enduring. "But you'll need stitches." Stitches she had no idea how to apply. Though she'd seen Eliza stitch wounds a dozen times, she'd never done them herself. She drew a deep breath and faced him again. She had no choice. They were at least a day or more from New Hope and she couldn't very well leave Hayden's flesh hanging open to the insects and filth of the jungle.

Gathering her strength, she poured water on a cloth and wiped blood from the gashes. He winced. "Sorry, but I need to clean the injured area."

He took one glance at his arm then swerved his gaze to the jungle. "I'm suddenly glad you learned nursing from Eliza."

"Some." Her heart scrambled into her throat. "Enough." She hoped. "Here, hold this."

Hayden pressed his hand on the cloth while Magnolia retrieved the flask of rum.

"This is hardly time for a drink, Princess." His grin turned into a grimace.

"Alcohol prevents infection."

"You would waste your precious rum on me?"

She uncorked it. "Hard to believe, isn't it? Now, this will hurt."

His jaw knotted but he gave her a nod.

She poured the pinga on his wound. He didn't move. Didn't scream. But pain seared in his eyes. What had this man endured to make him so tough? "You don't have to play the valiant hero for me," she said.

"You're not impressed?"

Of course she was. More and more each day. "Does it matter what I think?" She rose and sifted through her valise, not wanting to see, by his expression, what his answer was. There. She found the tiny leather purse and pulled out the thread and needle she'd brought just in case she needed to mend her skirts. Not that she'd ever mended anything herself before, but in lieu of a lady's maid, she was sure she could figure it out.

When she returned to his side, his eyes were squeezed shut. So he wasn't as tough as he pretended. After pouring rum on both needle and thread, she sat beside him and drew a deep breath. "This will hurt." Her hand trembled. Doubts flooded her. Who did she think she was? She couldn't do this. Other than her mother's failed attempts to teach her to embroider beads onto her skirts, she'd never sewn a stitch. Let alone human flesh! Her father's words pierced her confidence: *"Magnolia, God gave you one gift and one gift alone, and that is your comely appearance. So, focus on that, my dear, and forget the rest. Then you'll attract a wealthy man worthy of such beauty."*

She gulped. Firelight flickered over the needle, taunting her to continue. Somewhere in the distance, an owl hooted.

As if sensing her hesitation, Hayden opened his eyes, their intensity diving deep into hers. "Go ahead, Princess. You can do this. I trust you."

Trust me? Yet there it was in his eyes. Faith. Belief—belief in her abilities, that she was more than a face and figure. Warmth swirled through her, bolstering her courage.

He reached up and tucked a strand of her hair behind her ear. The gentle gesture nearly melted her on the spot. She dropped her gaze to the wound. *Focus, Magnolia. Focus!* "No distractions." Her nerves ignited like flint on steel.

"Then I *do* distract you."

"Be still."

"Aye, ay—"

She pierced skin and slid the thread through. His Adam's apple plummeted. A tiny moan reverberated in his chest. She hated hurting him. Making another pass, she looped flesh together. He faced her. His rapid breath spread hot waves over her cheeks.

He grabbed a lock of her hair and twirled it between his fingers. He smelled of sweat and blood and. . .Hayden. "I told you to be still."

"Touching you helps keep my mind off it."

She shifted her eyes between his. She still could not believe he'd risked his life to save her. Could not believe he'd leapt between her and a ravenous wolf.

She tugged on the thread.

Wincing, he ran the back of his fingers over her cheek. She allowed the familiarity if it helped him cope with the pain. What it did to her insides was anything but painful. She slid the needle through again. "Almost done."

The fire cracked and spit.

He fingered the lace at her collar and brushed fingers over her neck.

Magnolia's skin buzzed beneath his touch. She finished the stitch, snapped the thread, and tied it off. "I don't know how long that will hold, being common thread and all." Taking clean shreds of petticoat, she wrapped them around his arm, his muscles still rock hard even with the wounds. "But that's the best I know to do." She just prayed it wouldn't get infected. Prayed she'd done it right. Done something right when it mattered most of all.

Hayden couldn't take his eyes off Magnolia. Instead of curling up into a ball and whimpering as he would expect someone of her station to do after they'd nearly been eaten by a wolf, she'd taken charge, hadn't faltered in her task, and had stitched up a wound that would make most women swoon.

"You are a brave girl."

Shock blinked on her face. "Hardly." She washed her hands with canteen water and gathered the bloody cloths.

Placing a finger beneath her chin, he lifted her gaze to his. Those blue eyes, normally flashing like lightning, were soft, even timid. "You didn't run when you had the chance. You stayed. Risked your own life to knock the wolf off me." He eased a thumb over her chin, not wanting her to move and rob him of the look of ardor in her eyes.

"How could I do any less after you saved me?"

"Any other woman would have run. And most men I know, as well." He snorted.

She jerked her chin from his touch, one brow arching. "You always said I was crazy. Now you have your proof." She bundled the bloody cloths in her arms, inching away from him.

Yes, crazy and brave and charming and wonderful. And apparently uncomfortable beneath his complements. He flexed his arm, not showing the pain in his face. Though the wounds still throbbed, the bleeding had stopped. With his good hand, he tore off the remainder of his shirt and tossed it aside. "Guess that leaves me without a shirt." Since he'd returned the one he'd "borrowed" in Rio. When he looked back at her, she was staring at his chest.

A flood of pink crawled up her neck, and she fumbled with her skirts in an attempt to stand.

He gripped her arm, gently, yet firmly, keeping her beside him. "Thank you. For stitching me up. You did a good job."

She gave a little smile and stared into the jungle. A breeze stirred her loose curls, tossing one onto her cheek. "Why did you come after me, Hayden? You haven't spoken to me for days. I thought you hated me. Couldn't wait to be rid of me." She moved her gaze to his chest then quickly dropped it to the ground between them.

He took her hand and raised it to his lips. So soft. "I could never hate you." Before he'd even entered the clearing, he had heard the wolf's growls, knew she was in mortal danger. Yet, oddly, not a single thought of self-preservation had entered his mind. The great Hayden Gale who always put himself above others had rushed headlong into certain death to save another.

She searched his eyes, as if trying to assess his sincerity. There, the affection he'd seen moments ago returned. Was it possible that a woman like Magnolia could care for him?

"But you—but I thought—" she stuttered. "Didn't you just say, not moments before, that you blame me for not having enough money to. . . ?"

But Hayden wasn't listening anymore. Her rambling faded into the background as he absorbed her with his gaze, longing to take her in his arms. Zooks, the woman could argue about anything, even their affection for each other.

". . .and when I asked you to look in the mirror, why the very sight of me caused you to run off into the jungle. And every time I've tried to stir up conversation you. . ."

He grinned, delighting in her feminine gestures and expressions while she prattled on.

"So as you can clearly see—"

His lips met hers.

Chapter 24

Hefting the heavy book they'd found at the temple, James trudged through the jungle back to New Hope. Behind him, Blake and Eliza discussed what to do with Mr. Graves, while behind them, Dodd and Lewis argued about the best way to extract the gold moon and stars from the temple wall. But James didn't care about the treasure. Or Graves, if he were honest. He was still trying to shake off the foreboding presence he'd felt in the tunnels. In fact, he hadn't been able to get away from that place fast enough.

A flock of blue-and-green parakeets chattered above him as a swarm of gray butterflies flitted between thick hanging vines. The melancholy *caw caw* of a toucan sounded in the distance. A lizard skittered up a tree trunk beside him then stopped to bounce up and down on all fours. James smiled, took a deep breath of the musky air, and allowed the rhythm of life to settle his nerves.

That was when the crackling started. At first soft and slick like the sifting of grain through a sieve. Despite the humidity, the hair on James's arms prickled. One glance over his shoulder told him Blake and Eliza didn't hear it or perhaps, so engrossed in conversation, didn't notice. He faced forward again and swatted a leaf aside, scanning the jungle. A flash of periwinkle blue caught his eye, a glimpse of raven hair, graying at the temples. His heart cinched. Continuing forward, he kept his gaze on the vision, for that was what he knew it was. Just a vision, a dream from his past. His mother stopped and glanced over her shoulder at him, at first smiling with that I'll-always-love-you-smile a mother gave her only son, but then sorrow squeezed the life from her expression. She looked so real, James's eyes filled with tears. He shifted them away and continued onward. He wasn't going to make a fool out of himself again.

"You left me," she said as he passed her. "You went off to war." Her voice floated on the edge of sorrow.

James plodded forward, but she kept pace with him, walking through ferns and trees and vines as if she were made of nothing. Of course she was made of nothing. She was a vision. A mist. Then why did she look and sound so real?

"Don't leave me, Jimmy, not again. I died of a broken heart, you know. Died because you left me." Tears trickled from her eyes.

You're not here. You're not here. You're not here, James repeated in his head, keeping his gaze forward. *What is happening, Lord?*

"Jimmy, oh, Jimmy." She began to sob, and James could stand it no more. He stopped and stared into her swimming brown eyes. Oh, how he'd missed those loving chestnut-colored eyes. God in heaven, help him.

Then she disappeared. But not before he saw a tiny smirk lift one side of her lips. Gripping the book to his chest, James bent over, nausea welling in his stomach.

"What is it?" Eliza caught up to him.

"Have some water, Doc." The colonel handed him the canteen. "This heat can get the best of a man."

James pushed it away. "No." He straightened himself. "Let's just get back to town."

Eliza's look of concern transferred into one of understanding. "You saw something, didn't you? A vision?"

James nodded and stormed forward, ignoring further questions.

A few minutes later, they emerged from the jungle onto the path leading back to New Hope. Taking advantage of the widened trail, Blake and Eliza slipped beside James as they made their way past fields speckled with sugar cane sprouts. Finally the thatched roofs of their huts came into view. The sight brought a smile to James's lips. After the macabre gloom of the temple, their quaint settlement was like a ray of sunshine.

"Seems you have some studying to do." Blake gestured toward the book.

James ran his hand over the aged leather, faded and cracked. "Indeed. If I remember the Hebrew my father taught me."

"I was surprised when you told me it was Hebrew. I would have never recognized it," Blake said. "What baffles me is how a book written in Hebrew, an archaic language not used in centuries, ended up in Brazil. And buried beneath a pagan temple, of all places."

James sighed. "I quite agree. It doesn't make sense."

Eliza leaned forward, peering at James from Blake's other side. "How did your father know Hebrew?"

"He studied it. Wanted to understand the Old Testament better. My mother thought he was a bit overzealous." James chuckled but suddenly sobered. Was that why he'd seen a vision of her? Because the Hebrew had brought her to mind?

Blake rubbed his sore leg. "And now Graves wants you to translate it for him."

"I'll do it," James said. "But only to satisfy my own curiosity. Whoever wrote this was well educated." He'd already determined that from the few pages he'd perused.

Blake swatted a bug. "Perhaps it will give some clue about the purpose of the tunnels."

"And who or what was chained up below."

"I just wish we could help Mr. Graves," Eliza remarked as she stepped over a massive root. "And I'm still worried for Magnolia. It's been two weeks, and we've not heard from the scout we sent after her."

"Yes, I'm concerned as well." Blake raked a hand through his hair. "Yet if she ran after Hayden, he'll take good care of her."

James chuckled. "And no doubt bring her back as soon as he can. There's no love lost between those two," he said as they entered the town.

Blake halted, lifting a hand to keep Eliza back. Dodd and Lewis caught up with them and stopped.

"What is it?" James followed their gazes to the meeting shelter.

The rest of the colonists were huddled together on the dirt floor, surrounded by a band of armed men, muskets and pistols at the ready. James blinked as shock sped through him. Upon seeing them, a tall man with curly black hair sauntered their way. Jeweled pins decorating his silver-embroidered waistcoat sparkled in the sunlight as he continued toward them, sizing them up with his gaze.

Halting, he placed one hand on the hilt of a short sword hanging at his side. "I am Captain Armando Manuel Ricu of the pirate ship *Espoliar.* Now, tell me where is the gold?"

At the very least, Hayden expected a slight protest from Magnolia, a feigned indignation, perhaps even a slap when his lips descended on hers, but instead, she moaned in ecstasy and pressed her curves against him. He wrapped his good arm around her and deepened the kiss. She moaned again, ran her fingers through his hair, gripping it in bunches as her passion grew. She tasted fresh and sweet, and he grew thirsty for more of her. Not just more of her physically, but more of her in every way. She'd become a part of him and he needed to feed that part with knowledge of her, with her laughter, her fears, her hopes and dreams.

He gripped her face and rubbed his thumbs across her jaw, directing her mouth to move with his, leading her in their passionate dance. She withdrew, her eyes brimming with desire as they shifted between his. Releasing her face, he brushed hair from her cheek. "Magnolia," was all he could think to say. "Sweet, sweet, Magnolia."

The air between them thickened, charged with a power that made his heart swell, his blood pulse, his head spin. Time slowed as their eyes searched each other's. A breeze stirred leaves into a dance. Branches swayed. Fireflies sparked in the darkness. Something connected between them. Something deep and abiding.

She leaned her forehead against his, her breath puffing over him like warm fog. "I can't believe this is happening." She gave a little laugh and reached up to touch his good arm, hesitating at first then running a finger over his rounded bicep.

"That you enjoyed my kiss?" Hayden took her other hand and planted his lips upon it. "Or that you are kissing a man who's wearing no shirt?" He grinned.

"Both." She smiled, caressing his stubbled jaw.

"Sorry. I haven't shaved since we left Rio."

"No, I like it." She smiled. "It feels like sand on my cheek."

Everything inside Hayden that was real—his heart, soul, and spirit—ached. With an exhilarating, pleasurable ache. What was happening to him? Was this what it felt like to fall in love? Both thrilling and terrifying at the same time? Now as she gazed at him with such admiration, with such longing, he wanted nothing more than to wrap his arms around her and protect her, keep her safe, and give her all his love forever.

He kissed her cheek, then trailed kisses down her jaw and back to her lips, finding them as sweet as ever.

"Thank you for saving me, Hayden," she breathed out.

"My pleasure."

She backed away. A tear slipped down her cheek. "No one has ever risked their life for me."

He eased a curl from her forehead. "Because no one has taken the time to realize what a treasure you are."

At this, she melted in his arms and began to sob. Unsure if he had said something wrong, he embraced her, burying his head in her hair that smelled of moss and orchids.

When she'd spent her tears, she kissed him, deep and powerful, and he realized he'd said the right thing. But her passion soon stirred his own to near boiling, and against everything within him, he nudged her back.

"We should stop."

"Yes, of course." She seemed embarrassed, leaned forward on her knees and started to rise. Hayden stood and helped her to her feet, bringing her hand to his lips for another kiss. He'd love nothing more than to continue kissing her all night, but she was unlike the other women he'd known. She was special, precious, and he didn't want to ruin things with unbridled passion and regrets.

He stretched his wounded arm. "Thank you for tending my wound."

"It was my first." She gathered her salve, clean strips of petticoats, and thread and needle, and returned them to her valise. "Good night, Hayden."

"Good night, Princess." And for the first time, as he watched her walk to her shelter and cast a loving glance at him over her shoulder, he meant the title in the purest sense of the word.

Halting just a few yards from New Hope, Magnolia glanced down at her attire. She still wore her cleanest gown, the one she'd purchased in Rio, though it was anything but clean anymore. She'd pinned her hair up as best she could—without using her mirror—and scrubbed most of the dirt from her skin. It was going to be hard enough facing her father without looking like a filthy street waif. As it was, her nerves were in so many knots, they resembled the tangled vines crisscrossing the canopy. She knew he'd be mad, furious even. What she didn't know was what her punishment would entail, nor how much debt would be added to her already massive bill.

Hayden stood beside her, allowing her a moment. No doubt he knew how nervous she was, had listened to her fearful chatter all day, had apologized more than once for bringing her back home. But all she could think of now was how exquisite he looked without his shirt. He shook his hair, raked a hand through it, and winked at her as sweat glistened on the rounded muscles in his arms and chest. Heat flooded her belly and she looked away. The jungle was good for Hayden. He seemed to thrive in the wildness of it. Oh, mercy me, the shame! She'd been raised with more manners than to stare at a man's chest or the muscles rippling in his back as he moved through the jungle like a cougar. Just as she'd done all day from her position behind him.

"Are you ready?" He reached for her hand. She took it and allowed him to lead her forward as she remembered their kisses from the prior night. She'd never experienced such sensations—had never known they existed. Neither had she felt such deep affection for a man. The emotions had consumed her, filling every crack and crevice of her need to be loved, cherished, adored. He had said she was a treasure worth having. No one had ever said that to her before. And it made her want to never leave his side.

Thank God Hayden had the strength to stop kissing her. He truly was a gentleman. More than she ever realized. More than most of the sophisticated men who'd courted her. Yet now she feared for her heart even more than she feared her father's wrath, for she had no idea whether Hayden harbored any true feelings for her. No doubt he'd kissed dozens of women before. He was a charmer. And she'd already had her heart broken once by a charmer. And once was more than enough.

On their right, Hayden pointed out the green sprouts of sugarcane and coffee plants rising from rows of rich dirt. They'd barely been gone two weeks and the fields looked completely different. Magnolia wondered where the men were, but realized it was nearing supper and everyone would be back in New Hope.

They skirted a large puddle and memories assailed her of the time she'd been so enamored at the sight of Hayden working in the field, she'd tripped and fallen into the mud. Of course, he'd come to her rescue. At the time she thought he was nothing but a plebian oaf.

But now she realized he'd rescued her from far more than a little mud.

Brushing aside the final leaves of a large fern, he escorted her into town. At first glance, things seemed normal. Quiet, but normal.

"Everyone must be eating super," Magnolia said as they made their way down the main street, though no smell of cooking food reached her nose.

Her chest tight, she slowed her pace, dreading seeing her father, dreading the looks of censure she would receive from both him and the other colonists, the sordid rumors that would fly when they saw her with a bare-chested Hayden. Hayden was taking his time as well. She hoped it was because he didn't want to release her to her father's care, because he loved her and wanted to stay with her. Oh, why didn't they just turn around and disappear back into the jungle where they could be together? Where they could frolic and play in the waterfalls and sleep under the star-lit canopy. One word from him and she would do it, she would give up being clean and sleeping on a bed and having her belly full. Just to be with him. But he'd not said much to her all day.

They approached the meeting shelter. The sight that met Magnolia's eyes halted her on the spot. Sent her heart vaulting into her throat. A band of colorfully-dressed men armed with pistols and swords circled the colonists. Magnolia shook her head. She must be seeing things. Hayden gripped her arm and tugged her back. He'd seen them too. But it was too late.

They'd been spotted.

Before Hayden could draw his pistol, a group of men swamped him, forcing his arms behind his back and ignoring his cry of pain. Another foul-smelling man dragged Magnolia to the others and tossed her to the ground. Her stomach twisted in a knot. She gulped for air. Terror sped across the faces of the colonists, all held at gunpoint.

Magnolia's mother shrieked and started for her, but one of the assailants barred her with the barrel of a musket. She collapsed, quivering, into her husband's arms. Magnolia couldn't tell if her father was happy, angry, or ambivalent to see her, his stare was so benumbed.

It took four men to drag Hayden to sit on a stump. Their eyes met. His brimming with fury, hers pleading for help. He gave her a nod as if to assure her all would be well. But she knew that wasn't true. Gathering her skirts, she struggled to stand, grimacing when the assailants laughed at her attempt. Finally she rose, brushed off her skirts and swallowed down her fear.

An ostentatious brute with the swagger of a dandy approached. His lips slanted at an odd angle as he placed a jeweled finger on his chin and took her in with his vulgar gaze. "What have we here?" he said in a heavy Portuguese accent.

"Just another one of our colonists," she heard Blake say.

Magnolia peered around the man to see Eliza clinging to Blake, terror shadowing her face. The colonel's jaw bunched as his eyes sped across the group, no doubt planning some means of defense or escape. Angeline trembled beside James, who moved to shield her from the monster's view. The rest of the colonists gathered their children close and cowered beneath the weapons pointed their way. A few women sobbed. But at least everyone seemed in one piece.

"Since no one tells me where is the gold. . ." The brute spun around and waved an arm through the air, his lacy cuffs fluttering in the breeze. "And I know you found it. I will take a woman for myself. One every night until you tell me the truth." He turned and slid a finger down Magnolia's cheek. The man reeked of sweat and filth.

Disgusted, she turned away.

"Starting with this delicate flower."

Blood abandoned her heart. Her knees began to quake. Before Magnolia could move, he hoisted her onto his shoulder and stomped away, his men following after him. The last thing she heard was her mother's scream and Hayden's growl before someone silenced him with a thud.

Chapter 25

Magnolia struggled against the ropes binding her hands to the captain's bed. Yet for all her toil, she gained only bloody wrists and searing pain. Stretching out her legs, she adjusted her bottom on the hard deck. What sort of man kept a lady tied to a bed frame and sitting on nothing but wood that felt like stone for hours?

A pirate.

She shivered as the sounds of drunken revelry filtered through the deck head: a vulgar ditty accompanied by an off-key fiddle, shouts, curses that bruised her ears, random pistol shots, and the distant clang of a sword. The same raucous din she'd been hearing all night. Ever since Captain Armando Manuel Ricu had kidnapped her from the colony and dragged her on board his ship and into his cabin. When he'd tied her to his bed, sunlight angled over his oak desk and mahogany paneling. But hours ago, a curtain of black dropped over the stern windows, encasing the room in darkness. How long could these pirates carry on with their revelry?

She hoped a lot longer.

Terror gripped her at the thought of what the captain had planned for her when he retired for the evening. How could the colonists have allowed these horrid men to steal her away? How could Hayden? They'd all just stood there, staring wide-eyed at the barrels of the pirates' pistols... doing absolutely nothing. Even her own parents! Even when the vile pig-of-a-captain flung her over his shoulder and carried her away.

And for what? *Gold.* Magnolia grimaced. Dodd and his infernal gold! He must have found it. He must have buried it where no one would ever think to look. She could tell by the malicious twinkle in his eyes when the pirates had demanded it be returned or they'd start kidnapping the women one by one.

The ship rolled over an incoming wave. Magnolia braced herself against the deck, but her weight pulled against the ropes. Pain shot through her wrists. The wood creaked and groaned, voicing her inward protest. Why, when anchored mere yards off shore, did the ship insist on pitching and lurching as if it was out at sea? The same familiar smells that had haunted her on the long voyage from Charleston to Brazil now saturated her lungs: moist wood, mold, salt, tar, waste. . . and something else, something new that made her nose twitch. She couldn't place the foul odor, but surely it emanated from the beasts who inhabited this putrid bucket they called a ship.

Hanging her head, she stared at her soiled gown. Her eyes burned, but no tears came. She'd already spent every last one of them—could feel their salty tracks drying on her cheeks and neck. Mercy me, she must look a fright. But what did it matter?

She was about to become a pirate captain's mistress. Lose her innocence to that vulgar Philistine. And maybe her life. Ah. . .there the tears were. *Crack!* A pistol shot snapped her gaze to the deck head. Her ears perked, desperate to hear the sounds of a battle as her friends stormed aboard to save her. But instead, the cackle of sordid laughter accompanied the return of the discordant fiddle.

And Magnolia began to sob again.

Why wasn't anyone rescuing her? Tears spilled down her cheeks. One dropped onto her wrist, seeping beneath the ropes, stinging her raw skin. Why wasn't Hayden coming to save her? Had their kiss meant so little?

Perhaps she had not been the kindest person in the world. Yes, she had often complained about her situation. She had sabotaged the ship that brought them here, had told a few lies, grumbled at the lack of food and comforts. Yes, she'd tried to swindle Hayden into taking her home. She often drank too much, though most of the colonists weren't privy to that particular vice. Her eyes locked upon a half-empty bottle of port sitting atop a chest at the end of the bed, and she licked her lips. Drat. . .just out of her reach.

Regardless, she was a nice person, wasn't she? She had assisted Eliza in the infirmary many times. She had hauled water from the river. She had gathered wood and picked mangos a few times for breakfast. She'd even saved Hayden from a wolf! Surely those things—huge efforts for someone of her station—made up for her occasional bad humor.

The ship rolled. Boot steps thundered outside the door. Magnolia's heart charged through her chest as if it were looking for a place to hide. She wished she could do the same.

The door burst open, slamming against the bulkhead, and in walked Captain Armando Ricu—all sinewy six-foot plus of him. Tawdry music and laughter swirled in behind him like a hellish minion. The deck tilted, and he gripped the door jamb, a perplexed look in his glassy eyes as he lifted his lantern and surveyed the cabin. Curly black hair that would be the envy of any woman flowed halfway down his back over a waistcoat embroidered with silver and pinned with so many jewels and diamond-encrusted brooches, it made him look like a floating candelabra.

Trophies from his conquests, no doubt. Magnolia gulped.

He staggered into the room and set down the lantern. Then planting his fists on the wide belt at his waist, he focused on Magnolia as she attempted to curl into a ball small enough to avoid detection.

It didn't work.

"Ah, there you be, *amor*." His broken English was only further befuddled by the slur of alcohol. "Time to join the *festa*."

If by festa, he meant festivities, Magnolia would have to decline—wanted so desperately to decline, to blink her eyes and wake up in the middle of the jungle, sitting around the fire with Hayden, eating fruit and bantering back and forth as they so often had done.

Instead, the toe of the man's boot—made of some kind of repulsive reptile—appeared in her vision then landed on a fold of her skirt, marking her taffeta gown.

If only that was all that would be stained this night.

Tiny specks of light spun at the edge of her vision. Her breath huddled in her throat. *Oh, God. Help me. Please help me.* That was twice she'd appealed to the Almighty in the last few days. More than in her entire life. In truth, she rarely had much need to ask for anything. Except when her parents had dragged her to Brazil. And by then she had just been plain angry at God for allowing such an atrocious thing to happen.

Captain Ricu plucked a knife from his belt. Lantern light gleamed on the blade as it plummeted toward her. Magnolia tried to scream but only managed a pathetic whimper. The sound of splitting hemp reached her ears. Her wrists flew apart. Fingers as thick as bamboo grappled her arms and yanked her to her feet. Pain etched across her shoulders. The pirate thrust his face into hers, measuring her with eyes that seemed afloat in barrels of rum. Rum. The spicy scent of it filled the air between them and caused Magnolia to lick her lips, despite her predicament. What she wouldn't give for a drink or two, or eight, right now. Anything to send her into the bliss of unconsciousness, that secret place wherein existed no pain, no pressure, no insect-infested jungle, no pirates!

"Yes, *muito bonito*. We have fun, you and I, *é*?"

The cabin spun in her vision. *This can't be happening.*

Laughing, the captain shoved her onto the bed, slammed the door, and returned to her in one stride.

Magnolia scrambled backward across the ratty mattress. Hard wood knuckled her back, preventing her retreat. There was nowhere to hide. Nowhere to escape.

Captain Ricu slipped out of his jeweled waistcoat and tossed it onto a chair. Reflections from the gems twinkled on the deck head like stars. And for a moment, Magnolia dreamed she was far away in a small boat drifting at sea, staring at the night sky. Far, far away where no one could touch her. . .

But the pirate's belch broke her trance. He removed his sword and pistols, tore off his stained shirt, and leaned on the bed frame, eyeing her like a tiger eyeing a hunk of meat.

Magnolia squeezed her eyes shut. Seconds passed, yet no meaty claws seized her. Instead, a latch creaked and a blast of briny wind sent a chill down her back. Boot steps and a grunt of surprise from the captain opened her eyes. He had risen to his full height and spun around toward the now open door.

A stream of angry Portuguese shot from his mouth.

Whatever he said, it did not deter the intruder. Mercy me, was she now to be fought over like prey? All hope drained from her. Her eyes landed on the bottle of port and she started for it. Not for a drink, but to use it as a weapon. Battling against layers of petticoats, she was almost there when a voice, a wonderfully delicious voice, brought breath back into her lungs. She almost dared not look for fear she'd slipped into madness.

"Step aside, *Capitão*, I'm taking the lady back."

Magnolia peered around Captain Ricu's massive frame to see Hayden dressed in black trousers, a white open-collared shirt, a red neckerchief at his throat, and pointing a cutlass at the captain.

Her heart surged.

Captain Ricu chuckled, hesitated, and stared at Hayden as if he'd just told a joke. But when Hayden's blade poked the captain's chest, his stance immediately stiffened. In a speed that defied his inebriation, the captain ducked and charged Hayden, knocking the blade from his grip. It clanked to the deck.

Shrieking, Magnolia scrambled to the edge of the bed and reached for the fallen cutlass, but the captain kicked it beneath his desk and dove for his sword. Hayden charged forward. He shoved the captain. The man toppled backward over a chair. Kicking the broken seat aside, Hayden jerked the man up and slammed him against the bulkhead. Before the pirate could react, Hayden shoved his muscled forearm against his throat until the man's face transformed into a bloated beet.

"I said I'm taking the lady back," Hayden seethed. Lines of red appeared on his shirt from where the wolf had bitten him.

Heart slamming against her ribs, Magnolia jumped off the bed and grabbed the bottle of port. Captain Ricu sputtered and blubbered, his eyes wide. Hayden released him and slugged him in the stomach.

Bending over, the pirate coughed and gasped for air. For the briefest of seconds, Hayden's eyes flashed to Magnolia. The concern and affection within them nearly brought her to tears.

Would have brought her to tears if she hadn't seen Captain Ricu straighten and raise his arm to strike Hayden, a malicious smirk on his lips.

Hayden groaned and dropped to the deck. Magnolia screamed. The pirate captain rubbed his neck, spit on Hayden, and headed for her. Clutching the bottle to her chest, she backed away, but a thick wardrobe blocked her retreat.

A slow predatory grin lifted the captain's lips. "Sorry for *interrupção*, amor."

The grin vanished. Shock sparked in his eyes before he toppled like a felled tree. He struck the deck, and the ship seemed to tremble with the impact. Releasing his grip on the pirate's ankles, Hayden pounced on top of him and landed a punch to his face. The captain growled like a bear, clutched Hayden's throat, and tossed him aside. Both men leapt to their feet.

Captain Ricu slammed a fist across Hayden's jaw. The impact spun him around, squirting a circle of blood through the air. Magnolia shrieked and started toward him. Wiping blood from his mouth, Hayden glared at the pirate.

"Is the woman worth your death, Capitão?" Hayden's voice held the sarcasm of victory.

Captain Ricu's chuckle defied the fear racing across his eyes. "Is she worth yours, *idiota*?"

Hayden charged the pirate, landing blow after blow against his jaw and into his belly. Groaning, Captain Ricu raised his hands to block the assault. By his size and ruthlessness alone, he should have had the advantage over Hayden, yet it was Hayden who now had the pirate's back pinned on his desk, a stranglehold once again on his throat.

The pirate coughed and sputtered as his hands groped over the surface, knocking over quill pens and trinkets. He found his pistol. Magnolia tried to scream, but her throat slammed shut.

The pirate leveled the barrel at Hayden's head as the sound of the weapon cocking echoed in the room. Hayden froze. Releasing the beast, he stood and backed away.

Captain Ricu, one hand on his throat, one hand on his pistol, got up from the desk as a victorious grin played on his lips. "Any last words, *imbecil*?"

Chapter 26

Magnolia's heart beat so hard, her chest hurt. Without so much as a thought, she charged toward the pirate and slammed the bottle of port atop his head. Shards of glass and maroon liquid sprayed over her, and for a moment, she thought her assault had no effect, for the man simply stood there, unmoving. But finally, his shoulders drooped, his breath escaped in an eerie moan, and he slumped to the deck, striking Magnolia with his arm in the process.

She fell backward and landed on the mattress, the severed bottle neck in her hand. Tossing it aside, she tried to settle her breathing.

Boots crunched over broken glass and a strong, bloodied hand appeared in her vision. She gazed up to see Hayden, looking more like a pirate than a gentleman, grinning at her. He winked. "I've come to rescue you, fair maiden."

She gripped his hand. Warm, strong fingers curled around hers and lifted her from her seat, pulling her into an embrace that sent ripples through her belly.

"Your stitches!" She shrieked, pulling back and staring at the red blotches on his shirt.

"They're fine. Eliza saw to them." He glanced at his arm and shrugged. "Just bleeding a little."

She fell into him. "I didn't think you were coming." All the tension, the fear, released in a shuddering sob.

He kissed her forehead, took her face in his hands, and locked his eyes upon her. "I will always come for you, Princess."

Emotion clogged in her throat as she searched those eyes for any hint of insincerity, any hint that he was playing her for some selfish purpose. What she saw there instead caused more tears to fall. This time, tears of joy.

She ran a hand over his jaw, still red from the pirate's strike. "Have a care, Hayden, or a lady might think you seek something more serious than passionate kisses."

"And what if I did?" His lips quirked into a smile as he wiped moisture from her face. "Would the lady be agreeable to such a notion?"

The words shot straight from her heart, past her good reason, past her care for Samuel Wimberly, past her parents' approval, and spilled from her lips. "The lady would."

Hayden's wide smile sent her head spinning, and he drew her into his arms again, barricading her with his strength.

Reminding her of their precarious situation.

She tugged from his grip, her gaze snapping to the open door. "The pirates! How will we get past them?" Oddly, however, the ship had grown silent.

He smiled. "Don't worry about them." He took her hand and assisted her over Captain Ricu's prostrate form. "I expect they'll be unconscious for several hours. Thank you, by the way, for knocking this particular one out."

"Well, I couldn't very well let him shoot you, now, could I?" She gave a coy smile. "Even though you do look like a pirate, yourself."

He led her up onto the main deck. "As it turns out, the other pirates were of the same opinion. There were so many of them aboard the ship, they didn't even realize I was not one of them."

Even in the dim moonlight, Magnolia could make out bodies strewn about the deck in various poses as if they'd dropped in the middle of their revelry. If not for the loud snoring, she would have thought them dead. "Did you drug them?"

"Only with pinga." Hayden took her hand and assisted her over the fallen fiends. "Turns out Thiago had made a particularly potent batch. And lots of it. After bringing it on board, it was only a matter of persuading the pirates to overindulge." They reached the railing. He chuckled. "As easy as convincing babies to drink their mother's milk." A salty breeze and the sounds of waves lapping against the hull greeted them. Hayden stuck two fingers in his mouth and let out a shrill whistle. "Of course, once I saw the captain go below, I knew I didn't have much time."

All of her worries, all of her fears had been for naught. She fell against him, never wanting to leave his side. "Why aren't you as besotted as they?"

"I only pretended to drink. The more inebriated they became, the easier it was to fool them." He stroked her hair.

A moist thud sounded from below. Hayden leaned over the railing. "Ahoy there."

"Ahoy," a muffled yet familiar voice drifted up from the water. "Ready here."

Grabbing the rope ladder, Hayden leapt over the railing and assisted her onto the bulwarks. Then side by side, he helped her clamber down the shifting cord to the waiting boat. She really was going to have to get rid of this crinoline! Wobbling, she crawled to take a seat beside Colonel Blake, who smiled her way. James sat at the bow, lantern in hand.

"A rescue party. I am very grateful, gentlemen."

"We had fun," James said.

Hayden grabbed an oar and shoved off from the hull then hooked it in the oarlock.

Magnolia's gaze swept up the massive ship that seemed like an impenetrable mountain rising from the sea. "But won't the pirates simply come back ashore when they wake up?" Even now, dawn's glow curled over the horizon.

"We cut the anchor chain." Hayden grunted as he plunged the oar through water. "Good thing the ship is old and it was made of hemp."

"Then we tied it around the rudder," James added with a chuckle.

Magnolia gazed back at the *Espoliar* already drifting out to sea with the morning tide.

Leaning forward, Blake heaved his oar, propelling them through water that purled against the tiny craft with gurgles and splashes. "By the time they wake up, they'll be far away and have no way to steer."

An incoming wave struck the boat and Magnolia held onto the thwarts. "But they'll fix it, of course."

"Eventually, but by then, hopefully they'll have moved on to other conquests."

"I suppose Dodd may be right about his gold," James said, "if these pirates are so intent on finding it."

Blake sighed. "Perhaps. Many a foolish man has wasted his life searching for buried treasure that is never found."

"What happens if they do return?" Magnolia asked, dreading another encounter with Captain Armando Manuel Ricu.

The boat struck sand and Blake hopped into the shallow waves. "Then we'll be ready for them."

Propriety tossed to the wind, along with the fear of Mr. Scott's inevitable protests, Hayden flung an arm around Magnolia's shoulders and drew her close as they walked back to New Hope. She leaned her head on his chest and snuggled beside him, causing his heart to leap. Was it possible she returned his feelings? Was it possible she loved him and not that ninny of a solicitor back home? From the look in her eyes, he could see no other possibility.

Yet, now as the sun peeked over the horizon and unrolled its golden fingers over the landscape, Hayden knew he'd have to release her to her parents. He hoped they had missed her enough to forgive her for running away. He hoped they'd be kind, but when he saw them standing before their hut, his hopes vanished.

"Unhand her this minute, you officious reprobate!" Mr. Scott stormed toward Hayden, his jowls quivering.

"Papa!" Magnolia clung tighter to Hayden, but he pried her fingers loose and nudged her forward. Though Hayden would love nothing more than to get into a tussle with the man, it wouldn't be proper. And he was just too tired.

"This officious reprobate just rescued me from being ravished by a band of pirates!"

Her mother gasped in horror and drew Magnolia into her arms.

"Yes, yes, I knew he would." Mr. Scott waved the comment away. "Especially with the colonel's help."

"I assure you, sir," Blake said as he approached. "It was Hayden who risked his life."

"Oh, dearest," Mrs. Scott blubbered. "I'm so happy to see you. The pirates didn't harm you, did they?" She ran her hands over Magnolia's face and arms.

"I'm all right, Mother. Thanks to Hayden."

"But why did you leave us in the first place?" her mother continued, her lip quivering. "We were so worried. We sent a scout after you, but he hasn't returned."

Magnolia exchanged a glance with Hayden. "We saw no sign of anyone. I hope he didn't fall into trouble."

"Indeed." Blake's tone bore concern. "I'll send a few men to search for him."

Mr. Scott snorted. "I wouldn't bother. He's, no doubt, as much of a liar as this man."

"Papa, Hayden rescued me. Saved my life more than once. And he took good care of me these past two weeks."

But Hayden doubted the man heard her. Instead, he held up a lantern and stared in disgust at the stains on her dress and the dirty hair dangling about her shoulders. "He also stole you away."

"I ran away, Papa. He had nothing to do with that."

He shifted malevolent eyes to Hayden. "But I'm sure he took advantage of the situation."

Hayden's jaw began to twitch. "I return her to you, sir, pure and unscathed. Otherwise she would be on a ship bound for the States."

"Humph." Mr. Scott grabbed Magnolia's elbow, turned, and headed toward the door of their hut. "Her reputation is ruined. Completely ruined. Now, no one will have her."

Mrs. Scott blithely followed them inside.

Hayden hung his head and whispered into the wind. "*I* will have her."

Chapter 27

Two nights later, something startled James out of his sleep. Tossing a shirt over his head, he grabbed his pistol and darted out of the hut. He was sure he'd heard a woman's scream. It sounded like Sarah, the teacher, whose hut was next door to his. Stumbling in the dark, he spotted a man holding a woman in a tight embrace.

"What is the meaning of this?" He shoved the man aside. Patches of moonlight shifted over his face.

"Thiago, what on earth are you doing? Explain yourself at once."

Blake and Eliza appeared out of the shadows, their hair askew and concern lining their expressions. Several colonists followed in their wake, carrying torches and rubbing eyes filled with alarm.

"I do nothing." Thiago's expression was defiant.

"Then why was she—?"

"James, no." Sarah stepped between the men. "Thiago was helping me. I had a terrifying dream. . .a vision. . ." She pressed a hand to her forehead, stumbled, and seemed to melt before their eyes. Thiago captured her in his arms then gently set her down on a stool and knelt beside her.

The tender display caused emotion to rise in James's throat. He hadn't realized that a bond had formed between the teacher and the Brazilian guide.

"I hear her scream," Thiago said. "I come running. She is frightened, trembling. All I do is hold her."

Some of the colonists moaned and shuffled back to their beds.

James retreated. "Forgive me, Thiago. I thought. . .it looked like. Well, never mind."

Colonel Blake shifted his weight. "It seems to be a night for dreams."

"You too?" James said. Out of the corner of his eye, he spotted Angeline heading toward the group, eyes puffy with sleep and russet hair spilling down her back.

"Yes." Blake swung an arm around his wife and drew her close. "A nightmare about the war. I haven't had one of those in quite some time."

"I've been having dreams as well." James sighed. "Events from my past. Odd."

Lydia began crying, and before Sarah could get up, Eliza slipped inside the hut to retrieve the baby and handed her to her mother.

"I don't think it was a nightmare." Sarah rocked her daughter. "I was awake, couldn't sleep all night. I stepped out of the hut for some air and that was when I saw him."

"Who?"

"My husband. My dead husband. Only he wasn't dead." She glanced over the crowd. "I'm sorry to wake everyone."

Eliza shared a knowing look with her husband.

"I've seen visions too," Blake said, lifting his voice for all to hear. "My dead brother for one."

"Me, as well," one of the colonists added.

"And me," Angeline spoke up.

Several of the remaining colonists offered their own stories, and soon the air was filled with tales of various sightings. Despite the frightening accounts, an odd relief swept through the crowd as each person realized they weren't alone.

Yet James couldn't shake the dread settling like a stone in his stomach. If they weren't crazy then. . .he fingered his chin and stared at the ground.

Blake eased beside him. "What is it?"

"Just something I read in that book from the temple."

Blake hushed everyone. "What?"

"Something about visions. No, it was delusions. I didn't think about it until now. My Hebrew is a bit rusty. I can't make out all the words, but it said something about four generals, Deception, Delusion, Destruction, and Depravity."

"Generals? From what army?"

James shook his head. "I don't know, but there was an entire section on Delusion that used words like vision, memory, manipulation, torture. . . . Not pleasant stuff at all."

"Perhaps it's just some account of a war the Portuguese and Indians fought long ago," Dodd offered.

Eliza hugged herself. "Do continue to read and let us know, won't you, Doctor?"

"Of course."

"Superstitious rubbish," one colonist grumbled and ambled away.

"I see things too." Thiago crossed himself. "It comes from temple. There is evil there. We should leave. Find another place. My charms not strong enough."

"God can protect us, Thiago," Eliza said.

"Exactly," James added. "We have nothing to fear." Then why did he suddenly feel so terrified?

The orchestra wasn't at all like the one Magnolia had enjoyed at the soiree in Rio, but the fiddle, guitar, and harmonica, accompanied by a young lad slapping a beat on a wooden stump, delighted her ears nonetheless, drowning out the normal thrum of the jungle. As well as her father's constant castigation. She wished the music would delight her spirit, but that, along with her body, had been kept locked behind a prison of her father's wrath and her own guilt for three days. Three long, miserable days during which he had not let her out of his sight. Not even at night. Though she'd tried twice to escape.

The first day she'd been home, her father had worked himself into such a frenzy yelling at her about what a spoiled hoyden she was, he'd nearly collapsed from exertion. In fact, Mable, their slave, had been forced to run into the jungle and pick fresh fruit just to revive him. Once back to sorts, however, he continued his castigation, stating how Magnolia had not only broken his heart but her mother's as well—though the woman didn't seem heartbroken at all, simply upset that her husband was shouting so much. Then he growled on about how she'd worried them sick, though for the life of her, she found no evidence in his tone. But finally he got to the crux of the matter—the real reason for his anger. Magnolia had run out on her debt to them. Her debt to make up for her courtship with Martin. For bringing him into their lives, for falling for his schemes. For allowing him to ruin her family.

"Your beauty is our only hope to reinstate our wealth and name in this new land," he had said, stomping back and forth on the dirt floor of their home-in-progress, barely a frame of wood and stones. But of course he hadn't wanted to shout at her in town where everyone could hear. "And then you run out on your mother and me, leaving us destitute and without hope. You ungrateful girl!"

She should have shown him her reflection. That would certainly crush his hopes to toss her as bait into the pond of rank and fortune. How his face would wrinkle in disgust and his eyes pop out in horror if he saw the image she saw in her mirror. For some reason the thought brought a smile to her lips, though it quickly faded at the remembrance of that reflection earlier when she'd been dressing for the party. So upset at the sight, Magnolia had decided not to look at it ever again. Besides, now that she was home, she had Mable to fix her hair and ensure her face was clean.

Torches were lit and couples began dancing across the cleared area beside the meeting shelter, drawing Magnolia's gaze. She envied their happiness, their freedom. Their peace. At least her father had given her a slice of that peace today. He hadn't said a word to her. No doubt he'd exhausted not only himself but his store of insults. For the time being, anyway. However, his silence had finally given Magnolia a chance to steal away and tell her mother what had happened. Though obviously hurt that Magnolia ran off, her mother seemed to understand and even sympathize with the harsh treatment Magnolia received from her father. Regardless, the woman refused to say anything negative about her husband, always kowtowing to his needs, his wants, while ignoring her own. Magnolia wondered how she could be related to such a weakling. But the truth was, even if her mother wanted to leave, she had nowhere to go and no money to get there.

Just like Magnolia.

So now, she sat, squished between her father's stiff presence on her right and her mother on her left—like two sentinels guarding their most precious asset.

Worst of all, she'd been forbidden to speak to Hayden. Ever. At least they had allowed her to attend tonight's celebration—in honor of her return and the pirates' defeat—though she was sure it was only to save face.

One of the ex-soldiers came up to ask her for a dance, but her father waved him off before the man uttered a word.

The scent of roasted wild boar still lingered in the air from dinner. Although delicious, the food hadn't settled well in her agitated stomach. She scanned the couples, seeking the one face she so desperately longed to see. Had he meant what he'd said on the ship? That he'd always come for her? That he wanted something more than a frivolous dalliance? Or was he simply playing the part of the charming gallant in order to woo the lovely lady? She had to know. Must speak to him.

Before he left tomorrow.

Which frightened her all the more. He was leaving her. Magnolia's mother had heard from Mrs. Matthews who had heard from Sarah that Hayden was going on an excursion to seek this Mr. Godard, and he didn't know when he'd return. Or if.

"It's for the best," her mother had said, patting Magnolia's hand. "You know how your father detests him."

Perhaps he wouldn't if he knew that Hayden had saved her life more than once, cared for her and protected her. But that probably wouldn't make a difference. Hayden lacked the two things her father sought the most—wealth and rank.

Blake swung Eliza past in a polka, and she smiled at Magnolia from her husband's arms. The colonel's hobbled gait was barely noticeable when he danced with his wife. The sight warmed Magnolia.

As did the sight of Thiago, one hand on a tree trunk, leaning over to smile at baby Lydia in Sarah's arms. Across the way, James extended his elbow for Angeline and led her onto the makeshift dance floor. Mr. Dodd leaned over a table beneath the meeting shelter staring at a map in confusion. Perhaps he hadn't found his gold, after all. Lewis, ever the cheerful besotted soul, sat on a wobbly chair drinking from his flask and bobbing his head to the tune. Of course he was happy, he had spirits to numb his soul.

She raised her hand and noticed the slight tremble. Another thing she'd been denied these past days. Finally Mable returned with a tray of drinks. Not the kind Magnolia needed, but warm lemonade would have to do. She took a sip, her lips puckering. They were running short on sugar.

Moses headed toward them, across the clearing, hat in hand. Magnolia's attempt to warn him with her eyes failed as his were locked on Mable. He stopped before them. "Missah Scott, would it be all right if I ask Mable to dance? If she wants to, dat is."

Mable's eyes lit up as she gazed up at the tall black man.

But Magnolia's father had a way of crushing any happiness that crossed his path.

He waved him away. "Slaves don't dance."

"Oh, let her dance with him, Papa," Magnolia said, resisting the urge to pour her lemonade on his head.

"I said no! Why the colonel allows these freed Negroes to attend our party is beyond me. Now, go fetch the frond fan, Mable. I'm getting hot. And you"—he flicked his fingers at Moses—"run along."

Dejected, Moses trudged away. Magnolia opened her mouth to say something she'd probably regret when the sight of Hayden stopped her.

He strode into the clearing as if he owned the place. No longer looking like a pirate, he wore gray trousers tucked into high boots, a white shirt, a black waistcoat, and a string tie. Unlike in the jungle when he wore his hair loose and wild, he had combed it and tied it behind him, so unconventional for the fashion of the age, but one of the things she adored about him.

Their eyes locked and he winked at her as if he knew a grand secret. And her heart nearly beat through her chest.

Still he made no move toward her. No doubt he knew the effort would be fruitless.

The dance ended and people scattered for refreshments. Blake approached. "Mr. Scott, if I may intrude on your time, something has come to my attention regarding your home. A few of the farmers passed by the other day and told me there may be a flaw in the frame that will compromise the integrity of the entire structure."

Her father jumped to his feet. "Absurd! I know what I'm doing and have inspected every inch.'"

"Would you like me to show you, sir?"

"In the dark?"

"We have torches," Blake said, his expression grave. "I fear we should not wait."

Her father tugged on his waistcoat. "Very well." He turned toward his wife. "Look out after her." He nodded at Magnolia. "She is not to dance."

Mrs. Scott agreed, her shoulders slumping. Yet as Blake led the man away, Magnolia saw a slight grin lift the colonel's lips.

Moments later, Eliza asked Magnolia's mother to taste an orange pie she'd made with mandioca root, begging the accomplished woman's advice on the taste of the flour substitute. After Magnolia insisted she'd behave, her mother left, seemingly oblivious to the sparkle of mischief in Eliza's eyes.

For the first time in three days, Magnolia was alone.

No, not alone. Hayden appeared before her and offered his hand. "Would you care for a stroll?"

Chapter 28

Hayden led Magnolia away from the party, relishing the feel of her delicate hand in his once again. It had been pure torture not being able to speak to her the past three days. Especially after he'd made up his mind. But she was with him now. His plan had worked, thanks to his friends. Unusual nervousness buzzed through him as he shoved through a fence of leaves and led her into a small, private clearing. Two torches, planted in the soft bank of a bubbling creek, cast flickering light over the water.

Magnolia smiled. "Did you prepare this for me?"

"Of course."

She stared almost shyly at the reflection of golden flames bouncing across the dark water as if she were afraid to face him.

"I've missed you," he said, caressing her fingers.

She swung her blue eyes to his, the shield over them dissolving. "I have missed you too." Her voice was filled with longing. "Thank you for getting rid of my parents. Very clever." She grinned.

He shrugged. "How else was I to speak to you?"

She lowered her gaze. "Papa has been horrible."

Hayden squeezed her hand, tugging her closer. "I'm sorry. You don't deserve that."

"Maybe I do." Rare contrition shrouded her features.

"None of us are perfect," Hayden said. "But no one deserves to be treated like a commodity. Especially not from a father." It would almost be better to grow up without a father like Hayden had than to be reprimanded daily by an unloving one. His heart strung tight.

A breeze whistled through the canopy, joining the gurgle and splash of the brook and the buzz of katydids. She gazed into the jungle, sorrow shadowing her face, and he longed to bring the life back into her eyes that he'd witnessed on their journey. But it seemed every drop of hope had been squeezed from her these past three days. Magnolia attempted a smile. "Regardless, you have stolen me away from him for a brief time, and I thank you for that."

"I hope to steal you away for much longer," he said. Flames glinted in her eyes. He searched their depths for her response. Desperate to know. Feeling as if he teetered in the balance between life and death.

Then delight sped through him at what he saw in those sapphire pools.

"Whatever are you implying, Hayden Gale?" She thickened her Southern drawl.

He raised her hand to his lips. "I would like to court you properly, Magnolia, if you'll accept my suit."

The lace at her neckline rose and fell like the beat of angel wings, breathless, eternal, full of promise. Finally, she flung her arms around his neck and kissed him. A passionate, hungry kiss that revived his heart and sent flames down to his toes. Enveloping her in his arms, he drank in her sweet savor, never wanting the moment to end. When they parted, he leaned his forehead against hers. "I have something for you."

Reaching into his pocket, he pulled out the carving he'd just finished that morning.

Magnolia held it to the light. "It's a toad." Surprise heightened her voice. She looked at him. "This is what you were carving on our way back to New Hope?"

"Your nickname for me."

"I never meant it."

He tapped her chin with his finger. "Come now. You meant every word of it."

"Well, perhaps." She smiled and fingered the carving as if it were made of gold. Then lifting it to her lips, she kissed it. "We shall be good friends, shan't we, little one?"

"Now you're making me jealous. It wasn't meant as a substitute for me. Just a reminder."

"I need no reminders. Ever." Lifting her hand, she traced his jaw, her touch so gentle, so full of affection, his head grew light. But then the sparkle in her eyes dulled, and she glanced down. "My father will never permit a courtship between us. He has other plans for me."

The night song of a whippoorwill trilled its agreement. Hayden hefted a sigh. "Plans that don't include an impoverished con—broker, I'm thinking."

"He's forbidden me to ever speak to you again." Thankfully, she missed his near blunder, which reminded him that he should disclose his true profession—or his former profession—to her if they were to be courting. But later. Not now. The sound of music and laughter drew her gaze back to town. "Father will be returning soon. I shouldn't stay." She kicked the leaves by her feet. "It's hopeless Hayden, don't you see? I have nowhere else to go." Her voice broke as tears filled her eyes.

Placing a finger beneath her chin, he raised her gaze to his. "Ah, but you do. I have already spoken to Sarah. She would be happy for you to move in with her in exchange for help with baby Lydia. And Eliza is offering you a position at the clinic. Your work there will more than pay for any food and other necessities you need."

She stared at him as if he'd asked her to swim back to Georgia. "*Work* for a living?"

Hayden clenched his jaw. How could he want to kiss her one moment and strangle her the next? "Yes, work. Like most people must do to survive. Do you want to be free, Princess?"

"Of course." A tear slipped from her eye. "Yes, of course. But you don't understand—I owe my family."

"Whatever it is, we will pay them back. Together."

Another tear joined the first. "You would do that for me?"

He cupped her face in both hands. "I would do anything for you."

"Magnolia!" Her father's voice echoed off branches and leaves, clamoring like a gothic gong and drowning out the pleasant music.

Hayden took her hand in his. "Shall we go announce our good news?"

Magnolia's joy was soon swallowed up by apprehension as they made their way back to town. She feared not only what her father would say but what he would do. If her courtship with Hayden ended in marriage—ah, dare she hope?—she might never be able to pay back the money she owed her parents, and she'd certainly never gain them the prestige of title or position.

She fingered the toad carving in her pocket. But to become the wife of such a man! Was it possible? When she was with Hayden, everything seemed possible.

Breaking free from her father and living independently as a single woman, for one. It simply wasn't done. At least not for a genteel lady. But could she do it? Could she rise from her bed every morning and spend her days working like an impoverished washerwoman? She *had* enjoyed helping Eliza in the clinic, but it had been her choice to be there and her choice when she would leave. Yet. . .she had felt useful for the first time in her life. And Eliza said she had a gift for nursing. Wouldn't it be wonderful to have value beyond her appearance? Perhaps that would cause her reflection to transform back into one of beauty.

The thought elated her. Along with being loved by such a strong, courageous, kind man. And of having a lifetime to love him in return. It was too good to be true. Too much to hope for! Yet there he was, walking beside her, his warm, rough hand enveloping hers, the taste of his kiss lingering on her lips, his manly smell wafting in the air between them. And she knew she could face anything, even her father's wrath, with Hayden by her side.

He squeezed her hand and gave her that wink that melted her heart before they burst into the center of the square.

Her father, his face bloated like a jellyfish—with a sting just as potent—charged toward her. Her mother followed, ringing her hands. "Where have you been? I told you to stay away from that man!"

Before her father could yank her away, Hayden released her hand

and stepped in front of her. Equal in height, the men stared each other down, one snorting like a bull, the other calm and determined.

The music faded into contrary chords before ceasing altogether, giving way to protests and grunts as all eyes swerved to the brewing altercation. Still, Magnolia's father kept his eyes locked on Hayden's, like cannons about to fire. Magnolia knew that look. It was a look that had caused strong men to wither and staunch women to cry. But Hayden did not falter.

"You will step aside at once, sir, and hand me my daughter."

"Only if she wishes to come to you." Hayden's voice bore neither rancor nor intimidation.

"Of course she wishes to come to me, you hawkish popinjay!" With narrow, seething eyes, her father peered at her around Hayden. "Magnolia, come here this instant!" Her mother stepped beside her husband, a strength in her expression Magnolia had never seen before.

Gathering her own strength, Magnolia stepped forward, slipped her hand once again into Hayden's, and lifted her chin. "I cannot, Papa. Hayden and I are officially courting."

He let out a guttural laugh and glanced at the gathering townspeople. "Rubbish! There's nothing official about such nonsense."

"And I am moving to town," Magnolia continued. "Taking a position at the clinic." She feared he would read the tremble in her voice as doubt.

But he seemed not to notice as maroon exploded on his face. "A position? Moving!" He loosened his necktie, his chest pitching like a ship on high waves.

A gust swirled through the square, sending the lanterns sputtering and casting patches of light over the crowd. Magnolia thought she saw her mother smile.

Colonel Blake and James pushed through the mob to stand beside them.

Magnolia's father gave a bitter chuckle, casting another incredulous glance over the bystanders. Then leaning close to her—so close she felt his spittle on her neck—he said, "You will stop this foolishness at once! You are embarrassing your mother and me. We will discuss this at home." He clutched her arm.

Magnolia winced, and Hayden grabbed her father's wrist. So tightly, her father's jaw twitched with the silent struggle until finally he released Magnolia. Rubbing his hand, he gave Hayden a look that would have killed him if he had been armed.

Magnolia drew a shaky breath. "I have made up my mind, Father."

For once, her mother wasn't sobbing. Instead, she stared at Magnolia with pride.

"You ungrateful girl," he hissed. "This is the second time you have walked out on your bargain, and it will be the last."

Hayden took a step forward. "We will pay you what she owes."

Her father measured him with a scornful gaze then glared at his daughter. "You are a bigger fool than I thought, Magnolia, but do not take me for one." He tugged on his waistcoat, stepped back, and waved them away. "You are no longer my daughter."

Gasps sped through the crowd.

Eliza eased toward them. "You can't mean that, Mr. Scott."

A tangible pain speared Magnolia's heart. Her mother began to sob. Hayden squeezed her hand and drew her close as her father strode away, head held high, ordering her mother to come along. But Magnolia didn't have time to consider the implications of his words before the sound of crunching leaves—a multitude of crunching leaves—rose from the jungle. Blake, James, and most of the men, including Hayden, headed for their rifles and pistols, leveling them toward the noise while ushering the women behind them. Magnolia joined Eliza and Angeline as everyone watched to see what new dangers emerged from the trees.

Seconds passed like minutes. The leaves parted and a group of men marched into town. No, not just men, women and children too, their clothes torn and stained, their faces weary and frightened. Eyes widening, they froze at the sight of the guns pointed their way. Some of the men in the group plucked out pistols and returned the favor.

But Magnolia's gaze fastened upon a single man leading the pack, his arms raised and an impudent grin on his lips. Her heart seized. It couldn't be. It simply couldn't be. Surely, it was just another vision.

"Hold up there, gentlemen," the vision spoke, his slick voice confirming her fears. "We come in peace. We are settlers from the Confederate States, just like you."

"Martin!" Magnolia managed to growl the name. She started toward him, but her father stormed past her. "Mr. Haley? Mr. Martin Haley!"

The man lowered his arms. His eyebrows shot up over eyes filled with shock. Magnolia's mother shrieked.

"No, sir. You are mistaken. That is not my name." He spoke with his usual aplomb.

But the closer Magnolia got to him, the more she recognized the cultured goatee and thin mustache, the gray streaking the temples of his black hair. Those firm cheek bones and stark green eyes. Handsome, charming Martin.

Her father stopped before him. "I don't care what you call yourself. You stole all my money, sir! And I demand it back."

Wondering where Hayden was, Magnolia glanced over her shoulder to find him staring at Martin as if he were a ghost. No, worse. A monster, from the look of fury blazing in his eyes.

Blake approached the group. "What is the meaning of this? Who are you and who are these people?"

"Ah, you must be the man in charge." Martin faced the colonel with the same smile he used on everyone he wished to deceive. "As I said, we are but settlers like yourself. In fact"—he waved an arm over the town— "we are the ones who inhabited these huts before you."

"This man stole from me and I demand reparation!" Magnolia's father bellowed.

But Magnolia was tired of talking. Barreling forward, she planted her hands on Martin's chest and shoved him backward. He stumbled but quickly righted himself. Brushing off his coat, he smiled—a sweet, sickly smile that made her stomach turn. "Ah, dear Magnolia, how good to see you. Of all the places to find each other. . .Brazil." He chuckled.

A few of the newcomers took up positions at their leader's side, weapons raised, and defiance written on their faces.

"I am not your dear," Magnolia spat. "You are a liar, a cheat, and a thief!"

Seeming to forget he had an audience, her father shoved a finger in Martin's face. "You charmed my daughter into an engagement, wormed your way into our family's graces, and took me for everything I had with some spurious investment! You owe me, sir! You owe me, and you will pay. By God, you will pay!" Lunging for Martin, he locked fingers around the man's neck and squeezed.

Martin's eyes bulged. He clawed at her father's hands, gasping and croaking. Several women in his group screamed and the two men at his side cocked and pointed their pistols at her father's head.

"That's enough, Mr. Scott!" Colonel Blake shoved his way between them and pried them apart. Martin gasped for air. "Settle down! Everyone, lower your guns!" Blake shouted to the colonists.

But Magnolia didn't want to settle down. She wanted to gouge Martin's eyes out for what he'd done to her and her family. She was just about to attempt that very thing when Hayden nudged both her and her father aside, cocked his pistol, and leveled it at Martin's forehead.

Martin retreated, real fear skittering across his eyes for the first time.

"Hayden, no!"

"What are you doing, Hayden?" Blake grabbed Hayden's arm but he shrugged him off.

"Put the gun down." James came up from behind.

But Hayden didn't move. Didn't breathe, as his eyes remained locked on his target. A drop of sweat slid down his cheek onto a jaw strung as tight as a sail under full wind. Magnolia had never seen him this enraged, this focused. It frightened her.

"Please, sir, whatever you have against me, let us settle it like gentlemen." Still Martin's voice was as slick as oil.

With an ominous growl, Hayden flipped the weapon, raised it, and slammed it atop Martin's head. The odious man toppled to the dirt with a groan.

Shock filtered through the crowd as Blake knelt beside Martin and gazed up at Hayden. "Why did you do that? Who is this man?"

Hayden stuffed the gun into his belt. "He's my father."

Chapter 29

Shoving aside the bamboo door, Hayden headed into the night. Unfortunately the air was just as heavy and oppressive outside as it was inside his hut. Or maybe it was seeing his father that strangled the breath out of him. After he'd flattened the heinous man, Hayden had stomped into the jungle, trying to gather his thoughts and smother his anger. But after hours of batting aside leaves and slapping insects, his thoughts were even more convoluted and his fury hotter. So he'd had a drink of that pinga Magnolia loved so much and had gone to bed. Yet sleep taunted him with heavy lids that would not shut and a wounded heart that kept him awake.

Taking in a deep breath of air, thick with musk and earth, Hayden stretched the kinks from his back and gazed down the dark street. Not a single light shone from any hut. Nor were any watchman in sight. This would be the perfect time to visit his so-called father at the clinic, where he was spending the night after Eliza dressed his head wound.

Yet as Hayden plodded down the street, it was Magnolia who consumed his thoughts. Though he'd been frozen with rage at the sight of the man he'd been so desperate to find for fifteen years, Hayden had heard everything that transpired.

Magnolia had been engaged to his father!

He still couldn't believe it. His stomach lurched even as the thought twisted a cyclone of impossibility in his mind. How could she have fallen for such a scoundrel? A born liar, a charlatan of the worst kind. A shark who preyed on people's hopes and desires only to gobble them up at the last minute. How could she be that foolish? And more importantly, how could he court a woman who had once been in his father's arms, perhaps even kissed him and who knew what else? Disgust sent acid into his throat as he passed Blake and Eliza's hut. The sound of night creatures joined the rush of the river in a cadence that was usually soothing, but tonight the noise only clanked and gonged against Hayden's shock and fury.

His father had swindled the Scotts from all their wealth. That was the debt Magnolia spoke of so often. Now things began to make sense. Still, what kind of parents blamed their innocent daughter for being tricked by a master manipulator? And then used her mistake to enslave her with guilt into obeying their every command. He squeezed the back of his neck, his muscles coiled tight.

He was too confused to deal with his feelings toward Magnolia at the moment. Right now, he had to focus on the only thing that mattered—honoring his promise to his mother.

Pushing aside the canvas flap, he entered the clinic. It smelled of blood and lye and herbs. He groped for a match and a lantern and brought light to bear on the sleeping form of his father. A pile of cloths sat on the table, tempting Hayden to place them over his father's mouth and nose and finish the task quickly. But that wouldn't be a fitting punishment. His father must know who was killing him and why. Hayden wanted to see the fear, the realization in his eyes, and perhaps even a spark of regret.

"Wake up." He poked him, noting the bandage wrapped around his head. "Wake up."

With a growl, Patrick—for that was his real name—peered through tiny slits. But upon seeing Hayden, he jerked to sit up. Rubbing his forehead, he blinked as if trying to focus. "Come to finish me off?"

"Something like that." Hayden crossed arms over his chest.

Patrick glanced over the room as if looking for a weapon and, upon finding none, released a sigh. "Well get on with it then or get out." He swung his legs over the bunk.

If anything, at least the man was no coward.

"You don't recognize me?" Hayden heard the fury strangling his own voice.

"Should I?"

"Perhaps the name Hayden Gale will spark your memory, *Patrick*." He spit the name like the dirt it was.

Every muscle in the man's face stiffened. All except his eyes. They shifted over the dirt floor as if wishing a tunnel would open up beneath him. Seconds passed before he let out a ragged breath, attempted a grin, and lifted his gaze to Hayden, allowing it to wander over him. "You grew up well, lad."

Hayden huffed. "Is that all you have to say?"

With a diminutive slant of his lips, Patrick shrugged. "What else is there?"

A muscle twitched in Hayden's jaw. "You. . .left"—he squeezed out the words, barely able to contain his rage—"when I was only two. Mother. . ."

Patrick rose, stretched his back nonchalantly, all the while keeping a wary eye on Hayden. "Ah, yes. Elizabeth. Lovely lady. How is she?"

"Dead."

His brow folded, and he plopped into a chair beside the examining table. "How?"

"Run over by a carriage on her way home from slaving all day as a seamstress." Veins throbbed in Hayden's forehead. "Too exhausted to even look where she was going."

Genuine sorrow shadowed Patrick's face. Or was it a ruse? "A shame," he said.

"A shame?" Hayden started toward the man, intending to slug him, then stopped. "A shame!" Spit flew from his mouth. "You left her without means to survive. Forced her to toil her life away from dawn till dusk just to feed us."

"She was a resourceful woman. I knew she'd make it."

"But she didn't!"

Patrick flinched. "Listen, lad, I was a different man back then." He ran a finger across his finely coiffed beard, a shadow rolling across his expression. "I made a mistake marrying her. I loved your mother,

I truly did, but a man like me couldn't possibly be tied down."

"You mean a liar, a cheat, and a scoundrel like you."

"Perhaps." He jerked his head to the side and sighed. "In the end, I knew she deserved better."

"In the end you thought of no one but yourself."

Hayden's words seemed of no effect on the man as he pressed fingers on the bandage around his head and winced. "She had family. A father and a brother, I believe."

"Grandpa died of smallpox, and Frederick took to sea to find his fortune."

He seemed to ponder the information for a moment. "How was I to know that?" His indignant tone further infuriated Hayden.

"You would have known if you had bothered to check on our welfare. Even once. Did you check even once?"

Patrick shifted his gaze away. Lantern light glinted in green eyes that held a hint of remorse before he straightened his shoulders and faced Hayden again. "Well, boy, it appears you turned out just fine." He slowly rose and slapped Hayden on the back as if they were old friends—the confidence man at his finest. "How odd that our paths crossed all the way here in Brazil."

"Not so odd." Hayden jerked away from him. Was Patrick so dimwitted that he didn't understand what Hayden intended to do? What he'd sailed across an ocean to do? "I came looking for you."

"Me?" Patrick's brows pinched together, but then a hint of fear slowly claimed his features. "How did you know what I looked like?"

Reaching into his pocket, Hayden pulled out the tintype, snapped open the leather case, and showed it to the man.

Patrick took it, eased fingers over the portrait, and smiled. "Your mother had this made of me."

"And she gave it to me on her deathbed."

He touched the gray at his temples. "I'm older now."

"Yet you haven't changed one bit."

"Everyone changes, lad." He handed it back to him.

Hayden held up a hand. "Keep it. I don't need it anymore."

With a shrug, Patrick set it on the table.

"Do you have any idea what I suffered?" Hayden stretched his fingers, itching to strike the man. "I was only ten when she died. I lived on the street, hungry and cold, sleeping in refuse."

"You can hardly blame me for my ignorance." One brow arched over an expression of annoyance.

"You wouldn't have helped me even if you *had* known, would you?"

Patrick's silent stare was all the answer Hayden needed. He fisted his hand, intending to strike him, strangle him, whatever it took to wipe that smirk off his face. Patrick cringed, bracing for the attack. Fury pooled in Hayden's fist, throbbing through each muscle and bone, until it felt like it would explode. But no. Not yet. He lowered it, stretching out his fingers, gathering his control. Hayden must first find out about Magnolia. Taking a deep breath, he stared out the window.

"No doubt those hard times made you the strong man you are today." Patrick's tone had lost its edge, bordering on conciliatory. Good. He was starting to understand the danger he faced. "Perhaps I did you a favor," he continued. "I wouldn't have been much of a father anyway."

"Why are you here in Brazil, Patrick?"

"For gold, lad!" His eyes glittered greed. "I have a map given me by a reliable gentleman who told me there's a fortune buried near here. Why else would I subject myself to this bestial jungle?"

Wealth, of course. Hayden should have known. "You'll have to fight Dodd for it first."

"Dodd, who's Dodd?"

"Never mind." Hayden shook his head. "So you dragged these poor settlers here on the guise of starting a colony when in truth you plan on finding the gold and abandoning them?"

"I needed funding for the trip, didn't I? Besides, they'll be quite all right. They truly believe they can recreate the South here." He chuckled.

"You're still a monster who uses people," Hayden growled, disgust curdling in his belly. "And what about Magnolia?"

"Miss Scott?" Patrick grinned. "A rare treat, that one. I would have loved to have stayed and sampled more of her wares, but alas there was money to be had."

This time Hayden *did* slug him. Right across the jaw, sending him tumbling backward, arms flailing, and finally dropping to the ground with a thud. He moaned, rubbed his jaw, but managed to swing out his legs and trip Hayden. He fell beside his father, but quickly leapt up and struck Patrick again. Blood spilled from Patrick's nose as he scrambled to rise. Hayden clutched his collar, lifted him, and slammed him against the wall. The bamboo cracked. Palm fronds quivered above them.

"When I find the gold, I'll split it with you," Patrick screeched, his eyes sparking in terror. "Anything you want."

"I don't want your money."

"What do you want? To kill me for something I did over twenty years ago?"

"No, I'm going to kill you for the man you are today. And for the promise I made Mother on her death bed to avenge her untimely death."

Tossing Patrick to the ground, Hayden wrapped his hands around the man's neck and squeezed with all his might. His eyes bulged. His face grew purple as he tried to seize Hayden's fingers, desperate for release, desperate for life. As Hayden's mother had been when she'd gasped her last breath. *This is for you, Mother. Finally, you will have justice.*

A plea for mercy seeped from Patrick's eyes. Hayden searched for the joy, the thrill he expected to feel as he squashed the final breath from the man who had ruined his life. But instead, remorse pinched him. Guilt. And a sense of evil he'd never felt before. Still he squeezed, unable to release his hold. He would have continued, too, if strong hands hadn't pried his fingers away and shoved him off the man. Blake gave Hayden a look of horror as he pushed him back. Patrick coughed and sputtered and gasped for air, rubbing his throat.

Eliza darted in, glanced at the scene, and went to check on Patrick.

"Blast it! What is wrong with you?" Blake shoved Hayden outside.

Hayden paced back and forth before the clinic, clenching and unclenching his fists, struggling to restrain his fury before he did what every fiber in him longed to do—barge back into the hut and finish the job. Before he could do just that, Blake dragged him down the street, stoked the embers in the main fire pit, and ordered Hayden to sit on a stool.

"What's this all about, Hayden?" Blake glanced toward the clinic where Eliza was still tending the monster's wounds.

Hayden stared at the flames.

Selecting a log from a nearby pile, Blake tossed it onto the fire. "I tried to find you, to talk about what happened, but you disappeared."

"I needed to think."

"Think about how you were going to kill him? Blast it, man!" Blake limped around the fire and rubbed his leg. "Is he the reason you went to Rio?" He halted and stared at Hayden. "Is he the reason you stowed away on our ship?"

Hayden nodded. "Back in Charleston, I heard he was in town, heard he'd signed up for your colony."

"Hmm. But, apparently, he started another colony and arrived sooner than we did," Blake said.

"He must have taken a steam ship." Hayden ran a hand through his hair. "What does it matter? You don't know what he's done to me."

"Then tell me. Tell me so I understand." Blake pulled up a stump and sat down. The look in his eyes was one of true concern—a look that said *I care. You can trust me.* Hayden had never seen that look before, except recently in Magnolia's eyes. And perhaps glimpses of it in some of his friends here, but never like this. Sincere concern. Holding the power to lure all his secrets out from hiding.

A breeze whipped through the clearing, stirring dried leaves into a spin and dancing through the flames. A monkey howled in the distance. Hayden hung his head, released a heavy sigh, and slowly began to spill the story of how his father had abandoned them, how his mother had been crushed beneath carriage wheels, how he lived on the street, hungry and cold. And with the telling of each devastating event, Blake's shoulders sank lower and lower.

Leaning forward, Hayden planted his elbows on his knees and stared at the leaping flames. "I promised Mother on her death bed I would get revenge, that I would find my father and make him pay."

Blake squeezed the bridge of his nose. "Was that what *she* wanted?"

The question shocked Hayden. He shot Blake a venomous look. "She was unconscious by then and slipped away an hour later. But I know she would have wanted retribution for dying so young. Who wouldn't?"

"Really? From what you've told me of her, I doubt she would have wanted this kind of life for you."

"You know nothing of her," Hayden snapped.

"No. But I know much about revenge."

Hayden nodded. Indeed. He'd heard Blake's sad tale. How his entire family had died in the Atlanta burning, how his little brother had been killed on the battlefield. He had seen the fury in the colonel's eyes when he'd discovered Eliza's dirty little secret. Yet Blake had changed. Changed so much he ended up marrying a woman with the blood of his family on her hands.

"I don't know how you overcame your anger, your need for revenge, Blake. I could never forgive what my father did to me. . .to my mother. Her memory depends on it."

"If your mother was a godly woman, she's happier now than she's ever been." Blake's smile in contrast to the morbid topic confused Hayden.

"For over a year," Blake continued, "I wanted to kill any Yankee who crossed my path. I almost did kill a few." He chuckled then locked eyes with Hayden, the lines on his forehead deepening. "The only way I overcame my bitterness was by handing my need for revenge over to God. By understanding that if He could forgive me for so much, I had no right not to forgive others. Besides, when you receive God's love and forgiveness, it changes you. Makes you a better man."

Hayden flattened his lips. He'd be a better man when his father was dead. "God's never been there for me. Perhaps for someone like you—a West Point graduate, a colonel who served your country courageously, a man of honor." He shook his head and stared at the ground. "You don't know what I've done."

"I don't have to know. And God doesn't care about your past. He only cares that you turn to Him, ask His forgiveness and His help to forgive others."

Hayden studied the ex-colonel. When he'd first met him on board the ship, Hayden thought he'd found a kindred spirit and immediately became friends with the man whose bitterness and rage Hayden understood. But now that rage was gone, and a joy and peace surrounded Blake that Hayden envied. What would it feel like to be at peace? He had no idea—no remembrance of a time when he'd been at ease with himself and with life. But he would know soon enough. When justice was served.

Rising, Hayden grabbed a stick and tossed it into the fire. Perhaps forgiveness would bring him peace. But he'd have plenty of time for that after he got his revenge. "My father must pay for what he's done. If your God is so forgiving, He'll no doubt pardon my father's offenses as well. But, for my mother's sake, I cannot let that happen. Don't you see? It is up to me to see that her murder is avenged."

The fire hissed and crackled, sending sparks into the night.

"Hayden, you're not judge and jury of the world. That's God's job. Let Him handle it."

Hayden grew tired of all the God talk. "What are you going to do about Patrick?"

"Patrick. Is that his name? Hmm. Well, I can hardly turn him and his colonists away. You saw how hungry and worn they looked." Blake rubbed his eyes. "Besides, we could use the help, and they *did* inhabit this town before us."

"But they didn't build the huts," Hayden argued, his mind refusing to believe Blake could be so fooled.

"No, Patrick said they found them like this."

"Then let the colonists stay and banish my father."

"I can't do that and you know it. The man has done us no wrong."

Blood drained from Hayden's heart and fired through his veins. "He's a confidence man. A swindler! He's only here for the gold. He'll charm his way into this colony and infect it like a plague. And like a plague, he must be isolated, cut out with a knife, before we all fall ill."

Blake's gray eyes assessed him. "Perhaps. If so, he'll show his true colors soon enough. Either way, killing him is not the answer." Blake rose. "Rest assured, I will keep an eye on him. And so will James. We won't allow him to harm New Hope or anyone in it."

Hayden repressed a laugh. Though Blake was a competent leader, he had no idea who he was up against. But Hayden did. And he had no intention of allowing that man to stay. Perhaps Blake was right about not murdering him, but Hayden had other ways to exact his revenge.

Chapter 30

Babies made the sweetest sounds when they slept. Or at least Lydia did. Little gurgles and tongue clicks and grunts of innocence bubbled through Sarah's hut. Though the sound was far more soothing than Magnolia's father's snores, she still could not sleep, envying every second of the babe's worry-free existence—the sweet repose of innocence. If only Magnolia were a child again on her parents' plantation, when her mother and father were happy and her father doted on her as if she were a princess. Before she'd grown up and disappointed him. But those days were gone. They'd been gone for a long time. And now her father had disowned her.

Rubbing her aching head, Magnolia sat up in bed. Thoughts flitted through her mind, scattered and jumbled, some too painful to light on. Others too thrilling to ignore. Such as the one she embraced now, the one where she had accepted Hayden's suit! She could barely remember the joy she felt at that moment, so brief had it been before Martin had barged into camp, strutting like a bloated goose as if he owned Brazil. Just like he always did everywhere he set his imperious boot. *Hayden's father!* How could it be? Swinging her legs over the cot, she dropped her head into her hands. The Godard man he'd been searching for. The man he'd given his life to find was her ex-fiancé. A putrid taste flooded her mouth.

Shouts drifted through the bamboo and mud walls, and she wondered who else was having trouble sleeping. Flinging on her robe, Magnolia glanced at Sarah and Lydia sleeping side by side on the cot and smiled. Moonlight fluttered silver ribbons on both their faces, as if God Himself gently caressed them while they slept. Was that what it took to get God's affection? To be as good and sweet as Sarah? If so, Magnolia would forever be in His disfavor. Just like she was in her father's. Shoving her feet into slippers, she headed outside. To walk. To think. To clear her head. Anything to soften the ache in her heart.

After Hayden had struck his father, he'd stomped off, not once looking her way. Not once! Magnolia knew he was angry. Knew he was as shocked as she at their twisted, vile association. What she didn't know was what he thought of it all. What he thought of her. Mercy me, she didn't even know her own thoughts anymore. Martin had ripped her heart in two and stolen everything from her family. So desperate to be loved, to be cherished, to be of some value to someone, she'd ignored the warning signs along the way: the twinkle of greed in his eye, the twist of doubt in her gut, his sudden interest in investing in new racetracks in Kentucky.

Yet now those doubts rose once again. Was his son any different? Wasn't Hayden just as much a swindler as his father? Hadn't he tricked her with the same sugar-laced words and rakish grins and idle flattery? Perhaps even his offer of courtship was just a part of some nefarious plan to discredit her family again. Although how he could cast any further reproach on them, Magnolia could not imagine. Ah, she was just being silly. Hayden was nothing like his father, and until he gave her a reason to believe otherwise, she would trust him.

Night insects and birds hummed atop a cool breeze swirling off the river. Wrapping her robe tighter, she started down the street when the flicker of a fire caught her gaze. A few more steps and she saw Blake sitting on a stump, Hayden pacing before him deep in conversation. She knew that pace, knew that stubborn cut of his jaw. Her traitorous heart leapt at the sight of him, and she longed to run to him, to know his thoughts, to comfort him in his pain, but instead she just stood there watching.

Soon, Blake rose, said something to Hayden then walked away.

Hayden rubbed the back of his neck and stared at the fire with such anguish, it brought tears to her eyes.

Slipping from the shadows, she entered the clearing, halting when her footsteps brought his gaze to hers. Eyes the color of the jungle assessed her as if she were some unearthly being. Pain clouded them before they hardened like jade.

"Hayden, I. . ." Magnolia took a step toward him, but he held up a hand.

He faced the fire again, his Adam's apple diving in his throat.

"We should talk," Magnolia said.

"I can't."

"I had no idea he was—"

"I know." His cold, distant tone carved a hole in her heart.

"I'm so sorry, Hayden. I'm sorry he hurt you. He hurt me too. Lied to me. Ruined my family."

The strident rasp of crickets filled the air. Above her, a cloud cloaked the moon, stealing away its milky light. "Are you angry with me?"

"You were engaged to my father." He breathed out the words as if still in shock.

Magnolia swallowed, forcing back tears. Only a few hours ago Hayden had gazed at her with such love. Now his eyes were cold and hard. "What does it matter?"

"You and he, you—" Again repugnance braided his expression. "Every time I see you. . .every time I look at you, I will see him. I will see him and you. . .together."

"Well, we are *not* together now!" Magnolia fumed. "And we haven't been for years. Are you going to be equally repulsed by every man I've ever courted?"

He kicked a rock and fisted hands at his waist. "No. Just my father."

A terrible fear began to wind its way through her soul. "How can you be angry at me for something I did in complete innocence? Surely if either of us has a right to be mad, it is I, since it was one of your relatives, your very father, who ruined my family."

Snorting, he raked his hand through his hair and moved to the other side of the fire as if he couldn't stand being close to her.

"Do you think this is easy for me?" Though she'd wanted to sound angry, her voice came out a whimper. "You already swindled me once. Perhaps you *are* your father's son, after all."

He crossed arms over his chest, steely and defiant. Why was he behaving this way? She hadn't done anything wrong. Desperate, she reached out to him, clinging to the hope of his love. "But I want to trust you, Hayden. All you need do is tell me I can. Tell me one more time that I can."

Nothing but the crackle of fire and buzz of katydids met her ears. "Please, talk to me." A tear slid down her cheek.

Still no response.

Dread sank in her gut. "What does this mean for us, Hayden?"

His eyes rose to hers over the fire, the flames reflecting his pain. "I don't know if there is an us."

Knife in hand, Hayden whittled a fresh piece of wood, his anger chipping away at the branch with no design in mind. Much like his life. Lots of cuts and chips and broken parts that formed nothing but a nonsensical shape without beauty or reason. Dawn had broken an hour ago and still he sat in the same spot, ignoring everyone around him and even refusing a plate of fruit Eliza had offered. One thought consumed his mind, and one thought alone—revenge. Even as one feeling consumed his heart. Pain. Pain at the loss of Magnolia. Yet the two were so inextricably connected, he could not separate them. Both cut through his soul, leaving him bitter and empty. The former with a ravenous desire to fill, the latter with a hopelessness he'd never experienced. He hated hurting Magnolia, hated the anguish in her eyes when he'd proclaimed an end to their brief courtship. But what choice did he have? He couldn't look at her without envisioning her in his father's arms.

Speaking of the monster, Patrick finally strolled into the clearing, nodding his greeting at everyone and thanking them when they expressed concern for his injuries. As he passed to grab a plate of fruit, his eyes brushed over Hayden. A new confidence—a smugness—made its home deep within them as if he knew Hayden could not touch him.

Unfortunately for Patrick, he was wrong.

"You aren't getting any ideas." Blake's voice speared conviction through Hayden's thoughts as the colonel took a seat beside him.

"No." He continued whittling. None that he'd tell Blake. Unless Blake agreed to toss Patrick from the colony so Hayden could hunt him down like the animal he was. But he knew the honorable colonel would never do that. No, Hayden would have to wait to find his father alone. Then he'd knock him out, tie him up, and deposit him in the middle of Brazil far away from New Hope. The cultured coxcomb wouldn't survive two days in the wild. A fitting punishment for someone who stripped his victims of all their comforts and security and left them to die.

Patrick's laughter drew Hayden's gaze. His father sat with two women from his colony, both staring at him adoringly and giggling at his every word. The seductive curve of his mouth, the gleam of interest in his eye, his engaging chuckle, the way he looked at each woman as if she were a rare treasure, Hayden knew those tactics well. He'd used them on countless women himself.

"What are you going to do about Mr. Scott?" Hayden asked, noting that the colonel's gaze was also locked on Patrick. "I'm not the only one who wants Patrick Gale dead."

Before Blake could answer, the man in question barreled into the clearing like a steaming locomotive, Mr. Dodd at his side. The two men halted before Patrick. "Arrest this man at once!" Mr. Scott pointed at Hayden's father.

With a groan, Blake excused himself and headed toward the altercation. Hayden followed, the irony of his agreeing with Mr. Scott, for once, not lost on him.

Blake halted beside Dodd. "What's all the fuss?"

Several colonists stopped eating and glanced at the group, while others gathered around.

"The fuss, if you must know"—Mr. Scott gave him a superior look—"is that I'm having this thief arrested. Mr. Dodd was a sheriff back home. Ergo, he is best suited to be the law here. At least until we can set up a proper election or however they work it in Brazil." He scanned the mob and, upon realizing he had an audience, raised his voice. "We have three witnesses who can testify that this man robbed me and my family of all we owned."

"Absurd!" one of the women at Patrick's side exclaimed.

Patrick plopped a slice of orange in his mouth and smiled.

Dodd scratched his head. "Well, I suppose I could oblige you if we had a proper jail."

"We can lock him in the tunnels you told me about, Mr. Dodd. You mentioned there were chains down there."

"No one is arresting anyone," Blake said.

Patrick nodded. "At last, a word of reason." The ladies breathed a sigh of relief.

Mr. Scott bunched his fists. The lines framing his mouth seemed to have deepened overnight. "Colonel, this man is a criminal and must be punished."

Hayden stepped forward. "I couldn't agree more."

Mumbles of both protest and agreement thundered through the colonists.

"Hold up, everyone." Blake raised a hand. "Is anyone here a witness to the theft of Mr. Scott's wealth?" When all grew silent, Blake continued, "I thought not. Then, Mr. Scott, I'm afraid it is your family's word against Patrick's."

"Are you calling me a liar, Colonel?"

"No. I'm simply saying we don't have enough proof." Blake shifted weight off his bad leg. "Besides, as Mr. Dodd said, we have no jail, no judge, and no jury. If you want to see justice done, I suggest you escort Mr. Gale back to the States."

"Why would the man come with me, when all that waits him is the noose?!" Mr. Scott shouted, his baleful eyes narrowing upon Patrick.

The man merely shrugged and rubbed his goatee. "Why would I leave Brazil to waste time and money on a trial that would surely declare me innocent?"

Mr. Scott lunged for Patrick, but James leapt between them and forced the old plantation owner back.

"You can't just let him run free!" Mr. Scott blazed.

Blake rubbed his forehead. "What would you have me do with him?"

"String him up on a tree."

"Here, here," Hayden agreed, drawing his father's reptilian eyes.

"You know I cannot do that." Annoyance edged Blake's tone.

"I appreciate that, Colonel." Patrick smiled. Handing his plate to one of the women, he rose, brushed off his waistcoat, and gazed over the crowd. "Your colony has chosen a wise and just leader."

Ah, now the flattery began. Hayden's stomach curdled. But, thankfully, Blake didn't seem to fall for it.

"However, Mr. Gale." The colonel stared the man down with that I'm-in-command-and-you-will-obey look he must have given his troops on the battlefield. "That something unlawful occurred between you and the Scotts, I have no doubt. Simply because I don't have the means to discover what that is, doesn't mean I won't be keeping a firm eye upon you and your activities in our town. Should I find even the slightest hint of anything nefarious in your dealings with anyone, you will be banished from this colony. Do I make myself clear, sir?"

A flicker of anger, a promise of defiance, crossed Patrick's eyes before they clouded over with seeming compliance. "Of course, Colonel. I wouldn't have it any other way."

The lady to Patrick's right stood and brushed aside her chocolate brown curls. "Colonel Blake, is it? You are quite mistaken about Owen. . .this man you call Patrick. He is a noble man of the highest character." She sent a spiteful glance toward Mr. Scott. "He couldn't possibly have done what this man claims."

Other members of Patrick's colony shouted their agreement.

Mr. Scott seemed about to lose his breakfast. Patrick, on the other hand, nodded his thanks to his admirers before he turned to address Dodd. "Mr. Dodd, I heard you were searching for gold, sir."

Suspicion clouded the ex-lawman's face as he clipped his thumbs into his belt. "What's it to you?"

"Well," he began, drawing the man in. "I happen to have a map. . . an old pirate's map." Patrick raised dark brows.

"So do I." Dodd twitched his crooked nose, studying the man.

"Great news, great news. Precisely what I'd hoped." Patrick rubbed his hands together. "You see, my map is one of three. Perhaps yours is another?" Reaching into his waistcoat pocket, Patrick pulled out a crinkled piece of vellum, carefully unfolded it, and showed it to Dodd, whose eyes widened at the sight.

"It does look similar to mine," Dodd said. "But I found nothing at the spot it led me to. Just another piece. . .of. . ."—Dodd's words slowed as realization rolled over his face—"a . . .map."

"Indeed?" Patrick grinned. "Mr. Dodd, I do believe we need to talk." He glanced over the crowd. "In private."

Mr. Scott jerked from James's grasp. "What does this have to do with this man's arrest?"

Patrick thrust out his chin. "It has everything to do with your complaint, Mr. Scott. For here is what I propose. You say I stole money from you. I say I did not. However, I am a fair and generous man, and I do feel badly for you and your wife and, of course, your lovely daughter."

At the mention of Magnolia, his gaze brushed over Hayden, and the look of victory in his eyes nearly caused Hayden to draw his pistol and shoot the man on the spot. But that would be too nice a death.

"And besides," Patrick continued. "Whatever sort of man you thought I was before, by the very testimonies of the people who have spent months living with me, you can see that I am different—transformed, as it were." One arm drawn over his chest, he bowed toward Mr. Scott. "I wish to make amends for whatever harm you perceive I've done to you."

Hayden glanced over the crowd, expecting to hear rumbles of laughter, or at the very least, see eyes rolling in disbelief, but they all stood mesmerized by the man.

"Mr. Dodd and I will find this gold, I assure you." Patrick raised his voice for all to hear. "And when we do, I shall pay you and your lovely wife every penny you say I stole. How does that sound?"

"Why would you do that if you aren't guilty?" James eyed the man with suspicion.

"Because I am generous. And because if the information regarding this treasure is true, there'll be more than enough gold to pay this man and make us all rich!"

Nausea clambered up Hayden's throat. How could anyone believe such nonsense? But Mr. Scott made no protest. Instead, a hint of greed flashed in his eyes.

"Those pirates certainly thought there was a fortune here," one of the colonists said.

"But the gold is mine." Dodd frowned.

"Not if you need my third of the map to find it." Patrick grinned. "So, Mr. Scott, you can either have the colonel banish me from the colony and remain poor forever, or you can allow me to find the gold and make you a rich man once again."

Hayden chuckled, drawing everyone's gaze. "The man is lying. Can't you see that?"

Mr. Scott glared at Patrick, a vein throbbing at his temple. "I am not a man to be trifled with a second time, Mr. Haley or Gale, or whoever you are. But at the moment, I don't see that I have a choice."

Hayden shook his head in disbelief.

"Find your gold, sir," Mr. Scott continued. "If it even exists. You have six months to do so before I take matters into my own hands" —he swung a determined gaze at Blake—"regardless of what you say, Colonel."

"I would expect nothing less." Patrick gave a placating grin. "You shall have your money, Mr. Scott"—he lifted his chin and scanned the assembled group—"and then I will invest the rest of my share in this town and make it the Southern Utopia we all came here to embrace."

Ah, such seductive words frothing from devious lips with such aplomb that everyone cheered and smiled at him like the puppets they were. And he, the puppet master, skillfully pulling their strings. Hayden frowned. Yet, how many times had he, himself, lied to people, persuaded them with the same laud and puffery, put on a facade of honor and integrity while placating them with the same reassuring smile? All the while robbing them behind their backs of everything they had. Sometimes in front of their eyes.

A horrible realization struck him. One he should have seen long ago. In his quest to find his father by entering the man's world, Hayden had become just like the man he hated.

Chapter 31

Squeezing through the rotted gate, Hayden entered the temple square. How Blake and James had talked him into coming here again, he couldn't say. It seemed like a good idea at the time—a chance to get away from bumping into Magnolia everywhere he went, as well as from stewing in fury while he plotted revenge against his father. But now, as he glanced over the gruesome faces carved into obelisks and the huge fire pit whereupon those faces, along with their bodies, had been roasted, he much preferred his own internal angst than this temple of horrors.

But sweet Eliza had insisted that she check on Graves and bring him some food, and Blake would not have her come alone. In fact, he organized a regular posse consisting of Thiago, Moses, and of course James, who was anxious to return due to his reading of some ancient book Graves had given him. However, now as James entered the courtyard, he moved with the determined, wary look of a warrior rather than the interest of a scholar. The preacher-doctor was a constant surprise to Hayden for he knew the man harbored secrets from his past. Yet he played the part of a respectable man of God so well, Hayden couldn't help but admire him.

Thiago and Moses entered in after Hayden, looking less than pleased to be there, with Blake and Eliza bringing up the rear.

"Let's get this over with." Hayden started toward the temple stairs. "Though I don't see why you care so much for Mr. Graves, Eliza. If it were up to me, I'd leave him to his own devices."

Releasing her husband, Eliza slipped her arm through Hayden's. "We all have moments of insanity in our lives, do we not?" Her coy smile made him wonder if she referred to Hayden's recent attempt to murder his father. If she only knew the other horrid things he'd done, she wouldn't dare to touch him now. "Perhaps if someone had cared for us during those times," she continued, "we would have come to our senses sooner."

"You can't argue with my wife's compassionate heart." Blake leapt on the stairs, kicked aside a piece of crumbling stone, and helped Eliza up. The adoring way he looked at her clouded Hayden with sorrow. His chances at loving and being loved like that had died with the revelation of Magnolia's relationship with his father.

James faced the young interpreter. "Thiago, will you join us inside this time? There are some carvings I need you to look at."

The Brazilian's chest bellowed like the wind, but his jaw remained firm as he followed James up the stairs.

"I'll wait here," Moses said.

Blake nodded at the man, flung a sack of food and water over his shoulder, and led his wife inside the temple. Hayden followed, wondering if he shouldn't wait outside with Moses. But his curiosity got the best of him. The last time he'd been here, they'd gone no farther than the altar in the back. Since then, he'd heard Graves had managed to excavate tunnels beneath the building.

Minutes later, the oppressive heat in those tunnels threatened to melt Hayden on the spot. The deeper they went, the hotter it became. Eliza wilted in her husband's arms as he led her along, while James and Thiago discussed the odd carvings on the wall. Put there by the cannibals who built the temple, Thiago guessed, and telling a tale about a huge battle between the gods.

"And these." Thiago held up the torch and pointed toward drawings of figures that looked like giants with wings. "These are powerful beings who fought." He ran his finger over the rough stone. "Here see, they are put in chains. Defeated."

Sweat stung Hayden's eyes. He wiped it away, moving past them.

What difference did some ancient fable make when one was roasting alive? With each step he took, more air seeped from his lungs, while his damp clothes clung to him like tarpaper. And what in tarnation was that smell? A smell that got worse when, at the bottom of two sets of stairs, they entered a torch-lit cave. All the chamber needed to complete Hayden's vision of hell were volcanoes of fire belching from the ground.

Leading her to sit on a boulder, Blake handed Eliza his canteen. The woman shouldn't be here at all, but Hayden knew Blake oft had difficulty bridling his stubborn wife. Which reminded Hayden of Magnolia. Despite how things ended between them, a smile tugged his lips. A smile that soon faded when James lifted a torch to reveal strange symbols scrawled above two alcoves.

"Yes, yes. Deception and Delusion," he mumbled to himself as he knelt to examine the broken chains at the bottom of a long pole. "They are in the book. *The Judgment of the Four*. They are two of the four mentioned."

"I don't understand," Eliza said.

Hayden ran a sleeve over his forehead. "What nonsense is this, Doc?"

James shook his head. "I haven't translated it all yet. But they were some kind of powerful beings."

"Like the carvings on wall." Thiago's gaze skittered about the eerie cave. "The defeated ones."

Hayden snorted. "Where is Graves?"

As if on cue, sounds echoed from an opening to their left and out crawled Mr. Graves. Though he'd been sinister-looking before landing in Brazil, the dust-laden, long-haired, rag-attired man who emerged into the room now harbored such a macabre aura about him, Hayden's sweat turned cold.

"Ah, Mr. Graves." Eliza approached him. "We've brought you some food and water."

"I have no need of it." He waved her away, but by the way his clothes hung on him, Hayden thought he should reconsider.

"Still, we will leave it for you," Eliza said as the man brushed past her, his suspicious eyes flitting over her. "What are you doing here? Come to spy?"

Blake drew his wife back. "We were worried about you."

"No need." Graves swatted dirt from his stained and torn shirt. Cuts marred the skin on his arms and neck. "Unless you hear them and wish to help, it would be best if you didn't come at all." His dark glance roved over them. "Good. Just four of you." He wiped sweat from his forehead, leaving a streak. "There can never be six," he muttered, his expression suddenly tightening.

James and Hayden exchanged a glance that said they agreed the man was mad. Or at the very least, he couldn't count, though their fifth member, Thiago, now remained at the entrance as if ready to bolt at the first provocation.

The anxious twist of Graves's lips soon raised into a sinister grin. "I tried to stop you, you know."

"Stop us from what?" Eliza asked.

"From coming to Brazil. But I was wrong."

Hayden stepped toward the crazy man, his curiosity roused. "How did you try to stop us?"

A maniacal gleam crossed his eyes. "Don't you remember? The storm, the mists, the illness, the first mate's injury, the fire"—he paused, thinking—"oh, and the birds."

Of course Hayden remembered. That voyage from Charleston to Rio had been fraught with one odd disaster after another. Even Captain Barclay had commented that in all his years of sailing, he'd never seen such bad luck. Which was all it was. Just bad luck. "You cannot expect us to believe you caused any of that," Hayden said.

One brow arched in imperious delight. "You'd be surprised what kind of power is available for those willing to call upon it."

James rubbed the scar on his cheek. "There are only two types of power on this earth. The power of God and the power of the devil."

Graves chuckled. "Indeed, dear doctor, indeed."

"But why?" Blake asked. "Why would you want to stop us?"

"For revenge, of course!" Graves erupted in fury, fisting his hands. "I was to be a senator, then president someday. If not for the South seceding, I would have been!"

Whether it was the scorching heat, the stench, or the lack of food for days on end that had done it, Graves had gone undeniably insane.

"Someone had to pay, you see." Graves's hurried tone spiked with anger. "So I tried to destroy your hopes, your dreams, as you destroyed mine. But I was wrong. We were meant to come here." He waved a bruised, filthy hand over them. "Besides, you will soon suffer enough, and I will be more powerful than any president could be."

Blake gathered Eliza close. "Then, we will leave you be, sir."

Breaking free from her husband, she stepped toward Graves, extending a hand. "Mr. Graves, please come back with us. You aren't safe here."

"You are dabbling in things you don't understand," James said. "Dangerous things."

"Evil things." Thiago added from the entrance.

Eliza took another step. "Please, we care about you. Come back with us."

For a mere second, the evil glint in Graves's eyes softened, replaced by a look of pleading, as if a part of him, buried deep within, cried for help. But then it was gone, hardened into granite as black and infinite as a bottomless pit.

"Ah, but that's where you are wrong," he said. "You'll see. When I gain my power, I will crush your little colony to dust."

The next evening, Hayden sat whittling in the center of town, longing for some peace after a long day's work. But that was not to be. He could hear his father returning from his treasure hunt. The fiend's spurious laughter grated over Hayden—that gloating I-don't-find-you-amusing-but-I'll-laugh-anyway-to-win-your-favor chuckle that Hayden knew too well. Why? Because he had perfected it himself. Trying to ignore the grating sound, he chipped away at the piece of wood in his hand. He still didn't know what he was making. Other than a mess. But whittling kept his hands from doing what they longed to do—wringing his father's neck. Why hadn't the man fallen off a cliff or been bitten by a poisonous snake, or better yet, devoured by a wolf? Surely that would be a just end. But apparently God wasn't just, or surely He would have punished Patrick long ago.

Which meant it was still up to Hayden.

All around him, the townsfolk clustered in groups after supper, talking about the day's events and their plans for tomorrow. Both Blake and James had tried to engage Hayden in conversation, but his mood was too dour for company. He'd spent hours with them, chopping down trees for a barn and a dock, hoping the hard work would get his mind off of his situation. But all it had done was delay the inevitable confusion and despair that haunted his evening hours. The more Hayden sought to catch his father alone, the more people surrounded him like a fortress of worshipping toadies. It was as if God protected Patrick, while leaving his victims defenseless.

The odious man now sauntered into the clearing, a lady on each arm, conversing in his cavalier tone and looking none the worse for wear after a day of hunting gold. Dodd, on the other hand, followed behind him, carrying shovels and pick axes and appearing as if he'd wallowed for hours in the mud with pigs. Amazing. His father had even charmed Dodd into doing his work for him. Hayden scored another slice of wood and flicked it aside as colonists gathered to hear news of the treasure hunt.

A captive audience was the golden goose to a man like Patrick. Swinging about, his eyes twinkling, he began an embellished account of their adventures, drawing gasps from the ladies and admiring grunts from the men. Mr. Dodd, however, shook his head and circled the group to get his supper.

Hayden's own meal rebelled in his stomach. Rising, he slipped the knife into his belt and wood in his pocket and made his way to the edge of camp. Plunging into the jungle, he kept going until he could no longer hear his father's voice, until the familiar buzz and hum of night creatures suffused all other sounds. He sat on a log and breathed in the thick air, scented with orchids and lemons and musk. Dim light from a half-moon spread a dusting of silver on branches and leaves. Brazil truly was a beautiful place, teeming with life. But Hayden couldn't stay.

Once he got his revenge—in whatever form that took—he would go back home. In fact, depending on the type of revenge he exacted, he might be *forced* to go back home. The thought unnerved him, and he shifted on his seat. He would miss his new friends, his honest work. And most of all, he would miss Magnolia. But what choice did he have? Every time he looked at her, his mind conjured up a myriad of sordid images of her in his father's arms. Even worse, she seemed to be enjoying herself. Hayden shook the pictures from his head. No, he must start anew. Perhaps help his friend in his furniture shop in Savannah, learn how to survive on honesty and integrity rather than lies and deceit.

Like his father.

Visions of the man pranced tauntingly through Hayden's mind—his mischievous grin, swaggering gait—along with the wake of hapless victims fawning over his every witticism. Especially the females. Yet how was Hayden any different? He dropped his head into his hands, not wanting to consider the question, yet not able to avoid the suffocating truth of its answer. Crackling sounds echoed, louder and louder, finally fading into female moans and sobs. Hayden looked up. A mass of pearly moon-dust materialized in front of him, glittering in the starlight. It floated through the air like a cloud that had lost its way, uttering the woeful cries of a woman. Hayden could only stare at it, transfixed in confusion as it began to twirl and spin in a mad rush that soon took the shape and form of Miss Grayson.

Hayden swallowed. His heart raced.

"Hello, Joseph," she said, a vacant look in her once lustrous brown eyes.

Joseph Murphy, the name he'd used all those years ago.

"What? Nothing to say? The charming Joseph, with ever a witty retort on his lips, has suddenly gone silent?" She raised her chin, that pert little chin he had so adored—at least for a time.

"I'm sorry, Julianne."

"Oh, *now* you're sorry." Clutching her skirts, she sauntered about the clearing as if she were strolling through a ballroom. Yet not a twig snapped, not a leaf stirred beneath her silk slippers. "But you weren't sorry when you ran off with my dowry." She swirled to face him, her hooped-skirt bobbing. "Left me with a ruined reputation and no prospects."

Just as his father had done to Magnolia.

The words spun a tempest in Hayden's mind. Shame fisted in his throat, threatening to strangle him. He gripped his neck and forced himself to breathe. Julianne wasn't real. She was only a figment of his guilt-laden mind. Yet, as he stared at the agony folding her beautiful features, he suddenly wished she *were* real. Then he could tell her how sorry he was. Then he could somehow make up for what he'd done.

"What I did was wrong." He slowly rose.

"Wrong?" Her voice spiked, her eyes flashed. "It was more than wrong. It was cruel, heartless, and wicked. You don't know what happened to me, do you, Joseph? After you left?" Gathering her pink satin skirts, she floated across the clearing like a lily on a pond. "I never married, of course. Watched all my friends find love and have babies. But worse than that, I became the laughingstock of Williamsburg. A cursed woman whom the Yankees found easy prey when they stormed in to occupy our town."

Nausea bubbled in Hayden's gut. "No."

"Yes."

"I'm sorry." He stepped toward her, but she withdrew. "I didn't mean to. . . I didn't want to hurt you."

"Then why *did* you, Joseph? Why?" A tear spilled from the corner of her eye.

Visions didn't cry, did they? Hayden sank back onto the log. "I was trying to find my father."

"And you have finally found him, haven't you? A man after your own heart."

Hayden stared at the dirt. "No, I was only pretending to be like him, penetrating his social circles. It was the only way to find him."

He kicked a rock with his boot. How his mother would have hated that. "No!" He hung his head. "I'm nothing like him."

The swish of skirts sounded, and Julianne knelt before him, studying him. Her eyes, now devoid of tears, turned hard as quartz.

"Then you must kill him. It is the only way."

Up close, she looked so real. The shimmer of her skin in the moonlight, the wisps of hair dangling over her forehead, even the locket around her neck. "How will killing him help you?"

"He started this. He's the reason you swindled me, ruined my life. He should pay."

Which was exactly what Hayden had planned to do. Yet there was something familiar in Julianne's face. An expression. . .a madness. . . that brought a memory of Graves to mind.

Revenge. Was Graves's insanity the destiny for all those who sought revenge?

And what of Blake? The man had every reason to seek retribution from the Yankees, but he'd forgiven. The comparison between the two men shook Hayden to his core.

As if she could read his thoughts, Julianne's face contorted. Flames flickered in her hard eyes. "Kill him," she hissed. "It's what you've wanted your entire life. Now's your chance."

"I don't know what I want anymore."

"You fool! You weak, pathetic fool." She rose and brushed off her skirts, her face angular and harsh. But then it softened back into its familiar graceful curves. A glaze covered her eyes. "You must do it for me. The price for my forgiveness."

A breeze swept through the trees, swaying leaves and bringing shadows out from hiding. Dark mist slithered over the ground, swirled around her feet, and rose to circle her skirts like a cobra beneath its master's flute. And for the first time in his life, Hayden sensed pure evil. Dark, heavy, powerful, all-consuming. And with it came a heady lust, an irresistible yank on his heart to obey her words. To murder his father.

"Do it!" she shouted, her eyes fiery coals.

"Oh, God." Hayden dropped to his knees. "Help me!"

All went silent. All save the frogs and crickets and night herons. He lifted his gaze. Julianne was gone. So were the shadows. Instead, a spire of moonlight lit the spot where she had stood. "God?" Hayden's breath tangled in his throat. "Jesus, are you there?"

A breeze played upon his face, spinning through his hair and cooling the sweat on his neck. "You exist. All this time I thought you were a fable, a myth." Burning traveled from his throat to his eyes. He would not cry. He hadn't cried since his mother died.

"I'm so sorry, Lord. I've hurt so many people. Ruined so many lives." A tear escaped. He batted it away. "I don't deserve Your attention. I deserve nothing but judgment and pain."

Palm fronds fluttered, like angels laughing. No, not laughing, singing! Soft words sifted through his soul, "I love you, son. You are forgiven."

Son? No one had ever called Hayden that before.

A father of the fatherless, and a judge of the widows, is God in his holy habitation.

The verse blared in his mind from a time long ago when he'd sat in the back of a cold, dark church in Tennessee and listened to the first sermon he'd heard since his mother died. Yet now as an overwhelming feeling of love and belonging fell on him, he could not deny that God was present, wrapping His arms around the little orphan boy shivering and starving on the streets of Charleston.

God had been there all along. He'd always had a Father. One that would never abandon him.

Rising, he closed his eyes to the moonlight and allowed the wind to dry his tears.

He was a new man.

Chapter 32

Is that everything?" Magnolia corked the bottle of plantain tincture and placed it on the shelf, straightening the others beside it.

"Yes," Eliza said. "It's more than enough. However did I run this place without you those two weeks you were gone?" She stuffed a loose strand into her bun then wiped down the examining table. "You are such a huge help."

Magnolia smiled, feeling a lift in her heart for the first time in four days—four days since Patrick Gale had arrived in town and ruined her life. Again. Yet, in the meantime, she had more than proven her service to the colony—that she could earn her keep, take care of herself, and have no need for her parents' support. The realization was exhilarating. Or it would be if she weren't so melancholy. "Truly? Or are you just being kind?"

Eliza gave her a look of reprimand. "I wouldn't lie to you, Magnolia. You have a real knack for nursing. And you're a hard worker. At least you've become one since your trip to Rio."

Had she? Had she been that lazy before? "Don't tell my father that. He considers *work* akin to profanity." She chuckled.

"Good to hear you laugh again." Eliza threw the dirty cloth into a bucket.

Magnolia gazed out the window where the setting sun angled through palms and lined the floor with wavering strips of light. "As long as I don't think about things, I'm all right. Which is why I truly appreciate you allowing me to help in the clinic. It keeps my mind off my problems." Untying her apron, she drew it from her waist.

"Which one? Patrick or Hayden?" Eliza gave her a teasing smile.

"Both, I suppose. Though I'm relieved Patrick has been spending his days with Dodd hunting gold, sparing me the discomfort of his presence." Yet as relieved as she was of their absence, she'd been equally dismayed that Hayden had been absent as well.

"I don't know whether to pray that Patrick and Dodd find the gold soon, or that they never find it." Eliza began picking up dirty scissors, knives, needles, tweezers, and other medical instruments. "Hayden doesn't believe his father will stay long after they do."

Of course he wouldn't. Magnolia would bet her life the charlatan would break his promise and run off with any treasure he found, leaving her still indebted to her parents. But the worst of it was Hayden would leave as well, ever in pursuit of his blasted revenge.

Eliza touched Magnolia's arm. "Your parents shouldn't have blamed you for what happened. You were all fooled by the man."

"Perhaps." Magnolia tossed her dirty apron into a basket and looked down. "I don't know. But that's kind of you to say." She bit her lip. "But, then, you've always been kind to me, Eliza. Even when I blackmailed you for liquor on board the *New Hope*."

Eliza's golden eyes twinkled. "It all ended well. And your issue with drink? Has that ended well?" She picked up the tray of instruments and gave Magnolia a questioning look.

"Truth be told, I still struggle with it now and then."

The door flap swept open and Angeline entered, thankfully cutting the conversation short. Smiling at them both, she handed Eliza a bundle of dried herbs, while Stowy, her cat, circled the hem of her skirts. "Suma root. Complements of Mrs. Matthews. For your medicine chest."

"Wonderful." Setting down the tray, Eliza skirted the examination table and set the plants on a shelf. "Perhaps if we don't have too many patients tomorrow, Magnolia, I can show you how to crush these and create a tincture."

"I'd love to learn." Though Magnolia tried to interject excitement in her voice, her doleful tone drew Angeline's gaze.

"Why, Magnolia, I just came from the meeting area and I'd swear Hayden wears the same sour face you do," she said. "Perhaps you both suffer from the same malady?" She smiled.

Magnolia picked up the tray of instruments and carried it to the side table where a bucket of clean water waited. She hated that the entire town knew Hayden had broken off their courtship. She hated the whispers that ceased when she came near, the smirks, the looks of pity. She did not want to be pitied. *"A Scott is never pitied,"* her father always said. And besides, what's done was done.

"His father's appearance has upset him greatly," she answered Angeline.

"No doubt." Angeline twirled a lock of her russet hair. "As I'm sure it has upset you. I just don't see the point of you both denying your affections for each other."

"He doesn't want me anymore. Not after discovering I was engaged to his father. In fact, you can have him, Angeline. He's never hidden his interest in you." Magnolia flinched when her voice came out more clipped than she intended, but Angeline didn't seem to notice.

"His gaze follows *you* everywhere in camp. He doesn't even know I exist."

Forcing Angeline's words from her heart where they would only cause more pain, Magnolia raised her gaze to find both her friends staring at her curiously. A loose strand of hair tickled her shoulder, and she tucked it in place. "I must look a fright. And look at the dirt in my fingernails." She held them up before her.

"You always glow, Magnolia," Eliza said. "Surely you know that. Besides, a woman's beauty doesn't come from hairstyles or jewelry or clothing. It comes from within."

Magnolia studied Eliza, half expecting to see the old woman from the church materialize in place of her friend. But it was only Eliza, with the usual approval beaming from her eyes. So accepting, so loving of everyone. So unlike Magnolia. *Beauty comes from within.* Could it be true? Could everything she'd ever thought or ever learned be so completely wrong?

Scooping up Stowy, Angeline bundled the cat in her arms. "I quite agree, Eliza. True beauty is more than fripperies and finery. Thank goodness, because it's far too difficult to keep up appearances in this jungle."

"Isn't that the truth?" Eliza chuckled, placing the instruments in water. "I do miss a few of the finer things back home, hot baths, for one."

"And perfume," Angeline added.

"And being fitted for a new gown. . ." Eliza said.

"And wearing satin slippers with no fear of getting them muddy."

"And—"

"But how does one adorn one's inside?" Magnolia interrupted, drawing both their gazes.

Eliza approached and squeezed her hand. "Only God can do that. All you have to do is ask Him. He loves you, Magnolia. He formed you in your mother's womb to be unique and talented and beautiful and. . . well, just to be you."

Eliza's statement followed Magnolia as she made her way down the main street later that day. Was that what the old woman in the church was trying to tell her? That she had to turn to God? It was all too confusing. Though the scent of roasted fish permeated the air, her stomach knotted. She had no desire to eat. All she wanted was to find someplace alone where she could nurse her broken heart.

A child's laughter drew her gaze to Mr. Jenkins, one of the famers, coming home from working in the fields. His little girl, Henrietta, ran into his arms without a care about the layers of sweat and grim covering the man. He spun her around, showering her with kisses as her giggles rose to join the birdsong above them. Frozen in place, Magnolia watched as he lowered her to a bench and sat beside her, listening with rapt attention as she told him about her day. He didn't rush to clean off the filth from the fields or dash to get his supper. No, he sat and listened as if she were the most important thing in the world to him—his special princess. Mercy me, he didn't even notice that her dress was stained and her hair was a rat's nest! Nothing but love poured from his gaze onto his little girl. Tears flooded Magnolia's eyes. Was that how a father was supposed to treat his daughter? Not with harsh words and impossible expectations? But simple adoration?

The vision blurred before her, and she started on her way again, lowering her gaze lest others see her crying. She dipped into Sarah's hut, lit a lantern, then took it, along with her flask of pinga, and dove into the jungle. She needed time alone. Time to think, to sort things out, to plan. And to cry.

Shoving aside leaves, she entered her favorite spot by a small creek and sat on a boulder beside the rippling water, finally allowing her tears to flow. One by one they slid down her cheeks and leapt from her jaw into her lap. She swiped them away. What good did it do to cry? She stared at the brook, her eyes drawn to a small pool of calm water by her feet. Dare she take a peek? Or would it just distress her further? Either way she'd better decide before the setting sun stole the remaining light.

Leaning over, she cringed at the reflection and jerked back. Still old and ugly. And she'd been trying so hard to be kind and think of others! Helping out Eliza in the clinic, assisting Sarah with baby Lydia, working in the garden the other women had planted. Even carrying buckets of water from the river. But she was still ugly inside.

Uncorking the flask, she gulped the pinga. Burning spice sped down her throat and warmed her belly. She tipped the flask to her lips once again. Perhaps if she drank enough, the grotesque image would disappear from her mind.

Perhaps she should take her ugly self back to Georgia. Without Hayden, there was no point in staying in this uncivilized jungle. Yes, she had made friends—true friends—for the first time in her life. And she had employment—a trade. She was not useless as her father had always declared. But after tasting Hayden's love, how could she live in the same town with him day in and day out? Even if he did end up leaving, there were too many memories of him here.

And then there was Patrick. What if he didn't find his gold for months? How could she live in such close proximity with the monster who had ruined her life? It was too much to ask. If she could find a way home, she might be able to locate Samuel and at least have a chance at contentment and peace. And comfort. Not happiness anymore. She could never be happy with anyone but Hayden. She ground her fists on her forehead. "Oh." If only Patrick hadn't shown up and ruined everything!

Leaning back on the boulder, she plucked a leaf and fanned herself. "I'd kill him myself if I had the chance."

"Who's that, my dear?" Shoving leaves aside, Patrick Gale materialized out of the foliage and headed toward her.

"What are you doing here?" Setting down her flask, Magnolia jumped to her feet, feeling the rum crawl back up her throat. "Don't come any closer."

Yet Patrick continued onward, the ever-present grin on his lips. "Don't fret, my dear. I come as a friend not an enemy."

"You will always be my enemy."

"Always? I had hoped for a truce." Lantern light shifted over his face and sparked desire in his eyes. Eyes the same color as Hayden's yet devoid of the gleam that was uniquely his.

"You hope in vain, Martin, or Patrick, or whoever you are. Not another step. I'm warning you."

"Such threats. Tsk tsk. I well remember the days you longed to be near me. In my arms. With my lips on yours." He stopped before her—too close—eyeing her lips as if they were made of cake and he wanted a taste.

He smelled of the same lavender-spice cologne he'd always worn, and she wondered how he could still have some left after months in the jungle. But Martin had always been a resourceful man. She stepped back, fear clamping her gut. She shoved it aside, choosing anger instead. "Do you honestly expect me to run into your arms after you lied to me, cheated me, ruined my family, and broke my heart?"

"No." He fingered his graying goatee. "But you can't deny there is still a certain attraction between us." He reached up to touch her cheek.

She backed away. "I will deny it with my dying breath. Now, leave."

An animal growled in the distance, reminding her of the wolf that had attacked her. She shivered and stared at the beast hunting her now. His face was drawn in sorrow. But she knew it was a ruse. Everything the man did was a ruse to get what he wanted.

"I have come to apologize and to tell you I've changed. Can't a person change?"

Instead of charming, he looked sinister in the shadows of light and dark. Sinister and miserable. And old. What had she ever seen in him? "Some people do change, I suppose. Others never will."

He pressed the hair above his ears into place. "I want to make things up to you, dearest."

"Don't call me that!" Crossing her arms over her waist, she gazed over the swirling brook, envying its soothing dance. "I am in the middle of a savage jungle with no money, no prospects, and no future. All because of you. I doubt you can ever repay me."

"Ah, but I can. When I find the gold, I fully intend to repay your parents every dollar I stole."

She snapped her gaze back to his. "I hope that you do, sir, but I shan't count on it. As I shan't count on anything you say ever again."

He folded his lips in a smile—a patronizing smile—as if he had come to her rescue just in the nick of time. "We could run away together. Back to the States. You could have beautiful gowns and jewels and ladies' maids to service your every whim." He scanned her, frowning. "It would seem my offer could not have come a moment too soon. I've never seen you so out of sorts, dearest." He brushed something from his coat sleeve. "The jungle is no place for a lady like you."

Memories of their time together invaded like a cold mist. Magnolia's stomach shrank. She'd been so young, so impressionable, so eager to please this sophisticated man, that she'd allowed him to critique her every move, her every word, as well as her appearance.

Just like her father.

He leaned forward and sniffed. A victorious grin lifted his perfectly coiffed mustache. "I see you've done away with your prudish ways and have finally taken to drink."

"You thought me a prude?" She gave a bitter laugh. "Is that why you constantly pushed me to savor your spirits? Or was it to lower my defenses so you could have your way with me?"

He sighed. "But it never worked, did it?" Drawing a flask from inside his waistcoat, he tipped it toward her. "Scotch?"

Magnolia licked her lips and looked away.

Unscrewing the cap, he took a sip. "If you can find it in your heart to forgive me, dearest, perhaps we can start over?" He slipped the flask back into his pocket. "Begin a courtship anew. You always were my favorite."

"Your favorite what? Victim?" Magnolia snorted, suddenly wondering what *his* reflection would look like in the pond. "You sicken me, sir. I'd rather die a thousand deaths than tolerate one touch from you!"

"*Tant dramatique!*" The salacious glimmer in his eyes brightened. "I always loved your passion." He leaned toward her. "Perhaps a kiss for old time's sake?"

Magnolia raised her hand to slap him. He caught it and tugged it behind him, pinning her against his chest. Scotch and lavender combined in a repulsive odor that stung her nose. Her head spun. Her legs wobbled. She struggled to free herself and cried out. He grabbed her other arm and held it down. Lips descended on hers.

Then he was gone. Disappeared in a mad swoosh. Magnolia stumbled to catch her balance and peered into the shadows to see Hayden shoving Patrick to the ground.

"Haven't you done enough?" Hayden growled, then picked the man up by his lapels and shoved a fist into his gut.

Coughing, Patrick bent like a snapped twig and held up a hand to stay his son. When he recovered his breath, he stood upright and chuckled. *Chuckled!* Though Magnolia could see the hesitancy in his eyes. "Well played, son. Well played. But I had no intention of hurting her."

"Do not call me that." Hayden seethed, snapping hair from his face. "Now leave before I finish what I started the other night."

Patrick held up his palms. "You would murder an unarmed man?"

"You would ravish an innocent woman?"

Magnolia didn't know whether to be elated that Hayden had come to her rescue or frightened at the ensuing battle. She scanned the clearing for something with which to strike Patrick.

Hayden took a step toward his father, hands fisted at his sides. "Go!"

One corner of Patrick's lips twitched. "Very well. Calm yourself, boy. I'm leaving." Straightening his coat, he tipped his head toward Magnolia and started away. Hayden unclenched his fists and glanced at Magnolia. Just one tiny glance that took his eyes from Patrick for but a second. And the beast took advantage and slugged Hayden across the jaw.

His head jerked to the side. He stumbled backward. Yet even before Hayden recovered, he pummeled his father in the chest, knocking the man off balance. Grabbing his coat to keep him upright, Hayden slugged him in the stomach. A left and then a right before landing a final blow to his head. The vile man once again fell to the dirt.

Patrick rolled across the leaves, reaching inside his coat. Scrambling, turning, grunting, he finally leapt to his knees. Blood seeped from lips that formed a slow grin—a devilish grin that seemed to have a life of its own in the flickering light. Plucking a pistol from within his coat, he leveled it at Hayden. Hayden froze. The gun cocked. Magnolia's breath halted. Patrick pulled the trigger.

Chapter 33

The sharp crack of Patrick's pistol reverberated in Hayden's ears. Magnolia screamed. Gun smoke pinched his nose. Sweat dribbled down his neck as a numbness crept up his legs, his thighs, and onto his torso. He patted his chest, searching for the wound that surely must be there, all the while wondering why he felt no pain. Perhaps the absence was God's way of sparing those who were dying from last-minute agony. Yet, when he raised his hands, no blood appeared on them anywhere.

His father had missed.

Dashing to Hayden, Magnolia seemed equally shocked, her teary eyes scanning him from head to toe before falling into his arms. He absorbed her like a root absorbed water, her feminine scent wiping away the anger and smoke from his nose. It was good to hold her again.

Tossing down his gun, Patrick cursed and drew a knife.

Nudging Magnolia behind him, Hayden faced his father. "Killing your own son? I thought at least *that* was beneath you, Patrick."

"You've become a nuisance, Hayden. Besides, you already tried to kill your own father, so what does that make you?" Moonlight glinted on the blade as he flipped the knife expertly in his hand. "And it appears you've stolen my lady's affections. An insult that cannot go unchallenged."

Fingers twitching at the chance to put an end to this, Hayden slowly drew the knife from his belt. He could kill his father right here and now. And what better excuse? The man had assaulted Magnolia and shot at Hayden. No one would blame Hayden at all.

Patrick circled him, his eyes obsidian in the darkness—empty, hard obsidian that reminded Hayden of the vision of Julianne, the way her eyes had changed, the presence of evil surrounding her.

"Stop this at once! Both of you!" Magnolia shouted, her voice broken and desperate.

Patrick charged, his blade gleaming. Hayden sidestepped then barreled into the man's side, sending them both to the ground. Round and round in the mud and leaves they went. Patrick groaned and grunted, his spittle spraying. Pain sliced Hayden's arm. Releasing his father, he leapt back and jumped to his feet, holding back the blood beneath his sleeve.

"Hayden, no!" Magnolia cried.

Patrick bounced up with more agility than his age should have allowed. Brushing leaves from his coat, he stretched his neck. A malicious grin alighted on his lips. "How does it feel to have your father's cast offs?" He gestured toward Magnolia.

"How dare you?" Magnolia stomped her foot, bent to pick up a rock, and tossed it at Patrick. He ducked, chuckling. Groaning, she went off in search of another while Hayden assessed his enemy.

"If you're fool enough to release such a treasure what is that to me?" Hayden dove for the man, seeing nothing but the path from his knife to Patrick's heart.

But Patrick blocked that path with a quick thrust of his arm and then twisted to ram his blade toward Hayden's stomach. He would have succeeded in planting a fatal wound if Hayden hadn't lunged backward. As it was, Patrick's attack loosened the knife from Hayden's hand. It fell with an ominous thud to the dirt. Heart in his throat, Hayden searched the ground to retrieve it, but darkness kept it hidden.

"Aha!" Patrick sauntered toward him, his expression one of ravenous glee.

A flash of blue calico blocked him from view. "Stop this nonsense, Patrick!" Magnolia pounded on his father's chest. "He is your son. You beast! You horrible beast!"

Hayden charged toward her. Foolish woman. The man would take no thought to kill her if she became a nuisance. He reached out to shove her aside when Patrick grabbed her wrists and locked them together. "Ah, my dearest, how utterly quaint." She tried to kick him, but he sprang out of her way. "The woman fights better than you do, Hayden!"

The sight of Patrick's knife gleaming in the moonlight so close to Magnolia's throat kept Hayden in place. "Leave her be. Your fight is with me."

"As you wish." Patrick released Magnolia with a violent shove, sending her crashing to the ground in a puff of skirts.

Fury took charge. Hayden fisted Patrick in the stomach. His groan was but momentary. Leaning over, he grabbed something from the ground and then rushed Hayden. Hayden could barely react before something struck him over the head. His vision clouded. His legs liquefied. And he dropped to the ground, fighting to keep conscious.

Tossing a rock aside, Patrick pounced on him, jamming Hayden's shoulders into the dirt. Overhead, branches and leaves spun around a sprinkling of stars. He heard Magnolia's faint sobs. A glimmer flashed in his eyes and pain seared his neck. His father's face filled his vision, crinkled in rage. "Why did you have to find me? Why didn't you leave me alone? Now, you force my hand."

Hayden knew it was all over. His father would kill him. *God help me!*

His head began to clear. His strength returned. His father still hovered over him, knife to Hayden's throat, hesitating. Was there some goodness in the man after all?

"Sorry," was all Patrick said before he inhaled as if to gather strength for the task. In a burst of energy, Hayden kneed him in the groin and shoved him aside. Moonlight flashed on the knife as Hayden plucked it from his father's hand and held it to his throat.

"One move. One breath. And it will be your last."

Lantern light circled them as if they were performers in some gruesome play.

Terror etched across Patrick's eyes.

This was the moment Hayden had waited for his entire life. The moment he had planned, sought after, dreamed of during long, sleepless nights. This was the moment he would honor his mother's memory. This was the moment he would have his revenge.

The blade quivered over his father's coarse skin.

Magnolia groaned. Her skirts swished. If the man had hurt her!

A stream of blood trickled from the tip of the blade. Just another inch and Hayden would cut the artery that fed this vile man's brain.

FORGIVE.

Forgive? Had Hayden heard correctly? Forgive the death of his mother? Forgive the years he'd spent on the street, eating scraps not fit for rats. Forgive the frostbite and lice and sores and a belly that had clawed up his throat at the mere scent of food. Yet. . .hadn't God forgiven Hayden of all his wicked acts? Until now, Hayden had no idea how difficult that task must have been for God—forgiving those who hurt Him, who reject Him and renounce Him. Sending His own Son to die in their stead—Hayden's stead.

Hayden swallowed, gripping the knife tighter. Could Hayden send someone he loved to their death for this man? No.

But what of justice, God?

I AM JUSTICE.

Patrick swallowed, deepening the cut. His breath heightened.

Hayden's fingers trembled. Sweat dripped onto his father's chest. Hayden was not God. Not even close. He couldn't forgive him.

I LIVE IN YOU.

He ground his jaw together so hard he thought it would burst. But still he waited, seeking the strength of his new Father. If God *was* inside him somewhere, that strength would come.

And it did. Pity replaced anger. Sorrow replaced the need for revenge. And he shoved off his father and stood.

"Go." He waved the blade toward the jungle. "Go!"

Patrick struggled to rise and, without a word, dashed into the leaves.

After ensuring he was gone, Hayden searched for Magnolia but found only a lump of shadowy skirts. Terrified, he knelt beside her, reaching for her, praying she wasn't injured. Arms emerged from the darkness and looped around his neck. "Oh, Hayden, I thought he would kill you."

"So did I." He chuckled, feeling the blood trickle down his neck beneath his shirt. "Are you hurt?"

"I must have hit my head. I couldn't move. By the time I was finally able to sit, you held a knife to Patrick's throat."

"Can you walk?"

"I think so."

Hayden wrapped an arm around her waist and lifted her to her feet. She stumbled and leaned on him as he led her back to the creek and lowered her to a boulder. Grabbing the lantern, he examined her head. No blood. Just a slight bump. The sight caused his anger to rise again. He forced it down.

"I'm all right, Hayden, but you. . ." She touched the bloody gash on his arm and gasped when she saw his neck. Pulling a handkerchief from her pocket, she dipped it in the creek and dabbed the wound, her face puckering in angst.

He stayed her hand and engulfed it in his, searching her eyes, longing for things to be the way they used to be. She cupped his cheek, running her fingers over his jaw. "You didn't kill him. It's what you've always wanted. Why?"

Releasing her hand, Hayden stood. He drew a deep breath and stared at the moonlit water whirling and bubbling down the creek bed. "I've come to realize revenge only causes more heartache. Forgiveness is better." He shifted his shoulders and smiled. "Quite freeing, actually."

"Forgiveness? I never would have expected you to say such a thing."

"God has changed me."

"God? Now I know I'm dreaming." She stood and pressed the cloth to his arm. "We should have Eliza look at this."

He placed his hand over hers. "You took care of me when I had far worse injuries."

Her eyes lifted to his, liquid sapphires brewing with turmoil. "Would that we had never left the jungle, Hayden."

He'd give anything if that were true. If they could both go back to a time before Patrick appeared. Before everything changed. But they couldn't. And despite her care for him now, despite the look of love burning in her eyes, they never could. "I'm leaving Brazil."

Jaw dropping, she jerked from his touch. "Leaving? Why?" But then her hand was on his again, sudden joy lighting her face. "Take me. We'll go together. Like we planned."

Hayden shook his head and looked away, not wanting to see the pain in her eyes—not wanting to see his own pain reflected there. "I can't."

"I don't understand." Her voice etched with desperation.

Hayden made his way to the creek and stared over the water flowing past in peaks and valleys, much like his life. "Every time I look at you, I see you in my father's arms."

"Well stop seeing that, you stubborn fool! And see me only in *your* arms."

"Would that it were that easy." He faced her and was sorry he did. She'd never looked so lost, so completely and utterly lost. Not because of the dirt blotching her face. Not because of her hair tumbling over her shoulders. But because of the look of desperation, of hopelessness in her eyes. "You are a constant reminder of him. I've wasted fifteen years thinking of that man. I need to forget him for the next fifteen."

"He and I were engaged less than a year. Nothing untoward happened between us."

"I know that." Against his better judgment, he caressed her cheek. So soft. He never wanted to forget it. "You are a lady through and through."

She leaned into his hand and closed her eyes. A soft sigh spilled from her lips. Before they drew tight and she tore away from him. "So, God helps you forgive him, but you cannot forgive me!"

"There's nothing to forgive, Princess."

"You have no right to call me that. Not anymore." She took up a pace, bunching her skirts with her fists.

Hayden sighed. "I'm truly sorry." More sorry than she knew. For if he didn't leave soon, he was sure he'd toss aside his resolve and take her in his arms. But now he'd sparked her temper. Good. Her ire would aid him greatly.

"Sorry?" She shot him a feral look. "You are no better than my father—punishing me for succumbing to Patrick's charms!" A tiny vein pulsed in her neck. "And just like Patrick, you ask to court me one minute and the next you trample my affections beneath your traitorous hooves. You think you are different from your father. You are not!" She halted, spearing him with her contempt. "You are a man who lures women to fall in love with you only to break their hearts." The anger faded and the tears began. Grabbing her skirts, she took the lantern and darted from the clearing. Leaves swallowed her up like darkness swallowing light.

Chapter 34

James plopped the open book down on Blake's desk and pointed to the lines of Hebrew he'd finally managed to translate. "You need to know this."

"What? More ancient prophecies? More riddles we can't solve?" Blake laid down his pen and rose, stretching the kinks out of his back. "It's far too beautiful a morning for such dismal tidings." He glanced out the window where the rising sun flung spires of emerald through the jungle, stirring its creatures to life. "Besides, we need to weed the fields before it gets too hot. Then we can work on more irrigation troughs and start on the cane mill." Blake studied him. "You haven't slept, have you?"

"No." James rubbed his eyes and stared at the elegant Hebrew letters. Letters that couldn't have been penned by anyone other than a Hebrew scholar or a learned man. Certainly not the cannibals who had built the temple. "I had to figure this out."

Circling his desk, Blake shoved the book aside and leaned back on its surface. His eyes filled with concern. "You've become far too obsessed with these ancient fables."

James cocked a brow. "That's what they say about the Bible too."

Blake frowned. "Indeed." He glanced at the page and released a heavy sigh. "But this is not God's Word."

"No. But it means something. I know it. I feel it in my Spirit. Something important."

"Very well." Blake rose and walked to the window where a breeze brought the scent of mandioca cakes and boiled banana. James's stomach stirred. He'd been so caught up in the translation, he had skipped supper last night.

"What have you discovered?" Blake turned and gripped the back of his chair with both hands.

"From what I can gather, the judgment of the Four refers to four beings of enormous power. The first half of the book describes a battle that took place. The Four lost the battle, were judged, and then locked beneath the earth in chains." He glanced up at Blake. "The same story told by the pictures painted along the tunnel walls."

"But you don't know that for sure. Thiago could have guessed or even fabricated the story to match the book."

"He didn't know what was in the book."

"Hmm." Blake stared at the ancient manuscript. "So, I assume these beings were locked in the alcoves we found in the bottom chamber?"

"Yes. But, as you saw, their chains are broken. Do you remember their names?"

"Deception and Delusion."

James nodded.

"So, you're saying these beings were freed somehow?" Blake asked.

"That's what I'm thinking." James ran a hand through his hair, trying to curb his excitement. "Haven't we all been seeing visions lately? Delusions? Deceptions?"

Blake huffed. "Oh, come now, you don't think. . ."

"I do." James took up a pace, something he'd been doing all night long. "Something or someone has been reading our minds, conjuring up visions from our past, visions that are meant to torment."

"I don't know." Blake released the chair and rubbed his sore leg. "It sounds a bit farfetched. So, why can't we see these beings?"

"They live in the spirit realm. . .like angels and demons."

Blake snorted. "And the other two?"

"Hopefully still locked up." James halted as a breeze stirred the papers on Blake's desk. "You *do* remember that Graves was digging farther below."

"Humph." Blake eyed him with understanding. "All right, let's say I believe this nonsense. How were these powerful beings freed in the first place?"

"I'm not sure. But I believe this next section"—James planted a finger on the open page—"will tell me. I just can't quite decipher it." He scratched his head.

"And you think Graves is trying to release the other two?"

"I wouldn't put it past the man."

Blake rubbed his chin, lines furrowing on his forehead. "Continue your translation and keep me informed if you discover anything else. A year ago I would have laughed at all this, but now after what I've seen, after my encounter with God, I do believe there is another realm we cannot see."

"Indeed, the Bible speaks of it often."

"As I have discovered in my readings." Blake's smile soon faded beneath a sigh weighted with responsibility. "Speak about this to no one but me."

James nodded, happy his friend didn't think him a fool. He was about to thank him when one of the night watchmen stormed into the hut, his face aglow with excitement. "There are three men heading toward our town, Colonel. And one of them looks like Captain Barclay!"

James and Blake exchanged a puzzled look. The man who had captained the ship that brought them from Charleston to Rio? But as soon as they saw the old sea dog's ruddy, bearded face emerge from the greenery, hearty greetings were exchanged. In fact, everyone in town soon gathered around to welcome the captain and his mates, anxious for news from home.

"I didn't expect you back so soon, Captain," Blake said as everyone clustered near the meeting shelter to partake of breakfast and drill the seaman with questions.

"Nor did I!" Barclay laughed and drew off his neckerchief to dab his forehead. "I feel like a pig roasting on a spit! Is it always so hot here?"

James laughed as did many of the colonists. "You get used to it."

"I won't be here long enough, I hope," he said. "Ah, but yes, I picked up my cargo in New Orleans, delivered it to Norfolk and then passed by Charleston for another group of colonists headed toward Brazil. I just dropped them off in Rio and thought I'd gather your mail from the immigration office and bring it to you." He plopped a piece of mango into his mouth and groaned his pleasure as juice dribbled into his beard. "So here I am!" He reached into his pouch, withdrew a packet of letters, and began reading off names.

James hung back, sipping his coffee. There'd be nothing for him, of course. He had no one back home who would be writing to him.

His gaze landed on Angeline. She sat beneath the bamboo roof of the meeting house, her apron still on from helping prepare breakfast, a forlorn look on her comely face. He longed to know her story, for it appeared she had no one at home either. Nor did Blake or Eliza, though they seemed to be enjoying the colonists' excitement. Hayden was leaning on a tree at the edge of the clearing. James had heard the man intended to leave again, and he was sad for it. But he could understand in light of his father's presence. Would that Patrick Gale would leave instead, but they couldn't force the issue. They'd left the South to find freedom and it wouldn't be right to dictate who could stay and who couldn't.

"Miss Magnolia Scott. Magnolia Scott!" Captain Barclay shouted, and the lady emerged from the crowd to retrieve her letter, a look of confusion on her face.

Magnolia gripped the letter, still not believing the return address: Samuel Wimberly, 235 Washington Street, Atlanta, Georgia, United States. Her fingers began to shake as she left the others to find a quiet place to read.

My dearest Magnolia,

When I heard you had immigrated to Brazil, I could hardly believe it. What possessed your parents to drag you to such an uncivilized post? I sincerely hope it was not because of the way things ended between us, for I have been wallowing in misery ever since. The despicable war stole away the years we should have been together. But now that hostilities are at an end, at least the formal kind, I have found myself in a position of great influence in aiding the North as they rebuild our precious South. Great influence and great wealth, my dear. Enough to provide for you and your family in the manner in which you were accustomed before the unfortunate incident with that incorrigible confidence man. Do write back to tell me you'll return and marry me. Better yet, send no post but hop on the ship that delivered this letter and come back to me post haste. I wait with great anticipation to see your lovely face again.

You are ever in my fondest dreams,
Samuel Wimberly III Esquire.

"Oh my." Magnolia's mother flung a hand to her mouth as she perused the letter Magnolia had reluctantly handed her. Curiosity had driven her to Magnolia's side within minutes of receiving the post, had opened her mouth to finally speak to her. Something she hadn't done in days under the watchful eye of her husband.

"This is wonderful news! Just wonderful!" Her mother squealed. "I knew he wouldn't forget you."

"Why are you speaking to her?" Magnolia's father burst around the corner of the hut. "I told you—"

Giddy with delight, her mother shoved the letter toward him, stopping him in his tracks. "What's this?" he puffed out, his chin doubling as he perused it.

Magnolia waited while he read, her mind still whirling in shock and confusion. She'd never thought she'd hear from Samuel again. Mercy me, she hadn't even been sure he'd take her back if she *had* managed to return home. But this. That he missed her and still wanted her! It was wonderful news.

Wasn't it? It wouldn't be wonderful if Hayden loved her and still wanted her. The news would bear no effect on her whatsoever, except the pain at writing Samuel a letter of rejection. But that was only a dream.

"That settles it." Magnolia's father slapped the paper. His smile appeared at odds with his normally flat lips "We head home immediately!"

"This is my decision." Magnolia straightened her shoulders. "And besides, you disowned me."

"For accepting the courtship of that nincompoop!" He waved the letter toward the center of town. "This changes everything."

"If I accept, it does, yes." For once Magnolia returned her father's pointed stare. Yet no fear crawled up her spine at the fury blazing in his eyes.

"Surely you aren't still considering receiving the attentions of that ghastly man! Why, he's the son of the beast who ruined us."

"I'm well aware of that, Father." Despite that sordid fact, Magnolia would have Hayden if he wanted her. She hugged herself as the sound of laughter and gaiety drifted from the meeting area of town.

Her mother laid a hand on her arm. Was it Magnolia's imagination or were there more streaks of gray in her mother's brown hair since last she saw her? "We hear he's leaving town anyway, dear. Abandoning you just like his father did."

She tugged from her mother and backed away. "He's not abandoning me. He's hurt and confused." Then why did it feel like a boulder just dropped in her stomach?

"This is what you want!" Her father clenched his jaw to keep from shouting. "You've been complaining about coming to Brazil from the moment we set foot on the ship. You tried to sabotage the voyage, for Pete's sake. And all your poor mother and I have heard since we arrived here is how miserable you are."

"Then, why did you take me away from Samuel in the first place?"

"You know very well we couldn't locate him after the war."

"And he didn't have enough money or power to suit you. Odd how you've changed your mind now that he does." Magnolia cocked her head. She'd never spoken to her father with such an imperious tone. She'd always been so afraid of him. So fearful of his disapproval. But something had changed within her. And she found it exhilarating!

His dark eyes narrowed but not before she caught a hint of pain within them. "You've acquired a sharp tongue these past few days."

"I've acquired far more than that, Father. Confidence, for one. Freedom, for another. And along with both the realization that I can take care of myself."

"Bah!" He folded the letter and handed it back to her.

Magnolia took it as her mother's pleading eyes shifted between them. "Please don't quarrel. Not when we've received such good news."

"Your mother is right." Her father expelled his fury on a long sigh. "Let us put things behind us, dumpling. Finally, we can leave this jungle and live the life we were destined to live."

Magnolia didn't miss the use of her pet name, the one he used to call her when she was young and still in his favor. Nor did she miss the slight catch in his throat. For a moment, a brief, happy moment, he had looked at her like he used to before Patrick came into their lives. She swallowed down a burst of emotion. Perhaps things could be mended between her and her father. Perhaps he loved her just a little. She'd already made up her mind to return home anyway. Even if Hayden left, Patrick would still be here, and she couldn't stand to be in the same town with that man.

She glanced at the letter in her hand. She had loved Samuel once, hadn't she?

"What if Patrick finds gold?" she asked her father.

"Then he can send it to us. I'm sure Blake will see to it." She'd never seen her father's expression so soft, so placating. How quickly the power had shifted between them.

With or without the gold, if she married Samuel, her debt to her parents would be paid. And the idea of sleeping in a proper feather bed, of having steaming sudsy baths, a wardrobe full of the latest fashions, and a bevy of servants to wait on her every need was not without some appeal. No bugs. No thirst. No excruciating heat. She looked at her hands, once soft and white, now bruised and scraped. No mud. No hard work.

No purpose. No fulfillment. No love.

"Darling." Her mother tucked a strand of hair into her bun. "We must get you married before the bloom of youth is gone. Or it will be too late."

The bloom of youth, the bloom of youth, the words chanted over and over in Magnolia's mind as she strolled through a field of spring flowers, brushing her fingers over their colorful petals. Aquamarine, purple, gold, vermillion, amber, crimson—a thousand shades like dots of paint swaying on a canvas of green. A gentle breeze refreshed her skin and fluttered the delicate curls at her neck. She closed her eyes and breathed in the perfume-scented air. Sunlight blanketed her in warmth. Was there ever a more beautiful sight? Clutching her skirts, she ran across the field, dancing and laughing as the soft blooms tickled her stockings. Near breathless with glee, she stopped to pick one particularly beautiful blossom and drew it to her nose. A mixture of lilac and vanilla delighted her senses as she examined the crimson and orange petals, admiring their beauty and their silky feel.

The bloom of youth.

The flower began to shrivel in her hand. The petals browned and curled inward, then wilted into parched folds, drooping from the stem. Tossing down the blossom, Magnolia mourned the loss of such beauty when suddenly all the flowers around her began to brown and wilt and shrivel into dry, wrinkled twigs. Within minutes, the field became a crackling desert.

A chilled wind whipped the hem of her gown and blew the dried flowers away as if they'd never existed. Leaving nothing but gray, cracked ground. Leaving Magnolia all alone. In a dry and barren place. An ugly place. A tear slipped down her cheek.

A white speck appeared in the distance, gliding toward her. A person. A lady. The lady Magnolia had met in the church in Rio. The beautiful version with her glittering white robe, shimmering golden hair, and a face that would put Helen of Troy to shame. Halting before Magnolia, she smiled.

"Favour is deceitful and beauty is vain, but a woman that feareth the Lord, she shall be praised." Each word was as crisp and resonant as the plucking of a harp string.

"What does that mean?" Magnolia asked. "What happened to the flowers?"

"For what is your life? It is even a vapour, that appeareth for a little time, and then vanisheth away."

The woman smiled again and Magnolia smiled back, sensing only kindness, not judgment in her peaceful expression.

"Why are you telling me this?"

She raised a small mirror to Magnolia's face.

Magnolia turned her head. "I don't want to see."

"You must, child. You must." Grabbing Magnolia's chin she forced her to look at the hideous, wrinkled reflection. "This is—"

"I know. I know. This is my true appearance. What's inside of me." Magnolia squeezed her eyes shut against the sight and began to sob.

"Look again, child."

Magnolia shook her head. "No. Take it away."

"Look again."

Slowly prying her eyes open, Magnolia noticed the woman had flipped the mirror around to the other side. Beauty, pure beauty like she'd never seen before, stared back at her. The woman in the mirror glowed. She sparkled like a diamond, her skin luminescent, her hair spun silk, her eyes pools of glittering sapphires.

She couldn't pull her gaze away. "Who is she?"

"This is how God sees you when you turn to Him. When you accept the sacrifice of His Son, Jesus, you are cleansed, purified. You become His beautiful princess. Man looks on the outward appearance, but God looks at the heart."

Magnolia woke with a start, the lady's words echoing in her mind. *God looks on the heart. God looks on the heart.* A dream. A bizarre dream. Glancing to make sure she hadn't woken Sarah and Lydia, she swung her legs over the cot and rubbed her eyes.

Hadn't she discovered recently that she was more than a beautiful face? That she had value beyond her appearance. Besides, she was no fool. She knew her outward appearance would fade one day, that the bloom of youth would shrivel as her mother had said. And if Magnolia focused only on that, spent her time perfecting only that, what would be left when it was gone? Wasn't her soul, her character, more important? More lasting? Something that would never wrinkle or fade or die? But would only become more beautiful?

She'd once thought Patrick handsome but now that his true heart was revealed, she found him repulsive. And what of Sarah? She was no beauty and yet, she was the sweetest woman Magnolia had ever known, and more beautiful for it. Magnolia's heart shrank as she wondered how people truly saw her.

All these years her father, and oft times her many suitors as well, had spoken only of her appearance: complimenting, commending only her outside. Seeing her beauty as her only value. Making her believe she had no other redeeming qualities.

Rising, she grabbed her flask and tiptoed out of the hut, plopping on the bench.

"Oh, Jesus. I've been so wrong. About You. About myself."

She sipped the pinga and gazed up at the few stars peeking at her through the leaves above. "Do you truly see me as beautiful as I was in that second reflection?"

Wind stirred leaves by her feet into an exotic dance that tickled her legs. She giggled. "Is that You, God?"

"Precious one. Beautiful one."

Falling to her knees, Magnolia couldn't help the tears that streamed down her face. She tipped the flask to her lips again when the words "You don't need that anymore" flowed like warm water over her soul. Corking the flask, she set it on the ground and bowed her head.

"All this time I never spoke to You unless I wanted something. I never thought You cared. What a waste." She wiped her moist cheeks. "I'm sorry for being such a spoiled, vain, selfish girl. I don't want to be that way anymore. I want to be beautiful on the inside, not just the outside."

A whippoorwill sang in the distance as a sensation filtered through her. She had always been loved, regardless of what she looked like or what she'd done or what she would ever do. God's love was a gift that carried no conditions, no prerequisites, no debt. And even before she'd been born, He knew her. He'd fashioned her in her mother's womb as Eliza had said: special, unique, beautiful, and valuable.

And for the first time in her life, she felt all of those things as God's presence enveloped her.

Chapter 35

So you're going to let her get on that ship and sail out of your life?" Blake asked.

Hayden rubbed his aching eyes and stared at his two friends who had barged into his hut before the sun even had a chance to rise.

"You tell us you gave your life to God, forgave your father, released your need for revenge, which I'm very happy to hear, by the way"—James crossed beefy arms over his chest—"and now you're going to lose the woman God gave you to love. Just because of your foolish pride."

Hayden suddenly regretted telling Blake and James about his encounter with the Almighty. He wouldn't have even mentioned it if they hadn't insisted on knowing why he'd changed his mind about seeking revenge on his father and had decided to leave.

"Besides, if you're planning on going back to the States anyway, why not sail with Captain Barclay instead of walking to Rio?" Candlelight flickered mischief in James's eyes. "Not that I want you to leave. Not that I want either of you to leave. But if you're on the same ship with Magnolia, at least there's more of a chance you'll come to your senses."

"Or do something I'll regret the rest of my life."

"Like marry the lady? Why would that be so bad?"

"You don't understand." Hayden flung his shirt over his head and tucked it into his trousers. He'd hoped to sneak away that morning without anyone seeing. He'd said his good-byes to those that mattered the night before, painful enough as *that* was. More painful than he'd ever thought leaving people could be. Afterward, he'd had a fitful night of staring at the bamboo and palm fronds over his head, listening to the hoot of a nearby owl and the distant growls of jungle predators. A night of waiting for the first glow of dawn to give him permission to rise and slip away. But his friends had cornered him before he'd had a chance.

"I understand more than you think." The lines in Blake's forehead deepened as they always did when he was concerned.

Hayden studied him. Perhaps the colonel did know about revenge and forgiveness and the love of a decent woman. But his life had turned out well. His hopes had been realized. Hayden's hopes never would be. A breeze whipped through the window, ripe with the scent of orange blossoms and rain.

"She's leaving because she doesn't think you want her," James said.

Sitting on his cot, Hayden pulled on his boots. "She's leaving because she will finally get to marry her rich solicitor like she's always wanted." The news had carved a hole in his heart while at the same time giving him the peace of knowing she'd finally be happy.

Blake marched to the window, fists at his waist. "What other choice have you given her?"

"She could stay with the colony. Work in the clinic." Even as he said it, Hayden remembered how determined she was to repay her debt to her parents. Another reason to marry this Wimby fellow. He ran his hands through his hair and grabbed his only possession, his knapsack containing his knife, pistol, canteen, and the few supplies he'd purchased in Rio.

James released a heavy sigh and rubbed the scar on his cheek. "You could stay with the colony too. Why run away if she is gone?"

"You seem to forget my father is still here."

"If what you say about him is true, he won't be here for long."

Indeed. The man would either find his gold and leave or give up and move on to the next conquest. Regardless, even if his father left, New Hope was too full of memories. Hayden would see Magnolia's face everywhere he turned, catch glimpses of her flaxen hair among the leaves, picture those sapphire eyes staring at him from across the fire. No. He couldn't do it. Better to have a clean break, get far away from any reminders. Of her and his father.

"Look, I appreciate what you both are doing." No one had ever cared enough for him to look out for his best interests. The thought brought a burning sensation to his throat. He swallowed it down and glanced out the window. He would truly miss his friends. "But I must go."

Blake spun around to face him. "Do you love her?"

He wanted to say no. That she was just a passing fancy like so many other women in his life. But Magnolia was so much more than that. She was all spark and spunk and wit and courage, tenacity, kindness, and goodness. Besides, his newfound faith forbade him to lie. "More than anything."

"Then go to her, man," Blake said.

Hayden hung his head and stared at the packed dirt that made up the floor of his hut. "She was with my father. I cannot shake it from my mind. I don't think I ever can."

James gripped his shoulder. "Then you must ask God for help."

Blake nodded his agreement. "I understand what you are suffering. I thought I could never look at Eliza without remembering what her husband did to my brother. But God can heal all those memories, all those wounds. Like James said, you have but to ask."

"At least say good-bye to her." James raised a brow. "She inquired about you this morning, before she and her parents followed Barclay to the coast, wondering if you were awake."

"I've never seen a woman so distraught," Blake added. "Her parents had to drag her away sobbing. Doesn't seem like a lady happy about her upcoming nuptials, if you ask me."

"Sobbing?" Hayden shifted his boots over the dirt. Why was she sobbing? All she'd talked about during the entire trip to Rio was Samuel this and Samuel that. Could she really be that upset about leaving New Hope? About leaving Hayden?

"Truss it." James glanced out the window and groaned. "They've probably already set sail. Captain Barclay wanted an early start."

Hayden's gaze shifted between his friends, the urgency in their eyes igniting a fire in his heart. And then in his legs. Without a word, he dashed from the hut, tore down the street, and barreled into the jungle, all the while praying that Magnolia was still there.

A wave crashed upon the shore, reaching its foamy fingers toward Magnolia. For a fleeting moment, she thought to step into it—hoping the waves would grab her feet and drag her out to sea, down into the cool waters where all was silent and calm. Where her life would slowly leak from her body and abandon her to peace.

Her parents stood a ways off, chattering excitedly about finally leaving Brazil and returning to civilization and the lifestyle they deserved. But Magnolia drowned them out, instead focusing on the warble of birds, the buzz of insects, the flutter of leaves—all playing a melodious orchestra behind her. The delicate hum of life. A lump formed in her throat. She would miss it. How odd that she would miss it so! Those sounds would always remind her of her time with Hayden in the jungle. The best time of her life. She nearly chuckled at the thought. The entire trip she'd been nothing but hungry and tired and hot and sweaty and covered with bug bites. She'd slept on a hard bed of bamboo, had been attacked by bats and a snake and nearly eaten by a wolf.

And she'd been deliriously happy.

Pulling the toad Hayden had carved for her from her pocket, she fingered each curve and line. It truly looked like a toad. From the large eyeballs protruding from its head, to the thin dish-shaped mouth, to the rounded body, and the tiny webbed toes. Amazing talent. Memories of all the times she'd called him a toad surfaced to make her giggle even as tears slipped from her eyes. At least she would always have this part of him.

Shouts rang from the ship. Squinting, she ran her gaze over the silhouette of the brig, its masts stark against the rising sun. A beautiful ship, indeed. Then why, whenever she saw it, did her stomach sink to her shoes?

One of Captain Barclay's sailors began rowing the skiff to retrieve them after bringing his captain and the other men on board. It was only a matter of minutes now before her feet would leave the shores of Brazil forever. She should be happy, elated! She would marry Samuel, be well positioned in society, and live in ease and luxury. A month ago, this would have been the happiest day of her life. But a month ago, she had been a different person. Now, those things no longer mattered to her. She knew her value came from God, from the changes He wrought within her, not from adornments she placed without. She'd even looked in her mirror that morning, expecting to see herself old and wrinkled, but found some of the lines on her face had softened, some of the bald patches on her head had filled in with hair. It was a good start. But it came too late to save her relationship with Hayden.

She really couldn't blame him. Nor could she blame God. She, alone, was responsible for entangling herself with Patrick Gale. She would accept the consequences, no matter how bitter. And God's will would be done in the end. A breeze swirled around her, and she raised her face to the sun, basking in the warm fingers of heaven's love. Though her heart was breaking, she belonged to God now. All would be well.

The boat struck shore and the sailor leapt out, splashing through the water as he dragged it onto the sand.

"Come now, darling!" her mother shouted as the man hefted their portmanteau into the craft.

The sooner she left, the better. With a heavy sigh, Magnolia slipped the toad into her pocket and started toward them.

"Magnolia!"

She was surely hearing things, conjuring Hayden's voice from her memories, perhaps to instill it in her heart. But there was no need for that. She would never forget the deep, raspy timbre. When she reached her parents, their eyes sped behind her, widening in alarm.

"Magnolia!"

She turned to see Hayden marching toward her through the sand, his dark hair blowing behind him, his shirt flapping in the breeze, a look of longing and determination on his face.

Her heart stopped beating. The breath leached from her lungs. And elusive hope sprouted fresh within her again.

Hayden's overwhelming relief at seeing Magnolia was shoved aside by a much more powerful emotion—fear. Fear that he'd face her and see only his father, despite the petitions he'd lifted up to God on his sprint through the jungle. Fear that she'd come to her senses during the night and realized Wimby was a much better prospect. Fear he'd have to accept, once and for all, living without her. But as he drew close, the look in her eyes spoke of none of those things. In fact, he saw nothing but love and hope and pleading expectation.

Mr. and Mrs. Scott clutched both her arms and dragged her to the boat. "Time to go!" her father shouted. "We mustn't keep the captain waiting."

The sailor clasped Magnolia's hand to assist her into the wobbly craft while her father grabbed the other. And for a moment Hayden thought he'd lost her.

But suddenly, she tore away from them both, and clutching her skirts, headed toward him. How lovely she looked with the sea breeze dancing through her hair and the sunlight painting gold on loose strands about her neck, her pink lips slightly parted in expectation and a flush blossoming on her cheeks. Hayden's breath escaped him.

"Get back here at once, Magnolia!" Mr. Scott shouted, while Mrs. Scott held a hand to her mouth.

"In a moment, Father. I will speak to the man," she replied without turning around. Mr. Scott, his face red and blustery, started to follow her, but she swung to face him. "In private." The shock of her stern voice halted the man and put a smile on Hayden's lips. Turning, she closed the distance between them and stopped, all Chantilly lace and sweet Georgia peach. He could think of nothing else except that he wanted to kiss her. No vision of his father came to mind, no stench of him surrounded her at all. *Thank You, God.*

"I thought I'd never see you again." Her blue eyes searched his as if seeking an answer to a question deep within. "You didn't say good-bye."

"I couldn't."

He wanted to touch her, to brush aside the curl that had blown across her cheek, but he dared not. She had every right to be angry with him. To not want him after he rejected her love.

"I don't think I can ever say good-bye," he said, gauging her reaction.

Her lips parted. Her eyes moistened. "What are you saying?"

He took her hand in his and placed a kiss upon it. Then dropping to one knee in the sand, he gazed up at her. Maybe he was making a complete idiot out of himself, but he didn't care. For the chance to love Magnolia, he'd play the fool a thousand times.

Her eyes widened. Her chest heaved. Her parents groaned. And Hayden said, "Will you marry me, Magnolia? Will you stay here and start a new life with me?"

A tear slid down her cheek, touching the tip of her upturned lips. Was that a smile of joy or of mockery? She gaped at him as if he'd asked her to wed a wolf. Rising to his feet, he released her hand.

"I know I have nothing to offer you. No house or fortune. And especially not a good name." He gazed out to sea, his heart ready to implode. "You must think me rather presumptuous."

"Presumptuous? Always, sir. But at the moment I find you completely. . .completely wonderful and incredible and"—her nose wrinkled—"and wonderfully incredible." She giggled. "I can't seem to find the words."

"A first." He grinned, his heart daring to hope.

She frowned. Blasting that hope. "What about Patrick?"

"Patrick? Who's Patrick?" He feigned confusion then raised a brow. "And what of Samuel?"

She laid a finger on her chin. "I don't believe I know anyone by that name."

"But I fear your parents do." Hayden nodded their way, noting the horror on their faces.

"Then they can marry him." She laughed.

Happiness burst within him. Like none he'd ever known. "So, what is your answer, Princess?"

She fell so hard into his arms, it nearly knocked him over. "Yes! Yes! Yes! Forever, yes!"

Chapter 36

Hayden had never been this nervous. Not during his biggest scam when five thousand dollars, along with his very life, was at risk. Not even when he'd crossed blades with the notorious swordsman Monsieur de Chambolier after Hayden had entertained flirtatious dalliances of his wife. He shifted his polished boots over the dirt, eyed his clean, pressed gray trousers, straightened the black silk embroidered waistcoat he'd borrowed from Blake, and tugged on the cuffs of his pristine shirt—the sleeves a bit too short for his long arms. But nothing eased the knot in his stomach. He glanced at Eliza, standing off to the side, smiling at him with that pleased, knowing smile of hers. Hayden tugged at his black necktie. Why had he tied the thing so tight?

Women to his left giggled, joining the cacophony of birds and insects and the off-key thrum of Mr. Lewis's fiddle. Hayden glanced across the courtyard, seeking his bride, but all he saw were the cheerful faces of the colonists lined up to witness the nuptials. Angeline, cat bundled in her arms, smiled his way, as did Sarah, bouncing Lydia against her chest, Thiago by her side. Mr. Dodd nodded his approval with a sly grin. The Jenkins, their daughter Henrietta between them, stood at the end of a crowd of other colonists, several farmers, ex-soldiers, the blacksmith, the baker—all grinning like clowns. More colonists crowded together on the other side, even some from his father's group. Magnolia's mother stood on Hayden's left, flowers in hand and a pleasant smile on her face. Conspicuously absent were

Magnolia's father and Patrick.

Which was fine by Hayden.

He gazed at the strings of orchids festooning the thatched roof of the open-air meeting shelter, complements of New Hope's women, who had seemed more than excited to be planning another wedding. Vines covered with feathery flowers of white and scarlet circled support poles and tables, while violet petals littered the ground. A breeze flickered two rows of lit candles that formed a pathway from the main street to where Hayden stood. He gave a sigh of impatience as the scent of sweet lemonade and molasses cakes swirled beneath his nose.

Rays of a setting sun speared the jungle, dappling the area with glittering saffron.

James cleared his throat, drawing Hayden's gaze. The man stood in front of him, prayer book in hand, but his eyes were on something behind Hayden. He turned to see. . .

Magnolia.

Dressed in a shimmering white gown, trimmed in golden lace and embroidered with beads—complements of Angeline—and with her pearly hair swept up in a mass of curls, she looked more angelic than human. Her gloved hand rested in the crux of Blake's elbow as he led her through the rows of flickering candles. Their eyes locked, and he couldn't believe God had given him such a princess.

Releasing Blake with a nod of thanks, she stopped beside Hayden. The flowers in her hands quivered. Her eyes sparkled with love. A breeze tugged loose a single strand of her hair, sweeping it across her neck. She reached up to put it in place, but he took her hand in his and smiled. And he vowed right there before God and man to take care of her, protect her, and love her all of her days.

Thump-ump, thump-ump, thump-ump, the pulsating sound echoed in Magnolia's ear. As it had all night. Lulling her to sleep with its soothing cadence, while at the same time keeping her awake with the knowledge that it came from the heart of the man she loved. The man that lay beside her, his strong arm around her waist, his chest beneath her head where she had laid it after they'd become one flesh, just like the scriptures said. He'd adored her with his body and then adored her with his words of love and promises of care and affection and joy for a lifetime, until he'd finally drifted off to sleep.

The night had passed in a brushstroke of paradise as she lay ensconced in his warmth and strength, listening to his deep breathing, feeling the rise and fall of his chest, inhaling the male scent of him, and praying for God to bless and strengthen and protect this man forever. Closing her eyes against the glow of dawn creeping in through the window, she wished it would retreat, go back to the rising sun, and push it down beneath the horizon for just a little while longer. Just a little while longer in Hayden's arms, a little while longer absorbed in his love.

A parrot screeched outside the window. Hayden stirred. He reached up to rub his nose. Propping her chin on his chest, she watched him. His mouth twitched. He groaned and released a heavy breath. Then his arm tightened around her and he snapped his eyes open, shifting them to her as if surprised to find her in his bed. A slow grin appeared on his lips. "I thought I only dreamed last night."

"Do you often have dreams of such a"—she raised an eyebrow at him—"sensual nature?"

"Only about you, wife." Easing a lock of hair from her forehead, he propped himself up on his elbow, his eyes drinking her in. "Last night was magical."

Magnolia smiled, felt a blush rising, and lay back on the pillow, gazing up at him. "Let's never leave this cot. Stay here forever."

"Wouldn't that give the townspeople something to talk about?"

"Let them." She laughed, running her fingers over the dark stubble on his chin.

His gaze landed on the toad carving on the table. "So, now that I've spent the night with you, I suppose you must chop off my head so I can become a prince."

"It's two nights you must spend with me, Mr. Gale. After tomorrow, I shall have to see." She grinned. "But I do believe you are well on your way to becoming a prince, even with your head attached."

He rubbed his throat. "Good thing, Mrs. Gale. I've grown quite fond of my head."

"I rather like it myself." Propping herself up, she trailed kisses up his neck. "Especially this neck"—she continued on to his chin—"and this scratchy jaw"—she planted one on his nose—"and this nose and these ears"—she nibbled on his ear.

Groaning, he nudged her back onto the pillow and trapped her with his arms. "If you continue such provocative amusements, you will get your wish and never leave this bed."

"I don't believe you for one minute. Are you swindling me again, Hayden Gale?"

He grew serious. "Never again, for you have swindled the great swindler, Princess, and stolen his heart forever."

"I shall take good care of it, Hayden. You need fear nothing from me. I will cherish it forever and never betray your confidence, and I will—"

His lips met hers, and the rest of her thoughts flew out the window.

Epilogue

What in the Sam Hill are you talking about, Doc?" Hayden shook his head. "You're not making any sense." Besides, the man had dragged Hayden away from Magnolia on only their second night together as man and wife. He glanced down the dark street, lit in intervals by flickering lanterns, toward their hut where he'd left her sleeping.

"I know you're anxious to return to your wife," Blake said, drawing Hayden's gaze back to see him smile. "I am as well. To mine, that is." He chuckled at his faux pas. "But let's hear James out. He's been translating this book Graves gave him from the tunnels, and I'm sure he wouldn't have woken us unless it was important."

"Yes." James stared at the open book lying on the table in the meeting shelter. Light from a lantern perched beside it spilled onto the page littered with odd characters. The doc seemed unusually tense as he pushed from the table, took up a short pace, then stopped again. "I finally figured out what this section says." He nodded to the book. "The Latin phrase written above the alcoves is a key to release the powerful beings."

The impact of his ominous declaration was lost on Hayden. Just the preacher being a preacher, he supposed. But the news seemed to distress Blake. He planted a boot on a stool and leaned forward, his jaw stiff, his eyes intent.

"What powerful beings?" Hayden asked.

James gave Hayden a look as if he'd asked if the sun rose in the east. An event Hayden hoped he'd miss before he returned to his bed. "Ah, yes. Sorry," James said. "Remember those alcoves in the tunnels beneath the temples, the ones with the poles and broken chains?"

"Go on."

"This book tells how they got there. There was a battle. Probably on that scorched field we saw behind the temple." His eyes lit up as if he suddenly realized the connection. "Anyway, those powerful evil beings were subdued and locked below. Four of them."

Hayden had heard some rattlebrained tales before—had told a few himself—but this one could get a man locked in an asylum. "But there was nothing there."

"Two were gone. Yes." James scratched his thick hair. "I know how they escaped." He exchanged a look with Blake. "Remember the writing on top of each alcove?"

"Yes. Latin and something else written in another language." Hayden pointed toward the book. "Words that looked like this."

James nodded and shifted his gaze between them. "All someone needs to do to free the beings is say the Latin phrase out loud. Here, let me read this section. When the man of darkness in whom there is no light"—he slid his finger across the characters from right to left—"speaks the key to the four winds, the chains are broken."

Blake nodded as if James had just read facts from a scientific treatise. "But who released the first two?"

"Indians, pirates, cannibals. I don't know. The person merely has to say the phrase, not understand it. And he or she must be evil. A bad person in whom there is no light."

Hayden rubbed the back of his neck. "So who locked them up there in the first place?"

"I don't know. God. . .good angels."

Hayden snorted. "And you think these beings might be bad angels?"

James huffed his displeasure at Hayden's skepticism. "I know it sounds farfetched, but yes, I believe these beings could be angels who followed Satan in the fall."

Farfetched? Hayden shook his head. More like pure madness. "So, why would whoever conquered them make a way for them to be released?"

James flipped back a few pages. "It's hard to explain, but it says here that because the earth was given to mankind, fallen as he is, there had to be a way for man to release these beings. It had to be man's choice of good over evil. . .free will"—he looked up at Blake—"like we talked about before. God does not want puppets. If we choose evil, He allows us."

The excited way he spoke, the fear lacing his tone, brought Hayden's own fears to the surface. Were his two friends becoming as mad as Graves? Perhaps if Hayden simply excused himself and returned to bed, he'd wake up tomorrow to find their senses recovered. "Fascinating, gentlemen, but I have a new bride waiting for me." He turned to go.

"Graves is close to releasing the next being." James's forceful tone spun Hayden around and caused Blake to squeeze the bridge of his nose with a groan. "That's what he's been digging for," James continued. "Two of them were locked in the chamber we saw. Another two were locked below them. The worst two. More evil than you could possibly imagine." He gripped the edge of the table. "If what Graves said about sabotaging our journey was true, we know he was evil to start out with. But now, you've seen him. He's not only evil, but he's gone mad as well. If he knows any Latin at all, all he has to do is say the phrase above the open sepulcher out loud and the third being will be free."

Graves raised the lantern over the alcove he'd just uncovered. Finally. After weeks of digging, he'd finally removed enough rocks and dirt to clearly see the curved trench that ran from the muddy floor to the craggy roof of the cave. Water dripped and hissed all around him as steam rose from cracks. Sweat streamed down every aching muscle in his body and burned over cuts and abrasions. But he didn't care. Excitement set his hair on end. The chains were intact, suspended in midair as if still restraining something. . .or someone, yet now as he flooded the area with light, he could see no one there.

"I did what you said." He wiped sweat from his face, leaving a streak of mud on his sleeve. "I did what you said." He took a step closer.

Ah. . .there they were, the voices again. His friends, his companions for the last two months. Happy voices, praising him for his faithfulness, his hard work, his dedication, promising him rewards beyond his wildest dreams. Graves smiled. Finally all his work would pay off. Finally he would have immeasurable power.

Say the words. Open the chains.

Water dripped on his face from above—steaming water that smelled of sulfur and stung his skin. He leapt on a boulder and raised the lantern higher, illuminating the Latin above the sepulcher. Squinting, he tried to make out the letters, tried to remember their pronunciation from his lessons as a child.

The words sounded foreign on his cracked lips, but he shouted them aloud with glee. Their echo magnified and bounced off the walls with a power he would soon possess. A low rumble resounded from below. Louder and louder it grew until it thundered in the chamber. The walls shook. Dirt showered over him. Stalactites speared down from above. One struck Graves's shoulder, piercing his flesh. Crying out, he tumbled from the rock and landed in the mud. Another pierced his leg. He screamed in agony and raised a pleading hand to the sepulcher. Chains rattled. Iron split apart, and the dark outline of an immense being took form. Eyes as hot as coals stared down at Graves.

"Help me," Graves cried, reaching toward the creature.

The being pulled a sword with a blade as long as a man from his scabbard, stepped from his prison, and raised it over Graves's head.

Before he completely vanished.

Graves released a heavy breath. He never felt the blade on his throat until it was too late.

A loud boom like the roar of a cannon drew all men's gazes to the jungle. The ground trembled. The lantern wobbled on the table and slivers of thatch filtered down from above.

The three men exchanged wary glances. The shaking stopped. Night birds and crickets returned to their song, and a mighty gust of wind sent the lantern flame sputtering patches of light and dark over the prophetic Hebrew book.

"So what is the name of this third being?" Hayden asked, suddenly rethinking his position.

James pointed to a word in the book then eyed them both. "Destruction."

Author's Historical Note

For purposes of the story, I chose the location for the colony of New Hope to be roughly one hundred miles south of Rio de Janeiro, near a wide river that flows from the mountains down to the sea. The river and the colony are fictitious and are not actual landmarks in Brazil. There was, however, a colony named El Dorado, led by Frank McMullan, that settled south of Rio de Janeiro in the São Paulo province, near the São Lourenço River. Shortly after the colonists' arrival, Frank McMullan took sick and died, leaving his partner, William Bowen, a gruff, greedy man more interested in finding gold than planting crops, in charge. (Many legends abounded of a lake of gold near the area!) The resultant power struggle caused great dissention among the group. That division, along with sickness, lack of food supplies, money, and no way to get their crops to market caused the demise of the colony in 1870, three years after it began.

The fairy tale Magnolia recites to Hayden during their trek in the jungle comes from James Orchard Halliwell-Phillipps: *Popular Rhymes and Nursery Tales*. London 1849. I copied it here for your enjoyment.

The Maiden and the Frog

Many years ago there lived on the brow of a mountain, in the north of England, an old woman and her daughter. They were very poor and obliged to work very hard for their living, and the old woman's temper was not very good, so that the maiden, who was very beautiful, led but an ill life with her.

The girl, indeed, was compelled to do the hardest work, for her mother got their principal means of subsistence by traveling to places in the neighborhood with small articles for sale, and when she came home in the afternoon she was not able to do much more work. Nearly the whole domestic labor of the cottage devolved therefore on the daughter, the most wearisome part of which consisted in the necessity of fetching all the water they required from a well on the other side of the hill, there being no river or spring near their own cottage.

It happened one morning that the daughter had the misfortune, in going to the well, to break the only pitcher they possessed, and having no other utensil she could use for the purpose, she was obliged to go home without bringing any water. When her mother returned, she was unfortunately troubled with excessive thirst, and the girl, though trembling for the consequences of her misfortune, told her exactly the circumstance that had occurred.

The old woman was furiously angry, and so far from making any allowances for her daughter, pointed to a sieve which happened to be on the table, and told her to go at once to the well and bring her some water in that, or never venture to appear again in her sight.

The young maiden, frightened almost out of her wits by her mother's fury, speedily took the sieve, and though she considered the task a hopeless one to accomplish, almost unconsciously hastened to the well. When she arrived there, beginning to reflect on the painful situation in which she was placed and the utter impossibility of her obtaining a living by herself, she threw herself down on the brink of the well in an agony of despair.

Whilst she was in this condition, a large frog came up to the top of the water and asked her for what she was crying so bitterly. She was somewhat surprised at this, but not being the least frightened, told him the whole story, and that she was crying because she could not carry away water in the sieve.

"Is that all?" said the frog. "Cheer up, my hinny! For if you will only let me sleep with you for two nights, and then chop off my head, I will tell you how to do it."

The maiden thought the frog could not be in earnest, but she was too impatient to consider much about it and at once made the required promise. The frog then instructed her in the following words:

Stop with fog,
And daub with clay;
And that will carry
The water away.

Having said this, he dived immediately under the water, and the girl, having followed his advice, got the sieve full of water, and returned home with it, not thinking much of her promise to the frog. By the time she reached home the old woman's wrath was appeased, but as they were eating their frugal supper very quietly, what should they hear but the splashing and croaking of a frog near the door, and shortly afterwards the daughter recognized the voice of the frog of the well saying:

Open the door, my hinny, my heart,
Open the door, my own darling;
Remember the word you spoke to me
In the meadow by the well-spring.

She was now dreadfully frightened and hurriedly explained the matter to her mother, who was also so much alarmed at the circumstance that she dared not refuse admittance to the frog, who, when the door was opened, leapt into the room, exclaiming:

Go wi' me to bed, my hinny, my heart,
Go wi' me to bed, my own darling;
Remember the words you spoke to me,
In the meadow by the well-spring.

This command was also obeyed, although as may be readily supposed, she did not much relish such a bedfellow. The next day, the frog was very quiet and evidently enjoyed the fare they placed before him, the purest milk and the finest bread they could procure. In fact, neither the old woman nor her daughter spared any pains to render the frog comfortable. That night, immediately supper was finished, the frog again exclaimed:

Go wi' me to bed, my hinny, my heart,
Go wi' me to bed, my own darling;
Remember the words you spoke to me,
In the meadow by the well-spring.

She again allowed the frog to share her couch, and in the morning, as soon as she was dressed, he jumped towards her, saying:

Chop off my head, my hinny, my heart,
Chop off my head, my own darling;
Remember the words you spoke to me,
In the meadow by the well-spring.

The maiden had no sooner accomplished this last request, than in the stead of the frog there stood by her side the handsomest prince in the world, who had long been transformed by a magician, and who could never have recovered his natural shape until a beautiful virgin had consented, of her own accord, to make him her bedfellow for two nights. The joy of all parties was complete; the girl and the prince were shortly afterward married and lived for many years in the enjoyment of every happiness.

About the Author

MaryLu Tyndall, a Christy Award finalist and bestselling author of the Legacy of the King's Pirates series, is known for her adventurous historical romances filled with deep spiritual themes. She holds a degree in math and worked as a software engineer for fifteen years before testing the waters as a writer. MaryLu currently writes full time and makes her home on the California coast with her husband, six kids, and four cats. Her passion is to write page-turning, romantic adventures that not only entertain but open people's eyes to their God-given potential. MaryLu is a member of American Christian Fiction Writers and Romance Writers of America.